For Gareth, "I have your friendship. That is enough."

Place Names

Place names in Dark Ages Britain vary according to time, language, dialect and the scribe who was writing. I have not followed a strict convention when choosing what spelling to use for a given place. In most cases, I have chosen the name I believe to be the closest to that used in the early seventh century, but like the scribes of all those centuries ago, I have taken artistic licence at times, and merely selected the one I liked most.

Afen	River Avon
Albion	Great Britain
Bebbanburg	Bamburgh
Berewic	Berwick-upon-Tweed
Bernicia	Northern kingdom of Northumbria, running approximately from the Tyne to the Firth of Forth
Cantware	Kent
Cantwareburh	Canterbury
Dál Riata	Gaelic overkingdom, roughly

	encompassing modern-day Argyll and Bute and Lochaber in Scotland and also County Antrim in Northern Ireland
Deira	Southern kingdom of Northumbria, running approximately from the Humber to the Tyne
Din Eidyn	Edinburgh
Dommoc	Dunwich, Suffolk
Dor	Dore, Yorkshire
Dorcic	Dorchester-on-Thames
Dun	River Don
Elmet	Native Briton kingdom, approximately equal to the West Riding of Yorkshire
Engelmynster	Fictional location in Deira
Eoferwic	York
Frankia	France
Gefrin	Yeavering
Gwynedd	Gwynedd, North Wales
Hefenfelth	Heavenfield
Hibernia	Ireland
Hii	Iona
Hithe	Hythe, Kent
Lindisfarena	Lindisfarne
Mercia	Kingdom centred on the valley of the River Trent and its tributaries, in the modern-day English Midlands.
Muile	Mull
Northumbria	Modern-day Yorkshire, Northumberland and south-east Scotland
Pocel's Hall	Pocklington
Scheth	River Sheaf (border of Mercia and Deira)

Temes	River Thames
Tuidi	River Tweed
Ubbanford	Norham, Northumberland
Usa	River Ouse

ALBION
AND ISLANDS

Legend
- ○ Settlements
- ⋔ Fortresses
- † Holy sites
- — Roman roads

HIBERNIA

MAN

HIBERNIAN SEA

Din Eidyn

BER

RHEGED

GWYNEDD

POWY

ALBION
AD 635

PICTLAND

DÁL RIATA

BERNICIA   Bebbanburg

DEIRA

Eoferwic ○
ELMET

HIBERNIA

GWYNEDD   MERCIA

WEST SAXONS   CANTWARE
Cantwaraburh

FRANKIA

0   50 miles

0   100 km

N

Berewic
Ubbanford
R. Tuidi
Lindisfarena
Farena Islands
Gefrin
Bebbanburg

BERNICIA

NORTHUMBRIA

The Wall
Hefenfelth

Deira Straet

DEIRA

NORTH SEA

R. Usa
Eoferwic
Pocel's Hall
Engelmynster
Humber

ELMET

R. Dyn

R. Scheth

LINDESEGE

R. Maerse

R. Trent

Earninga Straet

THE
FENS

EAST
ANGELN

S

MERCIA

GYRWAS

Domoc

HWICCE

R. Afen

Waeclinga Straet

Dorcic

EAST SEAXONS

R. Temes

Lunden

Cantwareburh

WEST SAXONS

CANTWARE

ANNO DOMINI NOSTRI IESU CHRISTI
IN THE YEAR OF OUR LORD JESUS CHRIST
635

PART ONE
ALLIANCE OF BLOOD

Chapter 1

They attacked at night. Beobrand had known they would. The ragged group of Picts was driven by their desire for blood and death; their hunger for vengeance. And that was something he understood well.

The Picts descended on them in the stillest part of the night, as silent as the wraiths that haunt the burial mounds of ancient kings. Blades glimmered dully in the cool starlight. Approaching from the south, they were hopeful for the element of surprise. They had traipsed far to the west before crossing the river Tuidi and then circling round to move on Ubbanford from the desolate hills where few men lived.

The plan was good, but Beobrand was also cunning. Anticipating such a move from his enemies, he had set his men to watch the hills. At sunset, Attor, the most lithe and soft-footed of Beobrand's warband, had padded into the newly finished great hall.

"They are coming," he'd said, the glint in his eye from the hearth fire speaking of his thirst for battle-fame.

"How many?" Beobrand had asked, setting aside his

horn of mead unfinished. He would need his wits about him this night.

"A dozen. Mayhap more."

Beobrand had scowled. He hoped all the planning was enough. His warband would be outnumbered, it was true, but they would also be prepared, armed and waiting for the attack.

He had stood, pushing his freshly carved gift-stool back and looking at each of his warriors, his gesithas, in turn. He nodded, his face grim in the flickering flame light.

"We have prepared for this. Each take your position and await the signal. Attor, fetch Elmer from where he wards the river and have him get the women and children to safety."

Now, in the pre-dawn gloom of the summer night Beobrand watched as the shadows of men flitted between the buildings. They made their way towards the hill where the new hall commanded the valley. He straightened his right leg, tensing his calf muscle, testing it. He cursed silently. The arrow wound was still stiff, not fully healed. He could not run. He would have to spring the ambush sooner than he would have liked, or else he feared he would not be able to close with the enemy. Beobrand felt the throb of the leg wound and wondered whether Torran was amongst the Picts who crept through his settlement. Torran, son of Nathair, had loosed the arrow that had skewered Beobrand's leg. But not before Beobrand had slain his brother. He flexed his left arm, wincing. The skin pulled at recent scabbing where Broden's axe had bit deeply into his flesh. He bared his teeth in the blackness. The pain and memories of the battle at Nathair's hall only weeks before brought whispers of the battle fury into his thoughts. He had felt little these last few weeks. His lack of feelings frightened him more than the thought of bloodshed.

He signalled to Acennan who stood in the star-shadow of the smithy's forge. He could barely make out his friend's form in the darkness, but there was the slightest of movements in the gloom and then a piercing blast on a horn, as Acennan announced the moment of the ambush to the defenders who hid in the night.

Light flared suddenly as men uncovered torches and thrust them into prepared piles of kindling. Beobrand's gesithas burst from the shadows, their weapons and armour shining red in the sudden firelight. Beobrand too leapt forward, drawing his fine sword, Hrunting, from its fur-lined scabbard. He hurried towards one intruder, whose back was turned to him. He limped forward as quickly as he could, clumsy on the wounded leg. His arm felt naked without a shield, but he had decided before the fight that a linden board would hinder him in his current state. Both his arm and leg would heal, in time, but for now, he would need to fight without a shield, and hope that the Picts did not run away before they could be slaughtered.

The man who was the focus of his attention turned towards him at the last moment. His face was pallid. He was young, probably less than twenty years, perhaps the same age as Beobrand himself. But he was no warrior. He held a long knife, but had barely raised it to defend himself when Hrunting's blade sliced into his throat, splashing warmth over Beobrand's forearm and face. The young Pict fell back silently, his eyes wide, mouth opening and closing like a beached salmon.

With the first kill of the night, battle lust descended upon Beobrand. After the weeks of inaction, the numbness after

Sunniva's death and the events at Dor, Beobrand embraced the battle-ire, welcoming the familiar rush of power as a cold man clutches a warm cloak in a blizzard.

Casting around for another adversary, Beobrand saw that he had indeed sprung the trap too soon. The night was a chaos of dancing shadows. Men rushed between buildings. It was hard to discern friend from foe in the confusion. As he watched, one man sprinted away from the settlement on the valley floor, heading towards the new hall on the knap of the hill. Beobrand made a start to follow him, but instantly knew he would never be able to catch the Pict who was running fast. The light from the fires picked out the running man's form for a moment and Beobrand recognised him. Torran. So he had come, seeking the revenge he had sworn before his father's burning hall.

Another Pict, this one older, with full beard, screamed and threw himself at Beobrand. He wielded a broad-bladed sword, marking him as a warrior of some standing. He drove Beobrand back a couple of steps, leading with his shield. Beobrand gritted his teeth against the throbbing in his leg. He sidestepped as the man lunged forward. Taking advantage of his opponent's momentum, Beobrand dropped to one knee, grunting at the pain, and struck a terrible blow to the Pict's shin. Hrunting's steel shattered bone and severed sinews. The man stumbled forward once more, not yet realising his right leg had been destroyed below the knee. His limb buckled and he fell forward, eyes shocked, unable to understand what had happened. The agony hit him then and he squealed, writhing on the ground as his lifeblood gushed from the stump where moments before his leg had been. Beobrand did not allow him to suffer for long. He sliced down once, piercing the warrior's heart before flicking his attention back to Torran.

"Torran!" he screamed, his voice loud enough to carry over the tumult of clashing weapons.

"Torran, you goat-swiving son of a leprous whore! Fight me!"

Torran stopped and turned, his face aglow from the fires.

"Beobrand, your life is mine. I claim your blood as payment for my kin."

Beobrand threw open his arms, the blood from his kills already cooling on his skin.

"Come then, you maggot. Come and face me. Take what blood you can."

To Beobrand's left came a scream of pain. Beobrand recognised the voice and tore his gaze from Torran. Acennan had also been forced to fight without a shield. His shoulder had been smashed by Broden's great war axe. He did not yet have full use of the arm, but it had been healing well. Until now. A burly Pict, eyes white with fear or rage, was laying about him with a great club. The huge cudgel had connected with Acennan's shoulder and the stocky warrior was in trouble. The Pict swung his weapon again and Acennan deftly parried the blow. But the way he carried himself told Beobrand the story of how his shoulder fared.

Turning his back on Torran, Beobrand hobbled towards the fighting pair. Acennan was defending himself, but he was making no headway against the brute with the club. Beobrand drew close, but a heartbeat before he was able to reach the man with his blade, the Pict sensed the threat and spun round, flailing with his stout branch. Beobrand took a step back, avoiding the swing.

Acennan may have been injured, but he was a killer and he was still quick. Seizing the moment of his adversary's distraction, Acennan leapt forward and drove the point of his sword deep into the Pict's back. The man stopped and looked down in surprise at the gore-slick steel jutting from his chest. He lifted his gaze towards Beobrand, his mouth round in amazement, then fell forward.

Acennan stepped over the corpse. He nodded his thanks at Beobrand.

"I could have done with a few more weeks to recover," he said, grinning.

"You'll be wanting them to kill themselves next," replied Beobrand. The aches of his body had receded as the battle-fury took him. Now he wanted more blood. More killing. Perhaps blood could wash away his pain, as they said Christ's blood washed away sin. Yet all around them the Picts were falling. The fight was almost over.

But what of Torran? He searched for the son of Nathair on the darkening hillside. Behind the slope, the eastern sky was tinged with the grey of dawn. A flash of white caught his eye and he spotted the young Pict some way off. At the same instant he realised what the white was – the fletchings of an arrow. Torran had shot him before. He was a skilled archer; Beobrand's leg bore the witness to that. At this distance, Torran could not miss.

And neither Beobrand nor Acennan had shields.

Feeling hopelessly exposed Beobrand cast about for something to hide behind, but the nearest building was too far for him to reach before Torran could loose. He wondered whether the iron-knit shirt he wore would stop an arrow. He had heard tell of such shirts being pierced. At this close range, he fully expected an arrow to punch through the rings. He squared his shoulders. Well, if he could not hide from the bowman, he could give him less time to think. Less time to aim.

Stiff-legged, his right calf screaming, Beobrand walked purposefully towards Torran. Acennan walked at his side.

"Too scared to fight me, are you? Pissing your breeches at the idea of facing a real man?"

"I'm not afraid of you, Seaxon scum," Torran shouted, lowering his bow slightly. He nocked the arrow to the string, lifted it and pulled back the yew bow with great strength in one fluid motion.

For a heartbeat Beobrand saw the firelight glisten on the wicked iron point of the arrow. Torran aimed and held the arrow there momentarily. They were still too far away to attack. With every step though, his chance of missing, or of their byrnies protecting them, lessened.

"If you are not afraid, then lower your child's toy and face me with sword or spear."

Torran did not answer. His right hand let loose the bow string and the arrow thrummed towards Beobrand. It flew straight and true. Beobrand watched its flight, a blur of white in the dawn. He saw the arrow come but did not react. He closed his eyes and accepted his wyrd.

There was a crash and a clatter, but no impact. No searing pain as the arrow split through metal rings and the soft flesh beneath.

Beobrand opened his eyes. For a moment the scene was confusing in the dawn-shadow of the hill. Someone was sprawled on the earth before him. Was it Acennan? No, the short warrior was still at his side. Then the figure groaned and rose up. Teeth flashed in the dark as the face broke into a savage grin. It was Attor. He held a shield in his left hand. From its hide-covered boards protruded the arrow that had been meant for Beobrand.

"Seemed you needed saving, lord," he said, the glee of battle lending his tone a shrill edge.

Beobrand flashed him a smile and continued up the hill. Torran would waste no time and there was still a way to go.

Torran was preparing another arrow. It was nocked and he was drawing back the bowstring again as Attor rushed past Beobrand and Acennan, dropping the shield at their feet as he passed.

"You won't get away this time, you Pictish bastard," he yelled.

"No, I don't reckon he will," said a new voice, booming and strong.

Torran hesitated.

The voice came from behind, further up the hill.

Beobrand glanced at Acennan in surprise. Acennan shrugged. The voice did not fit any of Beobrand's gesithas.

Attor did not falter, speeding up the rise.

"Run or die, little Pict," the new voice said.

Torran glanced over his shoulder. A giant strode towards him from the gloom. Silhouetted against the paling dawn sky came a warrior from legend. Tall and broad, burnished helm reflecting the light from the dying fires in the settlement. The boss of the shield at his side shone. The warrior drew a sword and swung it as if it weighed no more than a twig.

Attor was close now, letting out a scream of battle-rage as he prepared to slice Torran open with his deadly seax.

The giant from the hill would be on the Pict in a moment, but Attor would reach him first.

Quickly making his decision, Torran pulled the bowstring anew, but did not have time for a full draw before loosing the arrow. The shot was rushed, his aim poor. It was not a death shot. The arrow clipped Attor's shoulder, throwing him off balance and slowing him.

The huge warrior was almost on Torran, sword blade red in the fires' glow.

Torran did not allow the man to use his weapon. The Pict turned and fled into the darkness of the valley that was still in shadow, even as the sun began to paint the eastern sky.

"Tiw's cock!" Attor screamed. "I will kill you, Torran. You can't run and hide forever." No answer came from the darkness but the sound of splashing as Torran forded the river.

The fight was over. A few other surviving Picts broke away from where they had been battling with Beobrand's warriors and disappeared into the morning gloom.

Attor gripped the shaft of the arrow, gritted his teeth and yanked it free from his flesh. He grunted.

A hush fell upon the valley.

"You have done well, Attor," said Beobrand. "Get Ceawlin to bind that."

Attor nodded, but did not leave. He turned his face to the giant warrior who still came towards them. The man's beard bristled beneath his helm. His shoulders looked strong enough to lift an ox. From out of the darkness came another figure. Slimmer, but still menacing, bedecked for war with shield, spear and helm. The two warriors walked down the hill together.

Attor held his seax tightly and moved to stand in front of Beobrand, placing his body between his lord and these two strange warriors.

"You are brave, little man," said the giant, "but if you mean to fight me with that tiny knife, prepare to meet Woden in his corpse-hall."

Attor bridled. The battle fury was fresh on him; certain death would not dissuade him from attacking.

Beobrand placed a hand upon Attor's shoulder, pulling him back even as he sprang towards the two warriors.

"Stay your hand, Attor."

Beobrand walked past the wounded warrior towards the two newcomers. Behind him, Attor and Acennan gasped.

"Wait," said Acennan, attempting to grab Beobrand's cloak, to pull him away from danger. Beobrand shrugged off his hands and continued.

Two paces before the huge warrior and his companion, Beobrand halted. He drove Hrunting into the soft soil, leaving it quivering at his side, and threw open his arms.

Acennan and Attor looked on in dismay as the giant warrior, even taller and broader than Beobrand, stepped forward. The massive man sheathed his own blade with a flourish and embraced Beobrand.

"I should have known I'd find you up to your neck in battle, Beobrand, son of Grimgundi," he said, his voice large and warm, like a roaring hearth fire.

Chapter 2

"This mead is good," roared the huge warrior who had arrived that dawn. He slammed down the horn he had just emptied, pushing the bench back and standing up. He staggered towards the door, almost losing his balance.

"Good and strong," said Beobrand, smiling. "Watch yourself, Bassus. I wouldn't want you tripping and hurting yourself, old man."

"Who are you calling old?" bellowed Bassus. He spun around to face the high table, arms lifted in mock fighting pose. Losing his balance, he reached out and grabbed hold of one of the hall's wooden pillars. "I'm not old," he said, shaking his head to clear it. "Drunk, yes, but not old!" He pushed himself away from the beam and walked unsteadily out of the hall.

The men gathered there, most as drunk as Bassus, filled the warm, smoke-filled space with laughter. Bassus, erstwhile hearth-warrior and champion to King Edwin, was known to them. He and Beobrand had fought shoulder-to-shoulder in the battle of Elmet. The older warrior was their lord's friend and had stood with them against the Picts in the darkness, and so they welcomed him.

Reaghan started at the raucous noise of the men in the great hall. They were full of cheer. Glad to be alive. Flushed with the morning's victory over the Picts. The air of celebration was clear in the expressions of men and women alike. They all felt it. Revelled in it. It was a warm day and the food and drink was plentiful.

And yet, the happiness did not reach Reaghan. She had been so afraid in the black stillness of the night, cowering with the other women and the bairns. Waiting for the sound of battle. For the flash of fire in the darkness.

Beobrand, sitting at the head of the room, waved to her, beckoning her to his side. She lowered her head and made her way past the men who lined the boards. She felt their eyes upon her as she approached her lord. She knew what they wanted. What all men wanted.

"More mead, my lord?" she asked in a soft tone.

He grinned and raised his cup.

It was the first time she had seen him smile since before lady Sunniva's death. Even when he looked upon Octa, his infant son, he displayed no emotion, save perhaps a brooding anxiety.

Reaghan poured amber liquid for him and stepped back, away from Beobrand. The fear of the previous night clung to her like a rain-soaked fleece. She shuddered.

The screams of the fighting, the clash of sword on shield and the crackle of fires had brought back to her the night she had been taken by Torran and his brother. She had not been as afraid since she was a child, when the Angelfolc had come on that autumn day, killing her family. But that was many years past and the memories had lost their edges, stones rubbed smooth in the stream of time. Her capture by the sons of Nathair had been recent, the wounds still fresh.

They had treated her hard. She was no stranger to the ways of warriors. She was a thrall. The property of Lord Ubba until his death, along with his two sons, the year before. All three of them had lain with her. Panting and pushing, grunting into her long auburn hair. Yet she had never feared they would truly hurt her. She had pitied them. Despised them. But she never believed they wished her harm.

The Picts were different. They had beaten her, slapping and punching her tiny frame. She had been powerless to prevent it, so had done the only thing she knew. Before they could knock her senseless, she had lifted up her dress, opening her legs, offering herself to them. They had stopped hitting her then.

What followed had been little better. The memories of that dark night threatened to engulf her with their black wings. She had passed out before they had finished with her.

She had awoken, battered and aching as the night erupted in flames and terror. The hall had filled with thick smoke and all about her men shouted. She recalled her own village all those years before, and the acrid smoke as her home was consumed. Her mother's screams. The Angelfolc, descended from warriors who had come from across the Whale Road, had murdered her family and enslaved her. And yet, these Picts, people who had long shared this island of Albion with her folk, had forced themselves upon her. They had kicked and hit her. For years she had dreamt of running away from Ubbanford. Escaping her life of thralldom. To leave the accursed Angelfolc behind and return to her people in the west.

Motion in the hall drew her gaze. Her reverie broken, she

watched as Beobrand drained his cup and rose to his feet. He craned his neck, seeking her out. Spotting her in the shadows, he offered her another brief smile before leaving the hall, following Bassus outside.

She watched him leave. His fair hair was long, his movements lithe and purposeful, even now, when dulled by drink.

The Angelfolc were a scourge on the land. So she had always believed. They were oafs who took what they desired by force. They had no honour and did not understand the ways of the goddess Danu and her children; the ways that Reaghan's mother had taught her.

Yes, they were a blight. Slayers of her kin who had enslaved her and used her all her life. And Beobrand was one of their thegns. A lord.

His muscular form was highlighted in the doorway for a moment before he stepped into the afternoon sun. She swallowed, her mouth suddenly dry.

She should hate him, as she had hated Ubba and his sons. She flushed.

Yet when she, a thrall, had been stolen away from Ubbanford, Beobrand had not forsaken her. She had awoken in that fire-filled night of death, alone and certain that she would die.

The next thing she remembered she had been sitting astride his horse, Beobrand's arms around her, holding her tight, his hands stroking her hair.

She should hate him, but she knew she never could. For when all was lost and she could see no way out, Beobrand had come for her.

*

"Octa would be proud of you."

Bassus stretched his legs out before him and leant against the bole of the oak. From where he sat he could see the new mead hall that Beobrand had built and the settlement that nestled in the loop of the river below. He belched contentedly, tasting anew the meat and drink from Beobrand's table.

"I leave you for a year and you become a lord with your own gesithas and hall."

Beobrand found a spot on the grass in the shade of the tree and lowered himself down with a groan. Bassus took in the way he favoured his left leg, not bending the right. A recent injury, he supposed. Beobrand's left hand showed sign of other battles. The smallest finger and part of the next had been severed. His face bore a savage scar under his left eye. Bassus remembered hearing the tale of how Beobrand had fled the battlefield at Elmet with the terrible wound to his eye, and how he had later been nursed to health by monks.

"But you clearly need to practise more with that blade of yours," continued Bassus. "You can hardly walk and you've lost half your hand."

"Yes, that was careless of me. Though Hengist lost more than I." Beobrand spat.

"I heard of the battle at Bebbanburg where you slew him. Tales of it reached us in Cantware. Your uncle was full of pride to hear of your sword-skill."

Beobrand looked up suddenly.

"Selwyn lives?"

"That he does. As tough as a boar that one, if I'm any judge of men."

"I was certain he had died," said Beobrand. "He had the fever when I left Hithe."

Bassus cracked his knuckles.

"Well, he yet lives and was hale enough. He was keen to hear of your exploits... and your brother's."

Bassus drifted into silence as he relived the moment when he had told the old warrior of Octa's death and Beobrand's quest for vengeance. Pride and sorrow was a potent mix.

"What did you tell him?" asked Beobrand, the slur of drink rapidly vanishing from his voice.

"The truth. That Octa had been a great warrior, killed by a coward and that you sought to avenge his death. When word reached us of Hengist's slaying and that you had also been present at the death of King Cadwallon, I took the news to your uncle."

Beobrand ran his hands through his hair. Bassus watched him sidelong. The change in the young man was vast. It was little over a year since last they had met, but Beobrand had changed from a youth to a man. His shoulders had broadened, his features had hardened. The fledgling fighter had been there to see before. He was skilled with weapons; was a natural warrior. The events of the last year had chipped away any softness in the boy, leaving the stone-faced warrior that sat beside him.

"The pedlar," said Bassus, "who brought the tidings of Cadwallon's defeat, spoke of the young thegn from Cantware who brought the Waelisc king before Oswald, King of all Northumbria."

Beobrand shifted uncomfortably, but did not reply. He stared out over the broad expanse of the Tuidi. The river glistened like burnished gold in the summer sunlight. Swallows darted and cavorted in the valley, preying on unseen insects.

"Still not much of a talker, I see." Bassus laughed. "Your new lord has rewarded you well. You are rich, Beobrand."

"I do not feel rich."

"Warriors follow you. You have land. A hall. Thralls. And what of that lovely girl, the smith's daughter? Did you bed her in the end? Was she worth staying for?"

As soon as he had spoken the words, Bassus knew he had trodden onto dangerous ground. When would he learn not to open his big mouth? Beobrand tensed and turned away from him.

"She died," said Beobrand, his voice barely audible.

"I am sorry. By Frige, I should learn to still my tongue. I let it flap like a goodwife's."

Neither spoke for some time. The sounds of laughter and conversation drifted to them from the hall's open doors. From a slope to the south came the distant whistles of a shepherd. They both watched as the man's dog drove the sheep towards Ubbanford.

At last, Beobrand spoke, his voice brittle as winter twigs.

"I burnt her here, on this hill. A pyre fit for a queen."

"How did she die?"

"The gods took her from me. They gave me a son and took my wife."

"A son!" Bassus blurted. "I didn't know."

"I named him Octa."

"A fine name." Bassus thought of Beobrand's older brother. His sword-brother. His friend. "I hope young Octa grows into as fine a man as his namesake."

Bassus wished to ask more; to seek answers to the questions that bubbled up, but the mood between them was heavy now. He swallowed his words and bit his lip.

Beobrand rose, wincing at the ache in his leg as he stood. He loomed over Bassus, his face in shadow, the sun wreathing his head in light.

"Enough talk of me," Beobrand said, his tone brisk in an attempt to lighten the atmosphere. "What of you and Gram? What brings you both to Bernicia? Are you on an errand for Ethelburga? Where are you bound?"

"Bound?" replied Bassus.

Misunderstanding his intent, Beobrand said: "Of course, you are welcome to stay in my hall as long as you both wish. I was merely curious."

Smiling, Bassus held out his hand. Beobrand grasped his arm in the warrior grip and pulled him to his feet. Bassus clapped him on the shoulder.

"I am not bound anywhere," he said.

Beobrand looked confused. "But where are you going?"

Bassus' smile broadened.

"I'm not going anywhere. We have arrived."

Beobrand's brow creased.

"You came to see me?" he asked.

"To see you, yes. But more than that, Beobrand. We came to serve you." Bassus was pleased that the mood had lifted. He almost laughed aloud at the expression of surprise on Beobrand's face.

"That is," he continued, with a glint of humour in his eye, "if you have a place in your warband for an old man."

Gram, lean, strong and sure of himself, flashed his teeth at Elmer. They circled, legs bent, shields raised. The high sun of morning glinted from their byrnies and helms. The blades of their weapons did not sparkle in the light. The swords were wrapped in leather and wool. This was a practice bout. It was Bassus' idea. Good to get all the men to bond as quickly as possible, and nothing better for that than a good fight.

Beobrand's gesithas, his growing warband, sat on the grass, cheering and jeering.

Most shouted support for Elmer. He was well-liked and had stood with them against many foes. Gram was a newcomer, friend of the giant Bassus. Their lord vouched for them both, and the two men drank, boasted and riddled as well as any, but they were still strangers. They were yet to prove themselves worthy of the warriors' respect. Or trust.

"Come on, Gram," shouted Bassus, "you move like a goat who's been fucked by a bull."

The men laughed. A good insult was always appreciated. Beobrand could not help but grin. The cloud of darkness still shadowed him, but Bassus' appearance had gone some way towards dispelling the gloom that had settled on him.

Maida, wife of Elmer, glared at Bassus. She was surrounded by children, the youngest of whom was Octa, Beobrand's infant son, cradled on her hip.

"Watch your tongue around the little ones," she snapped. "You are not much better than a bull yourself!"

"Nice of you to notice, my lady." Bassus smirked. "It is what many a maid has found."

More laughter. Maida's frown deepened. She looked set to respond, the colour high on her cheeks, but she did not utter any sound. For at that instant Elmer let out a scream and launched a withering attack.

Elmer was broad of shoulder, hale and strong, and his blows rained against Gram's shield. The dull thuds of the padded blade against linden board and the grunts of the combatants were almost drowned out by the men's raucous shouts of encouragement. Maida and the other womenfolk lent their own shrill voices to the cacophony.

Gram retreated, his footing fast and assured, his balance

true. Elmer pressed his attack. His eyes sparkled beneath his helm. He could scent victory. His opponent was on the defensive and his woman, children and all his friends looked on. There was a desperate edge to his attacks. Beobrand sensed it. Elmer had not forgiven himself for the death of Tobrytan. The old warrior and he had been left guarding Ubbanford. When Torran and Broden, the sons of Nathair, had attacked, Tobrytan had died, his throat spitted by one of Torran's arrows.

Elmer screamed again as he battered Gram's shield. There was something else in that scream now. Frustration. Elmer wished to prove himself before his friends and his lord, but this new warrior was deflecting all of his blows. He could find no opening.

In an instant, with no warning, Gram did what Beobrand had known he would do. He suddenly ceased his backwards movement, deflecting on his shield rim a savage blow that had been aimed at his head. At the same moment, he dropped his right shoulder, and thrust the point of his blade beneath Elmer's shield and into his groin.

The watching warriors winced as one. If the blades had not been covered, it would have been a killing blow. A man struck there bleeds like a pig sacrificed at Blotmonath. As it was, the blow would surely hurt. The blades were heavy and Gram had not been gentle.

Gram leapt back, dancing on the balls of his feet, ready for Elmer to counter-attack. But he needn't have worried. For a moment, Elmer looked ready to surge forward, and then his face paled and he crumpled to the ground, clutching between his legs. Maida rushed to him, but he waved her away angrily.

"Well done, Gram," said Beobrand. He limped into the area that the men had roped off for the bouts. His leg hurt. So did the big toe on his right foot. He glanced at the sky, but the wisps of clouds were white. There was no sign of the rain that twinges in his toe usually presaged. He looked down at Elmer. The man was struggling to catch his breath. Beobrand wished Gram had not beaten him. Elmer was a good man. Brave and true. But his belief in himself was damaged. Beobrand held out his hand with a smile.

"Rise, Elmer, son of Eldred."

Elmer reached for his lord's hand and allowed himself to be pulled to his feet.

"You fought well, Elmer." Beobrand slapped him on the back. "I see Gram had to resort to hitting a large target. Perhaps we should call you Elmer the Bull."

Elmer flushed as the men roared their approval. He looked to Maida and smiled sheepishly.

"Who is next to fight?" Beobrand asked. They had drawn lots, those who were not injured, and now Aethelwulf and Garr stepped over the rope. Aethelwulf, by far the shorter of the two, rolled his head, loosening the bunched neck muscles. Garr, tall and slim, stretched his arms up over his head and then touched his toes. He jumped high on the spot a couple of times.

Aethelwulf seemed unimpressed.

"Stop hopping like a flea and fight like a man."

Beobrand made his way back to the stool that awaited him between Bassus and Acennan. He nodded to Rowena, erstwhile lady of Ubbanford, before Beobrand had been gifted the land by Oswald. She sat in the shade of the oak with her daughter, Edlyn. The girl's eyes were wide, as Garr and Aethelwulf began to exchange blows.

Beobrand looked away. Sunniva had liked to sit under that oak and watch the construction of the hall. He swallowed the lump in his throat. He did not wish to think of her. It was too painful. Yet she was everywhere. The great hall, majestic and grand, had been her idea. The doors, with their lavish iron nails and extravagant metal hinges, were her doing. Forged with her small, yet strong and skilled hands.

A cry from the men intruded on his thoughts. Aethelwulf had landed a stunning blow to Garr's helmeted head. The tall man staggered drunkenly. He held his shield limply at his side and struggled to raise his sword. It was a brave display, but he had lost, that was clear. Aethelwulf, not wishing to shame his adversary, stepped in quickly and pulled the sword from Garr's grip.

"Come now, Garr," he said. "All that leaping about has tired you. Let's get some mead."

The onlookers applauded.

Ceawlin, flat face dour beneath thinning sandy hair that was pulled back and held in a braid, stepped up next. He took the sword and helm from Aethelwulf. They were firm friends and loved one another as brothers. Next to Beobrand, Bassus pushed himself up. His bulk was forbidding and Beobrand knew there was skill and cunning to match his size.

"Not too late to run away, little man," said Bassus.

Ceawlin answered something, but Beobrand did not make out the words. Some of the men who were closer chortled.

Movement near the hall drew Beobrand's gaze. Thralls and housefolk were bringing food and drink out into the sunshine. A swish of skirts and the sway of long dark hair held his attention, even as he heard the men cheer at the warriors' antics.

Reaghan.

She glanced in his direction and for a moment their eyes met, before she quickly looked away.

There was a clash of shield on shield and a roar of pain. Yet still he watched the slim Waelisc girl.

"Gods, man," said Acennan. "You would rather make eyes with a thrall girl than watch a good battle. Will you be joining the monks on Lindisfarena in prayer and contemplation next?"

With an effort, Beobrand pulled his gaze away from Reaghan. He did not have the same feelings for her that he had harboured for Sunniva. And yet, when he saw her, he remembered the feel of her fragile form trembling against him. The smell of her hair. When she had been taken by the Picts, he could think of nothing more than saving her. Now that she was safe, he found her in his thoughts all too frequently.

He shook his head and offered Acennan a smile. He could see that his friend was going to say more, probably a further jest, but Acennan closed his mouth tight and turned back to the fight. The events of the last months had left many scars and Acennan still trod lightly with him, scared of ripping scabs from recently healed wounds.

A sudden cheer erupted from the gathered men. Ceawlin had been sorely pressed, using all his sword-skill to parry and evade Bassus' powerful blows. But he could never hope to win. Bassus was too strong, his reach too long. And he was as fast as he was huge. But just when it had seemed Ceawlin would surely fall, it was the giant Bassus who tumbled, sprawling to the yellowing summer grass. Aethelwulf had crept up behind Bassus and then crouched behind him on his hands and knees. Ceawlin had seized his opportunity and bashed his shield into the big man's board, boss to boss. All it took then was a strong shove, and Bassus had tripped backwards over Aethelwulf's body.

Beobrand's gesithas guffawed and slapped each other on the back. It was a simple but effective trick. And they were pleased to see the massive warrior brought low.

Bassus leapt to his feet with a cry of rage.

"You whoresons!" he bellowed, swinging his padded blade in an arc around him. "That's not fair!"

Beobrand stood and shouted, lifting his voice above the tumult.

"Calm yourself, Bassus. You speak true. It was not a fair fight."

The noise died down and they all turned to stare at their lord.

"It was not fair," Beobrand repeated, "but Ceawlin did what you always taught me to do in a fight, Bassus."

The giant's face was red and sheened in sweat. His mouth was pulled down in a scowl.

"And what is that?"

"Win."

Chapter 3

The stink in the small room was one that Beobrand recognised all too well. The sickly tang of rot caught in his throat. He wanted to flee. The stench was almost too much for him. He had stayed away as long as he was able. Not wishing to witness that which he was sure would come, he had found tasks to fill his time and his mind. Disputes amongst ceorls had suddenly become important to him. The ownership of sheep or the theft of a loaf held his attention. He was the lord of Ubbanford, he told himself. It was his duty to see to his people.

But he had another duty. To protect his folk. He was ring-giver. Loaf-keeper. Hlaford. Lord.

He gave gifts, and in turn, his gesithas gave him their loyalty. Their oaths. It was a bond as strong as iron.

And yet iron could crumble; rusting into dust to crack and flake until the strongest of blades could be crushed in a fist.

It was two days after the practice bouts on the hill when Acennan had hurried to find him in the hall.

"You must come soon, Beobrand."

Beobrand had looked up sharply. He had been staring into

the embers of the hearth fire. Lost in memories of flames and death. Caverns and curses. He reached for the cup of mead and found it empty.

"I must come, eh?" he'd slurred.

Acennan had sighed, squaring his shoulders.

Beobrand's senses had been dull from the drink, but he could see his friend was readying himself for a fight. Beobrand had taken a deep breath. All too often Acennan had paid a heavy price for his lord's temper. But this was not Acennan's fault. His anger should not be directed at him.

"How bad is it?" he'd asked, softening his tone.

Acennan had relaxed.

"Bad."

He did not need to say more. Beobrand was lord of land and people now. He commanded men who would stand in the shieldwall for him. They would kill for him.

And they would die for him.

Beobrand had seen so much death these last months, he had hoped he would be spared more for some time. But such was not his wyrd. His wyrd it seemed was to watch those around him perish.

Steeling himself, Beobrand stepped towards the cot in the darkened room. A figure was hunched beside the bed, but now it stood and shuffled towards him. It was Odelyna, the old healer woman. She had not been able to save Sunniva.

"Elf-shot, my lord," she whispered, her stale breath adding to the miasma of the room. "The wound-rot has worked its way into the cut."

For a moment, Beobrand had a terrible urge to lash out at the woman. All she ever brought was sickness. Tidings of doom.

And yet she had helped bring his son into the world. The babe that had killed its mother.

Beobrand clenched his fists.

"Leave us," he said, his voice clipped and cold.

Acennan ushered the woman from the hut as Beobrand moved to the bed.

Attor's features were a-sheen with sweat. His pallor was such that he could have already been dead.

Beobrand sighed, closing his eyes. Torran's arrow had not pierced deeply, but soon after the dawn attack Attor's shoulder had begun to swell, red and raw. Now he would die. Another death to avenge. Another friend departing middle earth.

When he opened his eyes, Attor was staring at him from the gloom. His eyes were bright, glowing like moonlit meres.

"Do not be sad, lord," Attor said. "The Pict's arrow was meant for you."

Beobrand winced.

"I know that, Attor. But I would not have you die to save me. It is a price too high to pay."

Attor smiled thinly.

"I gave you my oath and you have been a good lord. How could it be otherwise?" Attor paused for a moment, gritting his teeth and holding his breath as a wave of pain washed over him. "I would have it no other way. I am your gesith. How could I live with the shame had I let you take the arrow?"

Beobrand thought back to that early morning fight. He had been wearing his byrnie. Attor had been unarmoured. Perhaps the arrow would not have wounded him should it have found its mark. Now they would never know.

As if he could hear his lord's thoughts, Attor said, "Do not dwell on what might have been. My wyrd has been woven."

Beobrand met Attor's febrile gaze and nodded slowly, his jaw set. Bassus always said not to waste time worrying about what you could not control. Scand, who had been a fine lord, had said similar. Beobrand knew he should not dwell on the past, on what could not be changed. He knew it, but was unable to heed the advice.

"You have been the best of warriors. Loyal and brave." Beobrand swallowed the lump in his throat. "We will honour you. And I will avenge you."

Attor's eyes brimmed with tears.

Beobrand reached out his hand. Attor gripped his forearm tightly in the warrior grip. His touch was hot and clammy.

In the silence three short notes from a horn could be heard outside in the valley.

Beobrand gave Attor's wrist a final squeeze and turned to Acennan.

"Quickly. Let's see who approaches Ubbanford. If it is those Picts, they will pay with their blood."

They did not see Attor's savage grin at his lord's words as they swept from the room into the sunlight beyond.

"Who are you and what do you want?" Beobrand's tone was harsh. He had no desire to play host to the bedraggled band of men before him. He had a good idea who they were. They wore the robes of the Christ followers, but he had never seen so many of the robed monks together outside of their monasteries.

There were thirteen of them. One, a skinny youth, was drenched. His robes clung to his bony frame and he stood shivering on the shingle beach. Several of the others were dripping too, though none was as wet as the boy.

Elmer stepped close to Beobrand. It was he who had sounded the horn.

"They just walked out of the trees and began to wade across the ford. Before I could get down here, that little one had slipped and went under as fast as an otter. He was lucky that big one has a fast hand."

Elmer pointed to one of the monks. He was a tall, broad man. He looked more like a warrior wearing robes than a holy man. Beobrand recognised him.

"Biorach!" he said, smiling in spite of himself. The big monk had paddled them across the sea to the lair of Nelda, the witch. Beobrand did not wish to think of that black time. His thoughts were already dark enough. He pushed the memories away and stepped towards the monk with open arms. "You are well come to my hall. What brings you and your brethren hence?"

The monk beamed with recognition.

"My brothers and I accompany the Holy Abbot, Aidan." He indicated a man of middling years. Like all of the monks the front of his head was shaven, leaving his greying hair hanging down behind his ears. He had a full beard and kindly, dark eyes.

Beobrand addressed Aidan as the leader of the group.

"Where is it you are heading?" he asked.

Aidan met his gaze and nodded slightly, but he did not answer. Beobrand shook his head.

Biorach spoke in the lilting tongue of the Hibernians. Aidan replied.

"Father Aidan does not yet know the words of the Angelfolc," he said. Aidan said something else and Biorach nodded. "But he is keen to learn. We are headed to Lindisfarena and we would welcome your hospitality for the night. We are weary, and foot-sore. And I believe young Conant may freeze if we do not get him dry soon."

"You have walked all the way from the isle of Hii?" Beobrand was incredulous. He had made the journey on horseback and would not wish to do it on foot. It was long and dangerous.

"We have. The abbot does not like to ride. In this way we are closer to God's land and His people."

Beobrand could scarcely believe they had traversed the isle of Albion from sea to sea on foot and with no warriors to guard them.

The young monk, Conant, suddenly sneezed. He was shivering uncontrollably now.

Beobrand did not wish to have to spend time with these men of Christ. But they were travellers in need of shelter, and they had fed and sheltered him when he had been on their island sanctuary the previous winter.

"Come, follow me," he said. "My hearth is warm and food and drink will be brought to you." He turned and led the way up the hill towards the new hall.

Reaghan was uneasy. She was unused to hearing so many voices speaking in the water-trickle pitter-patter of her native tongue. The sound stirred many memories. Distant visions of a small straw doll her father had made for her were conjured by the words that washed around the hall. The bitter-sweet recollections of her childhood were quickly engulfed by more recent memories. She closed her eyes for a moment and heard again the coarse voices of her captors in Nathair's hall.

"What are you doing, Reaghan?" The voice, sharp and

scratching as a chipped blade, pulled her back to the present. She opened her eyes.

"Can't you see that the men are awaiting their ale?" the voice continued. Reaghan turned and saw Edlyn.

The girl was several years younger than Reaghan and there had been a time when they had been close. But that time was gone. Blown away on the ashes of Sunniva's funeral pyre and Nathair's hall. Edlyn had looked up to Reaghan once. They had been playmates when Reaghan was spared from her chores. For a time they had almost been like sisters. Sunniva's arrival had changed that. In Sunniva, Edlyn found a new focus for her affections. Sunniva was beautiful, kind and the lady of a lord. Most importantly, she was not a thrall, and she was of the same race as Edlyn.

While Sunniva had lived, Edlyn had merely ignored Reaghan where before she would seek her out. After the lady's death, and Beobrand's interest in Reaghan, Edlyn's erstwhile friendship had changed into loathing. It was as if she blamed Reaghan for Sunniva's death. The more attention Beobrand paid her, the worse the abuse from Edlyn became. And worst of all, the other women seemed to follow Edlyn's lead. The girl's mother, Rowena, was waspish towards Reaghan, and had even beaten her once when she had dropped a freshly washed dress. She had never beaten her before. Even the other thralls and ceorl women were cold to her.

She had nothing to do with Sunniva's demise. And she could not stop Beobrand from bedding her. He was the lord of Ubbanford and she was a slave. What choice did she have? It was confusing, and unfair.

Yet she was used to unfair. Life had ceased being fair many years before.

The confusion she felt was not merely over how they

treated her, but how she felt. She glanced over at Beobrand where he sat at the high table. He was leaning in to better hear some comment from Acennan. Both were sombre of expression. The mood of all the warriors was dark. Beobrand seemed to sense her gaze upon him, for he looked her way. The sight of his ice-blue eyes sent a small tremor down her spine. She remembered the weight of him on her. The gentle ferocity with which he had taken her. So unlike other men she had been with. She felt a warmth in her belly. Yes, so different.

"What spirit has stolen your senses?" Edlyn screeched into her ear. "Do not make me take a switch to you before our guests."

Reaghan lowered her eyes and hurried to serve the monks and warriors at the lower tables.

Beobrand was restless. He watched Reaghan pour ale into mugs and drinking horns. Reaching for his own cup, he wished he could go somewhere away from all of this noise. Perhaps by the river. He liked walking there. The heron might be there, in its usual spot. He liked to sit and watch the bird. It was so still. So focused. He could take Reaghan with him. She was good company, seldom speaking. And she never complained. He snorted at his own stupidity. She was a thrall, of course she did not complain.

"Aidan is asking about your leg." Acennan was translating for the abbot, who sat at Beobrand's left hand. Acennan had spent long years in exile with the sons of Æthelfrith and had learnt the tongue of the Hibernians.

"My leg?" Beobrand had not been concentrating on the holy man. The cloud of Attor's impending doom shadowed his mood. He was a poor host this day he knew, but he had no time for these Christ followers and their soft god.

"Yes, he noticed you limping when you walked up the hill."

"Oh. Tell him it was injured in a fight with neighbours. But it is healing well."

Acennan spoke to Aidan, who nodded and smiled, before replying.

"He asks why we are so sad. Did one of your own die?" Acennan winced as he spoke the words.

For a long while Beobrand did not speak. Was his sadness so evident? He supposed it was. But he would not speak to this stranger of his loss. Of the agony of finding Sunniva and then having her snatched away from him forever. The abbot would be sure to speak of the will of his god or some such nonsense. If he did, Beobrand was not certain he would be able to control himself. He did not believe King Oswald would forgive him if he attacked his new bishop.

"Tell him we grieve for a brave warrior who is going to die of the wound-rot."

Aidan listened intently and then, with the vigour of a younger man, he leapt up.

"Where is he going?" asked Beobrand. He had already drunk enough mead to smooth the edges of his words. His leg no longer pained him.

"He wishes to see Attor," said Acennan, also rising from his stool. "He wants to pray for him."

Aidan spoke quickly.

"He says there is no time to lose. We are to take him to Attor."

Beobrand sighed. He stood, feeling the throb of the healing wound in his leg once more.

"Must we disturb Attor? He has earned his rest."

But Aidan was already striding away. Acennan struggled to keep up. The monks and warriors quietened as the abbot left the hall.

Beobrand did not wish to face Attor again in the noisome hut.

Squaring his shoulders, he limped after Aidan and Acennan. He caught Reaghan watching him as he passed and he frowned. If only he could slip away with her. Walk by the river. Away from troubles. Away from sadness.

But he was lord of Ubbanford and his duty beckoned.

Beobrand sighed again and walked into the cool air of the evening.

Beobrand stood in the doorway and watched Aidan. He admired the firmness in the abbot's step, the calmness in his voice. Aidan seemed not to notice the stench in the room. He swept in and went straight to Attor's bed.

Attor, his eyes gleaming in the darkness, looked up at the priest with awe.

They spoke in hushed tones, Aidan using Attor's name. Beobrand sometimes forgot that most of his gesithas had spent years amongst the Hibernians.

After a brief conversation, Aidan pulled back the bandage that covered Attor's shoulder. Even in the dark of the room, the swelling was apparent, the skin taut and red around the seeping wound. Beobrand wanted to recoil, but held himself still. He clamped his jaw tightly, his teeth grinding. That was a wound elf-shot and destined to bring painful death to Attor. Again he felt the pang of guilt. That arrow had been meant for him.

Aidan seemed unconcerned. He leant forward and sniffed.

He prodded the raw flesh and Attor was unable to prevent a small cry of pain.

Seemingly satisfied with what he had seen, the abbot turned and spoke in his native tongue. He spoke quickly and surely, as one who is used to giving orders and having them obeyed.

Beobrand did not understand the words. Thinking that Aidan had addressed Acennan, he expected his friend to reply, but was surprised to hear a soft feminine voice from behind him.

Reaghan was standing just behind him in the doorway. She must have followed silently behind them from the hall. She spoke to the priest and nodded.

In the last golden light of the evening she was beautiful, her pale angular face wreathed in her sprawl of dark hair. A tiny bat flitted past the door, briefly silhouetted against the opalescent sky.

She was about to leave when Beobrand reached out and gripped her hand. Did she tremble at his touch?

Her face flushed. Turning to Beobrand she said, "The holy man has asked me to bring hot water, bread, mead, honey and clean cloths."

"Does he truly believe he can save Attor?"

Aidan stood and, seeming to have understood the gist of Beobrand's question, responded in halting Anglisc. "Not I. Christ, the God."

Beobrand could not allow himself to hope. There was little in this world that he had seen that made him trust in gods. And still... There was the victory at Hefenfelth after Oswald erected a great cross and had all the men pray. Would they have defeated Cadwallon without the Christ god's aid? Or had they been victorious because of Thunor's storm? Who could tell?

Beobrand stared at Aidan for a long while. The abbot patiently met his gaze. His eyes were deep and dark, and kind.

It could do no harm to let the man call on his god. Beobrand nodded.

Realising he was still holding Reaghan's hand, he relinquished it with a slight feeling of loss.

"Bring him whatever he asks for."

Reaghan watched as Aidan's nimble fingers prepared the poultice for Attor's shoulder. She had brought what he had requested and then lingered in the hut. Several of the monks had followed her back and were now quietly intoning incantations to their god in a language she did not understand. But rather than be frightened of the magic of the holy words, she found their chanting comforting.

Beobrand and Acennan had returned to the hall, and the sounds of raised voices and song drifted to her. As the ale and mead flowed, the atmosphere of gloom that hung over the settlement lifted somewhat, though she knew that by morning the pall of doom would return again, with drink-fuzzed heads adding shortness of temper. She would do well to keep out of people's way then.

The smoke from the small fire in the hut stung her eyes. The room was crowded with people and the heat was stifling. Aidan ceased stirring the contents of the small pot over the fire for a moment and addressed his brethren.

"Your prayers are blessed and welcome, but I fear our patient needs some air to breathe if we are to allow God to bring him back to health. The night is warm. Please go outside and offer up your prayers directly into the heaven above. Thank you, my brothers."

The monks left, one or two grumbling under their breath.

The chanting started up from outside the hut and now, without the need for quiet in the confined space, they set to singing loudly in their strange tongue. Aidan chuckled and raised an eyebrow at Reaghan.

"Well, it may not be any quieter in here, but at least it won't be as hot and cramped."

Reaghan did not return his smile. He seemed kindly. Fatherly. But she did not know him and could not trust a stranger.

He made no further comment, merely setting aside the pot from the fire. In another pot he had placed some of the mead she had brought. He had asked for the strongest she could find and she had shyly asked Ceawlin, knowing he always had a secret store of white mead set aside for his and Aethelwulf's legendary late night drinking sessions. At first he had been suspicious, but when she had told him the drink was for the monks to try and heal Attor, he had quickly remembered where there was a flask of fine mead.

Now the mead was hot, but not yet boiling, and Aidan lifted it from the fire, his hand wrapped in a rag. He then took one of the cloths she had brought from the dairy hut. They were used to strain whey from the curds and were boiled clean. Dipping the cloth into the hot mead Aidan proceeded to wash Attor's wound. After wiping some of the pus away from the festering gash, he lifted the mead and poured it into the jagged flesh.

Attor had been dozing, but now he awoke with a whimpering scream.

"I know it hurts, my son," said Aidan, stroking the warrior's sweat-drenched hair away from his forehead, "but it must be cleaned."

Attor stared up at the abbot, his eyes glazed with the pain. He nodded and Reaghan saw the muscles in his jaw clench. He would not allow himself another scream.

Outside in the darkness the monks' voices rose in song as if seeking to drown out the sounds of Attor's torment.

The wound now clean to Aidan's satisfaction, the abbot picked up the poultice he had made. He had heated honey, bread and mead into a thick paste. He spooned the concoction into one of the cloths and then, before it could cool, he placed it firmly over Attor's shoulder. Attor drew in a sharp breath.

With dexterous fingers Aidan bound the poultice in place.

"The pain should ease soon," he said.

Attor relaxed, letting out a long breath.

"Now there is nothing more to do but pray that God will deliver you. I will check on you in the morning."

"Thank you, father," Attor said in the abbot's own tongue. His voice was thick with pain and fever, but Aidan beamed and patted the warrior on the hand.

Stepping out into the cool of the night, Reaghan realised she had no chores to do. She rarely had time to herself but she had had enough of the chanting monks. They may be holy men, but their eyes still followed her as she walked past where they knelt.

She walked away, leaving their strange words to drift heavenward. Would the Christ god really hear their prayers? Could it be possible that Attor would survive? She shrugged. Who could know? She hoped Attor lived. She cared little for the quiet, frightening warrior, but Beobrand was troubled enough with his recent losses. He would take Attor's death hard.

She recalled the warm touch of Beobrand's calloused hand

on hers that evening. The cool, ice-blue eyes. She often saw him watching her; could sense his need.

With a start, she found that her aimless steps had led her to the crest of the hill. The bulk of the new hall rose up before her. The scent of roasted meat reached her and her stomach growled. She was hungry, she told herself. That is why she had come to the hall.

There was nothing else that had called to her.

She thought of how the women treated her. As if she was to blame for something. She could not deter him from his interest in her. He was lord and she was thrall. She must abide by his command.

But perhaps the womenfolk saw something she had not dared to think of before.

Stepping into the shadow of the hall and nodding to Aethelwulf, who stood as door ward, she allowed a new thought to come to her. She may not have a choice when commanded by her lord, but he had not ordered her to return to the hall this night. She could tell herself that she sought food, but deep within, she knew she came in search of another kind of sustenance.

Beobrand's loneliness called to her. She could not bear to see him thus.

She walked into the heat and noise of the hall. Heads turned to see who had entered and then turned away quickly. It was only a slave.

At the high table sat Beobrand, his hair golden in the firelight. He fixed her with his piercing gaze across the hall.

He had come for her in the darkest of nights. She remembered the strength of his arms holding her to his chest as they rode back to Ubbanford.

Reaghan walked towards the high table, ignoring the hubbub of the hall. Beobrand watched her all the way.

She could not look away from him as she came ever closer. She felt a warmth in the pit of her stomach as she understood what had brought her back to the hall.

Beobrand had rescued her from darkness.

Perchance she could rescue him.

Chapter 4

Beobrand awoke with a sense of wellbeing that he had not felt in a long while. He stretched, careful not to disturb Reaghan, who yet slept beside him. Early morning light trickled into the chamber, picking out the shape of her slender neck; the soft swell of her small breast. Her hair was a dark, unruly tangle.

For a moment, a stab of guilt made Beobrand tense. It should have been Sunniva beside him. The hall was her dream and she had overseen much of its construction. He had seen the disapproving look on Rowena's face as he had led Reaghan to his sleeping quarters. But what was he to do? He was not one of the Christ monks, forgoing the touch of women.

Sunniva was dead. He drew in a long breath. She was gone. Perhaps Nelda's curse would prove true and he would die alone, but for now, he was yet living. And this quiet, slight Waelisc thrall made him feel alive.

When he had retired for the night, he had been surprised, but pleased that she had followed. She had not spoken, merely taking his hand and entering his bed chamber with him. He had been shocked at the response of his body to her touch. It was as if he had been asleep for weeks and was now woken by Reaghan's stroking fingers and warm lips.

They had coupled slowly at first, each unsure of the other's reaction. He was afraid of causing her pain. She was so much smaller than him. But as their passion mounted, she had seized his hips with her legs and pulled him into her.

"You cannot hurt me," she had whispered in his ear.

So he had thrust hungrily into her until they had both collapsed in panting exhaustion.

They had talked no more, each content to bask in the other's body-warmth.

The last thing Beobrand remembered was hearing the Christ monks' chants drifting on the night breeze. It reminded him of his time at Engelmynster. He had been alone and lost then too. There he had been saved from his darkness by the young monk, Coenred.

He smiled at the thought. Coenred was a good friend, but Beobrand preferred Reaghan's methods of reminding him that life was not over. He wondered how the monk was faring on Lindisfarena. Maybe he would travel there before the end of the summer. It would be good to see him again.

From the hall came the sound of running steps. Loud voices.

As quickly as a slap, his sense of calm was replaced with memories of blood and flames in the dark of a terror-filled night.

Had Torran and the Picts returned? Beobrand sprang from the bed. His leg protested at the sudden movement, but held. He pulled Hrunting from its scabbard. The sword's grip was cold in his fist, the blade a-gleam and sinuous with serpent-skin patterns in the dim light of the room.

The footsteps and shouts grew nearer. He readied himself to fight. Whoever came for him would regret it. He hefted Hrunting, prepared to make his assailant pay dearly. The door was flung open. For an instant Beobrand was set to lunge, to spit the man who dared attack him in his sleeping chamber. And then the truth crashed in, like ice water splashed on a slumbering face. This was no interloper. No marauding Pict. It was his friend, Acennan.

Trembling, sick at how close he had come to killing his most trusted warrior, Beobrand lowered his sword. He was shocked at his own actions. A lord should not be frightened in his own hall.

Acennan took in the scene, his gaze flicking from the battle-blade in Beobrand's hand to his lord's body to the thrall girl, face pale and startled, crowned in a dark tousle of hair, propping herself up on an elbow in the cot.

Beobrand was suddenly aware of the morning chill of the room on his skin. He had leapt from his bed naked. He felt his cheeks flush.

"Well?" he asked, anger tinging his voice. "What brings you to awaken me thus?"

Acennan struggled to stifle his smile.

"You should come with me. You will want to see this." He turned to leave, then stopped. "Oh, and you will not be needing your sword... Or Hrunting either."

Acennan could hold it in no longer. Beobrand was sure his friend's laughter would be heard all the way down to the river.

Aidan stood as Beobrand strode into the small room.

"Lord." The abbot inclined his head.

"What news?" asked Beobrand, his voice tight. He still shook from the sudden panic he had felt at Acennan's arrival. He covered his unease at his own reaction with brusqueness. "Has Attor gone?"

Aidan exchanged a look with Acennan.

"See with your own eyes," he said, stepping aside.

Beobrand's throat felt thick. He swallowed. Forcing himself to step forward, he looked down at the cot, expecting the ashen features of a corpse to be staring back at him. Yet Attor still lived. He offered Beobrand a thin smile, exposing yellowing teeth. Gone was the pallor of impending death. The sweat-sheen of elf-shot fever had departed. Could it really be? Odelyna had said he would die.

"How is this?" Beobrand would not have believed it, if he was not seeing it before him.

Aidan spoke in his soft voice and Acennan translated.

"The Lord God is merciful. We prayed and He has answered. It would seem Attor has more to do on His earth before entering the realm of Heaven." Aidan placed a gentle hand on Beobrand's shoulder. "Perhaps, Beobrand, you also have work to do for the Lord." Acennan did not comment on the words he spoke for Aidan, but his eyes twinkled in the darkness.

Beobrand and Aidan stared at each other for a moment. Beobrand wondered if it was his wyrd to be the plaything of gods. He looked away, back at Attor.

"It's good to see you on the mend. We thought we'd lost you."

"I fear I would have travelled a lonely path had not the good abbot come to save me." Attor grinned, then repeated the words in the Hibernian tongue for the abbot's benefit.

"It is not I who needs thanks, Attor," said Aidan, Acennan

46

again acting as interpreter. "It is the Lord our Father in Heaven. When you are strong enough, I hope you will be baptised."

"I will, and gladly," said Attor, eyes twinkling. Gratitude and happiness came off of him like heat from a hearth.

"Show me the wound," said Beobrand. He knew little of baptisms and the way of the Christ followers, but he had seen his share of battle-cuts and was keen to see how the arrow wound, that should have been black and oozing, was faring after a night of prayer.

Aidan unwrapped the bandage and peeled back the poultice. The scent of honey mingled with the odour of putrefaction. Aidan wiped the shoulder clean. Attor winced, but Beobrand could see that the swelling was down, the colour of the flesh close to normal, the skin less raw.

Aidan turned to some pots on the small fire.

He spoke quietly and waited for Acennan to repeat his words for Beobrand.

"He says he will prepare a fresh poultice. It will need changing a few more times yet."

Beobrand leaned forward and sniffed. The stench of wound-rot was gone.

Attor grinned.

"It is a miracle," he said.

Beobrand watched as Aidan heated mead, honey and bread, and then spooned the contents into a fresh cloth. Whether a God-sent miracle or some magic the Christ priest knew for curing wounds, Attor would live. Beobrand smiled at him. The trembling had receded now and his sense of wellbeing was returning.

"I am indebted to you," Beobrand said to Aidan. Acennan echoed the words in the abbot's tongue.

Aidan looked up absently from where he worked.

"You owe me nothing. I am God's servant. Thank Him."

"Well, I thank you and your god too." Beobrand took in the dark smudges under the abbot's eyes. "But I see a man who has not rested much this night. You must come back to my hall and I will have you and your monks fed like kings. And when you are ready to continue to Bebbanburg, I will escort you."

"Food would be most welcome, but simple fare is all we need. And we do not require an escort. God guards us as we travel the land."

It was true that they had travelled for many days and weeks through treacherous country to reach Bernicia, but Beobrand remembered Coenred's sister, Tata, broken and bloody on the altar of the church of Engelmynster. She had believed Christ would protect her too.

"You have saved one of my gesithas and I will have no ill befall you on the last stage of your journey. We will ride with you to Bebbanburg."

It was clear to all there would be no changing Beobrand's mind on this matter.

"Very well," Aidan said, through Acennan's Angelfolc words. "I give thanks to you. This is all part of the Lord's plan."

Beobrand snorted. He knew not if the Christ god had a plan for him. But wyrd would take him where it would.

This new abbot had done him a great service, and for now he would willingly allow their wyrd threads to be woven together.

*

"If you are to leave me here," said Bassus, his voice rumbling in the hall, "you will hear my oath first."

"I do not need your oath. I have your friendship. That is enough." Beobrand flushed. It embarrassed him to speak of such things, especially with his gesithas and Aidan's monks looking on from where they sat at the boards.

"You have my friendship, and freely given. But this is more. I would serve you as gesith. For that, you must hear me speak the words and you must accept me as your man."

Gram rose, to stand beside the huge warrior. Both stood straight as the oaken pillars of the hall.

"I would also swear loyalty to you," Gram said.

Beobrand looked at the faces of his men. Some nodded. Acennan raised his eyebrows, amused at Beobrand's discomfort.

"They speak the truth of it," Acennan said. "You should hear their oath. And you are right that they cannot come with us to Bebbanburg. Who's to say how the king would react to Edwin's right hand walking into the great hall on the rock. Best leave them here," Acennan eyed the two tall men who stood before them, "after they have sworn allegiance to you."

Beobrand sighed.

"Very well. I will take your oaths. Though I never thought I would be lord of one such as you, Bassus."

"What, a great champion?"

"No," Beobrand said, pulling himself to his feet so that he could look Bassus in the eye, "such an old man."

There was a moment's pause and then the men laughed loudly.

Bassus gave a twisted smirk.

"Once that leg of yours is healed, we'll have a bout or two

and we'll see how old I am. And there'll be no tricks next time." He shot a dark glare at Aethelwulf and Ceawlin, who concentrated on their bowls of pottage.

"I accept your challenge. When we return, I will cross swords with you." He felt a twinge of guilt at making jest of his friend in what should have been a solemn moment, but he felt light-hearted for the first time in what seemed an age. He had believed such feelings were lost to him, but the night with Reaghan and then the miraculous recovery of Attor had buoyed his spirits. He clung to his happiness, but forced his face into a sombre expression. "But first, I would hear your oath."

Bassus and Gram knelt before him.

"Let all here present witness the words of these two proud warriors."

A hush fell on the hall. Not all of the monks understood the words, but they could sense the import of the occasion.

Gram intoned the words steadily, seriously. An oath was no matter for merriment. A warrior's word was stronger than his sword. It was everything and he did not give it lightly.

Beobrand had spoken the words before and heard them from his own gesithas, but he still felt a tremor of trepidation at the enormity of the bond between lord and warrior.

Bassus spoke then. His voice rolled around the hall.

"I, Bassus, son of Nechten, will to Beobrand, son of Grimgundi, be true and faithful, and love all which he loves and shun all which he shuns, according to the laws of God and the order of the world. Nor will I ever with will or action, through word or deed, do anything which is unpleasing to him, on condition that he will hold to me as I shall deserve it."

Beobrand noticed that like the men who had sworn to him the year before in Bebbanburg, Gram and Bassus both referred to one god. The Christ god. Things were changing. Uncle Selwyn had taught him the warrior's oath and then he had talked of Woden, father of the gods. Beobrand looked over at Aidan, who returned his gaze with his dark, kind eyes and a smile. Well, one god was as good as any other for swearing oaths. It was the man's word, not the god's, that would be tested.

"I accept your plight gladly. Rise, Bassus and Gram."

He embraced each in turn. The hall resounded with the crash of the men thumping the boards and stamping their feet.

"Octa would be so proud of you," Bassus said, eyes glimmering as he held Beobrand's forearm in the warrior grip.

Perhaps it should have been his brother who stood here in this new hall, surrounded by his housefolk and warband. Octa had been a better warrior. A better man. And yet, he had perished at the hands of Hengist, attacked in the dark, and Beobrand lived. He pushed the thoughts away, like a man pushing the nose of a hungry dog that sniffs at table. He would not let darkness take sway. He held tight to the thoughts of happiness.

Later, when they had eaten their fill and were already loose-tongued from mead and ale, Bassus leaned close to Beobrand. The young man's eyes followed the small Waelisc thrall girl, as she served the men at the other end of the hall. She looked fleetingly towards her lord, a faint smile on her full lips.

"I am glad you have found someone to bring you joy," said Bassus.

Beobrand started, like a child caught at mischief. He watched Reaghan for a moment longer. She walked with a lightness of step he had not seen before. She too seemed happier.

"Yes," Beobrand said, "there is something about her…"

Bassus laughed. "I am sure there is."

"No. I mean… I don't know what I mean." Beobrand hadn't stopped to think about how he felt for the girl. He wasn't sure he wanted to dwell on it now. "I feel the need to protect her." He remembered the overwhelming panic when he had believed she'd died in Nathair's burning hall.

"Hmmm… Perhaps you need to protect her from some who are close by."

"What do you mean?" Beobrand sat up, suddenly alert, a wolf scenting a hare.

"It is probably nothing," Bassus waved his hand dismissively, "but I have seen the way Rowena and her daughter treat her."

"Well, she is a thrall." The words stuck in his throat, like unchewed gristle.

"Aye, she is that." Bassus rubbed his beard. "Living in fear cannot be easy."

Beobrand frowned.

"She has nothing to fear here."

"Perhaps not from you, but a thrall is always in fear of something. It is the way of things."

Beobrand took a deep draught of ale, all the while watching Reaghan. The men grinned and watched her hips as she passed. Then he spotted Edlyn. Her eyes too tracked Reaghan's steps, but where the young girl's face was usually demure and pleasing, now it was pulled into a scowl of loathing. How had he not seen this before?

The drink tasted sour on his tongue where before it had been pleasantly bitter.

He slammed the empty cup down with a clatter. His good mood had fled.

Chapter 5

The next day dawned warm and cloying. The sky was heavy with low cloud and the air swarmed with midges. Swallows dipped and careened over the river, beaks sometimes briefly slicing into the cool water. Beobrand's good humour of the day before had slipped away, driven out of reach by memories of the past and worries of the future. He knew he could alter neither, but try as he might to regain the pleasant feeling of contentment that had filled him, it was like trying to see the sun on a rainy day. You know it is there somewhere in the sky, but no matter how hard you stare, the most you can see is a lightening through the clouds.

Reaghan had visited his bed again. Unbidden she had slipped beneath the blankets and they had made love until sated. Yet even Reaghan could not dispel the gloom that had returned. Deep in the darkest marches of the night he had awoken to feel her warmth against him. For the briefest of moments he had thought she was Sunniva.

The whinny of a horse caught his attention. Acennan, mounted on his brown mare, trotted towards Beobrand. Some way distant, Aidan and the monks, accompanied by Ceawlin,

Aethelwulf and Garr, trudged up the path that would lead them to the coast and to Bebbanburg.

"I will wait for you," said Acennan, reining in his mount before Beobrand.

"No, I will not be long and Sceadugenga needs a good gallop. We'll catch up with you."

"Sceadugenga, or you?" Acennan raised an eyebrow.

"Both." Beobrand forced a grin. It was true that his black stallion would appreciate a run, but he too wished for some time alone with his thoughts.

"I should ride with you. I cannot protect you, if I am not at your side."

"Keep your eyes open on the road. I will be riding in your wake. Nothing will befall me. Besides, Sceadugenga could outrun Thunor's goats and Woden's steed, Sleipnir."

Acennan did not look convinced.

"If you are not with us by midday, I will come back in search of you."

"Very well. Now go. Look for me before the highest point of the sun."

Acennan nodded, tapped his horse's flanks with his heels and cantered up the hill towards the retreating backs of the others.

Beobrand walked through the small collection of buildings that was Ubbanford. The smithy was cold as he passed. Edlyn wished to light the forge and try her hand at what she had learnt from Sunniva, but Rowena would not allow it. It was not a woman's work, she said.

The rest of the settlement was abustle. A couple of men were hammering wedges into a log to split the wood into planks. These would be used in the construction of a new barn. Women carded wool, others were wrapping it onto their distaffs. From the hillside came the whistles of a shepherd and the thin bleating of the sheep. The calls of the withy men, making the fishing basket-traps down on the shingle beach of the Tuidi drifted to him.

It was a good place. A good home.

Arriving at his destination, he saw a woman standing outside her small house. She was spinning yarn. From time to time she turned to her daughter, a girl of eight or nine years, to show her how to tease the wool onto the spindle and whorl. On the grass at her feet played smaller children. One, a plump, pink-cheeked baby, lay on his back, chewing a smooth wooden toy.

The woman did not notice Beobrand at first. She had unpinned her sleeves against the stifling heat and her hair was loose. She was no beauty, but exuded a sense of solidity. Safety. She reminded Beobrand of his own mother. She had been dead these two years now. He missed her still. Probably always would. So many gone. Did they look on from the afterlife? He shook his head, again trying to peer through the clouds of despair at the pale sunlight of hope.

"Goodwife Maida," he said.

The woman, startled, dropped her spindle and distaff with a curse. The yarn fell to the earth in a tangle. She made to retrieve it and then seemed to change her mind. Leaving the wool where it had fallen, she scooped up the baby boy from the ground. The toy fell from his grasp and he began to wail. One of the other children started to weep too. Red-faced, Maida tried to curtsy to Beobrand, holding the screaming baby out towards him.

"Lord," she stammered, "your son is well. Do you see how strong he is?"

Beobrand smiled.

"He has strong lungs, of that there is no doubt." He winced as his son's cries reached new heights.

"Would you take him, lord?" she asked, her timid tone almost drowned out by the babe's protestations.

Beobrand hesitated. He had not thought to hold the boy. Did not know how.

Maida sensed his unease.

"Here, like this. Place your arm thus, carrying his head." She gave him no option, placing the child in his arms. "There," she continued, voice soothing, reassuring both baby and father, "that's right. You've got him now."

Octa ceased screaming and gazed into his father's eyes. For a time, both were silent, observing the other with interest. The baby was so light. So tiny. So defenceless.

"You've got him now," Maida repeated softly.

Beobrand was not sure if she was speaking to him or to Octa. Or both.

Octa reached out his hand and gripped Beobrand's calloused finger tightly.

"My son," whispered Beobrand. The boy's blue eyes stared back at him.

Beobrand said, "Maida, wife of Elmer, I know I have not shown my thanks for your care of my son."

Maida fidgeted nervously. Her cheeks reddened. The girl who had been helping to spin the wool stood behind her mother, her eyes wide. The other child who had been crying, now snivelled, clutching Maida's leg.

"It is my honour, lord," she said, her voice small.

"You have your own bairns to tend. You will not want for anything. If you suffer any hardship, come to me."

"One more babe is no trouble, my lord."

Beobrand looked down again into the blue eyes, lambent in the dull light from the sky. He could see himself reflected back. The same piercing gaze. The scar under his left eye. The strong jaw, bristled with thin straw-coloured beard. His was a hard face. He was shocked at his own scowling aspect. Would Octa one day look as dour? He hoped he would see less suffering. Less death.

"I am thankful for your kindness. A boy needs a woman to care for him. A mother." His throat tightened. He swallowed hard. "Sunniva would be thankful too."

Gently, he handed Octa back to Maida. She took him without a word. They were silent for a moment. She nodded to Beobrand.

Beobrand pulled the thong to open the pouch he wore on his belt. From it he produced a small object. He placed it in his palm and held it out to Maida.

There was no bright sunlight, and yet the object sparkled. It was a ring. Golden with a cut and polished garnet cunningly set in a mounting intricately carved with swirling patterns.

"A lord should give rings to his warriors, and to his most trusted servants. This was part of Sunniva's morning-gift. She cherished it and I am sure she would have wanted you to have it."

Maida was still. Her eyes drank in the lustre of the metal, the deep red of the stone. It was a thing of rare value. She made no move to take it.

"It is yours alone," Beobrand said. "To Elmer, I will give warrior rings and weapons of war. This ring is all yours. Take it, with my thanks."

She shifted Octa in her arms and reached out a trembling hand. The touch of her fingers on his palm was as light as feathers.

She felt the heft of the jewel and smiled broadly.

"I will not know what to do with such a precious thing," she said. Her pleasure at the gift tinged her words with a warm glow. She seemed to grow in stature.

"Would you care for a drink, lord," she said, perhaps not knowing what else to say. "Or maybe some food?"

"I thank you for the offer, but I must leave. I am to travel to Bebbanburg with the priest and his monks."

She inclined her head, sure that the meeting was over.

But Beobrand did not turn to walk away. Instead he said, "Yet there is one other boon I would ask of you."

Maida fingered the heavy gold ring in her hand.

"Anything, lord."

"You have been a true friend to me. To Sunniva. I would have you be a friend to Reaghan also."

Maida straightened. Her lips pressed into a thin line.

"But she is Waelisc. A thrall."

Beobrand sighed.

"She is. And yet, she is…" he hesitated, unsure. "She is dear to me."

Maida frowned, her disapproval clear.

"Reaghan is not to blame for any of this." He waved his hand to encompass all of Ubbanford. He was unclear about what exactly he was referring to. The violence? The deaths? Octa's birth?

"She is not to blame," he repeated. "She is a thrall, and you may make her work, but I would not have her mistreated in my absence. If you cannot be her friend, I would ask that you at least see that she is treated fairly. Can you do that?"

She met his gaze for a long moment, all the while turning the ring in her hand, before eventually nodding.

Beobrand revelled in the cool wind blowing his hair from his face. Sceadugenga, black coat glistening like liquid over powerful muscles, carried him easily at a gallop along the path. The stallion whinnied as it caught the scent of Acennan's mare in the distance. Beobrand pulled gently on the reins and the huge horse slowed, then halted. He was not much of a rider, but Sceadugenga seemed to sense his thoughts and had proven to be a faithful steed ever since Beobrand had ridden him in pursuit of Cadwallon, King of Gwynedd, after the battle of Hefenfelth. That had been scarcely a year before, but now Beobrand could hardly imagine riding a different mount. He patted the sleek neck. Sceadugenga blew hard, but Beobrand knew the stallion had much more to give before it would be tired. It still wanted to be given its head, to pound its hooves into the warm turf. To gallop freely through the clammy day, making its own breeze.

On the brow of a hill beyond a copse of birch trees, Beobrand could make out the group of monks and their warrior protectors.

They had made good progress. The monks must walk as fast as warriors on the march. Beobrand was glad of the extra distance. He would be upon them soon, but he looked forward to one final gallop.

He stroked his hand through Sceadugenga's greasy mane and said in a low voice, "One more run before we walk awhile, boy?"

Sceadugenga's ears flicked back, listening to his master's words. Then, without further encouragement, the horse sprang forward. Beobrand was almost unseated. He laughed as he grasped the saddle's pommel. The stallion's power always lifted his spirits. Riding the steed that Oswald had gifted him after he had delivered Cadwallon to the king, was one of the few times that Beobrand could believe he was truly a lord. From Sceadugenga's back he looked down on the world and was in control of great power. He grinned as he righted himself, pulling himself straighter in the saddle and finding again the rhythm of the horse's gait. Well, perhaps not in total control.

Horse and rider careened down the path, past bushes and a few scattered ash trees towards the valley between two hills. There, the path passed through the small birch wood. The trail was narrow and steep in places, but Sceadugenga knew no fear and thundered onwards. Its great hooves threw up clods of earth in its wake.

They reached the bottom of the valley and the stallion slowed momentarily, stumbling briefly at the change in direction from down to up before hitting its stride again and powering up the incline towards the trees. The foliage was lush and dense, the path a darkened tunnel surrounded by an archway of green. In the woods, Beobrand would need to slow Sceadugenga to a walk. It would be dangerous to rush through and there was no need for haste.

Just as they approached the tree line and the shadowed entrance of the path through the wood, Beobrand noticed something to the edge of the track. At the same instant, the horse seemed to see it too and shied away. The mount ceased its forward run and stepped quickly to the right, away from the object that nestled in the long grass and nettles. Beobrand lost his balance and almost fell. He gripped the reins tightly and clutched Sceadugenga's flanks desperately with his legs.

The horse circled twice before Beobrand regained control.

"There now, boy," he soothed, again patting the muscular neck with his mutilated left hand. The horse's skin trembled beneath his palm. Its ears lay flat on its head.

"Easy, boy."

Only then, when he trusted that the horse would not bolt, did Beobrand turn his attention to the object on the ground that had so frightened Sceadugenga.

Lying on a nest of fresh-cut holly branches was a huge skull. Long and angular, with great gaping holes where eyes once lived. It was a horse's skull, streaked and spattered with brown.

Dried blood.

All around the gruesome totem lay small trinkets. Crudely carved figures of wood, antler and bone. From some of the lower branches of the nearest trees and shrubs hung strips of cloth. They dangled limp and still in the oppressive warmth of the late morning.

On the crest of the skull, stark and white against the scabbed stains of old blood, were the fragile bones of a bird. The tiny skull stared at him with it empty sockets. Small dark orbs above the massive eye-caves of the horse.

A chill rippled over his skin. The echo of a winter's wind on the isle of Muile. The cavern-cold of a witch's lair. The hairs on his arms and neck bristled.

But surely Nelda, the witch who had cursed him, was far away; north and west in her distant island fastness. She could not have followed him here. Could she? No. Folk far and wide left offerings to the old gods. To the spirits of the land.

And to cunning women. To witches who could heal them, make them potions from secret wyrts.

Curse them.

A sudden sound, shrill and loud, made him start.

Tchack, tchack, tchack. The call of a jackdaw.

Sceadugenga tossed its head in fear. Beobrand shuddered.

Scanning the trees he searched for what he knew must be there, watching from the darkness. The living brother of the bird whose bones lay on the skull. For he was then certain that the bones belonged to Nelda's bird, Muninn. And where Muninn, Woden's raven of memory, rested, its brother, Huginn, was sure to be close by.

Yet there was no sign of the bird. The call came, shrieking from the trees again and then was silent.

Beobrand wanted to be away from this place. He imagined that eyes were upon him.

He peered into the shade of the copse. He had no desire to ride into the darkness. But he would not retreat from shadows and birds.

"It's only a bird," he whispered, repeating Acennan's words from Muile, to calm Sceadugenga. Or perhaps himself.

He had named the stallion after it had led him through the shadows of a benighted wood. Sceadugenga. Shadow-walker.

The horse was quivering. It longed to flee, yet held steady, awaiting its master's command.

There was danger in galloping under a roof of dense branches, but Beobrand lowered his head and whispered, "Come on, boy. Let us show them why you got your name."

He touched his heels to the steed's flanks and they surged forward into the gloom under the trees.

The shrieking cries of the hidden jackdaw followed them.

"I told you we should have killed her," said Acennan. He tossed a small log onto the fire. Sparks danced in the night air.

It was a warm night, but a fire was always good to allay men's fears. It kept wild animals at bay; held back the darkness.

Beobrand glanced up from the flames and looked at his friend's round face. It was craggy and hard in the firelight.

"Perhaps it is not her," he said, hearing his own doubt in the words.

"I hope it is not. But I fear it is. She means you harm, Beobrand. We must find her, and kill her."

A moth fluttered towards the newly kindled flames. For a moment it flew happily in the light before its wings set afire and it tumbled into the embers, adding its own tiny death pyre to the small blaze.

That morning Beobrand had traversed the wood and caught up with Acennan and the others without further incident. They had walked on quickly, making good time, and in the warmth of the afternoon, the terror of Nelda and her curse had abated. But like a poorly healed bone, the dull ache did not go away completely. Now, surrounded by the great blanket of a moonless night, the fear had returned, as the pain of a once-broken bone returns when the weather grows cold.

Beobrand rubbed his left side absently. At times, his ribs still hurt him, though they had healed nearly two years hence.

"Perhaps she is watching us now. From out there."

"Let her come," said Acennan, his teeth flashing yellow in the flickering light. "I will not suffer her to live. Besides, Aethelwulf is warding. He will let none pass unheeded." He drew his seax and whittled savagely at a stick.

"Who do you speak of?" said a voice.

They both started. Acennan, usually calm, leapt to his feet. He gripped his seax in a defensive pose. Ready for combat.

"Do not fear. It is I, Biorach." The huge monk stepped into the firelight, Abbot Aidan at his side.

Abashed, Acennan returned to his place on his travel cloak beside the fire.

Beobrand relaxed. He liked Biorach and Aidan. From behind them came the sounds of murmured conversation between Ceawlin and Garr. The monks were eerily silent following their chanting a while before.

Beobrand shifted his position, indicating for the holy men to sit. He handed a flask of mead to Aidan. As the leader of the monks, he must be served first.

"Thank you," Aidan said, his Hibernian lilting tone giving the words more music than was normal. He took a small sip, before passing the flask to Biorach.

The large monk took a long gulp and wiped his lips with the back of his hand. At Aidan's raised eyebrows, Biorach smiled and handed the drink to Acennan.

"The abbot frowns upon drinking more than a tiny amount." He chortled, a pleasant sound like a brook bounding over boulders. "I find it hard to abstain, but the Lord gives me strength."

For a time they sat in silence, until Biorach, at a nod from Aidan, spoke again.

"Who were you speaking of? We can speak freely, the lord abbot has given me permission to speak after Compline."

"Compline?" said Beobrand.

"The last office of the day for those who follow the Regula."

The strange words meant little to Beobrand, but he had heard similar things from his friend Coenred and the other monks at Engelmynster. He wondered if he would ever understand the ways of these holy men of the Christ.

"And you are not allowed to speak after… Compline?" Acennan asked.

"Normally we observe silence until Vigils."

Acennan and Beobrand both looked blank.

"The first office of the morning," said Biorach, smiling.

Acennan nodded as if he understood. Beobrand was sure he did not, but he didn't wish for a long discussion concerning the faith of the Christ followers, so he too nodded.

"So?" Biorach asked. Aidan looked on intently, his dark eyes twinkling in the fire-glow.

"We spoke of the cunning woman, Nelda," said Beobrand. A gust of wind made the flames flare and dance. The night had been still and warm until now. Beobrand did not allow himself to shiver.

Aidan must have understood the name, for he spoke to Biorach in hushed tones.

Biorach translated: "She has not been seen since the thaws in the north. Shortly after you left Hii, she was spotted by a shepherd walking eastward."

"And nobody saw her since then?"

Biorach shook his head.

"Not before we left Muile. And months had passed by then." He turned and translated to Aidan.

Beobrand caught Acennan's gaze.

"We believe she is here. Somewhere nearby."

"What makes you think that?"

Beobrand told of the horse skull, the bird bones. The ribbons and carvings.

Biorach made the sign of the Christ's rood over his body with his hand. Head to chest, shoulder to shoulder.

Aidan spoke in his calming voice and Biorach repeated the words in the tongue of the Angelfolc.

"Do not fear the ways of darkness, Beobrand. Light will prevail, as Jesus conquered death itself. This woman is a lost soul. She searches for meaning where there is none. She has been driven from this land before, I have heard. She will leave it again. The power of the one true Lord is too great for her weak, old gods."

The breeze stiffened, rustling the leaves in the trees nearby. The fire guttered. Beobrand threw on a fresh branch.

He had seen the power of this new god. It had cured Attor. Brought victory to Oswald at Hefenfelth. Or had that been Thunor, with his goat-pulled chariot and thundering war-hammer?

This talk of witches and gods was unnerving. He reached for the flask of mead and drank deeply. Who knew which gods had the most power? Whether Nelda had strong magic or not, he did not wish to have that witch always at his back; a threat to him and his own.

And, as he sat there by the wind-blown flames of the campfire, surrounded by the black of a night without moon, he was certain of one thing. Acennan was right. He should have killed Nelda when he'd had the chance.

Chapter 6

The dry weather held, the wind in the night blowing the clouds away and leaving a land bright with dew-sparkle. Fears retreated along with the shadows of the night, and the camp awoke in good cheer. The monks carried out their prayers and songs before they broke their fast and then, more quickly than a warband on the march, and with a lot less complaint, they were ready to move.

The holy men walked fast, settling into an easy gait that ate up the distance. The earth at their feet was dry and firm and the day was long. And so it was as the sun finally dipped towards the hills in the west that they saw the fortress of Bebbanburg. The rocky crag rose, as stark as a fist thrust from the earth, to stand guard over the gently rolling land around. Atop the rock was a wooden palisade and a section of stone wall that enclosed several buildings. Beobrand saw that the new Christ church that Oswald had ordered to be built was almost complete. Unlike the other buildings, it was made of blocks of stone.

To the east, the outcrop fell away down to the grey water

of the North Sea. The evening was clear, and they could make out the shapes of islands in the distance.

They walked past marsh flats that rolled out towards the sea. The setting sun licked the waters with red and gold, and a host of birds thronged over the grass and mud and brackish water, filling the afternoon air with a cacophony of calls. Beyond the marsh lay the island of Lindisfarena, low and dull green, with pale sandy beaches and a smaller crag on its southern tip to match that of Bebbanburg.

Beobrand pointed from his vantage point astride Sceadugenga.

"Your new home. Lindisfarena."

Biorach and Aidan talked for a moment.

"But is it not an island?" asked Biorach. "The mud and sand reaches it. We could walk there easily."

Beobrand smiled.

"It is an island when the tides are high. At other times the island can be walked to."

Biorach translated. Aidan nodded, seemingly pleased. The other monks whispered excitedly.

"The sands can be treacherous," Beobrand said, "and the tide comes in as fast as a galloping horse, they say. But you will learn of your new home soon. First, let us to Bebbanburg. To Oswald, the king."

"And some meat and fine mead," said Acennan. "And maybe even a comfortable bed and a nice young pretty house thrall to warm it for me!"

Acennan spurred his mare forward. Beobrand held Sceadugenga in check for a moment. He was surprised by the pang of longing Acennan's words had summoned. He hoped Reaghan was well. Maida would see that she was not maltreated, he was sure of it.

He watched for a heartbeat more as Acennan cantered towards Bebbanburg. Then, letting out a cry that sent a multitude of white birds flapping into the air in a fearful cloud, he dug his heels into Sceadugenga's flanks and the stallion bounded forward.

"Aidan, my old friend!" Oswald stood at the high table, gift-stool to one side, and held out his arms expansively. The hall was full of noise and movement. Darkness had fallen and the fire was stoked on the hearth, throwing light and heat far into the great room. Rush lights and candles added their own glow to the far corners. The boards were groaning under the weight of the feast prepared in honour of the new Abbot of Lindisfarena.

Aidan, dark eyes glistening in the red firelight, bowed, then walked the length of the rush-strewn hall and embraced the king.

They spoke quietly to each other in the lilting language of the Hibernians, while the monks made their way into the royal hall. They came sheepishly, unsure of their place and unaccustomed to such rich food and fine surroundings.

Once in the shadow of Bebbanburg, Beobrand and Acennan had ridden ahead to announce the arrival of the abbot and his disciples. Now Beobrand waved to Garr, who towered over all the monks except for Biorach. Garr returned the wave and led Aethelwulf and Ceawlin to a bench near their lord.

Aethelwulf and Ceawlin both sat and called for ale to the nearest servant, impatient for their first drink.

"I have such a thirst from all that walking, I could drink a lake," said Aethelwulf. "And my legs are burning from the pace those holy men set. Anyone would think they had a warm cunny waiting for them in Bebbanburg."

The young girl who was pouring his ale blushed.

"Still," he laughed, giving the girl a playful slap on her rump, "I cannot complain about what was waiting for us. The drink is not bad either!"

The girl hurried away, quickly replaced by a large woman of middling years. She poured ale into the remainder of the cups, a stern expression on her blotchy face. Then she fixed Aethelwulf with a grim stare.

"The only thing to be touched in this hall is the food and the drink. Any more wandering hands and I'll be adding some fresh sausage to the pot."

Aethelwulf gulped down a long draught of ale, but could think of no reply.

Ceawlin said, "Do not bother with his sausage, goodwife, it would not add much meat to the stew."

She turned her withering gaze upon him.

"Then perhaps I will be needing sausage from more than one to add to the stock. Keep your hands on the boards," she said, giving them all one final appraisal, "and your swords sheathed, or you'll answer to me."

With that, the burly woman waddled off to serve others. Or more likely to remonstrate with them.

"Well," laughed Acennan, "I don't fancy Aethelwulf's woman much, but I think she is in love."

Smiling, Beobrand looked to the high table. Oswald was addressing the hall. The hubbub abated as everyone turned to hear the words of their king.

Oswald, chestnut hair framing his angular, intelligent face, held his arms out to his sides as if imitating his Christ god on His death-tree. Beside him stood Aidan, face ruddy in the warmth of the hall.

Silence fell as all waited for Oswald to speak. Two hounds snapped and snarled over a bone. A swarthy warrior kicked one of the dogs away.

At last Oswald spoke. He did not raise his voice as one who declaims before a host. Beobrand had heard him speak many times before and he was always in awe of the way that Oswald commanded attention. His quiet tone made the listeners almost hold their breath in anticipation.

"My people," he said, "I am glad to welcome to my hall and to my lands, the Holy Father of Lindisfarena, Abbot Aidan."

This announcement was met with raucous noise. Hammering fists and the clatter of eating knives onto boards. Cheers. It was not that the king's gathered thegns, his comitatus, were overjoyed at the arrival of the Christ priest, they were simply relieved to be able to release the pent-up tension in the hall.

Oswald held out his hands again.

Hush. Silence.

"Some of you know that the monks who follow Christ lead a simple life. They do not eat rich meats. They do not drink like warriors at the mead-bench."

"The more for us," shouted a man from the back of the hall. Laughter rippled through the gathered throng. Oswald smiled.

"But tonight they will make an exception. Tonight I invite them to dine of my table as honoured guests who have travelled far at my behest. Aidan has given his permission for his brethren to feast with us. Treat them well and remember they are not warriors, but men of God."

The warriors cheered again. New faces in the mead hall was always a thing of interest. Perhaps they could learn news from afar. Or clever new riddles. Or games.

Oswald spoke to the monks who had congregated nervously at one side of the hall and explained to them what he had said. They relaxed and began to find places to sit. Biorach looked particularly happy, thought Beobrand. The large monk lifted a horn of mead and drained it in one gulp, to roars and laughter from the warriors nearby.

Aidan sat at Oswald's side at the high table. There also sat the king's brother, Oswiu. The atheling, solid and still like the crag of Bebbanburg itself, raised his drinking horn in Beobrand's direction, a thin smile on his lips.

At the far end of the table sat a lady of great beauty. Long, flame-red tresses tumbled down her back. Her eyes were downcast, hands folded demurely in her lap. Finola, widow of Eanfrith, Oswald's other brother. She was the sister of Gartnait, King of the Picts, and thus of great worth to Oswald. She sat now, as she always did when Beobrand saw her, quiet and still. A beautiful peace-weaver surrounded by men of war.

Beobrand felt sorry for her and her son, Talorcan, who sat at her side. They were both as good as prisoners of Oswald. And yet, their lot was not so bad. They had shelter, fine food and drink. Many would have killed to have the privileges they enjoyed.

For a heartbeat, Beobrand pictured Reaghan. Something about Finola reminded him of the slight Waelisc thrall. Both appeared fragile, their slim figures dainty and alluring.

And both were captives. Each thrall to their own wyrd.

A movement at the other end of the high table broke his reverie.

Oswald was looking directly at Beobrand, his eyes shadowed and dark. He held out his right hand and beckoned for Beobrand to approach.

"I see you have saved one of my men from a long ride," said Oswald, seating himself and reaching for a beautiful glass beaker.

"Lord King?" Beobrand stood before his king awkwardly. The last time he had faced Oswald had been at Dor, at the frontier of Mercia and Deira. A dark day following a night filled with lightning and spite. It had ended with Beobrand having to take the life of his servant, Anhaga, who had broken the King's truce, almost throwing Northumbria into war with Mercia. A war that Oswald had made clear he was keen to avoid. He had been furious with Beobrand and the warrior was unsure of his king's mood.

Oswald raised his glass to Beobrand with a smile. It seemed he did not bear him ill will. But it did not do to relax around kings.

"I was going to send a messenger to Ubbanford. You have saved me the trouble." Oswald indicated to a thrall to bring a stool for Beobrand.

Beobrand sat tentatively, uneasy at his presence at the high table. He cleared his throat. The slave proffered a wooden cup brimming with a dark liquid. Beobrand took a sip. His eyes widened. He had never tasted the like before.

Oswald laughed at his expression.

"It is wine. From Frankia, by way of Cantware."

"Wine?" said Beobrand, his mouth still caressed by the rich warmth left by the drink. He had heard tell of the stuff, but never before tasted it. "What is it made of?"

"Grapes. A fruit. In Frankia they drink it like we drink ale."

Beobrand took another mouthful of the wine. Both its spicy smoothness and the king's good cheer served to calm his nerves.

"It's good," he said. He savoured the taste of the drink in silence for a moment, then asked: "Why were you going to send for me?"

Oswald ignored the question.

"Word reached me of the burning of Nathair's hall." The king's eyes were suddenly hard; obdurate like flint.

Beobrand stiffened.

"They were my people, Beobrand. You cannot slay my people like you would slaughter cattle at Blotmonath."

The savage hatred of that night flooded back into Beobrand as quickly as a summer storm. With an effort he kept his tone low. His words came clipped and sharp.

"Those Pictish pigs had slain my people." From the edge of his vision he saw Finola's flame-red hair flick. For an eye-blink he felt sorry for his words. She too was a Pict. Then he remembered the red smear on Rowena's mantle. Tobrytan's blood. He recalled the trembling form of Reaghan as he had clutched her to his chest. He swallowed against the sour dryness in his mouth.

"They took my people. They had been warned."

"You should have come to me. There are laws. You should have asked for weregild for your slain. And for any object or thrall stolen from you."

Beobrand took a deep breath.

"You are right. There are laws for your people. But I did not see Nathair and his sons at Hefenfelth. Where were they when we slew Cadwallon and scattered his host?"

Oswald's eyes narrowed. He knew the Picts had not been

there. Many men had chosen to await the outcome of that fateful battle near the Wall before giving their fealty.

"Did you see them after that? Did Nathair's clan come to swear their oath to you, Oswald King?"

Oswald's face gave his answer.

"Then I have done you a service by ridding you of them. They were not men of honour. Heed my words, they will not be the last Picts we have to kill before this land is truly yours."

Oswald's anger flared again.

"You cannot judge which men should live and which should die. Only the Lord God has that power. And the laws of this earth must be followed or we are no more than animals."

Beobrand set down the cup of wine. His hand shook.

Squaring his shoulders, he said, "I have done nothing wrong. My people were attacked. I defended them and took payment in blood."

"You should have sought weregild. Gold in payment for the affronts on your own."

"I did nothing wrong," Beobrand repeated. "Has any man come to claim I have broken my oath or to seek weregild for a crime?"

The king finished his beaker of wine before replying. When he did, his voice was faint.

"It is hard to seek payment when you are dead."

Beobrand nodded. At last they understood one another.

"Yes. Nathair had to die," he said, his voice stony and chill. "As did Cadwallon of Gwynedd."

The King met Beobrand's gaze. For a time they stared at each other, neither averting his eyes. In the end, Oswald gave the smallest of nods and a flicker of a smile touched his lips.

"What of Nathair's sons? Did you slay them also?"

"He had three sons," Beobrand said, acutely aware of the ache in his arm and leg from the wounds inflicted by those sons. "Two are dead."

"And the third?" enquired Oswald.

Beobrand thought of white fletchings in the darkness, the stench of wound-rot from Attor's injury. Nothing good would come of speaking of these things with Oswald.

"Torran has fled like a kicked cur."

"You must be careful, Beobrand. You cannot kill whoever crosses you."

"Perhaps not," replied Beobrand, picking up his cup once more and draining it of wine. "But you have my oath, Lord King. And you know I will kill whoever crosses you."

The night drew on. Prodigious amounts of food were eaten. There was roast venison, oysters and a great pot of rich, tasty stew. All this was mopped up with freshly baked soft bread. The drink flowed as freely as water from a spring. And the men, warriors and monks alike, got drunk. The riddling began, and riotous laughter greeted the first of the bawdy word-games that were loved by all.

Beobrand had returned to his place with his men and now sat back, stomach full and drinking horn filled with good strong mead. Aethelwulf seemed to have worked some magic on the portly serving woman, for she attentively refilled their cups without being bidden and Beobrand was sure that she brought Aethelwulf the choicest cuts of meat.

"What did Oswald want with you?" asked Acennan.

"He wanted me not to kill people." Beobrand took a swig of mead. He was already past the point where he knew he would regret it in the morning, but the drink was sweet and fragrant, and like a man who is abed with a willing woman, there is a moment when there is no turning back.

Acennan choked on his ale.

"What? Nobody?" he spluttered.

"Said there are laws."

Acennan, also well on the way to drunkenness, nodded slowly.

"So no more killing then."

"We came to an understanding in the end," said Beobrand, with a thin smile.

"What?"

"I would only kill those who the king wants dead."

"Seems fair enough," said Acennan.

They watched as Conant, the young monk who had almost drowned fording the Tuidi, stood on a board, juggling three wooden cups. It was an impressive show of dexterity. The warriors howled and cheered. Moments later Conant lost his balance, took a faltering step to one side and tumbled from the table. He landed with a crash atop several of Oswald's house thegns. This got the loudest cheer of all.

As the noise died down, Acennan turned to Beobrand, eyes struggling to remain focused.

"Is that all he wanted?"

"No, there was more. He was going to send for me if we hadn't arrived today. We are to accompany him south."

"To Eoferwic?" The old city was in Deira, south of the Wall, and the location of one of the royal halls.

"No. Further. To Wessex."

"Wessex? Why are we going there?"

"It seems the king is in need of an heir."

"Well, he's not going to find one in Wessex, is he? Or do

77

they grow on trees there?" Acennan began to giggle at his own words.

"No," sighed Beobrand, "heirs do not grow on trees in Wessex. But that is why Oswald is travelling there. That and to strengthen ties with King Cynegils."

Acennan looked blank.

"Oswald seeks a peace-weaver."

Understanding finally dawned on Acennan.

"Not the heir, but the heir-bearer!" he said, words slurring.

"Yes," said Beobrand, reaching for more mead. The moment of no return had passed long since, and now was the time to seek oblivion.

"Oswald is to marry Cynegils' daughter. And we are to travel as his escort."

Chapter 7

Coenred drew in a deep breath and looked back towards Lindisfarena. Above the island, the sky was a dark blue, dotted with wisps of white cloud. From where Coenred stood, he could see his own tracks passing over the flat, wet sands that separated Lindisfarena from the mainland of Albion. He still marvelled at how the sea came rushing in to smother these sands with each high tide. He cast his gaze further to the slate-grey waves of the Whale Road. He knew he was safe. The waters would not return for a long time yet, but he was still uneasy standing on the sands that at other times would be the ocean floor.

Far in the distance, barely visible against the drab green of the isle, he could just discern the cells and chapel of the monastery. He had helped to construct some of those buildings; to dig the vallum around them. And to bury the abbot, Fearghas. He had loved the old man. Fearghas had given him so much; rescued him from a life of misery and offered him something to live for. A new God. Brothers in Christ. A family of Christian brethren.

A home.

He sighed. Above him wheeled sea birds. Many had swept down to the sands and were now pecking at the prints left by the monks for the worms unearthed by their steps. Coenred loved the island and its peace. The simple life of prayer and toil was a good one. And yet, he could not deny that he was excited to have been called to Bebbanburg again.

The king was to marry a princess of Wessex. And the king of that distant kingdom, Cynegils, was to be baptised into the Christ faith. These were important times. And King Oswald had asked for Coenred personally to travel with him to act as scribe for the events.

Coenred thought back to the meeting of kings at Dor. He had been there to write down the decisions and pacts made by Oswald and Penda. It had been a great honour. And yet it was there that he had begun to feel real doubt about his calling. When confronted with the injured Wybert, the man who had violated Beobrand's beautiful wife, an almost all-consuming rage had filled Coenred. When Wybert had shown no sign of repentance, it was all he could do not to slay the man.

The shrieks of the birds brought him back to the present. In a dark, hidden part of his mind the sound of birds always conjured memories of the previous winter. The cave on Muile. The witch. The jackdaw. Cormán.

"Come on, Coenred."

The voice of Dalston cut through his thoughts before they could pull him from the warm summer's day and back into the terrors of that frigid winter.

Coenred took one last look at Lindisfarena, and turned to follow Dalston and Gothfraidh. He had known Dalston since they were novices together at Engelmynster. They had never been close. There was something about Dalston that grated on Coenred's nerves. And yet, they had both seen much suffering; their old home destroyed and those they cared for killed. Neither was a boy any longer. They had each grown. Dalston was nearly a head taller than Coenred now, and the pimples that had so marked him in previous years had all but left his face, leaving little more than a shadowy pink memory on his pale skin.

They were not friends, but they had shared much. And shared hardship could not be easily ignored or forgotten. Coenred did not particularly like Dalston, but he did respect him. Dalston had not initially taken to the arts of writing and illumination, but he had worked ceaselessly until he was able to scribe as well as the most skilled monk of the monastery. In fact, he was far more adept than Coenred.

Gothfraidh was older; one of the monks who had accompanied the king from the isle of Hii. Though Gothfraidh was often taciturn and gruff, Coenred loved the man. When all had seemed lost, Gothfraidh had spoken up for Coenred. He had believed him over Cormán. Coenred would never forget.

Why did Oswald request his presence? Fearghas and the king had been close. And Oswald respected Gothfraidh. Coenred supposed it must have been Fearghas' and Gothfraidh's faith in him that made Oswald invite him to be his personal scribe. Perhaps the incident with Cormán was why Oswald favoured Coenred over the other monks. Whatever the reason, he was glad of the opportunity to once more expand his world. The events he had witnessed beyond the vallum of the monastery often frightened and saddened him. Yet he wanted to see more.

He caught up with Gothfraidh and Dalston.

"No time for dilly dallying, Coenred," said Gothfraidh. His voice was stern, but his eyes twinkled.

They walked on in silence for some time.

Before them, the westering sun threw the rock and fortress of Bebbanburg into shadow. They still had far to walk, but if they pushed themselves, they would reach their destination before dark.

"We are to witness a royal wedding," said Dalston, in his breathless voice that always sounded to Coenred equally fearful and enthusiastic. "And a royal baptism. Can you believe it?"

Gothfraidh snorted and strode ahead, leaving the youths to their chatter.

Coenred did not answer for a while. He thought of the portentous things he had seen. The future of kingdoms being decided. Abbots being chosen. Men elevated to positions of power by their lord.

What great events would they see in Wessex?

He shook his head.

"No," he said, surprised at the realisation, despite the many hardships and woes he had faced. "No, I can't believe it. We must be truly blessed."

Bebbanburg was crowded. Thegns and ealdormen gathered, answering their king's call. As each arrived with his own retinue of warriors and thralls, the atmosphere of the fortress reminded Beobrand increasingly of the time he had spent within the cramped confines of the walls. The previous summer had been a time of fear in preparation for battle with the Waelisc, followed by celebration and feasting. The air of the place now was closer to the festivities of victory than the gut-clenching nerves before war, but one thing was different for Beobrand.

The previous summer, when the noise and bustle of

Bebbanburg became oppressive, Beobrand had found solace and comfort in the arms of Sunniva. Now there was no quiet corner where he could forget himself, lost in his lover's embrace. There was no soothing word to cheer him when he doubted himself.

There was no Sunniva.

As he had done so many times before, he looked out over the sea from the eastern palisade. He watched ships being laded on the sands below. Men shouted, hefting bales and casks. Ropes were repaired. He was not looking forward to the journey south. He was no sailor and had no love for the rolling, shifting deck of the wave-riders that plied the routes of the Whale Road. Such was not his wyrd. Yet where the king led, he would follow.

He gazed southward, where the long shadows of the dying sun picked out the dunes in stark relief. Beyond the sand and marram grass he knew there lay a sacred place. A burial ground. His brother, Octa, mouldered there in a Christ follower's grave. But Beobrand would not go to him on this visit. The tree-lined area of canted grave markers and mounds unnerved him, and would do nothing to improve his mood.

He missed Sunniva. And he missed Octa. It was the living he needed, not the dead.

Perhaps sensing his dark mood, Acennan and his other men had left Beobrand alone to wander. They had been at Bebbanburg now for several days and as the fortress became more clogged with people, so Beobrand's humour worsened. He fretted over Ubbanford. Convinced that Nelda had travelled south and meant him and his people harm, he had sent Aethelwulf and Ceawlin back to Ubbanford with instructions for Bassus to set watches. They were to be vigilant. Should Nelda show herself, they were not to hesitate. She must be slain.

The two doughty warriors were not pleased to be sent home. They would miss the feasting that came with a royal wedding. "I've heard things about those Wessex wenches," Aethelwulf had said. "Good things, if you take my meaning."

"You will have to make do with Bernician lasses, for you are to stay at Ubbanford," Beobrand had replied.

"Picts and crones, that is all we'll get here," Ceawlin had moaned. "Not Wessex beauties."

"Pigs and kine is all you deserve," Acennan had said, with a grin. "Now, be off with the two of you. And don't drink all the mead before our return."

Having the extra men under Bassus' command, went some way to settling Beobrand's unease. But he knew he would not rest well until he was back in his own hall. And Nelda was no longer a threat.

"Hail, Beobrand, you ugly whoreson!"

Beobrand looked down into the courtyard to see who was shouting his name. A large man with a bristling beard had ridden through the gate at the head of yet more warriors and servants. He waved at Beobrand. Despite his bulk, he leapt easily from the back of his fine steed. His blue cloak shone in the dying sunlight, and rings glimmered on his muscular arms.

Beobrand raised a hand in response.

"Athelstan, you goat-swiving bastard, I didn't know you were coming with us to Wessex. I didn't think Oswald would want you to be seen outside of his borders." He made his way down the ladder from the palisade.

Athelstan strode towards him and clasped his arm.

"Well, the king has the princess already promised to him,

so I am no threat, with my good looks. Of course, the other women of Wessex will have to be wary, for they are wont to swoon at the sight of me." He grinned.

"Swoon at the sight of you?" Beobrand laughed. "I have heard that is the only way you can get a woman."

"We shall see, young Beobrand. We shall see. If you're lucky, perhaps I will teach you how to woo women."

For a moment, Beobrand's face clouded. Athelstan knew all too well of Sunniva's death. And what had befallen her before, at the hands of Wybert, at the time one of Athelstan's own gesithas. Beobrand frowned as he thought of the dark secret Sunniva had taken with her to the afterlife. How Wybert had violated her. Beobrand's hands clenched into fists. He had not been able to protect her and even the bitter salve of vengeance had been denied him when he would have slain Wybert at Dor.

Sensing the jesting had gone too far and had strayed from the path of mirth, Athelstan raised his voice so that all his men could hear.

"Now, enough of this talk of women. Where can a man find a drink in this place? You and I must raise a horn to old friends and fallen companions."

Chapter 8

"Will you never learn?"

The voice cut into Beobrand's head like a seax slicing into a ripe apple. He looked up from where he huddled at the stern of the ship. Coenred looked down at him. His face was split into a broad grin. The strakes of the vessel shivered as the bow ploughed through several small waves. The wind was brisk and the ship's ropes sung, thrumming and taut. The sail strained and cracked. From where he sat, the rushing water was muffled, but the sounds of the ship were amplified. It was as a living thing, groaning and creaking.

A wave broke on the bow and the chill spray splattered Beobrand's face. His stomach gave a lurch with the ship's motion, but he held his body still, breathing shallow breaths through his mouth. He would not disgrace himself.

His mouth filled with spittle in a rush. He swallowed it back down. It was bitter.

"Every time we meet, you are drunk or fighting," Coenred said. There was no real reproach in his voice and his smile remained. He held out a hand to Beobrand.

Beobrand thought for a moment, before grasping the

monk's arm and allowing himself to be hauled to his feet. Coenred had grown, his limbs now strong from building and working the land of Lindisfarena.

"You're almost a man," Beobrand said, trying to smile despite the churning in his stomach.

"I wager the monk can hold his drink better than you," roared Athelstan from amidships. Some of the sailors and warriors laughed. Beobrand did not find it funny.

"You're as pale as milk," said Coenred.

"I am fine."

"You don't look fine."

All Beobrand wanted was to be left alone long enough for his stomach to settle. By Woden, why had he allowed Athelstan to goad him into drinking so much? And why did Oswald always travel by sea?

Turning his face into the wind, Beobrand welcomed the cold air and spray. How he wished he had not been called upon for this journey. He would happily have stayed in Bernicia with Oswiu. The previous day Oswald had announced that his brother would not be travelling south for the ceremonies that were to be carried out in Wessex. There was unrest in the north of the land. It seemed Beobrand's neighbours were not the only Picts who resented the rule of the Angelfolc. Word had come to them of another hall-burning. A band of Picts, perhaps some of those whom Beobrand had displaced, had descended from the hills and killed all the inhabitants. Oswiu, grim-faced and solid, would put an end to the Pictish scum, of that Beobrand had no doubt. He hoped that Torran would try to confront the atheling. He would not survive an encounter with Oswiu.

"Have you come to scratch on your calf skins again?" Beobrand asked. He knew Oswald placed great importance in having all his decisions written down. Coenred had tried to explain the value of capturing the words in writing, but it seemed pointless to Beobrand. He spat the foul-tasting spittle from his mouth.

"Yes. Dalston and I are to record all that is agreed in Wessex. Gothfraidh travels with us."

"To see that you behave yourselves?" Beobrand offered a thin smile. "The ladies of the south had best keep their legs crossed around you monks, eh?"

Coenred flushed and frowned. Beobrand felt a twinge of guilt at his jesting.

"What of Abbot Aidan?" he asked. "Does he not travel south with you?"

"He is to stay in Lindisfarena," Coenred replied, his tone curt. "The king wished him to accompany us, but he said it was vital that he get to know his brethren here, in Bernicia."

The ship topped another wave and Coenred held out a steadying hand. Beobrand shook it off angrily. If only he had been able to stay with Oswiu.

"I'm fine, I tell you."

"If you say so." Coenred sounded hurt. They had not seen each other for many weeks, and he was clearly making an effort to rekindle their friendship.

"I am sorry, my friend," said Beobrand. "I am not myself."

The grin returned to Coenred's features. His robe flapped around him.

"I thought you said you were fine."

"Yes, I am." Beobrand smiled wanly. "I am fine."

And with that, he leaned over the side of the ship and noisily emptied his stomach into the foam-flecked sea.

*

The journey was not pleasant, despite favourable winds. The further south they travelled, the worse the weather became. The cold wind that drove their wave-riders through the surf brought with it darkening skies and rain. As the weather worsened, so the king's mood soured. He was on edge. What should have been a joyous occasion – the union of two kingdoms, both in marriage and under the same God – became a source of annoyance to Oswald. He had been exiled for years before returning to Northumbria to claim his throne. It had been a hard-fought reconquest. To leave now, while the Picts in the north threatened, stuck in his throat like the bone of a fish. The thegns told him not to fear. Oswiu would hold firm. Oswald would nod at these comments. His brother was indeed strong and determined in battle.

And yet, it was the uncertainty, the lack of knowledge of what might be transpiring, that needled and nagged.

Beobrand knew how his king felt. He could not turn his mind away from thoughts of Nelda working some dark mischief. In his dreams he saw Ubbanford in flames, as he had put Nathair's hall to the torch. He heard the screams of the dying. The shattered face of the woman he had struck down in that hellish night often flickered in his mind's eye, as if seared there by the conflagration of the hall. In the darkest moment of the night, he would sometimes awaken to find his cheeks wet from tears. But the men never saw him cry. He hardened his face. Grim, dour and scarred. His beard was yet thin, that of a young man, but no man would dare belittle him. Those who had seen him in battle were in awe of his skill. Those who had not, noted something in his gaze. He had the stare of a man who had seen more than his share of death, but would happily feed the ravens until they were too full to fly.

Beobrand's humour was not improved by the motion of the sea beneath the keel of the ship. After the first day, once he had rid himself of the excesses of the night's drinking, he was able to hold down some food. But he was no sailor and he was ever woozy, his bile threatening to rise.

After four days, they entered a land of fog and fens. They passed between small islets. Reeds and rushes sometimes loomed from the mist, causing the steerman to lean hard on the steerboard to avoid running aground. The wind died like the breath of a hanged man and the men were forced to the oars. Sounds in the fog were loud. Distant splashes drifted to them, but they never saw what creatures made the sounds. Birds shrieked and shrilled. Beobrand reached under his kirtle and clasped the Thunor's hammer that he wore on a thong around his throat. This was an evil land.

Oars creaked in tholes. Men spoke in whispers.

Athelstan spat over the side.

"This land is not fit for men."

"It had better be, Athelstan, son of Ethelstan," said Oswald, his voice as cold as the fog, "for it is the land of the East Anglefolc and we are to visit King Sigeberht at his hall. In a place called Dommoc."

"Do we not head for Wessex?" asked Beobrand. The sooner they were done with the wedding and the Christ rite, the sooner they could return to Bernicia.

"We will not tarry long in Sigeberht's lands, but he worships the one true God and he sent word for us to meet. He is our brother in Christ. We may well need to help each other to hold back the darkness from the lands."

"Well, with this fog," said Athelstan, "we'll be lucky if we find him. The darkness seems to have already overrun this Sigeberht's kingdom."

As if in response to his words, a flash of light blazed in the fog in the distance. A warm glow such as that cast by the setting sun hazed the horizon.

"See there," said Oswald, a spark of excitement creeping into his voice, "they have lit a beacon to guide their Christian brothers safely to Sigeberht's hall."

Athelstan glanced at Beobrand. Neither was as trusting as the king that this was the Christ god's doing. The fire could as easily have been lit to lure hapless seamen to their doom. Beobrand helped Athelstan into his byrnie, then struggled into his own. Most of the men not rowing did likewise. The fog echoed with the clatter of shields and spears being hefted.

Acennan growled from where he pulled at an oar, "See that my sword is close to hand, Beobrand. If we are attacked, I would not be unarmed."

"Do not fear," said Coenred, voice thin. "The king here fears God."

"And I fear cold iron and things I cannot see," said Athelstan, reaching to touch the hilt of his sword for reassurance.

They were drawing close now. They peered into the gloom, straining to make out details of the shapes around the fire on the beach.

Moments later they saw they should have trusted their king's faith. The fire had indeed been lit by Sigeberht's men, a surly group who awaited them on the pebbled beach. The Northumbrians were led with great ceremony by these desultory wardens to a long hall that nestled behind sand dunes. The hall was surrounded by several smaller buildings. All of them had reed-thatched roofs.

The fog was breaking up, and a watery sun forced its beams to shine briefly on the cluster of buildings. Oswald smiled to see that the hall was topped with the wooden cross symbol of the Christ.

His good humour was short-lived. They handed over their weapons, then entered the hall. But there they found no food to greet them on groaning boards, no fire crackling on the hearth. They had been at sea for days; were tired and hungry. This was no welcome for a king and his retinue.

"Where is your king?" Oswald asked one of the door wards. "Does he not greet us, with the cup of welcome?"

The man lowered his gaze, unable to look the Lord of Northumbria in the eyes.

"He is there." Scorn dripped from his words, like honey from a comb. "Praying."

At the far end of the hall, in the shadows, knelt a slim figure in a pale robe.

Oswald took a deep breath.

"Very well."

He strode forward. When Beobrand and the others made to follow, he held up a hand.

"No. I would speak with the King of the East Angelfolc alone."

He walked the length of the hall and knelt beside the king. There the two leaders remained for a long while, heads bowed, whispering in the gloom.

Beobrand, Athelstan, Acennan and the rest of the king's men stood stolidly waiting. They had not expected such a welcome. Treachery and steel was always a possibility when two kings met. Or feasting and noisy merriment. Boasting and gift-giving.

This indifference was unnerving.

The warriors, not used to being kept waiting, began to fidget.

To the door warden's obvious relief, Oswald finally rose from his knees and walked back down the length of the hall. The men looked at him expectantly. His face was unreadable, but Beobrand thought he noted a tightening around the eyes. Perhaps the jaw was clenched.

"We will sleep here tonight." Then, to the warden, "You are to order bread and salt fish be brought for my men. And clean water."

"Water? Fish and bread?" Athelstan bellowed, his outrage reverberating in the still hall. "We are warriors. Thegns of your comitatus. Not shepherds and thralls."

"Yes, you are my comitatus," said Oswald, his words clipped. "I am your king and we are in the realm of another. We are guests in this hall, and we will accept what we are offered."

Athelstan hoomed deep in the back of his throat, but said no more.

They spent a cold, mirthless night in Sigeberht's hall. The fish was tasteless, the bread gritty and hard. No fire was lit. Sometime in the evening, as the blaze of the setting sun outside made them yearn all the more for a roaring fire on the hearth, Sigeberht rose and addressed them in the language of the Christ priests.

Oswald bowed his head and nodded sagely. Gothfraidh, Coenred and Dalston spoke words in the ancient tongue in response to Sigeberht's words. Beobrand and the other men knew not what was said, but the King of the East Angelfolc beamed with pleasure at the sound of the monks' chanting voices answering his own sombre booming.

"This Sigeberht, it seems," said Acennan in a hushed

voice, "is more monk than king." His stomach let out a gurgling rumble. "This is no way for kings and warriors to live."

Several of the Northumbrians nodded and muttered their agreement. Oswald flashed them an ominous glower and they quietened. But Beobrand noticed the shame on the faces of Sigeberht's own retainers. They knew how a visiting king should be greeted. Their king brought them all into disrepute.

Beobrand thought back to the healing performed by Aidan. The victory at Hefenfelth. The Christ had real power, but was it necessary to eschew all pleasures of the flesh? A good king should above all things be generous; a giver of rings and wealth. That was gōd cyning. He wondered how long Sigeberht's gesithas would remain by his side. Glancing around at the frowning men and shuffling thralls of the hall of Dommoc, he doubted it would be long before this king was left alone with his god.

In the morning, they resumed their voyage, glad to be away from the gloomy piety of Sigeberht. Oswald did not speak of the encounter, but it was not hard to see he was unsettled. If he had hoped for a strong ally in Christ, someone to harry the Mercians on their eastern borders, he must now be questioning that likelihood.

The mist followed them south but burnt away in the late morning. The breeze did not return, so for that day and the next they made slow progress. The men, many unused to rowing, complained of blisters on their palms. Beobrand, pleased to be able to do something of use, took his own turn at the oars and quickly fell into a comfortable rhythm. At first, he believed he would be able to pull at the oar all day, but soon his shoulders and back began to burn. And his recently recovered left arm smarted with each pull. He gritted his teeth and stared at Garr's slim back, matching him stroke for stroke.

There was no merriment or jest in the ships. It was as if the last vestiges of humour had been sucked out of them at Sigeberht's hall. All they hoped for now was to arrive at their destination soon.

And that Cynegils, who they knew was to be baptised into the brethren of Christ, had not also become a shadow of a true king.

When they reached the wide estuary of the Temes, they turned to the west, and rode the incoming tide into the river that would lead them into the mainland of Albion, all the way to Wessex. To Dorcic. To the hall of King Cynegils.

But first they must pass through the lands of the East Seaxons.

They moored the ships that night, as the sun dipped below the horizon. Grey clouds streaked the western sky, laden with rain.

"The rest of the journey will be on the river," said Athelstan the next morning. The rain that had threatened now fell in an incessant drizzle. Their world became small, all distance hidden in the sheets of rain.

"Come on," roared Athelstan, "put your backs into it."

They heaved and pulled, and made their way, stroke by stroke, up the river. At first the river was so broad they could not see the opposite bank. Later, they slid closer to the shores. Shadows loomed through the mist. Stone and clay buildings, like those at Eoferwic. Buildings left by the mysterious Romans who had built so much, conquered all, and then disappeared like a dream that only the land itself remembered. As always, the sight of these edifices of stone made Beobrand uneasy. All that power gone and forgotten.

He shivered.

Without warning, the rain ceased. The sun, held captive behind clouds for so long, burst forth and shone its brilliance on the wide river. The crumbling ruins of the city that sprawled to the north of the river lost their mystery. But they were no less impressive. Some of the buildings had collapsed. Others showed signs they had been burnt. But many yet stood, and many more recent wooden structures also dotted the waterfront.

With the unveiling of the sun, they saw vessels all around them. Men rowed small skiffs towards them, raising up produce for sale. Buckets of fresh fish. Barrels of ale and mead. Trinkets. Rope. Baskets of reeds. All manner of food.

"This is Lunden," said Athelstan. "Once a great city, now a ruin."

It still looked great to Beobrand. The city was massive and the river around them now was loud with hawkers and fishermen.

One man bumped his boat against the hull of their ship. Athelstan pushed the bark away with a shove of his spear.

"Get away from us," he roared. "We want nothing from you."

They were slowed by the rabble, but after much jostling and shouting, the three Northumbrian ships managed to manoeuvre past the assortment of boats and continue upstream.

The only other incident that gave respite to the back-breaking rowing came shortly after they had passed Lunden. They rounded a bend in the river to find themselves confronted with three longships tethered together end to end, forming a barrier across the Temes.

Oswald had no intention of halting again to spend time with the king of these lands. But this was something he was prepared for.

"Arm yourselves," Oswald said. "Leave only half the number on the oars. The rest, to arms."

Beobrand wriggled into his byrnie with help from Acennan. All around them, men were once again donning their battle gear. This was what they were prepared for. Pulling on the oar might be good to build strength in shoulders and arms, but battle was where men could win fame.

They readied themselves for blood-letting. A sudden thicket of spears swayed on each of the Northumbrian ships. Watery sunlight glinted from helm and spear-point.

The barrier ships were likewise frantic with activity. The shouts of men being goaded into action carried over the water. Soon, men lined the barricade. Brightly painted shields shone. Polished bosses shimmered.

But there would be no battle-glory this day for Northumbrian or East Seaxon. No feeding of the beasts and the fish of the Temes. For Oswald did not wish to be delayed from his course.

He motioned to Athelstan and the two of them walked to the prow of the ship.

"Pull steady," said Athelstan. "Bring us in close."

The few men left on the oars did a good job, pulling fluidly to move the ship towards the barricade.

Within a spear's throw, Oswald held out his hand and called out to the men blocking their path up the river.

"I am Oswald, son of Æthelfrith, lord of Bernicia and Deira, king of all Northumbria. I request passage for my hearth-warriors and I."

On the middle ship of the barrier, a swarthy man with a

97

black beard and bulbous nose called out, "The river is closed to all unless they pay tribute."

Athelstan took a step forward as if he meant to let fly his spear at the man who demanded tribute from his king.

Oswald placed a hand on Athelstan's shoulder.

"I have told you my name. Who are you and on whose authority do you demand tribute?"

"I am Tredan, son of Tredan. My lord is King Sigeberht, and it is he who demands tribute."

The men in the ships murmured at the sound of the name.

Athelstan, incensed, blurted out, "Why that snivelling turd. That nithing. We sat in his hall not three days hence and now he sends men to steal from us. I'll have his heart. I'll rip out his entrails and make them into a belt. I'll—"

Oswald stopped his tirade with a raised hand.

"This Tredan," he said in a calm, quiet tone that would not be heard on the barricade, "speaks of another Sigeberht. Sigeberht the Little is leader of the East Seaxons. He is not a lover of Christ. I have heard rumour that he is often seen in the hall of Penda of Mercia. We must tread warily here. Stay your tongue, Athelstan."

The big thegn took in a deep breath, casting a murderous glare at Tredan, before nodding and taking a step back.

Oswald spoke loudly, for all to hear.

"Tredan, son of Tredan, I trust we are well met."

Tredan looked flustered, unsure how to respond. After a pause, he nodded.

"So, you will pay tribute to my king? To Sigeberht?"

"I will not," replied Oswald.

The warriors on both sides stirred. The afternoon air was suddenly tinged with menace.

"If you do not pay tribute to Sigeberht, you cannot pass. Turn your ships and return to the Whale Road."

"I am King of Bernicia and Deira. I am soon to be wed to a daughter of Wessex. I will pay tribute to no king."

Beobrand scanned the men on the barricade. Which one would he have to kill first when the fighting started? His stare met the eyes of an East Seaxon; a broad man with a small metal helm, a yellow shield and green cloak. For a few moments they held each other's gaze. Was the Seaxon thinking he would have to kill the tall fair-haired Northumbrian with the scar under his left eye?

Oswald continued speaking.

"I will not pay tribute to any king. But I will pay for passage on a river through a king's lands."

Tredan scratched at his beard, contemplating Oswald's words. In the end, he nodded. The tension washed away, as blood spilt in a river is diluted and then vanishes.

In the end, after much bargaining between Athelstan and Tredan, for it would be demeaning for a king to haggle over a price, the Northumbrians handed over a small chest of hack silver for Sigeberht and a finely crafted seax as a gift for Tredan.

The barricade was removed, and Oswald's ships were allowed to pass.

As they glided past the watching Seaxons towards a stretch of river that was flanked on both sides by dense forest, Acennan spat over the side.

"So, that's two King Sigeberhts. One gave us nothing but cold fish and water and the other takes pounds of silver so we can row up a river. I hope we meet no more Sigeberhts in the south."

Beobrand did not reply. He watched as the East Seaxon boats vanished around a bend in the river.

Darkness and cool air descended upon the Northumbrian ships as they moved into the tree-shadow of the forest. Beobrand felt a chill run down his spine. They rowed into unknown territory. Behind them they left two kings with the same name. One an ally of Penda who could blockade the river and halt their return to the sea. The other, a worshipper of Oswald's Christ, more akin to a monk than king, who would be of no use in a battle.

He was not sure which troubled him more.

Chapter 9

Torran took a slow, deep breath. He could hear rustling in the undergrowth. Deer often trod this path; he had seen the spoor. Another muffled crunch. The animal approached his position. Torran had been waiting quietly beside the small pool for a long while. His empty stomach grumbled and he tensed, hoping the creature would not hear the sound and be startled.

If it would only step into the clearing, his immediate problems would be over. He could not miss such a shot. Broden had always claimed Torran could take a sparrow in flight through the eye at a hundred paces, but his brother had liked to boast. Torran knew the truth. He was a decent archer. Perhaps even a good archer. But he was not a great archer. Still, he had been the best bowman of Nathair's people. Torran seldom missed his mark.

Until that Seaxon whoreson Beobrand came to Ubbanford. Torran clenched his fist tightly about the bow. If only it were Beobrand about to step from the shadow of the trees instead of a deer. For the chance of vengeance Torran would happily go hungry for another week. That Seaxon bastard had taken everything from him. First Aengus. Poor, foolish Aengus. What had possessed his youngest brother to attack Ubbanford? Beobrand had slain the boy with barely a word and had offered no recompense. No weregild for his death.

Torran's hands began to tremble, such was his rage. He breathed slowly again. He must remain calm, or he would miss again, as he had so often of late. It was as if his skill had fled with the arrival of Beobrand. After Broden's death and the destruction of the hall, Torran had fled north. Others had joined him, looking to the last son of Nathair to guide them. They had caused some mischief, preying on travellers and pedlars, but soon the desire for revenge was too great for Torran to resist. He had convinced his band of brigands to attack Ubbanford at night. They would burn Beobrand in his hall. Kill his retinue when they burst forth from their slumber, just as Beobrand had done to them. The men had not wanted to stand against the mighty warrior and his gesithas, but Torran had cajoled them. He had been so sure of their victory.

But somehow Beobrand had known of their coming. Instead of a night raid against sleeping men, Torran and his Picts had found themselves ambushed and facing warriors of great battle-fame, armed with swords and garbed in iron-knit shirts. The Seaxons had cut them down like barley at harvest. Torran cursed silently as he recalled that night of blood, failures and shame. His last shot would have hit its target if it had not been for that crazed bastard rushing him. He hoped that one had died from the arrow wound at least.

Later, the survivors had slipped away, leaving Torran alone. He had roamed the hills and forests for many days, too proud to seek refuge. He had always been a good stalker, able to bring down game even when it was scarce, but now he felt cursed. He had eaten no meat for days. Berries, roots and leaves was no food for a warrior.

Another hushed hoof-fall. The deer would step from the trees in a heartbeat.

Silently, using all his skill, Torran filled his lungs with air and drew the string of his bow back. He sighted along the shaft of his arrow, the iron tip glinting dully in the green light under the trees. He did not breathe for many heartbeats. His heart pounded in his ears and yet he stood as still as a rock.

At last, the deer, tawny coat sleek in the dappled light through the leaves, stepped cautiously from the gloom. Its head peeked out from behind the bole of a huge oak.

One more moment. He would wait for the perfect shot. Another step and the chest would be exposed. The tension of the bow pulled at the muscles in his shoulder and back. The cord dug into his fingers, but still he waited, ignoring all but the deer.

It raised its head, as if scenting the air. If it had smelt him, he would slay it anyway. From this range, he could not miss.

"Well, what have we here?" said a voice from behind him.

Torran let out a small cry of surprise and loosed the arrow. The deer bunched its muscles and sprang over the pool and into the trees on the far side of the clearing. A flash of fawn and it was gone. The arrow rattled off the oak trunk and disappeared harmlessly into the foliage.

Torran spun around, reaching for the sword at his belt.

"I will kill you, whoever you are!" he screamed, all his ire, hunger and disappointment focused on this newcomer who had caught him so unaware.

"You will do no such thing, Torran mac Nathair."

From the dense trees stepped a woman. Her hair was frost-streaked black, her face, half turned from him, was beautiful.

Her plump lips parted slightly in a smirk and she moved into a shaft of light. Her green dress was the same hue as the summer-bright leaves. It clung to her body, accentuating shapely breasts and hips.

Torran's mouth was suddenly dry. How had this woman come upon him so silently? She had made less noise than the hart. Could she be an elf? A creature of the woodland?

"Who are you?" his voice cracked. He had spoken to nobody in days.

The woman turned her head the other way and Torran's breath caught in his throat. The left side of her face was scarred and broken; a thing to bring fear to children in mead-hall tales. Her face was the moon. One side white, pallid and lovely, the other dark and evil. He suddenly needed to piss.

"I am Nelda," she said in the tongue of the Picts. "You have nothing to fear from me, Torran." Her voice was rich and sensual. His gaze drifted to the curves beneath her dress, only to flick up once more to the ruin of her face.

"How do you know me?" he croaked.

"I know many things," she smiled. The shattered teeth behind her rose-petal lips were hideous. "And I know what you seek, Torran, son of Nathair."

Torran shuddered as if a chill wind had blown through the trees. But the sun yet shone and the day was warm.

"What is it you think I seek?" he asked, his voice as small as a child's.

"I can help you find fame and fortune." She stepped closer. Her presence was intoxicating. He wanted to run from her, and yet he knew he would not. "And I know how you can wreak vengeance on your blood-enemy. On Beobrand, son of Grimgundi."

Nelda's eyes were as deep and cool as mountain meres.

Her tongue flicked over broken teeth, wetting her lips. He swallowed against his mouth's dust-dryness. He knew not whence this strange woman had come. Was she even flesh and blood? Perhaps she was a goddess, come to middle earth to walk amongst men for a while. But woman or goddess, she knew his name. And she knew his desires. His heart yearned for glory, but more than that, he burnt for revenge.

He looked fully on Nelda's face then. The two sides of the moon, the dark and the light. The perfect and the ruined. The good and the evil. She grinned.

He would see Beobrand bleed. He would see the accursed Seaxon dead for what he had done.

"Tell me how," he said.

Chapter 10

"I will kneel for no man!"

The bellowed shout was loud enough to cut through the general hubbub of the great hall of Dorcic. Beobrand looked up, setting down the fine drinking horn that had been passed to him moments before. It was filled with a heady local brew which cooled the throat and dulled the senses in equal measure.

At the high table, King Cynegils had stood up, knocking his finely carved seat over with a clatter. He was as different from the pious King Sigeberht of the East Angelfolc as fire is to ice. Tall and broad, with a wide red-veined nose, he did not strike Beobrand as one who would turn his back on the old ways of gift-giving and feasting.

On arrival at Dorcic, Oswald and his retinue had been treated with the pomp and honour expected by visiting nobles. The men had laughed and smiled as they had been led to a great hall, pleased to see such grandeur. It was as large as the hall of Gefrin, Acennan had said. Beobrand had nodded. It was a hall fit for a king, of that there was no doubt. He thought it was larger than Gefrin had been, and also more ornate. The lintel over the doors was carved with all manner of animals. They intertwined; a wolf bit the tail of a raven who in turn pecked at the claws of a great fire-breathing wyrm. The roof was topped with massive horns, larger than any bull Beobrand had seen.

"Perhaps they are the horns of an aurochs," Garr had whispered, awe in his voice.

They had been offered a warm welcome by the lord of the hall. Cynegils' daughter, Cyneburg, veiled and demure, offered around the cup of Waes Hael and they each drank heartily from the good, strong mead. In the absence of her mother, who had died some years before, the princess carried out the duties of lady of the hall with well-practised ease. She would make a good queen to Oswald.

The afternoon of their arrival had been warm, so the hearth was not aflame with crackling logs, but they saw firepits outside the hall where meat was being roasted. Cynegils had clearly had men watching the river so that his household could be prepared for this meeting.

Beobrand and the others had been cheered still further when they had seen the young women who served in the hall. Most were pretty, with swaying hips and easy smiles. A couple of them were true beauties.

"We must ensure we tell Aethelwulf and Ceawlin what they have missed," Acennan had chortled, as a girl with raven-black hair and startlingly blue eyes had filled his cup with ale. She had reminded Beobrand of Nelda, and tiny claws of ice scratched down his back, but he could not deny she was lovely. Acennan had beckoned to the girl and she had leaned in close, lips parted slightly, a smile in her eyes.

"Here," Acennan had said, holding out a dainty gold ring

inlaid with a small garnet, "something beautiful for the most beautiful girl in Wessex." Beobrand had no idea where he had produced the ring from.

The girl had eyed both Acennan and the ring suspiciously for a long moment, before taking it and slipping it into a pouch she wore at her side.

"So, you have seen all the girls in Wessex, have you?" Her face was stern now, but the smile still played in her pale blue eyes. "Do you say the same to all of them?"

"I do not need to see all the other girls to know that you are the most beautiful by far."

She had blushed, but dazzled him a radiant smile, white teeth between plum-plump lips. Then, with a swish of her skirts, she had bustled away to fill more cups from the pitcher she carried.

Beobrand had clapped his friend on the back.

"You work fast. You'll be wed before sundown at this rate."

The men had laughed. But Beobrand noticed with a pang that Acennan's features clouded slightly. Both he and Acennan had been wed before. Happy and in love. But things changed. And wives died.

Beobrand had been keen not to let his or Acennan's mood sour. The journey from Bebbanburg had been sombre. Now with good ale and mead in the horns, food on the boards and comely women to serve them, there was no reason for melancholy. He had slapped Acennan on the shoulder, forcing a grin.

"Let's drink to the women of Wessex."

The men had roared their appreciation of this fine toast and they all drank deeply.

The mood of the hall had been jovial since then.

Until Cynegils' outburst. Now all eyes were on him.

"I will kneel for no man," he repeated, his cheeks red with the flush of drink and his anger.

Another man at the high table stood. He wore the robes of a Christ priest and his hair was cropped in a strange way. Unlike Coenred, Dalston and the other monks from Hii and Lindisfarena who shaved the front of their heads up to the crown, this man had shaved a circle of hair from the top of his pate, leaving a ring of hair all round. This must be Birinus, the bishop from the southern lands over the sea whom they had heard would perform the baptism and wedding.

"My king—" Birinus spoke with a strange lilting, sing-song to his voice. He shook, voice tremulous, clearly afraid of the reaction to his words. "My king, we have spoken of this. In the baptism, you must kneel in the—"

"I will not kneel!" Cynegils boomed. He hammered a fist into the board before him to accentuate his words. Beobrand saw there were many scars on the king's forearms. This was a king who had stood in shieldwalls. He smashed both his fists into the board again, sending cups and plates crashing to the rush-strewn floor. His anger was terrible. This was not a man to take lightly.

A hound leapt up from where it had been dozing under the kings' table and sloped off, away from the furious man.

Oswald stood slowly beside Cynegils and placed a hand on the older man's shoulder.

"You will kneel," he said in a voice as cool as midnight.

Silence now in the hall. All strained to hear. Beobrand was suddenly alert. If the feast turned into a fight they were outnumbered. And worse, their weapons were stored for safety by the door wardens.

Cynegils turned to Oswald with a glare. He opened

his mouth to shout, but Oswald spoke again in his calm, cold tone.

"You will kneel. But to no man. You will kneel to the one true God and you will be washed in His Holy Spirit. For if you do not there will be no marriage. No alliance with Northumbria. And the next man you kneel to will be Penda. And believe me, the lord of Mercia is not so forgiving as Christ."

The hall seemed to hold its breath. The two kings stood face to face. Cynegils was panting, such was his ire. Oswald was still, slim and seemingly fragile next to the bulk of the Wessex king. And yet he stood his ground. Oswald's clever brown eyes never left Cynegils'. He may be slighter of frame, but he too was a force to be reckoned with.

After what seemed an age, Cynegils finally laughed. He reached for Oswald and embraced him, laughing all the while. Oswald appeared somewhat confused by the reaction for a moment, before he too smiled and returned the embrace.

"As I said, I will kneel to no man," Cynegils said, the anger in his voice replaced with mirth. "But I think even I, Cynegils, son of Ceol, son of Cutha, son of Cynric, King of all the West Seaxons can bend the knee to a god. And not just any god, the one true God!"

Night fell. Outside bats flitted between the buildings. The embers of the firepits glowed and flickered. Not for the first time that evening, Beobrand made his way to the midden pit to relieve himself. His pace was heavy, his steps weaving. Would he never learn? At least he would not be expected to take to the water in the morning. The mere thought of boarding a ship churned his stomach.

He grunted as he loosened his breeches and let out a stream of steaming piss into the stinking morass of the refuse pit. From the hall came laughter and singing. After the kings had embraced, the merriment had not let up. Scops sang. Men told riddles and tales of sword-play and battle. Barrels of ale and mead were consumed along with copious quantities of meat.

Beobrand looked up at the clouded sky. He could see no stars, but the moon's light paled the clouds. He fumbled with his belt and breeches, cursing under his breath at the clumsiness of his left hand. Turning, he staggered slightly, off balance. It would not do to partake any more of Cynegils' hospitality this night. He may not be going by ship in the morning, but they would all be going to the water. He had never seen a baptism, but Coenred had told him what would happen. It would not do for him to puke in the river while a king was being doused with sacred water.

Nearing the hall, he saw a man and woman briefly silhouetted against the doorway. The couple left the hall and Beobrand glimpsed the woman's pale face and full lips wreathed in black hair. The man was Acennan. Good for him. He had been giving the girl his attention all night and she seemed eager enough to give him what he wanted in exchange for his smiling flattery. And the garnet ring, of course. Beobrand felt a twinge of jealousy. He thought of the warmth of Reaghan's body next to his. But it would be weeks before he saw her again. Perhaps he too could find a willing Wessex girl.

He watched as the couple, arm in arm and leaning in close to one another, moved into the shadows between two buildings.

Smiling at Acennan's good fortune, he started towards

the hall once more, when he noticed four more figures leave the building. At first he believed they were going to relieve themselves of the ale they'd consumed, but there was something about their movements. Something in their bearing. They did not walk like drunk men looking for somewhere to piss. They moved with the stealthy silence of hunters. They were all large men and none of them spoke above a whisper as they followed Acennan and the girl.

Where moments before Beobrand had been befuddled by drink, now a calm stole over him. There was no time to seek help, or to fetch any weapons. But of one thing he was quite certain: these men were not pleased with the attention Acennan was receiving from the dark-haired beauty. And from the way they now stalked him into the darkness, they meant to make sure he would regret approaching her.

Quietly, Beobrand followed the men at a distance. If they meant his friend harm, they were the ones who would look back on this night with regret.

Into the darkness the four men walked, oblivious of Beobrand shadowing them. Acennan and the girl were clearly making for a destination far from the hall. Somewhere quiet. Secluded.

The couple darted between two buildings. The larger of the two seemed to be a byre, the scent of hay and manure surrounded it. The other building was dark and silent; perhaps a storehouse. Sounds of feasting from the hall carried into the night air, but were muffled at this distance. Further away, Beobrand heard the hushed murmur of wind caressing the leaves of the trees that lay at the northern edge of the fields that surrounded the settlement.

The four men sped up, closing the gap between them and

their prey. Beobrand caught the faint light of moon-glimmer on metal. A blade! He rushed forward. He would not allow Acennan to face these men alone. Or worse, to be surprised by them, unarmed and unaware. Something fluttered into his face as he ran, making him start. Just a moth, seeking the light of the firepits. He brushed it away absently and hurried forward. The men had disappeared between the two buildings now and no sound came from them.

As stealthily as he could while still moving fast, Beobrand rounded the corner. A horse whinnied and stamped in the byre. For a moment, he could make out nothing in the moon-shadow. He peered into the gloom. There was a shuffling movement and forms coalesced from the darkness, but he was still unable to make sense of them. Then, suddenly, someone fell backwards into him, with a grunt. Without thinking, Beobrand shoved and the man stumbled back between the buildings.

At the same instant, Acennan's voice came clearly from the shadows.

"Is that the best you can do? Did you think the four of you could take me?"

"We'll kill you, you Northumbrian shit." The voice was young. Brash and strong. Certain in the superiority of four armed men against one who carried no blade.

"There will be no killing here tonight," said Beobrand, voice as hard and cold as chiselled rock. He sensed as much as saw the faces turn towards him.

"Who are you?" asked the voice.

"I am Beobrand, son of Grimgundi, thegn of Bernicia and Lord of Ubbanford. Who are you?"

"Fuck off. Or we'll gut you too." Was there a slight tremor now?

"There are two of us, and four of you. Drop your blades and fight us like men."

"Why should we do as you say?"

"Our kings have just sworn to be allies. Oswald is to wed Cynegils' daughter. How do you think they will take to their gesithas slaying each other?" He paused for a moment to let that sink in. "Besides, if you start a fight with Acennan and me with blades drawn, I swear on Thunor's hammer we will kill all of you. Now, you choose."

He backed out of the darkness into the relative light of the path. He tensed his leg. The wound still ached, but the leg was strong now. He rolled his shoulders and winced slightly at the tightness of his left arm. The night hid his grimace. His arm would have to do. His course was set now. Whatever happened, there would be a fight.

Slowly, cautiously, the four men shuffled out of the shadowed alley. The squat figure of Acennan came behind them. They twisted this way and that, not wishing to turn their backs on either warrior.

"I still see seax blades. This is your last chance. Drop the weapons, or I swear they will taste your blood before this night is through."

After a moment's hesitation, they let their blades drop to the grass at the side of the path. As they did so, without warning Beobrand sprang forward, swinging his right arm towards one man's face. Sensing the attack, the man tried to duck but was too slow. Beobrand's elbow connected hard with the side of his head. He went down, as if struck with an axe.

Beobrand was aware of Acennan entering the fray. There was noise and movement, but he could not afford to lose his focus. His senses were perfectly clear now. The battle calm enveloped him and he welcomed it like the embrace of an old friend. He had hoped that his savage attack would give the second Wessex man pause, but it was not to be. Rather than being stunned, the man threw himself at Beobrand. A fist glanced against his cheek as he swayed back, taking most of the sting from the blow. The man came on without respite, seeking to wrestle and gouge. Beobrand slapped the man's arms away from his face.

He stepped back again, letting his adversary swing wildly. The man's eyes, wide and unblinking, shone in the darkness. Beobrand took a punch on his right forearm. A second blow came fast. He deflected it on his left arm, gritting his teeth against the pain. He allowed the Wessex man to throw two more punches, each time parrying them or stepping backwards. His opponent's teeth gleamed then, as his lips pulled back in a snarl of victory. He stepped quickly forward again, ready to land another blow. But this time, Beobrand did not step back. He raised both his arms before him, gripped the man's kirtle in his fists and pulled him on towards him. At the same moment, as fast as an eye-blink, he swung his head forward. He put the weight of his body behind the attack, folding from the waist. The man's blows went wide. They made less impression on Beobrand than the moth that had touched his cheek moments before.

Beobrand's forehead slammed into his enemy's nose with crushing force. Blood splattered black in the moonlight. The man swayed, but to Beobrand's surprise, did not fall. Beobrand shot a quick glance in Acennan's direction. He was down on the ground and wrestling with one of the men. The last one lay crumpled in a heap on the grass by the discarded seaxes.

Turning his attention back to the man before him, Beobrand was grudgingly impressed with his strength. The West Seaxon shook his head like a bear that has been stung by a bee, and then launched himself at Beobrand with a roar.

There was no more time for this. Again, Beobrand let the man come, but this time, he feinted a jab at his blood-slathered face. The man saw the punch and tried to block it. Beobrand let him. He took a brisk step forward and hammered his knee into the man's groin. The wind rushed from his attacker's lungs and he let out a groan. Beobrand shoved him hard on the chest. The man stumbled, tripped and fell, sprawling on the path. Beobrand finished him with a savage kick to the head.

He spun around, ready to help Acennan. But his friend was rising from the still form of his opponent.

Beobrand felt a strange mixture of disappointment and elation.

His heart pounded in his chest. He could hear its thumping. His arm stung. His forehead throbbed. He was vaguely aware of the ache in his big toe. He had broken it once before, kicking a man in the face. Perhaps he had done the same again. But despite all of the hurts and pains, unbidden his face split into a wide grin. For it felt good to fight. Every day he had held back his anger. The gods had laughed at him, taking all he loved.

He stood there, panting in the darkness, surrounded by fallen foes.

He had wealth. A great hall. Lands. A fine sword.

A son.

He had all these things, yet none brought him happiness.

Acennan staggered over to him, delivering a kick to one of the bodies as he came.

"Thanks for the help," Acennan said, "but I could have taken them on my own."

"Where's the girl?" Beobrand asked.

"Fled at the first sign of trouble. And I don't blame her."

Beobrand scanned the ground around them and realised something that sent a shiver down his spine.

"Pity there were only four of them," he said.

"Why?"

And he spoke the words that frightened him.

"I was just beginning to enjoy myself."

Chapter 11

Coenred narrowed his eyes at the bright sunlight that shone through the leaves of the willows. It was as if God himself looked down upon them. And of course, He did. If God was interested in anything that man did, surely he would care to witness the baptism of a king. The river bank was lined by ealdormen and thegns. Men of import and their wives. On the far side of the river stood a shieldwall of warriors, their backs to the king and the assembled dignitaries. Cynegils had insisted.

"If I am to kneel in the river in nothing more than a white shift," the King of Wessex had said, "I will have my hearth-warriors close at hand. I have many enemies and I am not certain that God can stop an arrow."

"God can do anything," Oswald had replied.

Cynegils had frowned.

"Perhaps that is so. But would He bother? I trust my men."

Cynegils and Oswald now stood on a shingle beach, flanked by several of those men. Each king had his most trusted thegns at his side. Coenred surveyed the warriors, all of whom were bedecked as if for war. Helms and byrnies gleamed in the hot sun. Beobrand stood stiffly near Oswald, his gaze flicking from one person to the next, as if they were all potential attackers. Beobrand's eyes met those of a Wessex warrior and lingered there. The West Seaxon glowered hatred back from puffy, swollen, bruised eyes.

So, it was as Coenred had thought. Beobrand was responsible for the beatings of Cynegils' men. At the height of the feast, four Wessex warriors had stumbled into the hall. They had all been bloodied and bruised. When Cynegils had asked them what had happened, they had dismissed the questions, stating that it had been nothing but a minor disagreement. Cynegils had nodded and let the matter lie. But Coenred had seen Oswald flick a glance at Beobrand where he sat with his friend Acennan. Both men had been flushed and in high spirits, but they had stopped their boastful jesting when the injured West Seaxons had entered the hall. They had sat upright and set aside their cups, listening intently to the exchange between the men and Cynegils. Coenred did not know if Oswald had seen, but the young monk's eyes were keen, and he had spotted a cut on Beobrand's cheek. And where Acennan's hand gripped his drinking horn, his knuckles were split, raw with fresh blood.

Now those same keen eyes were almost shut against the bright glare of the noon sun. All along the line of onlookers, others squinted in the light. There were many there who wished they had partaken less freely of the king's mead the night before. Two nights of feasting had proven too much for some, and they stood now, with downcast stares and hunched shoulders.

But Birinus was not one of them. He had fasted for the day and night following the arrival feast. The dark-robed bishop stepped forward into the centre of the beach, raising his hands for silence. This was his moment. He had come from far away to bring the word of God to these people, and now he was about to baptise their king. The pride of the moment glowed on his face. Coenred smiled as he could almost hear the thoughts inside the bishop's head. Pride was a sin. He was here to do God's work, not to take credit for it. Birinus fought to control his features. He removed the beaming grin of success and replaced it with a beatific, demure smile.

Coenred saw all this with great intensity of vision. His senses were as sharp as a spear-point. He recognised the acute awareness that came with fasting.

In the day and night since the feast, Coenred had fasted and prayed with Birinus. Following the incident with Cormán, Coenred found it hard to trust strangers. A new figure of authority within the brethren of Christ was especially difficult to feel comfortable with. And yet soon after meeting this foreigner, with his strangely cropped hair and unusual accent, Coenred had felt at ease. It was hard to describe, but there was a fundamental goodness that exuded from Birinus.

Gothfraidh agreed.

"Whilst Birinus differs in his beliefs to some of our ways," the grey-haired monk had said, when Dalston had questioned why the bishop wore his hair differently from the monks of Hii and Lindisfarena, "I cannot doubt that he is a true man of Christ. I believe the West Seaxons have found one who will shepherd them well."

Oswald had joined them for a large portion of the evening in which they had fasted, entering into the prayers and songs in a most pious manner. Cynegils had also been told to abstain from eating in preparation for his cleansing in the sacrament of water, but Coenred doubted he had. It was not his place to judge others, that was for the Lord to do. But it seemed to him that the King of Wessex had accepted Christ as a way to find favour with Oswald and to gain access to the power held in the Northumbrian king's grasp.

As he looked over now at Cynegils' daughter, Cyneburg, he could not help but think that Oswald was to take the victor's share in this bargaining for alliance between kings. Cyneburg was as beautiful as a sun-kissed summer morning. Her hair, like so many fine chains of gold, was secured upon her head in elaborate plaits. Her lips were full, pink and moist and looked as succulent as rosehips. Beneath her sumptuous blue mantle, Coenred could discern full hips, plump breasts...

Gothfraidh elbowed him in the ribs and shot him a sharp look. Coenred felt his face flush. Why was he tempted so? Why would the devil not leave him alone? He tried his best not to think such lewd thoughts, but he seemed incapable of focus when in the presence of young women. He shifted his body awkwardly, suddenly terrified that his arousal would be seen by those gathered at the riverside for this solemn occasion.

Birinus was speaking, and Coenred willed himself not to look or think more on the princess who was soon to wed his king.

"Who here is to be Godfather and sponsor of Cynegils, son of Ceol on this, his baptism into the church of Christ?"

Oswald stepped forward, resplendent in purple cloak, bejewelled clasp at his shoulder. His chestnut hair was held back from his face by a simple band of gold. He stood tall and proud. A king in every aspect of his being.

"I, Oswald, son of Æthelfrith, King of Deira and Bernicia, Lord of Northumbria. I will be Cynegils' Godfather."

Birinus inclined his head slightly towards Oswald. Such was the presence of the Northumbrian, none thought it strange. But in his current state of heightened awareness Coenred noted a tightening of the skin around Cynegils' eyes.

Birinus continued: "Step forward, King Cynegils. Step into the running water of this river, where your sins will be washed away."

Cynegils unclasped his cloak-pin and shrugged off his fine woollen cloak. The bruised-faced thegn took it from him.

The crowd of people was silent now. There was magic in the air. Magic of the new god, the Christ.

Birinus led Cynegils into the river. They halted when the cool water eddied over their calves.

"Now kneel before the Lord your God," said Birinus, his voice exultant, carrying to all onlookers.

Cynegils hesitated. For a moment, it seemed he would not kneel. He looked at Oswald, who gave a slight nod. Finally, as if struggling against a physical force, the proud King of the West Seaxons knelt in the river. The plain white robe he wore billowed around him like a lady's skirts in a strong wind.

Birinus signalled to Oswald.

"Oswald, as sponsor of Cynegils in this Holy sacrament, step forward and place your hand upon his shoulder. You are to be his support, his guide as he enters Christ's church."

Without hesitation, Oswald strode into the water. He placed a hand upon the kneeling Cynegils' shoulder and turned his face towards Birinus, who continued with the rite.

"Cynegils, what do you ask of the Church of God?"

Cynegils had learnt his part after much coaxing the previous night.

"Faith," he answered, his voice small, as if choked in his throat.

"What does Faith offer you?"

Cynegils seemed unable to speak. Perhaps he could not

recall the correct words. After a moment, Oswald whispered something to him.

Cynegils' face flushed scarlet, but he intoned in a clear voice: "Life everlasting."

Birinus nodded and said, "If then you desire to enter into life, keep the commandments. 'Thou shalt love the Lord thy God with thy whole heart and with thy whole soul and with thy whole mind; and thy neighbour as thyself.'"

The rite continued smoothly. The crowd watched in hushed awe at their king welcoming a new God and renouncing the old ones they had worshipped for generations. Most did not understand everything that was said, but they would all remember seeing the King of Wessex having river water thrice poured from a golden cup over his head as the strange priest from a southern land intoned about washing away sins. They would all recount how Cynegils had shivered as the cold water had doused him, plastering his plain white robe to his corpulent body.

But clearest of all, they would remember how their lord, Cynegils, son of Ceol had knelt before the tall and proud king of the Northumbrians.

Chapter 12

Beobrand scratched at his scrubby beard. His head ached with a dull throb. The day was still and humid, the sun heating middle earth as if it were inside a clay bread oven. There was no breeze, and scarcely any shade beside the hall where he sat. Some way off, Oswald walked stiffly next to his young bride.

Acennan slumped to the ground beside Beobrand with a groan.

"By Tiw's cock, if I have to eat any more boar, or drink one more drop of mead, I think I'll die."

Beobrand snorted.

"I'm sure you'll manage." But he understood Acennan's comment. Where the tedious journey from Bebbanburg had been sombre and full of tension, the days they had spent at Dorcic had suffered from a surfeit of merriment and celebrations.

The baptism of the king had been followed by feasting. And then, with barely enough time to recover, by the marriage of Oswald to Cyneburg. Despite the pain in his head, Beobrand smiled to remember the gasps from the men as the princess had been led to the altar, where Birinus performed the marriage rites. She was the most beautiful creature most had ever seen. Beobrand shook his head at the memory. Almost as beautiful as Sunniva. There was not a man there who was not jealous of the Northumbrian king at seeing him wed to this dazzling peace-weaver.

"I'm not so sure," said Acennan, rubbing his belly and stretching to work the kinks out of his shoulders. "I may take up fasting like those monks of the Christ."

"You'll wish for some hot meat and good mead when we are once more far from here on the whale's way. And I think we'll be leaving soon enough. Cynegils must be despairing of all the food we've eaten. His people will starve this winter if we stay much longer."

They were silent for a time, content to watch Oswald and Cyneburg. Behind the couple, a few paces back, walked Derian, the bearded thegn, leader of Oswald's hearth-warriors. Beside him, head lowered, walked the raven-haired girl from that first night. Her name was Eadgyth, and wooing her had become Acennan's obsession. After the fight, she would not approach him again, and any attempt he made at speaking to her in the hall, met with stony silence.

"Look at the king," said Acennan, scorn dripping from his words. "It is as if he doesn't know what to do with a lovely woman. Gods, instead of Derian I wish I could walk with Eadgyth. I could show Oswald how to treat a lady."

"Yes," Beobrand smirked. "You are doing such a good job with Eadgyth, I'm sure the king would welcome your assistance."

Acennan frowned.

"Well, how was I to know?"

"I suppose we could have asked."

"But her brother!" said Acennan. "Who could have foreseen such a thing?"

The thegn, who now bore the storm-cloud bruises of a broken nose from Beobrand's savage head-butt, was Wulfgar, brother of Eadgyth. Young and proud, he had not taken kindly to his sister receiving the attentions of a visiting warrior from Bernicia. Since the incident by the byre, Wulfgar and his companions had made no further attempt to confront Beobrand or Acennan, but the two friends were careful not to wander outside the hall alone. They could see the resentment burning behind Wulfgar's dark-ringed eyes. Beobrand knew what it was to crave vengeance, and worried that should the West Seaxon and his friends seek retribution, they would not set aside their weapons a second time. And with drawn blades there would be blood. And death. It would not do to shed the blood of their new-found allies. Beobrand had almost trod that dangerous path at Dor, when Oswald agreed a truce with Penda of Mercia. He did not wish to be forced into a situation that would go badly for them all, no matter the outcome of a fight.

They watched as Oswald pointed at something in the trees that they could not make out. Cyneburg's laughter reached them. Perhaps the king was making progress with his bride after all.

"We should count ourselves lucky that the king did not pry into what happened between us and Wulfgar."

"Why?" a new voice said, making them both start. "What did happen?"

Turning, Beobrand saw Coenred come round the corner of the hall. He offered the monk a smile.

"Nothing happened," Beobrand said quickly.

Coenred eased himself down to sit beside the two warriors.

"Really? The man's face says otherwise, and I have seen how he looks at you. His friends too. You should watch yourselves."

"Don't concern yourself with us. We're amongst friends here in Wessex. You know that."

"That is your problem," said Coenred, wiping beads of sweat from his shaved forehead. "You often turn friends to enemies too readily." He gave Beobrand a reproachful look, but was unable to hold it for long.

Acennan let out a short bark of laughter. Beobrand gave him a sidelong glance. Was he thinking of how Beobrand had knocked him senseless in that thunder-filled night, not so long ago?

"And your trouble, Coenred," said Beobrand, "is that you think too much. And see too much for your own good."

The king, his new queen and their entourage had walked out of their sight now, down towards the river.

Beobrand clapped Coenred on the shoulder. "Do not look glum, I was merely jesting with you. But best if you do not speak of Wulfgar and his friends. We are trying to keep the peace. Now, how goes your work?"

"It is done. Dalston and I have completed making the copies this very morning."

"Copies?"

"We have written down that which Oswald and Cynegils have agreed upon. Hides of tribute. Queen Cyneburg's brýdgifu, morgengifu and handgeld. All the quantities and values in their pacts. And so there is no confusion when the two kings are apart, we have made copies."

Beobrand had spoken of this writing with Coenred before. He could see little reason for it, but Oswald put great store in the scratched marks the holy men made on their sheets of stretched calf skin. Beobrand thought the writing made Oswald feel somehow more of a king, more than a warlord to be respected for his power in battle and shrewdness in peace. Beobrand was not very interested in the scratchings of the monks, but he had seen their writing on occasion and he could not hide his admiration for the craftsmanship. The lines of ink were precise. In places, the monks would add cunning drawings to the words. Animals and men, depicted with fine attention to detail. He cared little for the meaning of the writing, but he did enjoy looking at the pictures.

"And the copies are identical?" He could not imagine having the patience to scratch out the symbols on the vellum sheets once, let alone doing it all again.

"As near as we can make them. The content is the same. That is the reason for the copies."

"So," said Acennan, who had been sitting silently, "if the kings have made their agreements, and you have written your words, we should be leaving soon, no?"

"Gothfraidh says that is so. Oswald King was anxious to leave as soon as he was wed, but Cynegils bids him tarry a while longer."

"Why?" asked Beobrand. "Surely we have been here long enough for his hospitality to wane."

The distant sound of a woman's laughter drifted to them.

"Gothfraidh says Cynegils does not wish to say farewell to his daughter."

"She's no longer his daughter," said Acennan. "She's Oswald's Queen."

"That is true, but Cynegils would have one last feast in Oswald's honour before we leave."

Acennan groaned.

"Another feast? I will surely burst."

"Let us hope then," said Coenred, "that the Picts have settled down in the north and there is no war when we return to Bernicia."

Beobrand hoped for peace in the north too, but did not follow Coenred's thinking.

"Why?"

"Otherwise, with all this feasting, neither of you will be able to squeeze into your byrnies."

Another feast. Fresh ale had been brewed. Once more precious animals had been slaughtered, the meat roasted over great firepits, turned on spits by sweat-streaked children. Fresh eel had been brought up from the Temes. The hall was again awash with the sound of conversation. At the high table, the kings of Wessex and Northumbria presided over the gathered throng. At Oswald's side, sat his radiant new queen, her hair lustrous and golden. Many were the men who would catch themselves gawping at Cyneburg that night. Hers was a beauty that led to men dreaming. Beobrand gazed at her too, through the smoke-haze of the hall. But his thoughts were not full of lust for the daughter of Cynegils. Her shining tresses and flawless, smooth skin conjured images of Sunniva in his mind. She too had caused men to stare, to become ensnared in her dazzling beauty.

But she had gone, like all the womenfolk in his life. Well, not all. He had managed to save Rheagan. The memory of her dark mane of hair, her fragile, pale body, brought a secret smile to his lips. He yearned for the solace of her touch once more. To lie with her quietly in the dark sanctuary of his own hall.

He looked away from the queen. Lost in his thoughts, he stared into the fire that burnt brightly on the hearth, though the night was not cold. Smoke eddied and pooled around the wooden bones of the roof, where soot hung like blackened fungus growths on the beams. It reminded him of the blaze of Nathair's hall. That night of killing and blood.

He offered up a silent prayer to any god who would listen. Keep Ubbanford safe.

Surely he had done enough to protect his lands. Torran and his Picts were still abroad in Bernicia. But Bassus was strong. A good leader of men. And Beobrand had left most of his gesithas to guard his people. To keep them safe.

To keep Octa from harm.

To keep Rheagan safe. She was a thrall. Nothing more. And yet her face played in his mind at night. Sometimes he awoke with the shreds of his dreams tattering in the morning light. At those times, he knew he had dreamt of lying with a woman, but he was unsure with which one. Sunniva and Rheagan were as far from each other as day is to night, but both haunted his sleep.

No. Only one haunted him. Rheagan still lived.

Absently, Beobrand picked meat from the bones of the pigeon on the trencher before him. The flesh was soft and succulent, but the taste turned to ash in his mouth as he saw the remnants of the bird on the board. Bird bones, white and brittle. Like those left on the horse's skull on the path near Ubbanford. Nelda had left them there, of that he was certain. When he returned to Bernicia, he would seek her out, and put an end to the witch, once and for all.

He had done his best to push aside his worries. There was nothing to be gained from fretting about that over which he had no control. But now, as the moment for their departure drew close, it was as if a poorly built dam had collapsed and all his fears rushed back, flooding his mind.

Not long now. They would be leaving soon and the journey would not take them much more than a sennight, if the gods smiled on them and the calm weather held.

Beobrand looked about him at the assembled men. For the most part those from Northumbria and Wessex still sat apart. Bonds that were forged in battle were strong and hard to break. But in some cases new friendships had been made and Wessexmen and Northumbrians shared drinking horns and conversation. Willing himself to push aside his dark thoughts, he listened to Athelstan, who now stood, boasting before a group of West Seaxons.

"And so it was," the grizzled warrior said in a booming voice, "that we attacked the Waelisc host at night. Yes, your ears did not trick you. I said, at night. And Thunor's chariot crashed in the heavens and his hammer struck with savage fury. And Oswald led us down to their camp and we smote them with blade and spear in the flicker-flame light of the storm."

The warriors raised their cups and hammered their fists on the boards. Tales of battle were ever popular. And Athelstan was a good tale-spinner. He was no scop, but his voice was clear. His words clever. And he had been there at Hefenfelth. He bore the scars of many battles and wore the rings on his muscled arms that proved his worth. The hall quietened as people turned to listen to this brutish-looking thegn of the north. His beard bristled and he flashed his teeth in a grin at Beobrand, as he sensed the eyes of all on him.

"We fought all that long night. Cadwallon's host was huge. Their spears numbered more than all the trees in Albion. They thought to sweep Bernicia before them. To destroy us.

To push us back into the sea from whence had come our forebears. But Oswald had prayed to the Christ God. He had put up a great rood, before which we all bowed on the eve of the battle. God had promised him victory over Cadwallon, and the one God is true. He keeps his word."

At the far end of the hall, Oswald sat up tall and proud. He nodded, clearly listening intently to Athelstan's words. Cynegils turned to him and spoke; perhaps asking for the end of the tale. Oswald merely indicated with his hand to listen to his thegn as Athelstan finished his account of the battle of Hefenfelth. Off to one side, Beobrand saw Acennan and Derian, deep in conversation. He raised his hand to them, but neither noticed him. He heard his name and turned his attention back to Athelstan.

"... with only half a hand, this noble-hearted warrior from the south stepped forth from the shieldwall. Beobrand ordered the great steed to halt, and listening, the mount, a massive black beast, stopped before him, and allowed him to climb onto its back."

To Beobrand's embarrassment, eyes turned to him. Unsure what to do, he offered a thin smile and focused on Athelstan, willing them all to watch the older man, who revelled in the attention.

Athelstan, in total control of his audience now, told how Beobrand had chased down the King of Gwynedd and brought him back to Oswald. The story ended with Cadwallon defeated and Oswald, the Christ-worshipper, victorious and ruler of a united Northumbria. Athelstan recounted the victorious gift-giving feast, where Oswald rewarded his trusted followers.

Beobrand looked to the high table. Cynegils was frowning. The message was clear. Those who stood against Oswald were slain, and those who aided him were rewarded. Beobrand wondered whether Athelstan had been instructed to act as scop this evening, on the eve of Oswald's departure, to reinforce to the King of the West Seaxons that they were now allies and what that entailed.

The board creaked under Cynegils' weight as he pushed himself to his feet. He raised his hands to silence the cheering that had erupted at the conclusion to Athelstan's story. After a time, the noise abated and all present turned to hear what the lord of the hall would say.

The King of the West Seaxons drew in a deep breath and seemed prepared to address them all in his huge voice. But, before he could utter a sound, the silence of the hall was split by a shout from the doors.

"I must speak with my king."

The door wards, with crossed spears, held back a tall, lean man. He made to push into the hall, but they prevented him, laying their weight against the ash hafts of the spears.

"I have urgent tidings for my king," shouted the man.

Cynegils beckoned to the newcomer who had interrupted him. The man was clearly distressed, tension evident in his every move.

"Remove his arms and let him in to speak." Cynegils smiled complacently at Oswald. "A king must at times pause to listen to his people when they bring news."

The wardens allowed the man into the hall. He strode swiftly the length of the hall. His cloak was travel-stained, his leg bindings dusty. Upon reaching the high table the man gave a curt bow. Cynegils nodded expectantly.

The man spoke in a clear voice for all to hear.

"My lord King Oswald, I come with grave news. Finola and her son, Talorcan, have fled Bebbanburg. They were taken by the Pictish scum. Your brother, Oswiu atheling, has ridden in pursuit of them. He bids you return with your comitatus as quickly as you are able."

For a time after the messenger's arrival, the hall was in uproar. Cynegils, his face flushed with drink, was angered at being overlooked in his own hall.

"I am king here!" he had screamed. He had picked up an ornate drinking horn and flung it at the new arrival. He had missed, spilling mead over himself in the process. Someone had laughed and Cynegils' skin had turned such a deep hue of purple that it seemed he would either die or slay someone.

In the end, it took Cyneburg to soothe her father's battered pride. She placed her arm around him and led him from the hall.

Beobrand watched with eager interest as the messenger from Bebbanburg spoke with Oswald.

This was not good news. Finola was the sister of Gartnait, King of the Picts. Her son was one of the heirs to the throne of those people. Oswald would be furious to lose them. They were both important parts in the great game of tafl he played to rule the isle of Albion. The king would be angry, but there was good that came of this.

Beobrand drained his cup of ale and smiled despite the tension in the hall. With these tidings, they would be leaving straight away, and they would travel with haste. Soon they would be back in Bernicia. Back in Ubbanford. And he would once again see Octa. And Rheagan.

After a lengthy conversation at the high table, Derian approached Athelstan, beckoning to Beobrand to join them.

Acennan followed close behind, an expression on his features that Beobrand could not fathom.

"So, it is settled," Derian said, as Beobrand came within earshot.

"What is?" he asked. Athelstan's features gave nothing away. Acennan seemed to be struggling to hide a grin.

"We are to be Cyneburg's nursemaids," said Athelstan.

"What?"

"Yes, we, the heroes of Hefenfelth, are to escort the queen to Northumbria." Athelstan scowled, clearly unhappy with their lot.

Derian raised a placatory hand.

"This is a task that our lord the king would only entrust to his most worthy thegns. Besides," Derian's teeth showed through the thicket of his dark tangle of beard, "not all of the heroes of Hefenfelth are travelling with the queen. Most of us are travelling with the king by ship."

Athelstan growled and reached for a jug of mead.

"And you get to put those Picts in their place while we hold the girl's skirts out of the mud on a long ride north?"

"It is agreed," snapped Derian. "Oswald has willed it."

"Why us?" asked Beobrand, unable to keep the pleading tone from his voice. A moment ago he had believed he would be in Bernicia within a week; now, who knew how long until they would make it back.

"We are to hurry north," said Derian. "There can be no tarrying while the queen prepares her things. Besides, she says she does not wish to travel by sea."

"Well, that I can understand," said Beobrand. The mere thought of the rolling surf under the keel made his stomach twist. "But you still haven't answered me. Why us? There are others who could do this task. I need to return to my home.

The gods alone know what the Picts will have done in our absence. Couldn't some of Cynegils' men escort her?"

Derian nodded.

"They can, and they will. A group of them will travel with you. But as Cyneburg is now Oswald's queen, Lord Athelstan will lead."

Beobrand opened his mouth to speak, but Derian continued, anticipating the question.

"As to why you, that is simple. Acennan asked for the honour of escorting the lady Cyneburg to her new home. Oswald was most taken by the offer. After Athelstan's story of Hefenfelth, he believes it is a sign of how much he values his queen to leave the famed Beobrand Half-hand for her protection."

For a moment, Beobrand was unable to speak.

Athelstan laughed.

"Come now, boy. You look like a beached fish, mouth opening and closing. We will be home soon enough. Perhaps it will not be so terrible to travel with the queen and her womenfolk."

Suddenly, the truth dawned on Beobrand.

"Womenfolk, you say?" Then he asked the question to which he could already guess the answer. "Who is Cyneburg's handmaiden? Her gemæcce?"

Acennan stifled his smile and stared at the rush-strewn floor.

"I thought you knew," answered Derian. "The queen will travel with her closest companion, the lady Eadgyth."

Chapter 13

A smothering drizzle fell the next morning. It was still warm, but the summer was growing old. The heavy skies spoke of more rain to come. Perhaps storms. All about Dorcic, Oswald's men readied their gear for the short journey to the ships.

One of the younger warriors, a tousle-haired man with unusually long arms, stumbled and dropped his spear with a clatter. He was laden with his own belongings and battle-harness, as well as a sack full of provisions. Like all the Northumbrians, he seemed keen to leave, and so had attempted to carry everything to the waiting ships in one trip.

"Give us a hand with this," he called in a friendly tone to Beobrand and the others who stood watching him struggle.

"Carry your own damn spear," shouted back Beobrand.

Athelstan let out grunt of amusement.

"By the Christ and all his saints, you will not be a pleasant companion on this journey, unless you let go of your anger."

But Beobrand was not ready to forget his ire at having been left behind.

"If Acennan could have kept his mouth shut, we'd be getting aboard those ships soon."

Acennan said nothing, but Athelstan laughed.

"Acennan has his mind set on getting aboard something with softer curves than any sea-steed. And he can no more control his mouth when it comes to a beautiful woman than any man. A man will do anything for a warm cunny, but speaking sense does not come easily. There are some good tidings though." Athelstan grinned, and Beobrand knew that a joke was coming.

"What?" he asked, making no effort to hide his annoyance.

"Oswald is taking those monks with him. At least we won't have to pray day and night on the journey north."

Beobrand snorted. He cared little. It was true that the Christ monks were prone to being too sombre, but Coenred was good company. He actually thought he would miss the conversations he had with the young monk. Another reason to be angry for not travelling with the king and his retinue.

They watched on in silence as the preparations continued, until eventually, Oswald and his retinue were ready. The ships were low in the water where heavy treasure weighed them down. It seemed that Cyneburg's dowry was more substantial than just her father's promise of aid if war should come with Mercia.

Cynegils, face once more open and smiling, apparently mollified after the events of the previous night, walked down to the water's edge to bid his new ally farewell. His comitatus followed him, all resplendent in their finest jackets, cunningly patterned cloaks and gleaming buckles and brooches. The West Seaxon king did not want Oswald to quickly forget his strength or hospitality.

Cyneburg, Eadgyth and other womenfolk also walked the short distance to where the ships were moored. The rain was thin, but their fine-spun veils and braids were quickly bedraggled. They did not complain, but Beobrand noted the tight-lipped annoyance on the young queen's face. A quick glance at Acennan showed him that his friend was unaware of the queen or the rain. He only had eyes for Eadgyth. The dark-haired companion of the queen flicked an almost imperceptible look at the stocky Northumbrian warrior as they passed. Acennan beamed as if he had been given all the riches in the land of Wessex.

Beobrand sighed. He was still disappointed, but he could not remain angry at his friend. Acennan had stood by him in terrible times. Beobrand knew he had once had a wife. And a child. Both gone now. If he could find happiness with Eadgyth, he should seize it and hold on to it for as long as he was able. Before wyrd saw fit to snatch it away.

Beobrand clapped Acennan on the shoulder.

"Come, let us bid our king a safe journey."

Acennan smiled even more broadly, if such a thing were possible, pleased that Beobrand's temper was abating. Together, they all walked down to the river.

As they gathered at the river's edge, the rain ceased. The redolence of freshly trodden soil and wet grass was heavy in the air. The unbroken surface of the river reflected the iron-grey sky. A pair of swans glided past the watching men and women.

Oswald stepped forward and raised his arms in the now familiar posture he adopted when addressing a crowd. They quietened.

"Lord King Cynegils, son of Ceol, ruler of the West Seaxons, I give you thanks for your hearth, your board," a pause and a wink to their host, "and your heady mead and ale." A ripple of laughter from the listeners. Cynegils smiled and nodded.

"But of course, more than any of this, I give you thanks for tying our families and kingdoms with my marriage to your lovely daughter, Cyneburg." All turned to look at Cyneburg. As Queen of Northumbria and princess of Wessex, she must now be one of the most powerful women of Albion. She trembled under the gaze of so many, her pale skin showed clearly the rising blush of her cheeks. She looked down at the wet earth.

Oswald strode forward. Leaning in close to Cyneburg, he whispered something in her ear that only she could hear. She squared her shoulders, raised her head and offered a delicate kiss to her husband.

"Godspeed, my king," she said, her voice as soft as the kiss.

"Thank you, my queen, and I pray that God will speed your journey northward and keep you safe on the road." Oswald swept all those congregated on the riverbank with his gaze. "For it is the gift of our Lord God's love and protection that is the most cherished gift. I am overjoyed that the wise and mighty King Cynegils has welcomed the one true God into his heart and that of his people."

Birinus, standing off to one side of the royal retinue, pushed his chest out with pride. Then, awkwardly and with a quick flush of embarrassment, he bowed his head and slumped his shoulders. Although he looked downward, the dark-skinned priest could not hide his gleeful expression.

Oswald continued: "We share one God now. And yet Northumbria and Wessex are bound by more than just common beliefs. I am Godfather to King Cynegils, responsible for his spiritual guidance." Cynegils stiffened. "But wise Cynegils is the father of my bride, and will be the grandfather of our children. So it is that our two peoples are united by holy oath and blood."

Cynegils stepped forward, shoulders broad, face shining, still wet from the rain.

"May your journey be safe, son," he said, voice booming. One of the swans rose up to stand in the water, flapping its wings at the sudden loud noise. "As you say," Cynegils said, "we are bound by God and family. And yet let us not forget why we have sought this union. Penda of Mercia's power is waxing. The day will come when our truces will no longer hold and he will seek more land. Then, we will stand together, strong shield and sharp spear against the Mercians. Let all here remember and so may it be known to all of Albion, that Northumbria and Wessex are, from this day forth, bound by blood and blade."

The watching warriors cheered. Some crashed spear hafts into linden boards and iron shield bosses.

Oswald nodded. It was well-said. He embraced Cynegils, who grinned and slapped the younger man on the back.

The last thing Oswald did before boarding his ship was to approach Athelstan, Beobrand and the other warriors who would accompany Cyneburg north. He was smiling, but no mirth touched his eyes.

"Bring me my queen safely to Bernicia, Athelstan," he said. The king looked at each of them in turn, his face suddenly grave. "And do not tarry. I fear I will need all my swords before the winter snows."

PART TWO
TREACHERY AND TORMENT

Chapter 14

As if to remind them that the summer was drawing to a close, cold rain lashed them as they trudged north. Beobrand could scarcely make out Garr where he rode ahead of the small column, such was the intensity of the downpour. Garr had the best eyes of any of his men. He talked little, but watched much, making him perfect to scout ahead of the group in Attor's absence. One of the West Seaxons rode with him. They did not trust the Northumbrians to know their business. At least they knew the land well, so it would not hurt to have them around. Of course, they still rode through Wessex. Soon they would be in Mercia. Beobrand hoped they would not need to discover the Wessexmen's skill with shield and spear.

Cold water trickled down his neck and back. His cloak was sodden, heavy and plastered to his horse's flank. His byrnie would be eaten away by the metal-rot if he wasn't careful. He spat into the churned mud beside his mount's hooves. He was seated astride a dappled mare. She was smaller than Sceadugenga; less feisty. But she was nimble enough and obeyed his commands without hesitation. Cynegils had provided mounts for them all. Once the queen was safely in Northumbria, the Seaxons were to return home, escorting traders south. This was the agreement Cynegils had struck with Oswald, and it seemed a good bargain. All they had to do was get through Mercia without incident. Beobrand watched as a skinny thrall goaded the oxen to pull the queen's waggon up the small rise to where Beobrand waited. The beasts bellowed angrily, but finally the vehicle was over the hill.

Athelstan cantered through the sheets of rain, pulling his steed to a mud-splattering halt beside Beobrand.

"I thought you said the rain wouldn't last. If it goes on much longer, we will need a ship after all."

Beobrand sighed.

"It can't rain forever," he said. In truth he felt bad that he had convinced Athelstan to strike out north during the bad weather. He was anxious to get back to Ubbanford. The thought of being cooped up in the hall of Dorcic for days while the sky washed the world was more than he could bear. Cyneburg and the king had wanted them to wait until the rain passed, but Beobrand had swayed Athelstan, saying that the rain would cease soon and if it did not, the roads would only get worse, not better. Now the massive warrior looked less inclined to agree with him than when they had been sipping mead beside Cynegils' hearth fire. Athelstan rubbed the water from his face, his beard dark and dripping.

"Well, it looks like it might never stop." He raised a gnarled hand to shield his eyes and gazed upward. The dome of the sky was shrouded in a dense blanket of grey cloud. "I see no break in this rain. Not today. I'll ask Wulfgar where the nearest hall is." He spurred his horse forward to where the dark-bearded warrior, brother of Eadgyth, rode his fine steed. Beobrand swallowed back the sharp words he wished to speak. It would do no good, he knew. And yet he could not help but loathe the man. When Cynegils had announced the men who would be riding as the queen's escort from Wessex, Beobrand had almost laughed. Of all the men in the king's gesithas, Wulfgar and the other three from that first night in Dorcic, were all to ride north. The gods loved mischief, and to have Beobrand, Acennan, Wulfgar and Eadgyth all riding in the same group was clearly a great jest. So far, there had been no cross words between them, but the journey would be long and there would be many chances for vengeance from the warriors who had been bested in the dark outside the byre. Warriors did not easily forget, and they would be wanting revenge. Beobrand and Acennan would have to be wary.

Beobrand turned his attention to where the waggon now stood. The thrall and oxen both panted, breath steaming in the cool air of the day. On the wain, beneath a cloth and leather canopy, Cyneburg and Eadgyth were protected from the elements. So it was with surprise that he saw the slender form of the queen step out into the mire of the path. By the gods, she was a lovely creature; like a ray of sunlight on this gloomy day. She walked daintily towards him, picking her way around the larger puddles. Where possible she stepped on the remnants of the stone slabs that had once made the road great. Birinus said he came from the same distant land as the long-gone people, who had left such a lasting mark on Albion. With a jolt, Beobrand realised the queen was walking towards him. They had not spoken before. He had been content to observe her beauty from afar, as he would gaze upon a rare bird. She had seemed distant and withdrawn since Oswald's departure; seldom deigning to converse with the warriors. In his opinion, this was as it should be.

He felt suddenly foolish sitting astride a horse while his queen waded through the muck of the road. Swinging his leg over the saddle, he leapt to the ground. His right leg screamed in protest. The memory of Torran's arrow was still fresh to his muscle. The leg gave way, and Beobrand staggered forward, slipping and sliding in the mud. He lost the battle with his balance and fell to one knee before Cyneburg. Throwing out his hands, he prevented his face sinking into the mud. The taut skin of his left forearm gave a twinge of pain. But it was his pride that was hurt.

The sound of laughter reached him. Much of it the loud guffaws of fighting men who were cold, wet and tired and were glad of something to break the tedium of the day. From just above him came a softer giggle, and once again he was reminded of Sunniva. He was not sure he had ever heard Rheagan laugh.

He looked up into the smiling face of Cyneburg. Her hair wreathed her in a crown of finely spun gold. The rain and gloom of the day seemed unable to dampen Cynegils' daughter's beauty.

"No need to kneel, brave Beobrand," she said, the laughter still sounding in her words.

She knew his name. His face grew hot.

Pushing himself awkwardly to his feet, he shook his soaking cloak out behind him with one hand. He ignored the continued laughter from the men. He was sure he could hear Wulfgar's voice, but he did not look for him. He kept his eyes on Cyneburg.

"My lady," he hesitated. "My queen. Apologies for my clumsiness. But you are getting wet. Your fine clothes will be ruined out here."

"Never mind that," she said. "I heard you speaking with

Lord Athelstan. I know of a place where we could seek shelter."

"Indeed?" The thought of getting warm and dry was welcome, as was leaping back onto the dappled mare and galloping away. Hopefully never to look upon the laughing eyes of his queen again.

"Eadgyth's uncle, Anwealda, has his hall a short ride from here. He would welcome us and we could wait out this rain."

"Very well, my lady." The words felt as clumsy in his mouth as his feet had been on the slick cobbles of the road. "I will inform Athelstan."

She inclined her head in thanks.

"Of course, Wulfgar can lead the way."

For a moment, he watched the sway of her hips as she walked back to the waggon, before remembering they were not alone. He spun away, his face again burning as hot as if he had been struck with fever from elf-shot.

Fresh peals of laughter came to him as he grabbed the mare's reins and swung himself up onto her back.

Beobrand stretched his hands out to the fire that blazed on the hearth at the centre of Anwealda's hall. It was a strange place, reminding him of the chapel at Engelmynster. The walls were of stones, cunningly cut and laid by craftsmen of unmatched and forgotten skill. The walls showed elaborate paintings of people and animals. The paint was faded now, streaked with soot and dirt. Generations of Anwealda's family had probably sat in this very place and observed those images of scantily clad, slender women. On one wall, someone had attempted to repair a painting that had cracked and flaked with the damp. The result was splodges of muddy brown on the otherwise golden beauties; diaphanous clothes reduced to what appeared to be coarse woollen blankets. Beobrand wondered whether the artist was the same as the builder who had patched the roof. Much of it was yet covered with red tiles, but a large portion had collapsed and been replaced with thatch. The repair had happened a long time ago, judging by the darkened beams that supported it.

Beneath the thatch, rain dripped into a large cauldron that had been placed there for that purpose. The mood in the hall was subdued. They had slogged through streams and ditches to get here, all the while the rain had pelted them. Anwealda had received them with politeness, but not warmth. He had only returned from the wedding celebrations at Dorcic the day before and had clearly not expected to entertain a queen and her retinue of warriors. But he had kissed his niece on the cheek and, after only a moment's hesitation at his wife's nudge in his ribs, offered their sleeping chamber to Cyneburg. The thralls and servants had bustled around the hall and, without great delay, benches had been set and ale served. The lady of the hall, Osberga, brought the Waes Hael cup and bid them welcome.

Bowls of thin pottage were filled and served with good, fresh loaves. The simple fare was warming after the cold and wet of the day, and it was a welcome change from the feasting at Cynegils' hall. Perhaps Anwealda too had tired of the meats and mead. The men conversed in quiet tones. Wulfgar and the other West Seaxons at one end of the board, the Northumbrians at the other. Cyneburg and Eadgyth were at the high table.

"Well, I thought your bad temper would make this journey tedious," said Athelstan. "I did not count on the gods turning the weather against us, or Cynegils providing us with such sour companions."

Beobrand nodded absently. The dim firelight made Cyneburg's features dance and glow in the shadows. Her eyes were dark as she spoke to the lord and lady of the hall. Yet her hair shone more brightly than seemed natural in the gloom; lambent and reflective like a pond in moonlight.

Athelstan let out a sharp laugh, as harsh as a crow's call.

"It would seem," he indicated Beobrand and Acennan with one battle-hardened hand, "that neither of you find our companions sour. Though I was referring to the men. I can see the attraction in the girls. But," he lowered his tone, "you must be careful, lads. A queen's field is not to be ploughed by any, save for the king. And her gemæcce's land is best left untilled too."

Beobrand felt his face grow hot. He turned to Acennan, who had also been staring towards the high table at the object of his desire. Their eyes met and suddenly they were brimming with merriment. They laughed loudly, each clapping the other's back. It felt good. Athelstan smiled and drained his cup of ale.

The older warrior shook his head and muttered, "You young fools."

This only served to make Beobrand and Acennan laugh the louder. It had been a long time coming, and now the laughter welled up within Beobrand and he wondered if he would ever be able to stop. He clung to his friend and fought to regain control. He had barely sipped the ale, and yet he felt drunk.

After what seemed a long time, the two friends managed to rein in their good humour. Struggling for breath, they each wiped tears of mirth from their cheeks. All around them, faces stared. Conversation had stopped, while the two warriors had laughed uproariously. Wulfgar's look of utter disdain was almost enough to reignite Beobrand's laughter, but he swallowed it back. His gaze fell on Cyneburg and he smiled openly, his teeth flashing white in his summer-tanned face. She stared back at him for a moment, with an unreadable expression, before frowning and turning to her host once more.

The diversion over, people returned to their trenchers and cups. The sombre mood of the hall descended again, as thick as autumn fog.

Beside Beobrand, Athelstan swore under his breath.

"By the bones of Christ and the cock of Tiw, this hall needs more life." He rose to his feet, and slammed his open palm into the board before him. Silence descended once more.

"Hwaet!" he shouted. "Listen! And I will tell you the story of the evil and mighty Hengist, and how he was defeated by Beobrand, son of Grimgundi, who some know as Half-hand."

The men in the hall hoomed and stamped their feet. A tale of battle and the vanquishing of foes was something they all enjoyed.

Beobrand groaned inwardly. He hated to be talked of as some hero of legend while people stared and appraised him. The tales grew in each telling until he could barely recognise himself in them. He shot Athelstan a look of undisguised anger, but the big thegn just grinned and continued.

As he had proven in Dorcic, Athelstan was a good story-weaver, and despite himself, Beobrand found the words conjuring up dark memories. Athelstan recounted what he knew and what he had heard. He spoke of the fight in the mud of Engelmynster where Beobrand had split Hengist's face with a lucky strike. He spoke of the battle of Gefrin ford, where the river had run thick and red with the gore of foe and friend alike. He told of the ragged shieldwall before Bebbanburg where Beobrand had lost the best part of two fingers from his left hand. And then, Athelstan, clearly enjoying himself and pleased with the rapt attention of his audience, told of how Beobrand had used his brother's sword, Hrunting, to kill the very man who had stolen it and murdered its previous owner.

The listeners stamped on the floor and hammered fists into boards in praise of the tale. It had been well-told, of that there could be no doubt. And yet Beobrand felt the darkness of his past extinguish the lightness of the laughter that had gripped him so recently. Athelstan had recounted moments of great sword-play. Acts that warriors liked to sing of when the shieldwalls were a distant memory and they were glad to have survived them. But he did not speak of things that would not make such a pleasing tale. He spoke not of Cathryn's pleading eyes as she was violated on the gelid winter earth of the forest. He did not tell of her mutilated body, ruined and bloody on the frost-hard ground. Nor of the charred and smoking corpse of Strang, lying amidst smoking charcoal mounds. Athelstan did not recall the creak of the rope on the yew tree as Tondberct had been hoisted, gibbering and screaming, to his death.

No, Athelstan spoke of none of these things. Some he did not know of, but even if he had, he would not talk of them. Men wish to hear of the battle-glory of great warriors. Not the blood and shit and stench of death. They wanted to hear of the giant amongst men, resplendent in battle-bright byrnie and polished helm. Not the mewling boy with entrails escaping a gaping cut like so many writhing eels.

The warriors of the hall applauded the tale and Beobrand's part in the story. Athelstan grinned, content to bask in the praise; happy that the hall was full of sound. Beobrand was unable to bring himself to smile. To those watching, he was the perfect image of a warrior. Stern-faced, scarred, broad-shouldered and tall. A man who did not need to speak, for his sword's song was enough.

At the far end of the board, Wulfgar stood. The room was still once more.

"This is the second time that Lord Athelstan has told of your prowess in battle, Beobrand," Wulfgar said.

Beobrand took a deep, slow breath.

"Athelstan likes to spin a yarn," Beobrand said, his voice flat. He had known a moment of confrontation would come with Wulfgar, but perhaps he could avoid it.

"Nonsense," said Athelstan, still flushed from the success of his story-telling, "Beobrand is every bit the warrior I have said he is. He can best any man I have ever seen with a sword."

Beobrand sighed. Athelstan and his big mouth. When would he ever be quiet when needed?

"Well, you have not seen me with a sword," replied Wulfgar. And with those softly spoken words, the threat of violence and blood crept into the hall amongst them all.

"No, I have not," Beobrand said. There was no escaping this now. "I have only seen you fight with your fists... and I found you lacking."

A sharp intake of breath from the gathered warriors. Such words were as good as a slap in the face.

Beneath the healing bruises on his face, Wulfgar's skin grew pale.

"I would prove to you that I am more than a match for you with a blade." He turned to his uncle. "If Lord Anwealda will allow it, I would fight you here and now."

Anwealda rose to his feet. He surveyed his nephew with a withering look of tiredness.

"I do not allow it," he said.

"But, uncle—"

"I do not allow it," Anwealda repeated. "There shall be no combat in my hall. Tonight is a time of welcome. And need I remind you that we are allies? Friends? We are not foemen. Save your swords for the Mercians. I am sure one day soon Penda will seek to find more land and then we will need all the strong swords we can muster."

"But—"

"Enough!" shouted Anwealda. "There shall be no combat tonight. But I see there is a need for the two of you to settle some score. So, if the gods cease pouring this rain on us and you both agree, you may use wooden practice blades in a test of skills." He looked first to Beobrand. After a moment's hesitation, he nodded. What else could he do?

Wulfgar, smiling now, also assented.

"Very well," said Anwealda, "it is agreed. In the morn we shall see you cross blades and settle this once and for all."

Chapter 15

By the morning the rain had stopped falling. Though in the middle of the night Beobrand had been awoken by the crash of thunder and the roar of a storm that reminded him of the night they had attacked the Waelisc at Hefenfelth. Gusts of wind had buffeted the hall, rattling the beams and threatening to lift the old thatch from the repaired roof. A thin waterfall of rain had cascaded into the cauldron. By morning it had overflown and soaked the rushes strewn about it on the tiled floor. Beobrand had lain there in the darkness listening to the Thunor hammer-crash of lightning and the rumble of the god's chariot as it was pulled along by his great goats. He had shivered, in spite of the cloak wrapped about him and the warmth from the embers of the hearth. When he closed his eyes, he thought he could again hear the screams of those who had fallen south of the Great Wall. Perhaps he could. Maybe their voices would always come to him when storms raged.

When he awoke, Beobrand was stiff and unrested. His stomach grumbled at its emptiness, but he did not have an appetite. Shaking Acennan awake, he said, "Come on. Let's get this over with."

Acennan moaned and grumbled, but rolled over and pushed himself to his feet.

Beobrand stood and stretched. His leg did not feel right. He would have to be careful it did not give way as it had the day before. His arm was taut, but moved freely and seemed strong. He rolled his shoulders. He did not relish confronting Wulfgar. If he bested the West Seaxon he knew that the man's grudge against him would surely grow. But if he was defeated, he would lose the reputation he had gained before Athelstan, Acennan and the other Bernician warriors. And what else did a thegn have apart from his riches and his battle-fame?

He pulled his arms up over his head, working the life back into his sleepy muscles. A ghost of a smile played on his lips. Win or lose, the outcome of the fight would cause him problems. And yet, it would be a lie to say he was not excited at the prospect. He had beaten Wulfgar once without a weapon. It would feel good to show him that putting down his blade that night in Dorcic had been a wise choice.

"Awaken," Beobrand said in a loud voice. "The sun is in the sky and Thunor has gone to his bed. Awaken, that I may defeat Wulfgar and then I would break my fast."

Bidding Acennan to follow him, Beobrand strode to the end of the hall. Removing the bar from the doors, he swung them open, letting in a cool draught of watery morning air. This was met by curses and complaints, but throughout the hall men were rousing themselves. The womenfolk had retired to the sleeping chamber which lay behind a screen at the far end of the hall and he doubted they would ready themselves in time to watch the practice bout.

He stepped into the courtyard before the hall. In the distance, mist hung over a forest. The air was chill and still. The storm had gone, leaving a land that looked as if the gods had scrubbed it clean. A pair of crows flapped lazily overhead to land on the tattered thatch of the hall. Beobrand followed their flight with his gaze. Could it be that Woden himself wished to know the outcome of a contest between two mortals? Of course, the gods loved their mischief. Beobrand shivered. The presence of the birds unnerved him. What would his wyrd bring him this day?

Stooping, Acennan picked up a pebble from the muddy ground of the courtyard. He flung it at the crows. He missed. The stone skittered on the clay tiles, sending the black birds into the air, cawing angrily.

"I hope you do not mean to throw stones at me," said Wulfgar, stepping from the hall. "I am not a master of that skill. I leave the casting of pebbles to children and thralls." His three companions chortled dutifully at his poor jest. The warriors, who too bore the fading bruises from their fight with Beobrand and Acennan, were always at his side.

"A wooden sword will be enough," replied Beobrand, his tone as cool as the morning.

The rest of the men were stumbling from the hall bleary-eyed and tousle-haired. They rubbed their eyes to remove the grit of sleep. They grumbled, but without much conviction. They were all excited to see these two warriors face each other. Beobrand knew that some had wagered on the outcome.

He noted that, as he had expected, none of the womenfolk, with the exception of a couple of house thralls, had come to witness the bout. He wished that Cyneburg was there to witness his skill, but no matter, she would hear the tale of the fight soon enough.

Beobrand leaned close to Acennan. "Where is Athelstan?" he whispered.

"No idea. Asleep?"

"The man causes this, and then stays wrapped in his blankets while I fight?" Beobrand spat. He could not hold much anger against Athelstan. The man was brutish and loud, but he was a good warrior, and a good friend.

"Perhaps it is for the best," said Acennan with a wry smile. "If he was here, we'd be hearing the tale of this fight at every hall we stop at on this journey."

"True. Though not seeing it will not prevent him telling the tale. He'll be sorry he missed it." Beobrand's grin was wolfish now that the fight approached. No matter where Athelstan was, Beobrand wanted to fight now. He could feel the pressure building in him. It was as if there was an animal caged inside that was unleashed when he entered battle. Too long had the beast strained at its fetters. Beobrand shook his arms to limber them.

Anwealda walked to the centre of the yard.

"I see you are keen to test your sword-skills. It is early and we would all slake our night-thirst and fill our bellies." He waved to one of his gesithas who brought forward two plain shields and carved, oaken practice blades. Wulfgar and Beobrand armed themselves.

Beobrand swung the sword a few times. It was a comfortable fit in his fist, much lighter than Hrunting, with a very different balance. It was also a hand-breadth shorter. It would be a fast fight. The shield was simple, boards of willow covered in hide. The central boss was nothing more than a dull dome of iron, with a central handle to grip in the left hand. Beobrand missed the straps that Sunniva had fashioned for his own shield. He had grown accustomed to them and the way they supported the board. This shield felt clumsy in his half-handed grip. He hefted it, and thrust it forward, as if punching with the boss. His grip held.

"I know that I am not the only one who is hungry and thirsty," continued Anwealda, "so we shall keep this short." A few moans came from those in the crowd who wanted an epic battle. Most were quiet, their eyes wide and eager to see the two warriors spar. "The bout will be won by the first to strike seven times. A fall to the ground will be counted as a blow received. As lord of this hall, my word is final and neither of you is to bear a grudge against the other after this. No feud will be entered into. All previous scores are settled here. Are we agreed?"

Neither man responded.

"Are we agreed?" Anwealda repeated. "I am hungry and in no mood for the foolishness of young men." He turned to the dark-bearded Wulfgar. "And do not think I will find in favour of you, nephew, should this come to a dispute. The man who best wields a blade will win. Now, are we agreed?"

"We are agreed," said Beobrand.

Wulfgar nodded. "Agreed."

"Very well," said Anwealda. "Now, all of you form a circle in the yard." The crowd spread themselves into a ring, leaving an area of muddy ground that measured across its width the length of three men lying end to end.

Anwealda made his way to the edge of the ring.

"Prepare yourselves," he said, in a loud, ringing voice.

Beobrand raised his shield; readied his sword. His feet squelched in the mire. The ground was treacherous. This would be tricky.

Anwealda lifted his right hand.

"Remember, the first to strike seven blows is the victor."

Though hungry, the lord of the hall seemed more animated now; excited at the prospect of the entertainment. He held his hand up for a few heartbeats, clearly revelling in his role, then dropped it as he shouted, "Begin!"

Beobrand did not look to the lord. The people watching were mere shapes behind his foe. To lose concentration now would be to sacrifice victory. Looking over the rim of his shield, he fixed his gaze on Wulfgar's feet. He would not be the first to strike. He would allow the West Seaxon to make the first move. Beobrand wished to see what skill he possessed.

The two circled each other warily. Beobrand felt the tightness in his left arm, the twinge of pain in his right leg as his foot slipped a little in the mud.

Perhaps perceiving the slip as a weakness, Wulfgar chose that moment to attack. With surprising speed, especially given the soft ground, he bounded forward, aiming a blow towards Beobrand's midriff. Beobrand sidestepped easily, taking the blow on his shield and allowing Wulfgar to glide past. As he went, Beobrand cracked the wooden blade of his practice sword against Wulfgar's left leg. He did not put his full force into the blow, but Wulfgar winced.

"The first blow is struck by Beobrand," Anwealda said.

Acennan, Garr and Athelstan's gesithas let out a ragged cheer.

Beobrand grinned. It seemed this fight would not tax him as he'd thought it might.

Yet his gloating was short-lived. Wulfgar spun around to face him once more and instantly resumed his attack.

By the gods, he was quick. Beobrand shuffled backwards, soaking up the brunt of Wulfgar's attacks on his shield. But the mud and his leg hampered his movement. He was retreating too slowly. Wulfgar pressed home a flurry of blows on the shield. Beobrand wished to continue to move backwards but he sensed the watching men behind him. There was nowhere to go. So he changed direction, punching his shield forward and to the left to parry Wulfgar's sword, he lunged at his adversary's legs again. But this time, Wulfgar was not off balance. He had anticipated the move and twisted away from the shield, smashing his blade hard into Beobrand's outstretched sword arm.

The crowd gasped. It was a crippling blow, even with a wooden blade. Beobrand sprang away from Wulfgar, darting over to the other end of the area ringed off for them to fight. His arm was numb. It was all he could do to keep hold of his sword. He kept his eyes on Wulfgar. If he came on without pause again, Beobrand was unsure he would be able to do much more than defend himself with the shield.

"One blow apiece," shouted Anwealda, over the cheer of the West Seaxon onlookers.

Wulfgar wiped small beads of sweat from his forehead with his arm.

"If this had been a real blade, you'd have lost your arm then, Beobrand," he taunted.

It was true, Beobrand knew. His arm throbbed from the blow, but the feeling was returning and with it, movement. All he needed were a few more moments to get the blood flowing again. He swung his arm, willing his body to recover quickly.

"If we had used real blades, Wulfgar, you would have found it hard to attack with only one leg."

Wulfgar frowned. The watchers laughed. This was a rare entertainment indeed.

Both wary now, they circled once more. Beobrand twisted and flexed his forearm. The feeling returned slowly. He would have a bruise to remind him of this fight for a few days. He was lucky the bone had held. It could easily have shattered under such force. Perhaps it was his wyrd to vanquish Wulfgar today after all. The crows had settled on the thatch once more, and now let out a series of raucous calls. Was Woden watching? Were the gods laughing at the men and their sticks? Beobrand wished he could reach for the Thunor's hammer amulet that hung at his neck, but he dared not lower his guard.

He spat into the churned mud. Beobrand's arm throbbed. He recalled another, deadlier fight in the mud of Engelmynster. He had goaded Hengist then. Anger needed to be harnessed in battle. Unbridled rage was seldom a companion of victory.

"Well, Wulfgar, are you going to show me what great sword-skill you have? Or would you rather I turned my back? And perhaps your friends could join you. That is how you prefer to fight, is it not? Attacking from behind when your foe is outnumbered?"

"I am no coward," Wulfgar screamed, and launched himself at Beobrand.

Despite having hoped for the attack, Beobrand was once more shocked by Wulfgar's speed. The West Seaxon's oak blade passed a finger's breadth over Beobrand's head as he dropped to one knee, allowing his left foot to slide in the slimy muck. His right leg screamed in protest at the sudden jerking motion. Wincing against the pain, he thrust his practice blade forward and caught Wulfgar solidly in the stomach, bringing him up short, wheezing and coughing.

The audience whooped and cheered.

"To Beobrand, a second blow," shouted Anwealda.

Wulfgar, doubled over and clutching his middle, glowered at Beobrand. He was filled with rage now; that was something that Beobrand recognised all too well. But there was something else in the man's eyes. It was there for only the most fleeting of moments, quickly replaced with the flint-hard stare of the warrior. Yet, for an instant, Beobrand was sure he had seen the uncertainty of one who has given his best and has been found wanting. He was skilled; strong and fast. And yet Beobrand was faster and they both knew now, as did the warriors watching, that Wulfgar was outmatched.

Beobrand heaved himself up from where he knelt in the muck. He nodded as Wulfgar straightened and hefted his shield and sword once more. He had spoken the truth, he was no coward. Beobrand felt a pang of guilt. He had humiliated Wulfgar once. He had no desire to do so again, in front of all these people. The thought of the fight had enticed him, but the flame of his battle lust had died; snuffed out the moment he had looked into Wulfgar's eyes and realised he had no more need to prove himself.

But there was no way out of this now. Neither could cede victory without losing face. They began to circle again. Sweat trickled into Beobrand's eyes, making them sting. He may have nothing to prove, but if he did not give his all, Wulfgar would make him pay. Of that he was certain. There was nothing for it, but to continue and hope he could beat him quickly.

Perhaps the gods tired of the spectacle. Mayhap they saw that the warrior's hearts were no longer in the fight. But at that moment, a terrible scream echoed from the hall. Everyone turned to stare at the doors, as a young thrall girl ran into the yard. Her face seemed as grey as the sky above the roof, where the crows still perched, watching the proceedings with their unfeeling eyes.

The thrall looked about her, pale and trembling.

"What is it, girl?" asked Anwealda, stepping towards her. "What has happened?"

Sweat trickled a trail down Beobrand's back. It felt like the cold finger of death.

"Gone," the girl said, her voice as tremulous as her lower lip.

"Gone?"

"Taken," she replied.

"What has been taken? Speak sense now, Gitta." Anwealda's voice had lost its air of self-assurance.

"Not what. Who."

"What are you talking about?"

"The queen. Cyneburg's been taken."

Chapter 16

"By all the gods, what has happened here?" Anwealda's voice was barely a whisper. The sleeping chamber was dim. The thin morning light dribbled through the gap between the shutters on the window. The mass of bodies blocking the doorway impeded most of the light that could have filtered in from the main hall's hearth and rush lights.

Beobrand, still holding the wooden sword and shield, forced his way through the throng and joined Anwealda at the entrance to the chamber. He could discern little in the room. There was a wooden bed, and a couple of smaller cots stood to one side. The room was deathly still. He sniffed. A familiar scent hit the back of his throat. Shit. This had been the ladies' quarters. It was not the smell one associated with ladies and queens. Unless...

A groan. A shape he had assumed to be a pile of bedding moved. Anwealda rushed forward and bent beside the form.

"My dear," he said, the words choked.

The shape moaned again.

"I cannot see," Anwealda said, desperation in his voice. "I need light."

Beobrand strode to the window and pushed open the shutters.

Watery light washed the room in grey.

Anwealda held his wife, the lady Osberga, in his arms. There was a splash of blood on her face. Her skin was pale. And someone had tied a strip of cloth around her mouth to prevent her making a noise. Her hands and feet were tied with strong strips of hide. Anwealda tugged and fretted at her bonds for a few moments. Beobrand dropped the shield and sword with a clatter and knelt beside them. Pulling his small eating knife from his belt, he sawed through the cords. Anwealda pulled the gag from her mouth.

Osberga's eyes were dazed, unfocused. Anwealda smoothed her hair away from her face. It was sticky with blood.

"What happened here, my lady?" Beobrand asked, his gentle tone belying his pounding heart. Cyneburg, his queen, was gone. Taken. But by whom? And where?

Others crowded into the room behind him. Beobrand held up a hand to quieten them.

Slowly, Osberga's eyes focused on Beobrand. He watched as understanding came to her. Her mouth opened and her eyes grew wide.

"What happened here?" he repeated. "You are safe now," he added in the voice he used to calm anxious animals.

"They... they came in the night."

"Who?"

"I do not know. They came quietly. Quickly. They knew what they wanted. They took her. Oh, by Frige, they took her, didn't they?" She tried to sit, but moaned and fell back against her husband.

Beobrand struggled to make sense of this. They had been safe in Anwealda's hall. How could this have happened?

"You recognised none of them?"

She shook her head briefly, but her face crumpled with pain and she stopped moving.

"No. We were abed. Sleeping. There were enough of them to overpower all of us. Before we could do much of anything, they had tied Gitta and me. I screamed then. For help. That is when one of them hit me."

In the gloom of the room, the blood on her face and in her hair looked black. Beobrand found himself unable to look away from it. For an instant, he recalled the face of the woman at Nathair's hall. She had flung herself at him and before he had known it, she had lain dead at his feet. Slain by his hand. He loathed men who would raise a hand to women. They were the worst kind of craven. Hengist. Wybert. His father. Was he really any different?

Pushing the dark thoughts from his mind, he forced himself to look into Osberga's eyes.

"I will find these men and they will pay for what they have done."

For a moment she stared into his eyes. He did not know what she saw there, but after a time, she gave the tiniest of nods, and reached out to touch his arm. Her grip was surprisingly strong.

"You must bring back Cyneburg safely." She looked past him at the crowd of faces gazing down at her. "Is he well? Did he raise the alarm?"

Beobrand frowned. The savage blow to the head had

addled her thoughts. It was not uncommon for this type of wound. He hoped she would recover fully.

"She needs rest," he said to Anwealda, who nodded. Beobrand made to stand. Osberga gripped his arm more firmly.

"My lady, there is no time to waste," Beobrand said, trying to gently prise her claw-like fingers from his arm. "We need to ready the men to ride. We must hurry."

She ignored his words, digging her fingers in.

"Is he well?" she repeated, urgency in her voice. "He fought like a bear to protect us."

Cold dread gripped Beobrand.

"Who do you speak of?"

"The great warrior. I cannot recall his name. He came at my scream. He crashed into the chamber and lay about him with his fists. He downed one of the attackers with a punch. That was when I screamed for the second time. One of them must have hit me again. The next thing I remember is awakening now."

Beobrand leapt to his feet and moved further into the chamber. There was an unmoving bundle of clothes between the bed and the cots. The stench of shit was stronger here. He stepped cautiously forward and reached out a hand. He was certain now of what he would find. The shape before him was gaining form and sense in his mind as he moved closer.

With the trembling fingers of his half-hand, he pulled at the blanket that covered the body, for that was clearly what it was. Tugging at the cloth he revealed an ashen face. The teeth, surrounded by a bristling beard, were bared in a vicious snarl of anger.

His heart sank. Athelstan had not missed the bout that morning through laziness.

By his side, Acennan gasped at the sight of the thegn's unseeing eyes and death-pale face.

"By Woden, Thunor and Tiw, the bastards will pay for this."

The pungent stench of death was overpowering now.

Beobrand turned to the gathered men.

"Queen Cyneburg is taken, and Athelstan died trying to save her." Athelstan's men let out a moan of grief.

Dreogan, one of Athelstan's gesithas, a balding man, with a hard face made harsher by blackened lines on his cheeks where he had rubbed soot into cuts, stepped forward and said, "We should have stopped this. Or we should have died alongside our lord. Instead, we slept and played at fighting." He fixed Beobrand with a bleak scowl.

Beobrand thought of his dreams of screams in the storm. He took a deep breath. The taste of death stung his throat.

"Athelstan was a great warrior. A strong lord and a true friend. I share your grief, Dreogan. And I also share the guilt you feel at not preventing his death. But he died protecting his queen. It is a good death. And we should not dwell on what has happened. We must move. We find the men who did this and we avenge Athelstan." And salvage our pride, he thought.

Dreogan lowered his gaze.

Beobrand sought out Wulfgar amongst the watchers. "We must put our squabbles behind us and find Cyneburg."

Wulfgar nodded.

"There is no time for games now," the West Seaxon said. "Together we will seek out Cyneburg."

Neither Beobrand nor Wulfgar needed to mention what was at stake. Oswald of Northumbria's queen was gone, taken by men clearly capable of murder. Wars had started over less.

"What of my sister?" Wulfgar said, suddenly.

Acennan quickly, frantically searched the rest of the chamber, throwing aside cloaks and blankets in case they hid another grisly secret.

"She is not here," he said, an edge of panic in his voice.

Chapter 17

Beobrand sat astride his mount and waited for Wulfgar's man to speak. The horses were lathered with sweat, blowing hard. This rest would do them good. They would have to slow the pace or risk killing the beasts. He hoped their quarries did not have replacement mounts. If they did, there would be little chance of running them to ground.

Bitter spots of rain began to fall as they waited while the dismounted warrior walked back and forth over the churned track. Beobrand looked up at the iron-grey sky. It didn't look as if it would rain heavily. It would take a lot to wash away the tracks. The earth was soft and they were in pursuit of many riders.

How could it be taking the man so long to decide on which direction they had taken? Beobrand missed Attor. He had no equal in tracking and would have scarcely needed to dismount to track the queen's captors at this crossing of two paths. Thinking of Attor brought thoughts of Rheagan. He prayed she was well. He smiled grimly. He could almost hear Bassus' voice telling him not to fret about things he could not control. He knew the sense in those words, but he was ever unable to fully heed them.

As if he could also hear the voice from within his thoughts, Wulfgar said, "Do not fear. Hlisa is the best tracker I know. He will set us on the right path."

Beobrand did not reply, but gave a curt nod. He had asked Wulfgar to ride at the head of the small column of warriors with him. The men seemed happy enough to follow with them both in the lead. He just hoped that if it came to a fight, and surely it would, Wulfgar would allow him to lead. There could be no division in a group hoping to win a pitched battle.

Wulfgar seemed calm, the only sign of tension the tightness of his jaw and a slight pinching around his eyes. His sister was missing too. Beobrand suddenly felt sorry for him. Where he had despised the man before that morning, he had now seen how he reacted in the face of an armed opponent and adversity. He was a brave man, proud and vain, but courageous and a skilled warrior. Beobrand took in Wulfgar's rigid posture in the saddle, the warrior ring on his tensed arm. At his side hung a sword in a finely decorated scabbard. Wulfgar peered towards the wooded horizon for any sign of the men who had taken Cyneburg and Eadgyth. Watching him, Beobrand was sure that they would regret their actions soon enough.

A few paces to Beobrand's left, Acennan had dismounted. He paced back and forth, face like thunder, muttering under his breath. He too worried about Eadgyth and did not hide it as well as Wulfgar.

Beobrand nudged his mare towards his friend, out of earshot of Wulfgar and the others. The small horse tossed its head nervously at the rapid movements of the squat warrior.

"Save your strength, Acennan," Beobrand said in a soft voice. "When we find the bastards who took them, you'll have need for it."

Acennan strode to his own mount where it stood, reins trailing, cropping at the rain-soaked grass beside the track. He snatched up the reins, causing the horse to snort, then swung himself onto its back in one easy motion.

"Never mind me," he said. "I'll have strength to spare to split the skulls of the vermin who have done this."

Hlisa had reached a decision and remounted, spurring his horse over to Wulfgar. Beobrand rode back to where the two conversed, brushing away the annoyance that the tracker had not thought to wait until they were both able to hear his news. He was Wulfgar's man, not his.

"Hlisa is certain," said Wulfgar, as Beobrand approached, "they rode that way." He signalled the path that struck off between forested hills into the west and north.

"There can be no mistake?" asked Beobrand.

"None, lord," Hlisa replied. "There are several of them. It is hard to say the number with certainty, but I would say about ten. All mounted. Riding hard."

"Any extra horses?"

"From the depth of the tracks, I'd say not. Perhaps a brace of them, but not one per rider."

"Well, that's something, at least. Let us pray that some will go lame." Beobrand stared along the track until it disappeared between the trees. "This is your land, Wulfgar," Beobrand continued. "Where are they taking them?"

Wulfgar scratched at his beard absently.

"Yes, I know this area well. We would often come here to visit Uncle Anwealda. We hunted these forests, and he would entertain other lords from Wessex and beyond."

"Beyond?"

"Yes. For we are in the borderlands of Wessex here. Oftentimes there would be skirmishes with the neighbours. At other times, there was peace. Anwealda was always keen to make peace. Good for trade, he would say." Wulfgar shook his head, as if to clear it of memories. "I know this land well, but I have little enough knowledge of what lies over those hills."

"But you think you know why they have taken Cyneburg? Where they are taking her?" He saw the sharp look from both Wulfgar and Acennan and corrected himself. "You know where they are taking them?"

"I can think of no reason other than to cause war. We must ride hard and we must catch them before they reach their destination, wherever that may be."

"We are agreed, let us tarry no longer," shouted Acennan. And then he asked the question, the answer of which Beobrand had already gleaned from Wulfgar's words and his own rudimentary understanding of the isle of Albion and its kingdoms.

"But where are they taking them?"

Wulfgar dug in his heels and his mount bounded forward, throwing up gobbets of mud and water.

"Come, men," shouted Beobrand, not waiting for Wulfgar to respond to Acennan, "we ride with all haste. For they are taking the ladies to Mercia. To Penda."

Reaghan stood unmoving; quiet and as still as the great bird she watched. It was so tranquil here, with the wide waters of the Tuidi sliding silently past. She knew why Beobrand came to this spot. It was a good place to think. Not that she had matters of such import to ponder. She would not need to pass judgement over farmers who could not decide on their boundary stones, or whether a ceorl's tribute of cheese or grain was enough. Even so, her mind was full of thoughts, each vying for her attention like squabbling children.

She touched her belly under her peplos. Flat and slender. But that might change all too soon.

On the breeze, she heard the sound of voices from Ubbanford. At the distant noise, the snake-necked heron on the far bank shifted its position, tilting its head slightly, as if trying to understand words in the voices.

Reaghan was glad not to be able to hear any words. They would surely be ordering her to rush to some chore or another. She had crept away after finishing the milking. She had taken the bucket of warm goat's milk to the dairy, but Rowena had not been there as she had expected. So, without pausing to contemplate her actions, Reaghan had left the pail in the shade of the hut and made her way westward along the river bank.

Seeing the heron reminded her of Beobrand. He talked about the bird as if it were an old friend. She missed him. Her hand went again to her belly, nervously, like a butterfly unsure whether to settle.

Rowena would have her beaten when she returned to the settlement. Since Beobrand had left, Reaghan had been beaten more frequently than ever before. The only one who was kind to her was Maida. She would invite Reaghan in to sit with her while she spun or weaved. The chatter and play of the children reminded her of a distant childhood where the children spoke in a different tongue. Where she was loved. At these times she would recall her father's strength as he lifted her in his arms after a day harvesting hay. The scent of freshly cut grass would envelop her along with his warm embrace.

She was glad of Maida's kindness. And yet she secretly believed that Beobrand had ordered Elmer's wife to spend time with her. To watch over her. The thought of him caring enough for her to do such a thing troubled her. What did this mean? She was merely a thrall. Beobrand was a lord. There could be no more than that. But what if her fears were proven true?

She could run away. The idea came, as it always did, with a sense of dread. Memories of her family and the attack that had seen them slain all those years ago.

Where would she go? She had nothing to offer, save that which she did not wish to give to strangers. Better to stay here. The beatings would cease when Beobrand returned. He would not allow them to continue. And, despite the looks from some of the warriors as she served in the hall, none had dared touch her. Not while Beobrand was their lord. They knew she was his, and none was foolhardy enough to cross him.

The heron suddenly twitched, bringing Reaghan back to the present, to the shadowed bank of the river. A moment later, the bird spread its huge wings and flapped away downriver. She watched as it rose into the sky, grey against the grey. The summer was reaching an end. It was yet warm, but soon winter would be upon them. Beobrand had been away for so long.

A voice from behind her startled Reaghan.

"Well, girl, are you in some sort of trouble?"

Reaghan spun around.

A woman in a flowing green dress stepped from amongst

the alder and willows that lined the river. Her hair was long and black as a raven's claw, although there were streaks of white at the temples. She walked with animal grace, hips swaying. Slender limbs and soft curves. She would have been beautiful, but for the hideously puckered scar that ran from her mouth up her left cheek.

The woman smiled broadly. A dark gap where two of her teeth were missing made Reaghan reconsider. Perhaps she had once been beautiful, but no longer. But there was something alluring about her all the same. Reaghan could not take her eyes from the woman. Like watching Thunor's hammer-flash of lightning in a storm cloud, or the searing flames of a bone-fire.

Reaghan took a step backward, as the stranger walked towards her. The river lay behind; cold and deep. Nowhere to go.

"Do not be afraid, child," the woman said, her voice soft as rain on leaves.

"I'm not afraid," Reaghan replied, and hoped the woman could not hear the lie in the words.

The woman threw back her head and let out a laugh. It sounded as harsh as a jackdaw's call. Reaghan tried not to shudder. Without noticing, her hand had returned to her middle.

"Oh, but you are frightened, my dear. But you don't need to be."

"What do you know of me and my fears?" asked Reaghan, suddenly defiant.

"I know many things, child. I know things you could never comprehend. I have travelled the land, walking in the company of gods and spirits. Your fears are as clear to me as if you had told them to me yourself."

The woman's talk of gods and spirits sent a shiver of ice down Reaghan's back.

"Who are you?"

"My name is of no consequence. Just know that I can help you."

"Help me with what?"

The woman smiled slyly and took a quick step forward. Reaghan wanted to flee, but the river was at her back. The woman grasped her wrist with a painful grip. Reaghan stifled a scream.

The woman slid her other hand slowly over the coarse cloth of Reaghan's peplos. She ran her hand softly down her smooth stomach. There her hand lingered. Reaghan wanted to snatch it away, but instead she stared into the eyes of the woman. They were hazel, flecked with gold and madness.

"Help me with what?" Reaghan repeated in the tiniest of voices.

"What pretty unwed girls always need help with, Reaghan." Reaghan jolted. How had she known her name? "Do I need to say the words, Reaghan? Do I need to speak of the evil thing you are thinking of doing?"

Reaghan shook her head slowly, as if dazed from a blow to the head.

"No."

"Good," the woman's hand began to massage Reaghan's belly gently, softly, "then let me help you free you of your burden."

Chapter 18

The sun was low in the sky. It had been hidden all day behind the dark clouds, but now, as night drew close, it shone bright and glaring from under the band of darkness. The clouds had spat rain at times as they had ridden west, but nothing to rival the storm of the night before. But the dark sky and laden clouds spoke of further downpours to come.

Beobrand squinted as the dying light of the sun reflected from the puddles and pools of the path they followed. Far in the distance wound a river of molten gold. Against the glare of the sunset, they could not make out the men they pursued, but they could not be too far away. Hlisa had dismounted several times during the afternoon and swore the tracks they followed were getting fresher. They were gaining on their quarry.

Wulfgar reined in next to Beobrand.

"We must make camp, even if just for a short while."

Beobrand turned to him and nodded. They were all exhausted. His arm ached where Wulfgar's wooden blade had struck.

Acennan yanked savagely at his mount's reins, jerking its head round so that he faced Beobrand and Wulfgar.

"We should keep riding. If we halt now, we might lose them."

Beobrand saw the desperation in Acennan's eyes. He could feel it pulling at his own will. This was the curse of leadership. He could not show his fears.

"No, Acennan. Wulfgar speaks true. If we ride into the night, we risk the horses. Or losing the trail. The men we follow will need to rest too. Have the men make camp there, in that copse. We will ride before dawn."

Acennan glowered at him for a moment, before wheeling his horse around and shouting at the warriors. They rode towards a stand of oak and ash, leaving Wulfgar and Beobrand alone.

"Where do you think they are headed?" Beobrand asked.

Wulfgar scratched his beard, hawked and spat into the nettles at the side of the muddy path.

"I cannot tell. But whatever mischief they plan must be in Mercia."

"Do you know where we are?"

"My knowledge of these lands is not deep, but I have ridden here before. That river yonder is the Afen. We are near Grimbold's hall."

Grimbold. Why was the name familiar?

"I have heard the name, but cannot recall where. Is he a great thegn?"

"They say he is a good lord. I have met him a couple of times at Anwealda's hall. But I would have thought you would have remembered who he is. Word of the events of kings travels quickly."

Beobrand stared at him, frowning. What was he speaking of?

"Your wyrd is woven with Grimbold's. Or at least with one of Grimbold's gesithas."

Then, as sudden and as bright as the flaring sunlight had burst from the black clouds in the west, it came to him.

"Wybert," he said, his voice brittle and hard.

"Aye, Grimbold is Wybert's lord."

"I have sworn a bloodfeud with Wybert." His hand went to the hilt of Hrunting. His fingers tightened around the sword. He could ride now to this Grimbold's hall. The others could surely find Cyneburg; bring back the queen. The thought of vengeance almost overcame him. His mouth was suddenly dry. He licked his lips.

"I know, Beobrand." Wulfgar's voice was unusually soft. "I have heard what he did to you." He swallowed. "To your wife." Beobrand's jaw clenched, he did not meet Wulfgar's gaze. "There is no man who would not wish to seek the blood price for what Wybert did. But I fear your moment for revenge is not close."

Beobrand looked at him sharply.

"You said Grimbold's hall lies nearby."

"I did. But Wybert is not there."

"Where is he then? I will kill him. Tell me where he is, that I may search for him once we are through with this."

Beobrand could sense Wulfgar looking at him for a long while.

"I would not wish to be Wybert," Wulfgar said at last. "But I know not where he is now. All I have heard are rumours. The murmurings of visiting travellers."

"And what is it that you've heard?" asked Beobrand.

"That after he had recovered from his wounds at Dor, he rode south."

"South? Where?"

"I cannot say, but there are those who said he was bound for the coast. And then on to Frankia."

Frankia? What lay there? Was he fleeing Beobrand's wrath?

"If he thinks that putting a sea between us will protect him," Beobrand said, "I will prove him mistaken."

Wulfgar nodded.

"I hope the gods smile upon you in your quest," he said and spurred his horse towards where the others were making camp.

Beobrand tightened his grip on Hrunting until his hand ached. He sat thus, tense and angry astride the dappled mare, staring into the setting sun until his eyes began to water.

Heavy rain fell in the night. The ash and oak trees offered little protection so they spent a sad and wet time of it. They had few provisions and did not light a fire, making do with stale bread and some scraps of cold meat; leftovers from Anwealda's table. Beobrand set guards and ordered the men to get some rest. Taking his own advice, he had wrapped himself in his damp cloak, propped his back against the bole of a large oak, and sought sleep. Despite his discomfort, he fell into a light doze almost at once. His dreams were filled with thunder and the screams of innocents. When he awoke with a start, the only thing he could recall from his slumber were eyes. Staring. Imploring. The eyes of Cathryn, as she lay on the cold earth.

It was still dark and the rain had eased. Acennan was shaking him.

"It will be dawn soon," Acennan whispered. His face was a pale smudge in the gloom.

Beobrand grunted, and held out his hand to be pulled to his feet. Acennan's tension was palpable.

Beobrand stretched, wincing at the number of aches he felt. His rib and leg both throbbed dully. His left arm was stiff and his right hurt from the bruises Wulfgar had inflicted on him. The practice bout had only been the previous morning, but it seemed so far away. He stamped his feet and swung his arms to get the blood flowing.

He stepped out of the cover of the trees, the big toe of his right foot giving a twinge. The sky in the west was still dark, but there was a dim glow in the east.

"Wake the men," he said to Acennan, slapping him on the back. "We ride, my friend, and we shall make them pay for what they have done. Athelstan's death shall be avenged."

Acennan hesitated.

"What if…?" Acennan's voice trailed off. He could not say the words.

He did not need to.

Beobrand again thought of Cathryn's eyes.

He gripped Acennan's shoulders roughly.

"Do not think those thoughts. We will face those who have done this and we will make them pay for what they have done." But what had they done to Cyneburg and Eadgyth?

"Do not fear for the womenfolk," Beobrand said. "Now rouse the men. We will ride hard again today and should the gods will it, we will run them to ground."

Acennan nodded and stalked into the gloom under the trees. Sounds of men rising and gathering their belongings came to Beobrand.

Somewhere, in the darkness, a night creature shrieked, making him shudder.

He was almost certain that Cyneburg would be safe. Surely they had taken the queen for something more than to be the plaything for some warriors' lust. She was too important, the risks far too great. But what of Eadgyth? She was of no importance in the game of tafl played by kings. And she was a beauty.

Beobrand hurried back into the copse and helped Acennan get the men up and mounted. There was no time to lose.

Chapter 19

There was scarcely light in the sky when Reaghan awoke. She felt refreshed. The fears that had been troubling her had fled, like bad dreams or the spirits of the dead borne on smoke from a funeral pyre.

Rowena had not beaten her in the end. Reaghan had returned to find the lady of the hall fussing over some new cloth that Aart, the pedlar, had brought to Ubbanford. All of the women were flocking around the man, a stunted creature who looked as old as the hills themselves. He had a small handcart and he visited two or three times a year with his brutish companion. The big man who accompanied him never spoke, but his eyes were always vigilant. The man's size alone would be enough to deter most brigands from attempting to rob Aart, but if that were not sufficient, the hefty axe he carried was extremely persuasive.

A visit from Aart was always cause for celebration. He brought trinkets and fine thread; spices and herbs from faraway lands. His eyes would twinkle as he told of the places his wares came from, and Reaghan always wondered how much of it he made up. She was not interested in hearing his tales of distant lands, but, like all the other inhabitants of Ubbanford, she was hungry for news. She had remained at the back of the hall while the Angelfolc questioned him. She had not been keen on attracting attention to herself. Rowena might remember that she had disappeared before her chores were complete, and Aart and his massive friend always let their gaze linger on her. Nothing had ever come of their leering, but Beobrand was not here to protect her. It was best to be prudent. Besides, she did not wish them to discover her secret. She had not used it yet.

She held it in her hand; small, smooth and warm from her constant touch while she slept. The lady by the river had told her what to do. She traced its shape with her fingers in the dark. It was tiny. She marvelled at the skill to make such a thing. To construct such a delicate earthenware flask must be the work of a craftsman fit to serve a king. She felt where the opening at the top was stopped with wax. It was softening under her fingers, she must be careful not to warm it too much and break the seal.

She had clutched it in her hands, hidden from view last night as Aart had told tales of the kingdom of Bernicia and beyond. There was trouble in the north. The Picts had taken Finola and her son from Bebbanburg and fled to Din Eidyn. Oswiu had the fortress under siege.

"But what of our king?" asked Rowena. "Have you tidings of Oswald, and those who travel with him?" Women, men and children had stopped talking then. Their friends were with Oswald. Their husbands. Their fathers. They all listened intently to Aart's reply.

"Well, I am just come from Berewic, on the coast, and

yesterday I heard tell from a sailor friend of mine, that Oswald King is on his way back to Bernicia. He may already be home."

"This is joyous news indeed," Rowena had said, "the men will be returning to us soon." Reaghan had wondered what it was to the lady. Her men were all dead. Then she had caught the gaze of Edlyn. Perhaps the girl thought the same thing. Her look was dark. There was no joy on her face. Reaghan had turned away, as Aart continued, preventing Edlyn from one of her spiteful outbursts.

"They say that the king's marriage to the princess of Wessex was a glorious occasion. The ladies wore the finest cloth of green, just like this." He held up a bolt of dark green linen. "Would the lady Rowena be wanting some? It would make a wonderful dress for your beautiful daughter."

The evening had continued with the folk of Ubbanford asking for news. Sometimes the pedlar had quick answers that rang true, at other times he seemed to think a little too hard, and on those occasions, Reaghan noted, his stories always turned to the items he had for sale. There was no further news about Oswald or Beobrand, but it seemed there had been no trouble on the journey, so they were expected back in Bernicia very soon.

As the night had drawn on, Reaghan had smiled to herself. She carried food and drink, serving the men without complaint. Frequently, her hand would go to the small weight in the pouch she wore at her waist. Her man would return to her soon.

Not your man, said a small voice inside. Never your man. You are a thrall. Waelisc. You are nothing to him.

But he had come for her when no other man would have, so she pushed the sour voice into the darkest reaches of her mind. Beobrand was coming home and she would ensure that she did not spoil things.

Stepping quietly out into the overcast cool of the early morning light, she shivered.

How had the woman by the river known of her predicament? She slid her hand over her smooth stomach. There was no sign.

She had asked the woman, but she had merely smiled a crooked smile, made frightening by the scar and the missing teeth.

"I did not come here seeking you, my dear Reaghan. It was you who came to this place seeking me."

Reaghan had not understood, but had not spoken.

"And you have found me," the woman had continued. Then, she had produced the small container and handed it to Reaghan.

"You must find a place where you will not be disturbed and drink all of this potion."

"What will it do?"

"You know what it will do. It will rid you of your burden."

Something in the woman's eyes had frightened Reaghan and she asked, "Will it hurt?"

"I will not lie to you, girl. It will hurt and you will likely cry out for a time. But if you do nothing, you will feel more pain. In the chill of winter, you would scream as if your innards were being ripped asunder. And then what? Do you think they would let you stay here? You are a thrall. Nothing to them."

Reaghan had shuddered. Pain she could handle, but she did not wish to be turned out with nowhere to go.

"So why do you offer your help to me?" she had asked.

Again, a smile twisted the woman's face.

"Womenfolk should always stick together. Men understand nothing. Just swords and killing. We sisters know about life."

Now, as she walked into the shadow of the trees down by the water's edge, Reaghan wondered at the woman's words. "We know about life," she had said.

Her fingers once more stroked the smooth shape of the tiny wax-sealed jar, as she sought a place where she would not be disturbed. Her burden would be gone soon, and Beobrand would return. All would be well then.

Beobrand missed Sceadugenga's easy gait as they rode hard into the west. The dappled mare was sure-footed enough; more than once it slipped on the mud-slick track they followed, but on each occasion it regained its footing quickly. But it lacked Sceadugenga's confidence and the sense of control that Beobrand had when riding the black stallion was absent. There had been no setbacks apart from a brief disruption as they mounted. One of the horses had stepped on Renweard's foot. The warrior, a gesith from Athelstan's warband, had screamed like a child, before punching the beast squarely on the snout. Under other circumstances, the men would have laughed and teased him, but such was not the mood with them this day. They were wet, cold and tired, and above all else, they were grim and determined.

Now well into Mercia, they did not wish to stay there any longer than necessary. They passed ceorls who stood dejectedly leaning on scythes, surrounded by swathes of wet barley. Beobrand wondered whether those men might tell their lords they had seen a warband riding west. Perhaps even now, Grimbold, or other thegns of Mercia were amassing their warriors to hunt down the horsemen riding through their lands. As the rain once more began to fall on the already waterlogged land before them, Beobrand told himself that more than likely there was nobody on their trail. Penda had sworn a truce with Oswald. And yet, he could not shake the feeling of being ever more surrounded by enemies. After all, the men who had taken Cyneburg and Eadgyth must surely be Mercians. Could they be acting without Penda's knowledge? Of course they could, but would it be worth the risk? And for what reason? The raid on Anwealda's hall had been daring and dangerous.

This brought another question. One that he had pondered much, but with no answer. If Cyneburg had been their target, which seemed the only explanation, how had they known that the queen was there to be taken?

Hlisa and Garr had been scouting ahead of the column of riders, now they both crested a small rise and rode towards Wulfgar and Beobrand. Beobrand held up his hand, indicating for the band to halt. Wulfgar produced a leather flask and took a swig, before offering it to Beobrand. He took the flask with a nod of thanks and swilled some of the tangy water around his sour-tasting mouth. He spat and took a longer draught. In spite of all the water around them, and the now constant, drenching rain, he was terribly thirsty and he welcomed the drink.

Garr and Hlisa cantered up to them in a splash of mud and grimy water. Their horses were mud-splattered and sweat-lathered. Beobrand tossed the water flask to Hlisa. The tracker took a long pull on it and then handed it to Garr.

"We are upon them," he said.

"How far?" asked Wulfgar.

"Not far. If we push on now, we will close with them before they reach the Afen."

"And the women?" Beobrand asked. Acennan had ridden close, and Beobrand knew what question he would want answering.

"They are with them. Each is mounted. We must have been able to ride faster without the women to deal with."

Acennan scowled.

"How many men?" he asked, his voice gravel-rough.

Garr gave a sidelong look at Hlisa.

"More than we reckoned," he said, pausing to spit into the mud. "A score. Maybe a few more."

Wulfgar turned to Beobrand.

"This will be a bloody fight. If we force them to stand, they will not give ground."

"You speak true, Wulfgar. But you men of Wessex are brave of heart, are you not? We have not ridden through mud and rain to feast with the men we chase, have we?"

Wulfgar showed his teeth in a savage grin.

"No, we have not."

Beobrand stared up the rise. Dense forest crowded the path at either side. The foliage was thick with tangled brambles and hawthorn. No rider could penetrate that verdant wall.

"How far to the river?" he asked.

"Not far, lord," replied Hlisa. "The forest follows down to the valley. There is a ford there, though with the rains the water will be high."

"And beyond the Afen?"

For a moment, it seemed Hlisa would not respond. He stared into the distance, perhaps imagining the land in his mind. Eventually he said, "The land opens into water meadows, and beyond that more wooded hills. But the woods are not so thick there. There are many paths. If they reach those woods, they can lose us."

Beobrand gave it a moment's thought. They had ridden too far to let them escape now.

"We should ride them down, before they cross the Afen."

Acennan's mount circled and he drew his sword.

"What are we waiting for?" he asked. "There are some Mercians who need killing and we will not do that here."

Dreogan came forward. His legs trailed long on the small roan he rode. The dark scar marks on his face gave him a frightening aspect. This was enhanced by splatters of mud that could have been dried blood.

"Are my lord Athelstan's slayers near?" he asked.

"Aye," said Acennan, struggling to control his mount that sensed its rider's excitement. "And we stand here talking when we could be riding. And killing."

"Dreogan and Acennan speak true," said Beobrand. "We must ride now. To tarry, will see us lose our prey."

"Wait," said Wulfgar in a strong voice. "We know they outnumber us. To ride at them without a plan is madness."

Beobrand's heart sank. A divide in the leadership of the warband was what he had feared. Such a division would drive a wedge into the men's resolve.

"Wulfgar, a word," Beobrand said, his tone broaching no argument. He beckoned to the West Seaxon thegn and they rode a few paces from the gathered warriors, where their words could not be overheard.

"We are a long way from a safe hall," Beobrand said. "The Mercians are close and outnumber us, but we must act with speed. If we stop to argue this point, we will lose the womenfolk. At worst, we all perish. We must be united, Wulfgar."

"Perhaps we could follow them further, and then send men into their camp at night to rescue the women."

"And what if they stop in a hall in these lands? We are lucky they have not done so already. Woden alone knows where they are heading."

Wulfgar's jaw clenched. He was angry at the rebuke, or perhaps angry at himself, as he knew Beobrand's words to be true.

"And if we did take the women?" spat Beobrand, anger entering his voice. They were wasting precious moments. "Then what? We ride back through Mercia? Exhausted men on exhausted horses?"

Wulfgar seized on this.

"Whatever path we choose, how do we mean to escape Mercia?"

Beobrand glowered at the bearded thegn, his eyes the cold blue of winter ice.

"It will not prove so difficult if we slaughter all those who know we are here. We can afford to spend no more time talking about this, man. We must ride now."

"But—" Wulfgar began to form a retort, but his words dried in his throat.

The decision had been taken from them.

Over the knap of the hill, bedecked in the gear of war, spears waving, wet shield bosses gleaming dully in the rain, rode more than a score of warriors.

Beobrand grinned.

The time for talking was over.

Reaghan sat for a long while in the still of early morning with nothing for company but the occasional splash from unseen denizens of the river and the dawn song of the birds. She would like to have seen the heron, as it reminded her of Beobrand, but she had not gone westward along the Tuidi towards the great bird's usual haunt. She had headed downriver, towards a small shingle beach, where she knew she would not be troubled. The cunning woman had been at the heron's spot, and something made her turn away from that direction. A tremor of fear ran down her spine. She needed to steel herself to the task in hand. The woman had said it would hurt, but the alternative was much worse, she had been right about that.

Reaghan watched the mist curl over the sluggish waters of the river. A muted splish-slap sound made her turn her head, and she thought she saw a flash of silver before the ripples showed where a fish had leapt. The sun did not yet reach the edge of the river where she sat. The beach was in the shadow of the hills and the air was unmoving, and cold. Reaghan shivered and looked away from the water to the small flask in her hand.

All she had to do was break the wax seal and drink the contents. There would be some pain, and then all would be well again.

The echoes of distant barking tugged at her attention. If she was going to do this, she needed to get on with it. Ubbanford was waking. In her left hand she clutched the small sack that was full of scraps of wool. She was unsure how much blood there would be. Her stomach was still flat. Surely there could not be much. Perhaps nothing more than a normal monthly bleeding. But what of the baby? What would it be like? She hoped she would not look upon it. She would wrap up whatever came and throw it in the river. Or bury it.

Please, Danu protect me and take the sacrifice of my blood. Another shudder racked her frame. It was cool here in the shadow-gloom by the water. Yet that was not why she shivered.

She placed the sack on the ground beside her and took a deep breath. She was surprised at how much she was trembling. She must do this now. It would get no easier if she waited.

Without more hesitation, she clasped the edge of the wax that stoppered the clay jar and pulled the layer back. Her hands shook. Careful not to spill the contents, she raised it to her face. Her nose wrinkled at the scent of the flask. Acrid and bitter. There could be no doubt that the potion would taste foul. Danu only knew what was in the concoction.

She lowered the flask for a moment and took another tremulous breath.

It was not meant to taste good. It had but one purpose. To rid her of the burden she bore, that she could continue with her life in Ubbanford. Perhaps the Earth Mother would look over her. Mayhap the goddess had guided the cunning woman to her. Perhaps she had brought Beobrand to her too.

She closed her eyes, and raised the noxious brew. The smell burnt her nostrils and made her gag as the clay pot touched her lips.

Chapter 20

The Mercians reined in when they saw the horsemen gathered just beyond the brow of the hill. Not much more than a spear's-throw distant, Beobrand could see the mud and sweat on their mounts. The sodden cloaks. The weary dark circles around the eyes of men who had ridden long and hard. He recognised the look; the Northumbrians and West Seaxons around him bore the same signs of fatigue.

The leader of the band, a large man in a warrior coat of leather, was quick to assess the situation. Before Beobrand or Wulfgar could react, he had raised his hand and shouted over his shoulder. Despite their evident tiredness, the men riding behind him turned their steeds in a well-trained manoeuvre and galloped back the way they had come, quickly disappearing over the hill. The leader kicked his own horse into motion, tugging its head to the side. The beast sprang forward, throwing up clods of mud as it galloped in the wake of the last two riders of the band. They had been slower to react to the change in direction than the rest of the men, and then Beobrand understood why. The last two riders, who were now closely followed by the leader of the Mercian warband, were not warriors. They were Eadgyth and Cyneburg.

Beobrand sat straight upon his mount and raised his voice, so that all would hear.

"The gods have smiled upon us. Behold the men we seek. They have Cyneburg and Eadgyth. The Queen of Northumbria and her gemæcce. Both daughters of Wessex. Will we turn away now because they number more than us?"

"No!" roared Acennan. The other warriors echoed his cry a heartbeat later.

Beobrand nodded. The way a smith can discern the correct moment to strike a blade on the anvil, he sensed the resolve of the men hardening. Their will would be what would bring them victory. Or defeat. He could show no doubt. Certainty and belief won battles.

"Many of us have faced worse odds than these and we have prevailed. We will prevail once more. Those men have stolen our womenfolk and slain one of our brothers. They cannot go unpunished."

His horse, sensing the urgency in its rider, shook its head and made to break into a gallop. He yanked its reins and it turned a tight circle. He directed his gaze to Wulfgar.

"There is no time for plans. We must close with them now. We will face them in the shieldwall, and kill them."

The men roared their approval. They too, it seemed, wished to be unleashed to punish the Mercians.

"And then?" asked Wulfgar, in a voice meant only for Beobrand. "How will we flee Mercia with our lives?"

It was a good question, but Beobrand remembered the words of older, wiser warriors. There was nothing to be gained in worrying about the past. Or the future.

"One problem at a time, Wulfgar," said Beobrand with a grin. "First we fight. And, as I said, if we slay them all, there will be none left to hinder us."

He pulled Hrunting from its scabbard and flourished the blade above his head. It caught the dull sunlight, flashing in the drizzle.

"Come, men," he shouted. "We ride to save our women and to avenge our friend."

With that, and trusting that the men would follow, he dug his heels into the mare's flanks, and galloped in pursuit of the Mercians.

"What are you doing, girl?" The screeching anxiety in the voice made Reaghan's heart flutter. She quickly pulled the flask from her lips, spilling some of the precious liquid. Viscous and baneful, the honey-hued liquor dribbled down her chin. Guiltily, Reaghan wiped at her face with the back of her hand. She had thought she was alone.

Odelyna, brow furrowed under her wispy grey hair, crunched onto the pebbles of the beach. She bustled forward and held out her hand.

Reaghan began to move the clay pot behind her, but Odelyna snapped, "No use in pretending there is nothing there, girl. I may be old, but I am not blind and I am certainly not stupid. Now, give it to me."

Hesitantly, Reaghan offered the small receptacle. A bead of its contents adorned the rim where the wax had been broken. It glittered like amber. Odelyna took it from her and began to inspect the pot.

Reaghan watched in dismay. How could this be happening? She had been so careful. If only she had not tarried. If she had already drunk the brew, it would now be doing its work and nothing this old crone could do would stop it. She would have been rid of her troubles and nobody would have needed to know of her secret. Now everything was in ruins.

For an instant, Reaghan wondered if she could overpower Odelyna. Her hands tightened around a large smooth pebble. She could leap up and surely the pebble would be enough to do for the old woman. But then what? If she had troubles now, how much worse would they be if she killed one of the villagers? She would be slain for sure. She was a slave; unable to pay weregild. She swallowed back the madness that had consumed her for a heartbeat. Her fingers relaxed, letting the stone clatter back to the beach.

The sound seemed to remind Odelyna that she was not alone. She had been sniffing the pot, all the while frowning. Now, she turned her attention back to Reaghan.

"Where did you get this?" she asked.

Reaghan did not answer. Her life was in tatters now. There was nothing to say.

"Where," repeated Odelyna, "did you get this?"

Reaghan remained sullen and silent, but could not meet the older woman's stern gaze.

"You are a foolish girl, Reaghan. I thought you cared for our lord. We all know you have been warming his bed. Is he not kind to you, that you should think to do this? Does he deserve to be treated thus?"

Reaghan looked up at Odelyna sharply.

"He is not unkind," she said in a small voice. She felt her cheeks grow hot. "I could see no way out of this."

"Out of what?"

Reaghan did not reply. She pulled her knees in close to her

chest and buried her face in her skirts. She would not cry, but she did not wish to see this woman's face. The judgement in her scowl. Her loathing. Or worse: her pity.

The shingle grumbled and crunched as Odelyna sat down beside her. The old woman let out a sigh that was full of sadness, not hatred.

Reaghan flinched as Odelyna placed her arm around her shoulders.

"The ways between man and woman are never simple," Odelyna said. "When the man is a lord and the woman a thrall, matters are worse. But it need not end like this. He is a man like any other, with his needs. But he is not a bad man. If having to lay with him is causing you so much distress, I will speak with him. I must say I am surprised though. I thought you had been happier than I'd seen you for a long time. Happier than ever, really. I was saying so to Maida just the other day, that you seemed content with your lot, and Beobrand had found solace with you following the tragedy of Sunniva. I think if I had not stopped you, it may well have undone him when he returns."

Something in Odelyna's words confused Reaghan.

Lifting her head from her knees, she asked, "What do you mean?"

Odelyna frowned at the question, clearly trying to understand what she was being asked.

"Well, for the lord to return to find you dead, so soon after the death of his wife, I think it might have done for him."

"Dead?" Her voice came out as a squeak.

"You'd have been dead sooner than it takes to skin a hare. And it wouldn't have been pleasant, I can tell you."

"Dead?" Reaghan repeated, sounding stupid to her own ears.

"Well, what did you think would happen when you drank that? It is made from ðung, a plant as deadly as any blade."

"She said it would relieve me of my burden."

"Who did? What burden?" Odelyna's tone was sharp.

Reaghan's eyes brimmed with tears now.

"This one." She placed her hand on her belly. "In here."

Understanding dawned on Odelyna's face.

"Well, this ðung would have got rid of that burden for sure. And any other burdens you carried. You'd have never seen another sunrise."

"But she said…"

"Whoever she is, she lied to you. But do not fear now, Reaghan, you foolish child." She gave the thrall a squeeze with her meaty arm. "If the only problem you have is an unwanted babe, why didn't you come to old Odelyna? I can help you be rid of it. There now, child. Do not fret."

Perhaps her life was not ruined after all. Could it be that she would be able to stay in Ubbanford? That all would be well again?

She shook, like an animal that has been held in a trap for a long while.

Without thinking, she leaned into Odelyna's ample breast and allowed the tears to flow.

The path was churned and slick. The passing of many horses and the constant rain had made parts of the track a quagmire. Beobrand clung to his mare's reins and gripped the horse's flanks with his legs as the beast, seeming to feel its rider's eagerness, galloped with abandon down the hill. The horse skittered and slipped, but despite the danger of falling, Beobrand let out a bark of laughter. A calmness had come upon him and he recognised the joy of imminent battle replacing the fears and worries of uncertainty and the unknown. Gone were the questions of what they should do, of how they would escape Mercia, and why the womenfolk had been taken. Their foes were within sight. The Mercians had slain one of their own and stolen those they were oath-bound to protect. There was no doubt now. Their enemies must perish.

The cloud-laden sky and the shade from the forest that loomed on either side, made the path a gloom-filled tunnel. A tunnel filled with the thunder of horses, the rattle and clank of battle-harness and the shouts and cries of warriors, thirsty for vengeance and battle-fame.

Beobrand sensed the rest of the men crowding behind him, all riding recklessly down the hill in pursuit of the Mercians. The bellowing war-cry of Dreogan rose above the clamour of the charge.

"Athelstan!" he screamed, and Athelstan's retainers took up the call.

They may be outnumbered, but Beobrand was sure of these men. He had stood with all of the Northumbrians at Hefenfelth. They would not be frightened of a handful of Mercians. He was less confident of the Wessexmen, but that would have to be Wulfgar's worry.

Ahead of them, the Mercians pulled up their steeds in an abrupt halt. In the darkness of the shadowed path it was difficult to make out what was happening, but then, it struck him. The Mercians had come upon them at the brow of the slope because they had been riding back the way they had already travelled. And there could only be one simple reason for that: they could not go forward. Something had blocked their path. So now, with their pursuers snapping at their heels, and unable to continue along the trail, they had dismounted and were quickly forming a shieldwall.

For a heartbeat Beobrand thundered forward, and the battle-joy sang to him. Here was glory to be sung of in the mead halls of kings. He would smash through their ranks. He had broken a small shieldwall before. Then he had charged his mount into the tiny group of warriors who faced them. But there had only been four men standing in that wall, and they had been caught by surprise. In the dim light of the tree-shadows, Beobrand discerned the wicked flicker of steel. The shieldwall had formed quickly. The men they faced were well-trained. When they arrived at the Mercians' line, they would be riding into a thicket of metal-tipped spears. Outnumbered by battle-ready warriors who stood prepared with spears set and shields raised, only one thing awaited a rider galloping at that shieldwall.

Death.

Battle-fame would be better enjoyed by the living.

Beobrand held Hrunting high and bellowed in a voice that he hoped would be heard over the thunder of the hooves.

"Halt! Halt!"

He dared not yank his mount's reins hard, for fear of the men behind him not slowing quickly enough to avoid a collision. Instead he waited a moment, screaming again for the men to halt their charge, then pulled gently on the reins, checking the mare's gallop. Cantering now, he could see that in a matter of moments he would be upon the shieldwall of Mercians.

"Halt!" he roared again, and then, with no alternative, he tugged hard on his reins. The mare dug her hooves into the slimy muck of the road, ripping deep channels in the mud. He heard commotion behind, but was too intent on keeping himself in the saddle and watching the warriors before them to look over his shoulder.

A horse whinnied and a man yelled.

Beobrand's mount finally came to a stop. He risked a glance behind. The men following him must have heard his cries or understood what awaited them on the path, for they were slowing their mounts. One of the West Seaxons stood some distance away. He was plastered in mud, evidently having been thrown from his horse. Beobrand spotted the animal cantering riderless towards him. He leapt from the mare's back without thinking of his leg until he hit the ground. It reminded him quickly enough that it was not yet fully healed with a silent scream of pain, but it held him upright. Without pause, he took three quick strides and snagged the reins of the frightened horse. Beobrand braced himself to be dragged forward by the animal, but it was happy enough for him to take charge and stood, quivering, eyes rolling.

Around them, the men were reining in. The gods must have been smiling on them, for none of the other riders had fallen foul of the thrown man. And the unseated warrior appeared uninjured. He walked towards the gathered men, a sheepish grin on his mud-splattered face.

"You have the luck of a fox, Eldrid," cried Wulfgar. His cheeks were flushed. The gallop or the prospect of battle appeared to have kindled a spark of excitement within him.

Eldrid trudged through the mire left by the passing of so many horses. Mud caked his shoes and leg bindings, making his feet appear huge.

Beobrand took hold of his mare's reins and called to Garr, who was dismounting close by.

"Garr, you and Eldrid, secure the horses. Tie them to the trees. The rest of you," he raised his voice, "form a shieldwall."

He did not wait to see if his orders were obeyed. He turned his attention back to the Mercians. They were close enough to make out their faces. They wore byrnies and polished war-helms. Their shields bore bright painted sigils and patterns. These were no brigands.

Behind them, the path appeared to open out into a plain. But now, from this new vantage point, Beobrand saw why their quarry had not ridden on. The open area beyond the tree-tunnel of the road caught the light from the sun. The rain had stopped now, but its constant barrage over the last day had done its work and helped force the Mercians to stand and fight. For, what should have been open meadows running down to a ford of the Afen, was instead a lake. The rains had raised the water level and the river had burst its banks. The usually passable ford had become a wide stretch of lapping brown water that would require a boat to traverse.

The Mercians were trapped.

Beobrand grinned. They would push them down to the water's edge and kill them all. But a trapped animal was dangerous indeed.

As he watched, the enemy shieldwall parted and one of their number ran forward a few paces. At the end of his run, he let fly a short spear. It was a long distance for a spear throw, but Beobrand had seen Garr throw further.

For a heartbeat, he watched as the javelin flew high, narrowly missing overhanging branches and leaves, and then arced down towards its target. Incredibly, it was going to fall behind the shieldwall that was forming around Acennan and Dreogan.

Beobrand let out an incoherent cry of warning, unable to form words in the moment he realised what would happen.

Perhaps hearing the shout from Beobrand, Eldrid spun

round from where he was leading one of the horses. He never saw the spear that killed him. It fell silently from a shadowed tunnel of trees and pierced his throat. Eldrid was flung back into the mud once more. But he would not rise from this fall.

Beobrand watched aghast, as the West Seaxon's lifeblood pumped crimson into the black mud.

A great cheer went up from the Mercian ranks.

Eldrid's feet, huge in their viscid coating of mud, danced forlornly, splashing in a puddle.

Eldrid with the luck of a fox.

The ways of wyrd were unfathomable.

Chapter 21

Reaghan's stomach cramped again and she bit her lip so as not to cry out. Her mouth filled with the bitter taste of bile and the potion Odelyna had given her. Maida put her weaving to one side and came to her. She dipped a cloth into a bowl and wiped Reaghan's face with the cool, damp material.

"There you go, girl," Maida said, in the voice Reaghan had heard her use to her children. "The worst is over now."

Reaghan hoped that were so. The griping pains had been terrible. Worse than anything she had ever suffered before. The rags she had brought in the small sack proved to be pitifully inadequate. As her body expelled Beobrand's seed, thick, dark, glutinous blood came forth in such quantities that she feared she would die, as the woman by the river had intended.

Tears trickled down her cheeks, and Maida wiped them away, all the while making small humming sounds under her breath.

The ripples of pain from this last clenching of her stomach passed quickly. Perhaps she would survive after all. If childbirth was anything like this, she hoped she would never have to suffer it. Fresh tears came then as she thought of little Octa, Beobrand's son. Maida had given him to one of the other women to care for while she tended to Reaghan, who she said had been taken ill. She had killed Octa's brother or sister. She had destroyed life that had come from the man who had rescued her in the most horrific of nights.

Maida continued cooing and wiping Reaghan's face. Suddenly, Reaghan gripped her hand tight enough to make the older woman cry out in surprise.

"He can never know!" Reaghan said, her voice a hiss of anguish. Who could say what he would do if he discovered what she had done? He was a man of war. Quick to anger and slow to forgive. He solved his problems with the blade. "Promise me! He must never know of this."

Maida looked at her, sadness in her eyes.

"I will not speak of this to anyone, Reaghan. Beobrand wished that I watch out for you while he was away."

Reaghan had suspected as much, but to hear the words took some of the sting from the pains she endured. Beobrand wished her to be safe.

"I will not speak of this," Maida continued, "as I can see no good coming from anyone knowing of what transpired here. Men do not need to know of the secrets of women."

Reaghan shivered at the words, which closely echoed those of the stranger by the river.

"Thank you," she said, in a small, cracked voice.

"But we must tell the men of the woman you saw by the Tuidi. She must be the woman Beobrand feared meant us harm. The witch from Muile."

Reaghan nodded. She thought of the woman's scarred beauty. Her hair like a thunder storm. The blaze of her eyes.

"I am not sure that she is of this middle earth," she said.

Maida reached for the small Christ-rood amulet she wore at her neck.

"All the more reason to tell Bassus. We must be wary and allow nobody to travel alone."

"Hold your shields ready," Beobrand roared. "Forward!"

As one, the shieldwall trudged slowly towards the Mercians, who were raising a clamour fit to bring Woden himself to see what was afoot. They beat blades on linden boards and screamed insults at the small shieldwall that moved forward one step at a time. It was two men deep and five wide. Beobrand stood front and centre. The mud clung to his feet, just as it had to Eldrid's. Beobrand could feel it hungrily sucking and pulling him back, as if it had not yet had its fill of man's blood. He looked at the helmeted faces that scowled over the shields before him. Those men would not easily be made to step aside. If the earth was thirsty, it would drink more blood soon. Death hung in the damp air.

Acennan, standing on Beobrand's right, wore the granite expression of a death-dealer who knows his trade.

"You sound like Scand," Acennan said. "He could always make himself heard in battle."

Beobrand did not answer. He wished that Scand was there to guide them. Had the old thegn felt this way when he had led men; so unsure and confused? He doubted it. Scand had been a warrior lord; terrible in battle and generous in victory. Beobrand hoped he would one day attain such stature amongst his men. But for now, there was no time to ponder. The Mercians were close. If they chose to throw more spears, they would not miss.

Beyond them, the weak sun shone on the muddy waters of

the flood. The Mercian horses stood behind the shieldwall, heads lowered, exhausted from the long chase. Beobrand caught a flash of sunlight on hair the colour of molten gold.

Cyneburg.

She stood with the horses, face pallid and eyes dark with fear. Eadgyth was with her. Both looked terrified.

"Halt!" Beobrand raised his sword. The men stopped.

"I am Beobrand of Ubbanford," he said, in the voice he hoped was as certain as Scand's had always been, "Thegn of Oswald, son of Æthelfrith, Lord King of Bernicia."

A tall man stepped from the ranks of the Mercians. Clad in byrnie and warrior-jacket, a red belt cinched at his waist and full helm covering his head and face, he raised his hand and the Mercians fell silent. This was the leader Beobrand had seen directing the riders at the crest of the hill.

"You are a long way from your home, Beobrand." The man's voice was muffled by the intricately decorated faceplate of his helm. The helmet was a thing of wonder. An artefact fit for a king.

"You have taken that which belongs to my lord. I demand that you return it."

"It?" The man's scorn was clear, despite the muffling helm. "Is that how you Northumbrians refer to your queen?"

Beobrand felt the heat rising in his cheeks. He swallowed down the bitter taste in his throat.

"You know my name," Beobrand said, voice sharp as ice. "What is yours, Mercian?"

"My name is no concern of yours. You are outnumbered here. If you mount up and leave these lands, I give you my word you will not be hampered."

"The word of a man who will not give his name is worth less than dust in the wind. In the name of my king, I demand that you return Cyneburg, daughter of Cynegils, and her maidservant, Eadgyth."

The helmeted warrior shook his head.

"I will not."

Beobrand's knuckles showed white on Hrunting's hilt.

Acennan said in a low voice, "This is getting us nowhere. Let's just kill the bastards."

Beobrand silenced his friend with a glower.

"This is your last chance," he said, shouting the words now, so that all of the men listening would hear. "Return the queen and her woman to us now and pay the weregild for the men you have killed, or you will feed the ravens come nightfall."

In answer, the tall warrior returned to his shieldwall and, a moment later, the hurled insults recommenced, accompanied once more by the threnody of swords and spears beating against shields.

And so it came to this, as somehow he had known it would. From the moment they had found Athelstan's stiffening corpse, what other outcome could there be but that of warriors facing each other in the mud? Battle was not the glorious thing the scops sang of in the mead halls in the firelight. It was fear and blood. Shit and mud. The screams of the dying and the maniacal laughter of battle-joy.

And yet, Beobrand could not hide the smile that tugged at his lips. Battle may not be as it was recounted by bards, but Beobrand welcomed the chance to release the fettered animal that was held within him. Too long he had kept it in check. A coolness washed over him, as if a heavy rain had begun to fall again. The time for talking had gone.

Now was the time for killing.

He raised his sword high in the air once more and hoped

the men would follow him. He had told them his plan briefly and positioned the shieldwall so that those men he knew he could trust to obey were closest to him. These were men who had trained with him under Scand, men who had faced the Waelisc at Hefenfelth. He glanced at Acennan, who gave him a nod of assurance. Wulfgar's jaw was clenched beneath his beard, his mouth a blade's edge line of tension, but he too nodded.

"Now is the time to take back what is ours," Beobrand said. "Hold firm and hit them hard and keep moving forward."

He offered up a silent prayer to Woden and Thunor, and sliced Hrunting down towards the enemy line.

"Now!"

For a sickening instant, his feet slipped in the mud and he was unable to find purchase. He dug his left foot in and shoved hard, surging forward. Dimly, he recognised the aches in his leg and arm, but these were distant things. All there was now was the foe who stood before him. He was aware that Acennan, Dreogan and Wulfgar were just behind him, pressing him forward at speed. There was not much distance, and the earth was treacherous with the slime of the road, but Beobrand could see no other way. He had become the tip of a spearhead of men in the hope that they could break through the Mercian line. But for this to succeed, they needed speed and strength, or the attack would break on the shieldwall like a wave against a cliff.

Beobrand registered Mercians launching spears into the air. They had panicked, the missiles soared over their heads, sinking harmlessly into the mud behind them. Good. Throwing the spears may well have weakened the shieldwall momentarily as men adjusted their gear and lifted fresh weapons.

Beobrand ran faster. He screamed his rage at the Mercians. Behind him the roar of his men's battle-ire drove him forward.

He chose his enemy, a short, helmeted man, who crouched behind a red and yellow shield, spear thrust forward to meet the oncoming charge.

Beobrand fixed the man with his gaze and planned how he would kill him. An instant later, the sharp steel of the man's spear tip jabbed at Beobrand's face. He had anticipated this. It would have been better for the man to strike at his legs and trip him, but the spear had rested on the rim of his shield, so a low attack would have been impossible. Beobrand dipped his head, lifting his shield at the same moment. He did not hesitate in his onward rush. The spear scraped harmlessly over his shield rim and then Beobrand was too close to be concerned by it any longer. He bellowed and hammered his shield forward, putting his shoulder behind it.

His arm screamed in pain at the jarring shock as shield boss met shield boss. And yet he did not pause. Acennan and Dreogan added their weight to his and it proved too much for the Mercian to withstand. He slipped in the muck, until he lost his footing. He tumbled backwards, his eyes full of fear. Beobrand stepped onto the red and yellow shield, thrusting down with Hrunting as he moved. The blade pierced the man's neck. The eyes widened in shock and terror. Blood bubbled and spouted. And then Beobrand moved on.

All around him were enemy warriors. They had parted instinctively as he smashed into their ranks, but now they turned, intent on slaying this huge warrior with the serpent-skin bladed sword, that flickered and thrummed in the dappled shade of the forest path. A large man, long beard hanging to his chest, leapt towards Beobrand with a cry of rage. He wielded a heavy-bladed seax in his meaty hand as if it were nothing more than an eating knife. Beobrand stepped to meet him, ignoring the dangers to either side. He would have to trust to Acennan, Dreogan and the others to do their part.

"For Oswald!" he screamed, beating Hrunting's blade against the willow wood of the man's shield. The Mercian was screaming too, but his voice was lost in the tumult of the fray. All around them men shouted and cried out in rage and agony and fear.

The bearded Mercian lunged and Beobrand took the blow on his shield. He lowered his shield slightly, inviting the man to take another swing. The seax sliced at his neck once more, but Beobrand had the measure of his opponent now. He was a strong man, large and brave, but he was slow and unskilled. Beobrand again took the strike on his shield, but at the same moment stepped forward, raking Hrunting's long sharp blade under the Mercian's shield and along his thigh. He was unarmoured there and the sword sank deep into his flesh. Dark blood gushed from the killing blow in a great torrent. The man's face paled and his eyes filled with shock. Beobrand had seen the expression many times before. The embrace of death in battle always came as a surprise. Beobrand shoved with his shield, wary of a dying blow from the man. But he needn't have worried, the fight had gone from him as his blood soaked into the mud. The man fell backwards, and Beobrand hacked into his exposed neck as he fell. He did not wish for the fallen man to be able to kill from the earth even as his own life fled him. Such an end had come to Scand, who had always warned of the danger from under the shield. Beobrand had learnt the lesson well. He watched for a heartbeat as the bearded warrior slid into the quagmire, his eyes blank and sightless.

Panting from the exertion now, Beobrand's eyes stung as sweat trickled from under his helm. For a moment there was nobody before him to fight. He watched Acennan dispatch a broad-shouldered ox of a man, with a skilled sword-blow to the wrist. The huge warrior lost his grip on his sword, his hand almost completely severed. Acennan hammered home his advantage, smashing blow after blow into the man until he collapsed under the pressure and the loss of blood. Acennan finished him with a savage thrust of his shield rim into the man's face.

Acennan turned to Beobrand, face slick with gore and mud. His teeth flashed white. Beobrand felt the same gleeful expression stretching his own features.

"You never know, Beobrand," Acennan said, "we may just win this fight."

But Beobrand could sense more than see that elsewhere along the line things were not going as well. He scanned the warriors locked in combat, trying to make sense of what was happening. Along with Acennan and Dreogan, he had broken the Mercian line and they were now through to the other side. Yet, to the left, the West Seaxons and the remainder of the Northumbrians were not faring so well. The Mercians had coalesced around their leader. Wulfgar, who had somehow become separated from them after the initial charge, was sorely pressed there.

A few paces away stood Cyneburg and Eadgyth, both as still as carven totems, faces pallid and full of fear. The horses milled about behind them, white-eyed and whinnying at the scent of blood.

Acennan took a step forward.

"We have come for you, ladies. You have nothing to fear now."

The women did not reply, but seemed to recoil at the words. Perhaps they could not hear over the sounds of the battle, or the sight of the blood-soaked warrior frightened them.

"Later, Acennan," said Beobrand, urgency lending his tone a jagged edge, "we must aid Wulfgar."

Acennan dragged his gaze from Eadgyth.

"Aye. There is one sure way to end this."

"Yes," Beobrand nodded. "We kill that bastard with the grim-helm."

"To me," Beobrand yelled and as if from nowhere, Dreogan and Garr were beside Acennan and Beobrand. Men lay dead or dying behind them. Beobrand recognised the face of one of Athelstan's gesithas amongst the corpses. More bodies lay before the Mercian shieldwall that remained strong around the tall leader with the glorious helm that marked him out. In spite of having shattered this side of the Mercian shieldwall, they were still outnumbered. Beobrand could see their doom in the gleam of the Mercian leader's helm. Strong hearth-thegns surrounded him and none seemed able to approach without feeling the bite of their blades.

"Follow me, brave sword-brothers," Beobrand said, raising his voice. "This is where we take the day and seize our battle-fame."

They hefted their shields, and sprinted towards the side of the Mercian ranks.

Chapter 22

"For Oswald!" Beobrand screamed. Acennan, Garr and Dreogan added their voices to the battle-cry.

They lumbered forward, as fast as they could, feet weighed down with the clinging mire.

The Mercians either saw or heard their approach and three of their number turned to defend their lord from this new threat. They were stalwart thegns, not new to the art of killing. They raised their shields, held their blood-dipped blades high.

But they did not have more than an instant to prepare themselves and Beobrand urged his men forward. He flung himself into the still-forming side shieldwall with a guttural scream of unbridled ire.

The ferocity of his attack and the abandon with which he threw himself upon the Mercian shields once more proved enough to force a breach in their defences. Beobrand brought Hrunting down on the helm of the middle warrior. The blade rang like a hammer striking an anvil. The Mercian, dazed, staggered back, lowering his shield in confusion. Beobrand followed him, trusting Acennan to protect his flank. He raised

Hrunting again and hacked into the man's exposed shoulder. The iron rings of the man's byrnie burst asunder, Hrunting's blade cutting flesh and sinew and smashing the bone beneath. Blood welled up from the wound, and flowed down the iron-knit shirt in a crimson cascade.

"For Oswald!" Beobrand roared again.

The sudden attack from the flank sent a tremor through the Mercians and brought renewed hope to the attackers, who had seen Beobrand break their enemies' defence. Beobrand quickly checked behind him. Garr and Dreogan were exchanging blows with the two remaining men who had stood against them. Acennan smashed his shield at the left man, causing him to give ground, his attention divided as it was between Garr and Acennan. The moment's hesitation gave Acennan space, and he rushed through to join Beobrand behind the enemy line.

Panic was in the air now, but the Mercians had yet to fully comprehend that their doom was amongst them.

Off to Beobrand's left, Wulfgar bellowed a defiant war-cry, then sent a flurry of vicious attacks at the centre of the Mercian shieldwall. The West Seaxon spat insults as he smashed his blade over and over into the enemies' shields.

"Die, you dog-fucking, piss-guzzling cowards! I will rip out your hearts, feast on your brains, drink your blood!"

Wulfgar's attack was so furious, his taunts so loud, that all eyes turned to him. The Mercians lifted their shields against the torrent of sword blows and insults. Beobrand grinned.

Without hesitation, he leapt forward at the distracted leader of the Mercians. Acennan came with him.

Before any of the Mercians could react, Beobrand was upon the tall lord. The man's head was protected by the finely decorated helm, so Beobrand swung his blade at the

Mercian leader's back. The sisters who weave men's wyrd surely did not wish for this Mercian to die that day, for in the instant before Hrunting's bright blade connected with his broad, leather-clad back, he spun towards Beobrand, raising his shield. What sense had told him of the impending cut, none but the gods could say, yet even with the luck of the gods themselves, the man was too late to stop Beobrand's attack completely. The shield edge clattered into the sword blade, but such was the strength of the blow, the sword carried on, pushing the shield with it. It swung around the edge of the shield and sliced into the lord's right side. He stumbled slightly, but held his shield firm. He had not fully turned, so his own sword arm was away from Beobrand.

This was the chance. Beobrand could feel it. If he could defeat their leader now, the Mercians would crumble. If they rallied around him, they would prevail and Cyneburg and Eadgyth would be lost. Athelstan's death would have been in vain. Beobrand would not allow that.

He sent an overarm strike with Hrunting towards his foe's fine helm. The man's vision would be hampered by the face-guard, but he was skilled. He would see the attack. And he would defend against it.

As Beobrand had anticipated, the Mercian lifted his shield to parry the sword. At the instant the blade connected with the hide-covered board, Beobrand took a quick step forward and kicked the man's left knee with all his strength. He heard the howl of pain from behind the helm and the man who had stolen Oswald's queen in the night fell sprawling to the mud. Beobrand sprang forward, stepping on the flat of the Mercian's sword blade, squelching the patterned steel into the grime.

Around him Beobrand could hear the clash of weapons. Men yelled. He heard Acennan roar in anger. But he did not look up from his prize. He could end this here. Now. Dropping Hrunting into the mud, Beobrand fell atop the Mercian, pinning the man's shield arm under his body weight. Unable to shed his own shield that was strapped to his arm, Beobrand fumbled clumsily at his belt with his right hand. His fingers found the hilt of his seax and he pulled it free of its scabbard.

The Mercian was squirming beneath him, fighting for his life. In the flailing of arms and legs Beobrand finally shook his arm free of the linden board and hammered a punch with his half-hand into the man's stomach. Scrabbling, he clutched at the cold metal of the helm, yanking it back to expose the man's sweat-drenched beard and neck. And so it would end, wrestling in the mud. Not the glory-death of the tales. Their two fine swords wallowed in the quagmire as the small seax flashed.

Then, once more the gods took pity on this lord of the Mercians. Or perhaps he was destined for greater things. For a sound echoed in the forest that stayed Beobrand's hand. A sound that pierced the clang and crash of battle-play. A sound sweeter and yet more terrible than all the other screams, shouts, groans and death-cries of the shieldwall.

The high-pitched shriek of a woman.

"No! Do not kill him!"

A dark memory fluttered in Beobrand's mind. A Pictish woman running at him in the dark. Her face smashed and ruined; destroyed with a blow from his sword.

He looked up towards the female screams. Cyneburg, golden hair trailing behind her, flowing like the tail of a horse, was running towards him. Towards the men who battled and died to rescue her. To protect her. Her face was streaked with tears and she screamed once more.

"Do not kill him, Beobrand!"

All the men on that mud-splattered, gore-soaked path, hesitated. The queen's cries had reached all of their ears and they paused, unsure. Warily, and without a word, the men parted, stepping back from their foes. They welcomed the respite. Once a safe distance, some of the warriors bent forward, hands on knees and panted like hounds that have harried a boar.

Beobrand felt the man beneath him tense, readying himself to resume his struggles. Quickly, Beobrand placed the seax blade against the bearded throat and said in a voice of iron, "Move, and you die."

Cyneburg let out a small cry of anguish. She halted a few paces from them. Looking around her, she suddenly seemed to become aware of all the battle-hard warriors staring at her. She looked back at Beobrand, her face a mask of despair.

"Do not kill him," she said for the third time, her voice now little more than a whisper.

For what seemed a long while, Beobrand stared at her in disbelief. What could the meaning of this be? But now was not the time for questions. He offered a small nod and said, "As you wish, my queen." Then, raising his voice so that all there would hear, he said, "Mercians, drop your weapons. Your leader is my prisoner and his life is forfeit should you continue to fight against me."

None of the Mercians moved.

Beobrand jerked the leader roughly up into a sitting position. Tugging at the helm, it came free, revealing a handsome man, still young but some years Beobrand's senior. He had long braided hair and a full beard. His face was awash with sweat. He glowered at Beobrand, his eyes burning with fury. Wrapping his half-hand in the lord's braids, Beobrand pulled his head backwards savagely, exposing the throat and placing the sharp edge of the seax against it once more.

The Mercians seemed set to rush him. Several took a step forward, unable to see their lord treated thus.

"Please," Cyneburg said, "do as he says, or he will kill your lord."

For several heartbeats Beobrand held his breath, fearing that the Mercians would attack him. With Wulfgar and the others having stepped back from the shieldwall, and where he was in the mud, straddling the lord of the Mercians, he would be cut down in an instant. He raked them with his gaze. Aye, that gaze said, you may slay me, but I will take your lord with me to the afterlife.

One by one, the Mercians let blades and spears fall to the muck at their feet.

Beobrand let out his breath. He looked at Cyneburg's distraught face and was unable to make sense of what had happened.

Around him the Mercians were being herded together by the West Seaxons and Northumbrians. Wulfgar came over to where Beobrand yet held the Mercian lord by his hair.

"If you do not mean to slice his throat, I believe you should let the man get to his feet." He glanced at the blood that trickled from the wound in the Mercian's side. It did not appear deep. "And perhaps we should tend to his wounds. After all, this is no way to treat those of royal blood."

Beobrand's hands began to shake, as they always did after combat. To hide the tremors, he got to his feet and pulled the man roughly up.

"Royal blood?" he asked, confused. "What do you mean?"

"I mean, Beobrand, you must think long and hard before killing this one. You may not be able to pay the weregild for his death. And, by Woden, you certainly do not wish to make an enemy of his kinfolk."

"Why?" Beobrand said, sizing up his foe's commanding presence, his fine sword and the helm fit for a king. "Who is he?"

"This," Wulfgar said, an unreadable expression on his sweat-streaked face, "is Eowa, son of Pybba. His brother is Penda, Lord King of all Mercia."

Chapter 23

Bassus twisted his head at just the right angle to produce a welcome clicking in his neck. He grunted with pleasure and rolled his shoulders, loosening the tension there.

"An old wound?" Gram asked.

"No," replied Bassus, his tone gruff. In truth his body ached from the scars and injuries suffered in battles over the years, but this was something else. A tightening of his neck and shoulders that came when he was unsure of himself. He did not like to dwell on things he could not change, but he did wonder whether coming back to Bernicia had been a mistake.

They strode along beside the Tuidi for a while in silence. The leaden sky reflected in the broad river, turning the water into polished iron. Insects buzzed and flitted above the water. Occasionally, small ripples appeared, where some denizen of the river broke the surface.

"Do you think this witch is truly a threat?" Gram said.

Bassus shrugged.

"Who can say? Beobrand certainly believes it. And if what Maida and Odelyna say is true, she came here seeking to kill that girl."

"Why bother killing a thrall? Just because Beobrand is swiving her?"

Bassus glanced sharply at Gram. The slim warrior always spoke his mind. It was one of the things Bassus most admired in him.

"Perhaps. If she means to hurt Beobrand, I believe that would have the effect she seeks." He paused to clamber over a small but deep stream channel that ran into the Tuidi. There were many such burns that fed the waters of the large river. Safely across, he waited for Gram to join him.

"And yet," Bassus said, his face grim, "if I had an enemy such as Beobrand, I would not seek to anger him."

"And if we find the woman? What then?"

Bassus ground his teeth, but did not reply. What indeed? He had not come north to wage war on women, no matter how evil they may be. He had heard tales of Beobrand's exploits and recalled what it had been like to stand in the shieldwall beside his friend, Beobrand's brother, Octa. Surely he was not yet too old for more battle-fame. By all the gods, he was as strong as an ox still. And as stubborn? Perhaps.

They were approaching the small stand of willow and alder where Reaghan had said she'd spoken to the cunning woman.

"Will we kill her?" Gram asked, never one to let a silence deter him.

"I know not. Scaring her off would be better." Killing a woman was never a good thing. And to slay one who had the ear of the old gods was reckless or foolhardy. "I do not wish to kill women. And it seems to me, this woman has done no real harm."

"The women seem convinced that she is a witch intent on evil. And Beobrand was clear what we should do should she cause mischief."

"Well, Beobrand is not here, and the women of Ubbanford are full of spite, and are keen to see others do their killing. I have little stomach for the murder of women." And yet, he had sworn his oath to Beobrand, and he was certain that Beobrand would wish to see this woman gone. But, Beobrand was far away. He had left Bassus in charge, so the decision would be his until Beobrand's return.

He rolled his shoulders and neck again, trying to ease the tension. He hoped they would not find the woman. There was little chance that they would, unless she decided to approach them. He was good for battle, for the clash of sword and spear. The sword-song and the battle-glory. Not for this. Warriors were not difficult to control. But their women! By the gods, how the women bickered and nagged.

He spat into the river and silently cursed coming here. It had been good to see Beobrand again. The boy had grown into a man; a warrior of renown. He was a thegn now, valued and respected, and Bassus took pride in his part in Beobrand's journey. Octa would have been proud of his younger brother, and they were enough alike that Bassus enjoyed the young man's company immensely. Beobrand was taciturn and seldom jested, but he was loyal and strong, a man to be trusted. Bassus remembered the glow of pride at seeing Beobrand seated on the gift-stool of his own hall. He recalled the warm joy of being given the role of trust to lead Beobrand's gesithas while he was away. To be given the command of the men and his lands was something that Bassus did not take lightly. But he wished he had not made the decision to return north.

He shook his head to clear it of these thoughts. They were like the flies and midges of the river, they buzzed and circled his head, but there was nothing to be done about them.

"Do you wish we had not come here?" asked Gram, no sign of his usual light-humoured tone in his words.

Bassus sighed. They had been shield-brothers for a long time. Gram knew him well. And he was no fool. He must be feeling it too. Each night they sat alone. Beobrand's gesithas had fought together against a common enemy, forging them into a hardened unit. They served Oswald, and some of them had followed his brother, Eanfrith, before him. Bassus and Gram had been King Edwin's men. King Edwin who was the sworn foe of Oswald and all his kin. It was easy to understand why Beobrand's comitatus did not warm to them. And yet understanding did little to sweeten the bitter taste. And it was worse for Gram, mused Bassus. The men offered Bassus respect and did his bidding without complaint, as their lord had ordered them to. They saw Gram as an interloper in their midst.

"There is nothing to be gained in talking of what could have been. We are here now."

Gram nodded, as if he had expected this answer.

Bassus turned and faced him.

"Things will be different once Beobrand returns. There will be war soon. We'll be joining Oswiu in rooting out those Picts. And once we have stood shield to shield with the rest of the men, they will forget our past."

"I hope that is so," Gram replied, but his words were distracted, distant from the focus of his thoughts.

"What is it?" asked Bassus.

Gram bent down and parted the foliage at the river's edge so that he could better see something that lay there.

Bassus pushed in close.

"What is it?" he repeated.

For answer, Gram held back the leaves and merely pointed.

Bassus peered into the shade beneath the elder bushes and his heart clenched. He could hardly believe Gram had spotted this thing, half-hidden within the tangle of branches and leaves. But find it he had, and there was no doubt in his mind now that the cunning woman Reaghan had spoken to yet lurked somewhere nearby. Perhaps she was watching them even now. His skin prickled as the first claws of fear scratched down his neck. Yes, she was yet somewhere near Ubbanford, and her purpose was clear.

Bassus sighed.

Betwixt the twigs and green of the elder, a small doll dangled in the dappled light. It was a crude thing, made of straw and twigs. Not much larger than his hand, there was little on the doll to distinguish it from any other such plaything that parents made for their children. And yet, Bassus knew that this was meant to be Beobrand. It was crowned with a golden sprig of barley chaff to resemble the young thegn's blond hair. The hands were just rough sprays of hay, splayed out like fingers. The left hand had clearly been cut in half.

Bassus suppressed a shudder. He had hoped the witch might have fled. He spat. He caught himself once again wishing he had not returned to Bernicia, for now he knew he must kill this woman.

The doll Beobrand twisted on the end of a thin cord. It had been hanged from a noose round its neck. Piercing its heart was a tiny arrow. Perhaps that is what had caught Gram's attention. For the delicately cut white fletchings of the minute arrow winked and glimmered as they caught the light.

*

Beobrand clenched his fists against the trembling. He sat on the trunk of a fallen elm at the edge of the path. Before him, where the path normally ran down to the Afen, brown water lapped. Here and there trees and bushes jutted from the murky waters, like the hands of drowning men.

"I have set men to watch at the brow of the hill."

The voice startled Beobrand. He turned quickly to see Wulfgar.

He nodded at the West Seaxon.

"That is well done," he said. He should have thought of it himself. Nobody could approach from the waters of the swollen river without the aid of a boat, and the forest at either side of the path was too dense for a group of men to traverse, especially with horses, so danger was unlikely to come from that quarter. But they were in Mercia, and now had the brother of the lord of the kingdom as their captive. By the gods, how had this happened? It made little sense. Beobrand shook his head to clear it and pushed himself to his feet. On the other side of the swirling, muddy waters he could see a small group of people. They were staring. He saw no spears, no shields. Probably thralls or ceorls working the land. They must have heard the fighting. Where there were men working the land, there would be a hall and a lord close by. And lords had gesithas.

They could not stay here. It seemed Wulfgar was still content to allow him to lead, but that would quickly change should he appear unsure of what to do next.

To hide his uncertainty and to give him time to think, he snapped at Wulfgar.

"Have the men strip the bodies of all of worth. Let the Mercians tend to their own, but see that they do not claim sword or spear from the fallen. They are our prisoners. If one of them tries anything, kill him." Beobrand took in the scene of carnage on the mud-churned path. The wolves would feed well tonight.

One of the horses further up the track whinnied pitiably. A spear had pierced its side and still dangled from its flesh. The beast stood trembling and snorting, its white-rimmed eyes bright in the forest gloom. Its flank was awash with blood.

"Kill that horse," Beobrand said. "We will need meat. But do it fast. Each man must carry what he can." He remembered butchering such an injured creature after another skirmish, and the slow trudge they had made through the wilderness of Bernicia with more men than steeds to carry them. "We will take the rest of the horses with us. Fresh mounts will serve us well."

Beobrand looked about him for a moment. What was he missing?

"Bring Eowa to me," he said at last, then, after a brief hesitation, "and Cyneburg."

Wulfgar stood motionless for a moment, as if he was going to say something. In the end, he said nothing. He turned away and barked orders to the men.

Beobrand watched as Acennan left the side of Eadgyth to begin the process of collecting weapons and treasures from the corpses. The instant the battle had finished the dark-haired beauty had rushed forward into Acennan's arms. Wulfgar had frowned at his sister's actions, but there was little he could do. Beobrand was pleased for Acennan. He had been concerned that the girl would not return his friend's affections. He clearly did not understand women.

The thought brought a grim smile to his lips. Cyneburg, his queen, walked gingerly through the mud towards him.

Her fine dress was ruined, splattered with blood and mud. Her hair had fallen free of its braids and hung wet and lank down her back. And yet, she was still stunning; a flash of sun on a stormy day. No, he really did not understand women. He probably never would.

Eowa followed her. Proud and noble he came, holding his head high. Despite his injuries, he walked with grace. Beobrand met his eye. He wondered if they could have been friends in other circumstances.

"So, you are Penda's brother?" Beobrand asked. He searched the man's face for similarities with the King of Mercia. If there were any, they were not strikingly obvious. The eyes perhaps. The same savage glare in them. Like an animal stalking prey.

"I have that pleasure," Eowa answered. A slight raising at the edge of his mouth lent the words irony. "It seems to me," Eowa continued, still smirking, "that you are in a tight spot here. Days of riding from the borders of Mercia, and not enough men to guard all of your prisoners."

"I could have them all put to the sword right now," said Beobrand, his voice as harsh as the clash of shieldwalls.

He half-turned towards Wulfgar and Acennan, as if about to give the order. Eowa's smile faded, his eyes seemed less certain. Oh, so perhaps the atheling lacked his brother's iron will too. Beobrand was sure that Penda would not have cared for an instant at the death of a handful of warriors.

For a moment, Beobrand watched as the surviving warriors went about the bitter business of retrieving valuables from the dead. It was a dark task that nobody relished, but the men knew their work. The pile of weapons and trinkets was growing. Beobrand counted nine dead, seven Mercians, the unlucky Eldrid and one of Athelstan's gesithas. A Wessex man led the injured horse up the path away from the other steeds. Beobrand looked back to Eowa.

"But enough good men have died this day. I am content with the blood price paid for my friend, Athelstan. You must see whether Oswald will be satisfied with the death of a few of your gesithas in payment for the loss of one of his most trusted thegns. A thegn who died protecting Oswald's queen."

Beobrand flicked a look at Cyneburg. She stood off to one side, head down, shoulders slumped. Tears glistened on her cheeks.

"I am sorry that Athelstan had to die. It was not my intention. There should have been no bloodshed." Eowa's words sounded hollow in that darkened tree-tunnel path, beside the murky waters of the storm-burst Afen. Cold ire flooded back into Beobrand. His hand fell to the hilt of Hrunting and he took a pace forward.

Eowa stood his ground, but tensed, preparing himself for a blow. But none came.

Mustering all his will, Beobrand released his sword, letting it slide back into its scabbard.

"Athelstan was my friend. Soon enough you will tell me why he died." A sob from Cyneburg drew his attention for a heartbeat. "Aye, I would hear that tale. But first, you will give me your oath that you will not attempt to flee."

"And what of my men?"

"They must give the same oath. And any who breaks it will forfeit his own life, and yours. They will be allowed to ride their mounts, but will not bear arms."

"And if I refuse these terms?"

"Then all of your men will be killed. Here. Now. And I will take you bound and gagged, shamed and beaten, before

Oswald." Cyneburg let out a whimper. This time Beobrand ignored her.

Beobrand held Eowa in his ice-chip blue stare. There was no self-doubt in those eyes any longer. He was sure of what he must do next.

"Swear your oath to me now. Then command your men to do the same. And do it now. We cannot tarry here any longer."

And so the atheling of Mercia, brother of the formidable warlord, Penda, son of Pybba, plighted his oath that he would not raise arms against Beobrand or the men he rode with and that he would not seek to escape them. Beobrand made sure Eowa's comitatus witnessed their lord's oath. He then had the Mercians bend their knees in the mire and swear also.

There was much grumbling, but their lord gave the command, so they could not refuse. As they spoke the words, unhappily and disgruntled, Beobrand felt some of the burden of the situation lift from him. When the last had spoken, he addressed them all, while the West Seaxons and Northumbrians readied the horses and secured the new-found treasures they would carry home.

"Mercians, I know the words of this oath must have tasted bitter as poison on your tongues." A burly ox of a man, with a broken nose, spat a gobbet of phlegm into the mud close to Beobrand's feet. "I know you see us as your enemies. And perhaps one day, you will be free again to fight us once more in the shieldwall. But for now, you have sworn your oath not to raise arms against us, or to try and flee. And I know that I can trust your word, for I have seen you stand strong, shield to shield. You are brave men, one and all. And whilst we are not friends, I trust you. Now mount up on your own steeds, for we ride north. To Northumbria and King Oswald. There we shall learn your fate."

The men clambered onto their horses. Beobrand went to help Cyneburg up onto her gelding. She had not spoken a word to him since the battle. Now she flinched as he reached out to cup his hands for her to use as a step. He boosted her into the saddle, and then, while all around them was the noise and bustle of men preparing to ride, he held the reins of her mount tight, preventing her from moving away.

"We shall talk, you and I," he said, "when we are a safe distance from here."

Cyneburg's eyes were wide with fear. Tears brimmed there still.

"Yes, my queen," he whispered, so that only she would hear, "we shall talk of how you came to be riding unguarded and free amongst this band of Mercians. And why it was you who stayed my hand when I could have slain their leader."

He released the bridle and strode over to his dappled mare. Dreogan, flanked by two other men, awaited him there. They were unsmiling. Anger came off them like a stench.

"The Mercian must die," Dreogan said simply. "They should all die. We do not accept that the weregild for our lord has been paid."

Beobrand stepped close to Dreogan. He could smell the tattooed warrior's sour breath and his sweat.

"I have spoken. We take the atheling before our king. Oswald will decide Eowa's fate. Not you." Beobrand held Dreogan's gaze. Athelstan's man's jaw clenched, the muscles bulging.

"Make no mistake. I lead here," said Beobrand, "and you will not question my word again, Dreogan." Beobrand spat into the mud. "If you cross me again, we will be having more than words. Now mount up and ride. And save your anger for any more Mercians we might meet."

Beobrand stepped past Dreogan and swung himself into the saddle. Digging his heels into the beast's flanks, he set off back up the muddy hill.

Bassus cradled the straw doll in a fold of his cloak. He did not wish to touch the thing, unsure of what the witch might be able to do to him through contact with the crude figurine.

Gram had said they should cast it into the Tuidi.

"It will wash away any magic on it," he'd said.

But Bassus had stopped him. Neither of them really knew what would happen if they destroyed the effigy of Beobrand. Perhaps he would drop dead wherever he was. If they threw it into the river, he might suddenly feel his lungs filling with the cold waters. Bassus had shuddered at the thought of drowning on invisible water, conjured up by some witch's accursed magic.

"Should we remove the arrow?" he'd asked, knowing Gram would have no answer. "Maybe Beobrand can feel the stab of it."

In the end, they decided not to tamper with the thing, but to take it back to Odelyna, the nearest thing in Ubbanford to a cunning woman. Hopefully, she would know what should be done.

Bassus had held his cloak under the doll while Gram had used his seax to slice through the noose cord.

The two warriors hurried now along the riverbank towards Ubbanford, both eager to be free of the small figure and away from the muggy stillness that had settled on the valley.

Bassus slipped at one of the creeks that ran into the river. Gram caught his arm, preventing him falling.

Bassus took in a slow breath of air.

"Look at us," he said, grinning. "We are like two boys who have been told a tale of the elves in the forest."

Gram returned the smile, but Bassus noted it didn't reach his eyes.

"Aye, if any should see us, they would not think us strong spear-men, slayers of many foes."

They continued at a slower pace. Midges flitted into their faces in clouds. Bassus blew and spat, unable to swat them away, without releasing his cloak and dropping the doll.

The sky frowned and darkened above them. The river made no sound as the nettles and weeds snagged and snatched at their legs. Bassus noted that they had begun to walk more quickly again, as if the atmosphere of the river's edge were pushing them forward. His neck and shoulders ached from the tension there. Bassus knew that no amount of rolling and twisting of his muscles would bring relief now. What he needed was to get back to the hall, to be rid of this evil talisman and to have a drink of strong mead. Perhaps then he would be able to relax.

The hairs on his neck bristled and pricked. They were being watched, he was sure of it. He stopped and spun around, searching the trees and bushes for any sign of the woman they had sought. Gram also halted. He must have sensed it too, for he drew his seax and crouched in the warrior stance. Ready for combat.

But what use would steel and iron be against a witch? The skies continued to darken. A storm brewed in the heavens.

All was still. The only sound was Bassus' ragged breathing. Even the insects had grown silent.

A sudden burst of movement and sound made both men jump. Several crows flapped noisily from the trees on the far bank of the river. The slap of their dark wings broke the silence.

Bassus let out the breath he hadn't realised he'd been holding.

Just birds.

He watched as they flew upwards on soot-coloured feathers. But there was a flash of white amongst the dark. What was that arcing across the river?

Bassus understood he was seeing the white feathers of an arrow's fletchings in the same instant the iron tip pierced his flesh.

Searing agony followed a heartbeat later, and, as he fell to the earth, a single thought ran through his mind.

He knew it had been a bad idea to come back to Bernicia.

Chapter 24

Beobrand stood with his back to the small fire that shed its warmth and light on the exhausted men sprawled around it. The flickering glow did not reach further than the bushes and trees that sheltered their camp. He stared out into the darkness for signs of pursuit, but all was still. They had escaped the banks of the Afen without incident, retracing their steps and then heading northward to join the crumbling Wæcelinga Stræt.

A sudden burst of laughter from the men around the campfire shattered the quiet of the night. Beobrand frowned. Enemies could be approaching, hidden by the darkness. Still, it seemed unlikely. This land was sparsely populated and a large group of mounted and armed warriors would not attract thieves or brigands. The only men they would need to fear would be a sizable force of Penda's warband, and there was no reason to believe there were any of his gesithas nearby.

Beobrand turned towards the slightest of sounds, a rustle of cloth. Cyneburg stood there, face in shadow, hair a wreath of fire-licked gold. She had regained her composure. She held her head high once more, and despite the grime of hard travel, she was once again the image of a young queen.

He swallowed the lump from his throat, attempting to summon the anger he had felt back in the mud, surrounded by corpses. But he was too tired. He did not know how to broach the subject with her. As they had ridden, he had become less sure of himself. She was his queen. Oswald's bride. What right did he have to question her? He had made up his mind that nothing good could come of confronting her with his concerns. And yet it seemed she was not prepared to avoid talking to him.

"Where are we heading?" she asked. There was no echo now of the tremulous anguish in her voice he had heard at the battle.

For an instant, his anger bubbled up and he considered not telling her. But to what end? He would merely appear petulant. He swallowed again and resumed staring into the night rather than be dazzled by her beauty.

"We will follow Wæcelinga Stræt, then northward along Earninga Stræt to Eoferwic."

"We will not return to Anwealda's hall?"

"No." Beobrand had made that decision as they rode through the afternoon. He had consulted with Wulfgar and Acennan, who both agreed it was the best course. "To return would add many days to our journey. And all of them through Mercia."

"But what of my possessions? My waggon is there. All of my things."

"Your possessions are of less import than the lives of these men," he snapped, too tired to control his tongue. "We will send for the waggon once we are safely in Northumbria."

"But to ride so far. Eadgyth and I are already exhausted."

And then, as sudden as Thunor's lightning striking from a summer storm, his ire blasted away his own exhaustion.

"We too are tired from riding. Riding hard through the night and the rain. Our limbs tremble from standing strong in the shieldwall. Look around you, queen," he spat the title at her as though it were an insult. "All the men here, all of them, from Mercia, Northumbria or Wessex. They have all fought for you. Bled for you." He leapt forward and raised his fist.

It would be so easy to make her understand what a waste it had all been. He could make her see sense quickly enough.

Through the fog of his rage, he noticed the silence that had fallen over the camp. Cyneburg cowered before him. Acennan stepped forward from the warriors.

"Beobrand?" he said. And it was enough. Acennan knew him well. He had faced him before when anger coursed through his veins like molten hate. Beobrand remembered with shame hitting his friend. But more than that, for a terrible moment, he heard his father's voice screaming in his mind.

He unclenched his fists. Lowered his hands.

"Good men died for you," he said, his voice barely more than a whisper but shaking with emotion.

Very well. If she wished to talk, then she would know the truth of it. He was no longer unsure or tired. He looked over at Acennan and nodded his thanks. Slowly the conversations around the fire started up again. Eowa sat with his men, many of whom were already sleeping, wrapped in their cloaks. His eyes glittered in the firelight as he stared unblinking at Beobrand.

Turning back to Cyneburg, Beobrand said, "I am sorry for frightening you, my queen."

For a moment, he thought she would not reply. When she did, her voice once again trembled.

"It is I who should be sorry, Beobrand." Her lower lip quivered and her face crumpled as tears rolled down her cheeks.

"Walk with me," he said, "where we cannot be overheard. I would hear the truth of the matter from you."

She hesitated, then nodded.

He led her a little distance from the camp. They were still in sight of the fire, and a flickering of light reached them, but if they spoke quietly, they would not be heard.

Beobrand leaned against the bole of a birch and stared at the pale smudge that was her face in the gloom. Every now and again, the distant flames glinted in the tears on her smooth cheeks. He did not speak.

She sniffed and rubbed at her face.

"How could we have been so foolish?" she whispered.

"Who?"

A pause, then, "Eowa and I."

Beobrand let out a long breath. He feared that knowing the truth of this tale was going to bring him misery. No good would come of it. He knew it. And yet, he must hear it now.

"How is it possible that you should know each other?" he asked.

"I am the daughter of Cynegils, lord of Wessex. Eowa is atheling of Mercia. We have met many times over the years. Eowa would come as emissary to my father's hall." Her fingers absently played with her hair that Eadgyth had freshly braided. Beobrand glanced back at the fire. Eowa had not moved. He was staring into the darkness directly at Beobrand and Cyneburg, his eyes dark shadows.

"We met many times," she continued, "but it was last year that we…" She took a deep breath, preparing herself, as if for a leap from a clifftop into a frigid and rock-strewn sea. "That we fell in love."

Beobrand sighed. He wished he had not pulled on this thread. For his wyrd would soon be woven into this cloth of queens and athelings and kings. The weft and warp of this fabric might follow those of noble birth, but it would be the warriors who would drench it with their blood before the end. Of that he had no doubt.

"But there can be no love now. Not for a peace-weaver married to a stranger from a faraway kingdom."

"Perhaps you will grow to love Oswald. In time."

Now it was Cyneburg's turn to flash bright with anger.

"You know nothing! You just fight and kill. What do you know of love?"

The storm of his anger shredded and tattered and was replaced by a dark, hollow sadness. His chest ached at the memories that tumbled through his mind.

"I am no stranger to love," he said. "You would do well to know of what you speak before allowing your tongue to flap like the women washing their men's clothes by the river. You are no washer woman, you are a queen. A peace-weaver, as you say. You must start acting as such."

For a long while she was silent. He stared into the night and breathed deeply of the cool air. It was redolent of rain and damp earth. He should not speak so bluntly with her. She was his queen and yet he could not allow himself not to say the words she needed to hear.

He thought she would speak no further, when she said, "Tell me."

"Tell you what?"

"You are right, I spoke with no knowledge. Tell me of your love."

"There is nothing to be gained from dwelling on the past," he snapped, his voice harsh. "I do not wish to speak of it." He took a slow breath; calmed himself, softened his tone. "And my story is not important here. What happened between you and Eowa?"

Again a long pause.

"When he heard I was to be married, he sent word. He told me to ensure I would stop to rest at Anwealda's hall. It is close to the frontier with Mercia. He said he would come for me. And he did…" Her voice trailed off.

"And what did you believe would happen then? That you could ride away and Oswald would do nothing? You are both mad! Men have already died because of this madness, but this could lead to open war between three kingdoms."

Cyneburg sniffed in the gloom.

"I do not know." She sounded like a child now, unsure and fearful. "All I could think about was being with him. I have been blinded to all else."

"You are both mad," Beobrand repeated, but with less vitriol in his tone. Would he not have risked everything for Sunniva? Had he not ridden into a night of flame and death to rescue Reaghan? And for what? A mere thrall whom he did not even love. What might he have done if Cyneburg had been his?

"What will happen to us?" Cyneburg asked.

"I cannot say. That will be for your husband to decide."

"If you tell him this, he will kill us both."

Beobrand imagined Oswald receiving news of his queen's treachery. He recalled the iron in his king's will when they had faced the Waelisc at Hefenfelth. The flash of Oswald's sword as he had beheaded Cadwallon. In the darkness, Beobrand nodded. She probably had the right of it.

"You cannot tell him, Beobrand."

"I can do nothing else."

"But why? You say you know of love. If that is so, can you not understand the madness that overcame us? Why tell Oswald?"

"He is my lord and king." That was answer enough.

He heard his queen's sobs as he trudged back to the fire. He needed a drink of mead.

"Perhaps she is right," said Acennan.

Beobrand jerked the reins of his mare hard, bringing his mount to a halt. Wulfgar turned in his saddle, always alert, a question on his face. The rest of the men rode past.

Beobrand waved them all on.

"Keep riding. Acennan and I will catch up."

Wulfgar shrugged, too tired to ask more. They had been riding north now for six days and everyone was on the verge of collapse. Their provisions were running low. They had taken as much horseflesh as they could easily carry from the rapidly butchered beast, but they had not tarried, leaving precious meat behind for the forest animals. The previous night they had stopped at a farmstead and purchased some smoked cheese from the surly man who stood protectively before his wide-eyed children and sour-faced wife. The food was not much, but it would see them through to Eoferwic, if the weather held. Beobrand had contemplated slaying another horse, but had decided it was better to keep the fresh mounts in case of the need to flee from pursuit.

The rains had abated, but the grey sky bore the threat of more to come. Summer was dying. The wind had a bite in it, and the men pulled their cloaks about them as they rode.

Beobrand waited until the last of the band had plodded past. He scanned the horizon for any sign of an attacking force. There was nothing. This land was all dales and crags, tumbled rocks and scrubby heath. They had made good progress through Mercia. People who saw them approach either hid, or bowed to them as if they were oath-sworn thegns of Penda. One armoured lord was much like another. Such a large warband of mounted gesithas was not often seen, and nothing good ever came with such men. Beobrand offered up silent thanks to any god who would listen that this was so, and that Eowa and his men had kept their oaths. None of them had sought to run, and the atmosphere in the camps at night was becoming more relaxed. The night before he had seen Garr offering one of Eowa's thegns a swig of mead. The drink was precious, and the sharing said much about the attitudes of the men.

"So, you think I should lie to our king?" Beobrand said, sure now that they would not be overheard.

"I think, lord," said Acennan, using the title to reinforce the point that it was Beobrand's decision, "that if you tell Oswald of the truth of the matter between Cyneburg and Eowa, he will slay them both. Would you have the blood of such a beauty on your hands?"

"I do not wish her death. You know me better than that. But it is not for me to say what her husband, our king, should do with her." His stomach churned as it did before battle. They would soon be in Eoferwic, in Northumbria. If Oswald was there, Beobrand would need to make a decision.

Acennan shook his head.

"No, it is not for you to decide on the king's actions, but you know as well as I, that if you tell him, you are as good as condemning them both to death."

"Perhaps not. The Christ-god priests preach forgiveness," Beobrand blustered, grasping at anything that would make his dilemma simpler.

"Does Oswald strike you as a forgiving man?" Acennan gave a half smile.

Beobrand watched as the riders moved towards the brow of a nearby bluff. They would need to follow after them very soon if they did not wish to lose them from sight.

His vision blurred as he peered at Wulfgar and the others. Would that he could just put all of this confusion aside. He yearned for rest. For sleep. His eyes were heavy and the weight of responsibility was harder to carry than any iron-knit shirt. Perhaps Oswald would still be in the north fighting the Picts. That would at least give him some respite. Maybe he would even be able to return to Ubbanford.

To Reaghan. To Bassus. To Octa.

"How do things fare with Eadgyth?" Beobrand asked, wishing to shift the conversation from the thorny issue of Cyneburg and Eowa.

Acennan's face lit up as if a cloud had split and the sun's rays had illuminated him.

"She is a marvel, Beobrand," he said, grinning. "Who would have thought that travelling to Wessex would see me find such a gem?"

"You mean to marry her?"

The smile fell from Acennan's face, like a child caught stealing.

"I believe she would have me, but I will need to speak to her brother first."

Beobrand nodded. Wulfgar, as her older brother, could speak for her family, but he doubted the Wessex thegn would give her to Acennan.

"I'm sure he can be swayed... if you offer a large enough brýdgifu. If you have need of treasure, I can help you."

"I give you thanks of that, lord," said Acennan, suddenly formal, "but I hope to be able to pay for my bride's gift with my own worth."

Acennan was a proud man, as it should be.

"Just remember what I have said. I am your lord, as you seem so keen to remind me," he smiled wearily, "and as such, I must give rings and treasure to you. We took much from the Mercians. You will have your share, Acennan."

Acennan did not reply, but dipped his head in acceptance of Beobrand's words.

"Besides," said Beobrand, "if you do not manage to convince Wulfgar to give you Eadgyth in marriage, you will soon find yourself in the same position as Eowa with Cyneburg. And I do not wish to be sent to hunt you down."

Wulfgar was at the crest of the hill now. The rest of the group had already disappeared over the other side. Not wishing to lose them from view, Beobrand dug his heels into his mare's flanks. The beast shook its head at the demand for speed after so many days of travel, but the horse, while small, had a strong spirit and with a snort, she jumped forward and took Beobrand at a canter up the slope.

He turned back to see Acennan staring at him. His face was thoughtful. Beobrand hoped he had not sown the seeds of an idea in his friends mind.

Why did women always bring such trouble and confusion?

Chapter 25

Beobrand awoke with a jolt. The echo of a scream hung in the air and he looked about him nervously at the slumbering men scattered about the hall. Had he let out the cry of anguish into the silent darkness of the hall? No. Acennan snored from where he lay closest to Beobrand. None of the other men stirred. It must have been in his dream.

He stood quietly and made his way to the door of the hall. A dim light glowed under it. Dawn was close. The large doors creaked and the door warden turned to see who was up so early. The hooded figure nodded at Beobrand, but did not speak. In no mood for conversation, he was glad of the warden's silence.

Walking towards the soaring walls of Eoferwic, he picked his way through the mud-clogged courtyard, skirting black puddles.

His father had been in his dream. Sunniva too.

And baby Octa.

Beobrand's teeth ground together as he clenched his jaw. The dream was yet fresh in his mind. Grimgundi, that hate-filled brute, had first beaten Sunniva about the face, kicking her savagely after she fell to the ground. Then, tired or bored of the sport of hurting a woman, he had reached for the infant. All the while, Beobrand had been unable to move. His feet were as tree trunks, rooted to the ground. He had watched in horror as his father had picked up Octa from his small cot. In those huge, calloused hands that Beobrand remembered so well, Grimgundi had raised the child high in the air. A crazed smile split his face like a scar.

Beobrand had fought with all his will to move, to throw himself at his father. To stop the vile man from hurting anyone else. But he was frozen. Beobrand had started to wail when Grimgundi had dashed Octa's brains out against a wooden pillar. Blood and bone had splattered his face.

He climbed the crumbling stone steps up to the wall. A cold wind blew, cooling the tears on his cheeks. He swiped them away. His father could never hurt Octa. Beobrand stared north. The dawn lit brooding clouds there. Summer was nothing more than a memory now.

Just like Grimgundi.

Turning south, the land was all shadows and dull glimmers of water. The Usa ran broad and deep close to the fortress walls, beyond that there was no sign of life apart from a flock of starlings, way off in the distance; swirling flecks against the grey sky. He wondered where the Mercians were. Would they have ridden through the night, or risked camping so close to Eoferwic?

The previous day, when they had come within sight of the stone-walled fort, Beobrand had halted the riders. He had considered what to do long and hard as they had ridden north through Mercia, and he could think of no better course than this. He had sent Eowa's men away, with what was left of the provisions and the horses they rode. But no weapons.

He would not be watching his back all the way to Ubbanford. There were too many of them to guard. They had given their word and having travelled with them for several days now, he was sure they were good men, men of honour. But they were sworn to Eowa, and as they got ever closer to what would surely be the cutting of his wyrd-thread, would their need to protect their lord outweigh their oath to an enemy? It was an easy question to answer. Given the chance, they would turn on their captors and there would be further bloodshed. And there had been enough of that.

They had not wanted to leave their lord, but Beobrand had made up his mind and he would not be swayed.

"You have my word that Eowa will be treated fairly. Oswald is gōd cyning." The words had offered them little comfort. They knew what kings were capable of.

In the end, it was Eowa himself who had quietened them, convincing them to return to their home.

"Prepare my hall for winter," he had said to his gesithas, most of whom looked ready to weep, "prepare it for my return. For if I yet live, I give you my oath that I will return to you." At the mention of the possibility of his death, one of the warriors, Scur, had let out a moan. Eowa had raised his hands for silence.

"Await my return or tidings of my death, but know this. Should Oswald King take my life, it is as it should be." Scur had wailed then, and Cyneburg had lent her own sobs to the sounds of grief. Eowa had not looked at her.

"Do not seek vengeance for my death, for I have wronged Oswald, and my life is his to take."

It had been well-said and Beobrand had felt a lump in his throat as the Mercians rode away, shoulders slumped and heads down.

The breeze picked up, swinging his cloak about him. His hair, long and matted from the dirt of travel, blew into his eyes, and he turned his face northward once more, into the wind. There was the brittle promise of snow and ice in that wind. His ribs ached at the change in the season. He could feel the throb of his heartbeat in the toe he'd broken kicking one of Nathair's warriors.

"Winter is coming," said a familiar voice.

Beobrand made no show of the surprise he felt. He had not noticed Acennan following him through Eoferwic. For the first time in many days he had allowed himself to lower his guard. He would have to be careful. Perhaps they were safe enough in Eoferwic, capital of Deira, with its old Roman walls, and the fine oak hall and new Christ-god temple, but the north was far from safe. The aches he felt reminded him all too well of that.

"Aye, there will be snow before too long," Beobrand said, without turning to face Acennan. "There is a storm growing in the north. I can feel it. We must hurry. I fear Oswald will be in need of our swords before the winter snows."

"Would that we could tarry here awhile. I ache from being in the saddle."

Beobrand turned to him.

"Perhaps you ache for something else?" He arched an eyebrow.

Acennan let out a short laugh.

"Perhaps I do at that." Then suddenly serious, "It has been a long time for me, Beobrand."

"I am sorry, but you will have to wait some more, my friend. We ride north today. And the queen stays here."

"Can we not take her to Bebbanburg? Surely they will be safe there?"

Beobrand shook his head.

"Cyneburg and Eadgyth stay here. They would slow us down and I would leave them far from the Picts. We almost lost Oswald's queen once, I will not risk it again. I have spoken to the king's steward here. His lady is already doting on the queen and her handmaiden. There are warriors and walls here to keep them safe." He looked at Acennan's round face. Fingers of dawn light softened the cheeks, but he could not fail to see the tightness of the mouth, the anger and disappointment that lurked just beneath the surface.

"We will return as soon as we are able, Acennan. I give you my word."

Acennan said nothing, but let out a long sigh. His breath steamed briefly in the cold before the wind shredded it.

"But first, my friend," Beobrand said, clapping Acennan on the shoulder, "we must say our farewells."

"You ride north so soon?" asked Wulfgar. Beobrand noted that his dark beard was shaggier than it had been, less well-groomed. The ride through Mercia had taken its toll on them all. "You could not stay awhile to rest before continuing?"

Beobrand did not need to look to Acennan to know that his friend was listening carefully from where he sat at the ale-bench of the great hall.

"I wish that we had time to recover, but no, we must head northward today. Our king is in need of all the spears he can field. We are wasted here. Besides," said Beobrand, flicking a glance to where Eowa sat alone at the far end of the hearth, "we must take our guest to Oswald. His wyrd is in our lord's hands, and I would be rid of the burden of warding the atheling of Mercia."

Wulfgar nodded and sipped at the warm ale in his wooden cup.

"I will miss you, Beobrand, son of Grimgundi."

Beobrand's face clouded at the mention of his father; the dream was yet fresh in his memory. Wulfgar looked away quickly, perhaps misinterpreting the reaction to his words.

"I prefer to be known as Beobrand of Ubbanford now. My father is dead."

Wulfgar looked back at him, a strange expression on his face.

"We all live in our father's shadow. But we will be remembered by our own deeds, not those of our forebears. I know nought of your father's exploits, but yours are sung in halls across Albion. You need not worry about how people speak your name, Beobrand, Lord of Ubbanford."

Beobrand smiled at the Wessex thegn and raised his own cup to him in salute.

"I will miss you too, Wulfgar, son of Ethelbert." Even as he said the words, he realised it was true. They had not grown close, but the journey and battle in Mercia had changed how they each felt about the other. Gone was the rivalry and suspicion. It had been replaced by mutual respect. "Perhaps one day we will be able to finish our bout to find who is the better swordsman." He grinned at the West Seaxon.

"Perhaps," replied Wulfgar, also smiling. "I will ride south soon, but someone will need to bring the queen her waggon-load of goods that she left at Anwealda's hall. I will ask that it may be me who returns to Northumbria. Perhaps I will even travel to Bebbanburg, or your own Ubbanford, if I would be welcome."

"We have stood together against a common foe, Wulfgar. You will always be welcome in my hall."

They rose and gripped each other's forearm in the warrior grip.

Then, Wulfgar strode along the bench to where Acennan sat.

"And you, brave Acennan, do not think I am ignorant of the thing you would ask of me." Acennan made to reply, but Wulfgar held up his hand to silence him. "Do not ask it of me now. Go north, fulfil your duties to your king and lord. Then, should you still feel the same way when I return, seek me out and speak your wish. If my sister is agreeable, I believe we will be able to strike a bargain that will see us become more than friends and shield-brothers."

Acennan seemed unable to speak, a rarity indeed. Beaming, he leapt to his feet and offered his hand to Wulfgar. At last he found his voice. Turning to Beobrand he said, "Come, lord. We must be away. There are Picts to slay in the north."

Beobrand marvelled at Cyneburg's beauty. Gone was the grime of travel. The women of Eoferwic had spared nothing in making their new queen and guest comfortable. Her hair, brushed and freshly plaited, shone in the light of the expensive wax candles that flickered on the table near where she sat. She wore clean clothes, probably the finest that could be found in the town. Her blue gown had sleeves with cleverly embroidered grey stripes. Around her narrow waist was a woven girdle in green, white and indigo. At her neck shone a necklace of garnet and gold. She was stunning.

Oswald would have been a lucky man, had she not loved another.

Around her were gathered the ladies of Eoferwic. The

steward's wife sat closest to the young queen, but it seemed that all the women of any worth – wives of thegns and other freemen – wanted to spend time with Cyneburg. They had been chattering quietly, sewing and embroidering as they talked, when Beobrand had approached them with the news that he was travelling north.

Now, all the faces around the table were staring his way. He swallowed, feeling like a naughty child before all of these women. By the gods, this was worse than standing before Cadwallon's Waelisc in the shieldwall!

Clearing his throat, he began again.

"We leave today, my queen. We head north to lend our support to your husband, the king."

Cyneburg did not reply, but tears welled and glistened in her eyes.

Beobrand's mouth grew dry under the scrutiny of the watching women.

"A word, if I may, my queen," he said, indicating for them to step away from the onlookers. The women would gossip at them talking in private, but he feared the alternative was worse.

Cyneburg rose gracefully and followed him a few paces away from the table, out of the pool of light cast by the candles. Behind them, he heard the women murmur amongst themselves. No doubt they debated what he needed to say to her that they could not be allowed to overhear. He hoped they would not guess the truth.

"So soon? Can I bid... him farewell?" Tears brimmed now and one toppled down her cheek. Anger flared in Beobrand.

"You cannot speak with him," he hissed. Instinctively, she took a step away from the force of his ire. "And you must dry your eyes. None can know of your feelings. Do you wish death upon you both? Should anyone find out the truth, your deaths will be assured."

Another tear rolled down her face. But he saw her square her shoulders and take a deep breath. She dabbed at her eyes with a sleeve. Her face was still, impassive and cold now. The face of a statue. Perhaps she feared that showing any emotion would cause her true feelings to tumble out.

"Good. You are a queen now. Do not forget your place. Let nobody know the truth of what happened between you both."

"So you will not tell Oswald?" Her eyes pleaded with him. His heart leapt in his chest. Such beauty. Such perfection.

"I ride north. Eowa must answer to your husband."

To her credit, no more tears came, but her pain was plain to see, despite no change to her expression. He could see it in her eyes.

"You must do what your duty demands of you," she said, her voice flat and cold as ice on a winter lake.

Beobrand could find no more words. She had the truth of it. He must do his duty to his lord. He was oath-sworn. Nothing else mattered.

He turned abruptly and strode away. The eyes of many women followed him as he left the hall.

Chapter 26

One of the mounts whinnied in the gathering gloom of the night. The others replied with their own snorts and blows. Beobrand glanced over to them, but there was nothing amiss. They were safely tethered and were merely settling down for the night after another long day's ride.

Behind him, Garr and Acennan tended to the small campfire that guttered and smoked. It had taken them a long while to get a spark to catch and now they both leaned in close, bickering about how best to conjure the elusive flames they sought. The flames that would dry their sodden clothes, warm them and allow them to eat hot food this night. Darkness was closing around them like a cloak and if they did not succeed soon, they would have no light.

They had travelled for three days since Eoferwic, staying in halls and steadings where possible. They had left Dreogan and the rest of Athelstan's men behind. They could find their own way back to their lord's hall. He wondered whether they would hurry with the tidings they carried. He would have been tempted to tarry a while in Eoferwic.

It had rained heavily that morning, a harsh wind buffeting

their faces as if with pebbles, such was its force. The road was slick and treacherous; the streams swollen. At one crumbled bridge they had been forced to travel far to find an alternative crossing. They had covered much less ground than they had anticipated when they had left the hall of Beadurof that sunrise. The rain had ceased in the afternoon, but the chill wind still blew from the north. As the sun had begun to sink towards the western horizon, Beobrand had led them to a wooded hill that would provide them some shelter. If they could get the fire burning, it would not be so uncomfortable.

He turned away from the camp and stared into the north. The last rays of the sun picked out the edges of black clouds that rolled over the high hills of Bernicia. This would be his third winter in the north. Each had brought its own horrors. Cathryn, raped and mutilated on the frozen forest floor. Nelda's shrieked curse from within the depths of her cavern fastness.

He hated winters. He loathed being enclosed in smoky crowded halls. Sunniva had hated it too. They both loved the open spaces of the hills. The cliffs overlooking the slate-grey Whale Road. The forested valleys that followed the great rivers as they flowed forever towards the sea.

Sunniva. How Cyneburg reminded him of her. The queen had the same beauty. The same golden locks. And yet, Sunniva had a strength that was evident to all. It was encased in the soft, pliant flesh of woman, but Sunniva's heart was as strong as the iron she had forged with her father.

A fresh cloud of smoke billowed past Beobrand.

"Do not blow so hard, Acennan," shouted Garr. He was not one to lose his temper, but Acennan's lack of patience was clearly too much for him. "You will snuff it out before it can catch."

Beobrand ignored them. Sunniva would have had the fire blazing by now. She had always had a way with flames.

He shut his eyes against the sting of the woodsmoke. The twigs Garr had placed on the fire began to crackle and snap as the flames leapt into life. For a terrible moment, he could see the flames that had consumed Sunniva's body. Had those same flames burnt away something within him? He wondered whether the sound of flames hid the cackling of the vicious gods who laughed to see the despair that was woven into the wyrd of men.

Opening his eyes so as not to see the images in his mind he beheld that the sun had fallen behind middle earth now. Complete darkness would be upon them soon. A tear in the clouds showed the first star of the night, glinting like a fine jewel on rich, purple silk, such as that worn by kings and queens.

It would be a cold night. For a moment, he thought of Reaghan. Her long dark tresses. Her slim form pressing against his flesh. Was she also looking up at the first star? Beobrand felt a sharp pang of guilt, as if he was being disloyal to Sunniva. He thrust the feeling roughly away. Sunniva was gone. And the gods alone knew what that thrall girl was doing. Probably swiving one of his gesithas. He scowled into the darkening night.

The fire would have to be enough to warm him.

As if welcomed into his mind by the night, the tiniest of voices whispered to him. And what of Octa? Was he safe? Had the witch, Nelda, cursed him? Perhaps he had been stricken down like so many babes with the coughing sickness. Mayhap he was already dead. Perhaps they all were. Ubbanford could be a wasteland of blackened timbers and bones. Had Torran exacted his vengeance?

"You are nervous," the voice startled him and he spun around. Eowa stood close. He never talked much. The atheling rode alongside each day with scarcely a word being said. He did not complain, and he was helpful when the need arose. Fetching wood. Saddling the mounts. Two days before, he had even pulled Acennan from a bog after he had fallen from his horse. Acennan had been covered in thick black mud and Eowa had got himself caked in the stuff too. He was a good travelling companion, and yet, they were not friends. How could they be? They were taking him to his doom.

"Nervous?" answered Beobrand, angry at himself for not being aware of the man's approach. He was too distracted. It would be his undoing.

"The further north we get, the more anxious you become. You are like a cat before a thunderstorm."

Beobrand snorted at the description. He would never admit it to Eowa, but the Mercian was right.

"We head towards war," he said by way of explanation.

Eowa shook his head.

"There is more," he said, looking sidelong at Beobrand, "I do not believe you fear battle." Beobrand recalled the terror of awaiting the clash of shieldwalls. Many strong men were reduced to mewling wrecks, puking like children. He remembered the screams of the dying. The stink of shit and piss. The pallid, mud-splattered skin of the corpses left for the ravens to gorge on.

"Any man who is not a fool fears battle."

Eowa nodded slowly.

"And yet, you fear something else more than you fear the shieldwall."

Beobrand looked at him sharply.

"I am no fool. I fear many things."

Eowa placed his hand briefly on Beobrand's shoulder. Beobrand tensed, uncomfortable with the contact. What did Eowa's sudden closeness mean?

"All men are worry-struck at times, Beobrand. It is the way of life. Especially for one such as you. A leader."

Beobrand frowned.

"My worries are my own concern," Beobrand said, his tone curt.

"That they are," replied Eowa. "Perhaps you worry about a woman?"

"Perhaps," said Beobrand, his head once again full of Sunniva, Reaghan and the shadow of Nelda. "Or more than one."

Eowa laughed. Acennan and Garr looked up from the fire that now burnt bright and hot. None of them had ever heard the atheling laugh before.

"Women. Always women," he said. "We men may carry spears and swords into battle. Lords rule our peoples. And yet who has more power? The men who die and fight, or the women who bewitch us all, and bring our children into the world?"

Beobrand did not answer. He was unused to speaking of such things. Had Coenred been here, he would not have been so surprised. This was the sort of topic the monk would enjoy discussing.

"When I first saw Cyneburg, it was as if all other women vanished from the world," said Eowa, his voice growing soft and distant as his memories returned to him. "I could no more let her travel to Bernicia, than I could will the sun not to set at night. I was entranced." He sighed. His breath smoked in the cool evening air. "I would risk all I had for the chance of one more night with her."

"Was it worth it?" Beobrand felt ashamed of the question as the words left his lips. He understood too well the power of emotion that had led Eowa to act the way he had.

Eowa laughed again, this time a harsh sound, empty of mirth.

"It was cold and miserable. You pursued us like a pack of hounds on the scent of a stag. We could not rest. How had I believed we would escape? It was madness."

"Yes," said Beobrand, "but a madness I too have felt. Perhaps the gods enjoy watching us weak men losing our minds over women. Lucky for me the woman who bewitched me was not married to another. Not married to a king."

Eowa smile ruefully.

"The gods will have a fine time watching me then, for I truly lost my mind. And now, I fear it is too late to find it again. All I can do is face my wyrd with pride." Where did Eowa find such calm acceptance?

"That is no small thing, Eowa, son of Pybba," said Beobrand.

In the dim light, Eowa's teeth gleamed in a smile.

"Thank you, Beobrand of Ubbanford. Know this. If one of the things that preys on you is my fate, push it from your mind. You are doing what is right. It is I who did wrong to your lord king. My life is in Oswald's hands."

Eowa, atheling of Mercia, did not wait for an answer. He walked back to the warmth of the fire, leaving Beobrand staring after him, the perplexed expression on his face hidden by the shadows of dusk.

Beobrand patted the neck of the dappled mare he rode. The small horse had proven a steadfast companion on the long ride from Wessex. Now they were close to Ubbanford at last and Beobrand imagined riding once more on Sceadugenga. The huge stallion was stronger and brave, but the smaller mare would certainly have a place in his stables. At the moment, he could scarcely think of riding yet further north on any horse. His body ached, though his muscles were now accustomed to long days in the saddle. A rest would be most welcome.

And yet he knew that there would be little time to rest. At Bebbanburg, they had heard tell of the conflict that yet raged in the north of the kingdom, on the very borders of the land of the Picts. Oswald would not wish them to waste time recuperating. He would expect Beobrand to gather his men and ride to add his spears to the Northumbrian force.

They passed the trees where he had found the horse skull and bones. Beobrand scanned the bushes but could see nothing in the foliage. Had his gesithas captured Nelda? Perhaps the witch had moved on. Maybe Bassus had killed her. The thought of killing a woman sat heavily on him, but what else could be done? Hengist's mother had sought him out, followed him to his home. She would bring mischief, which would only mean one thing: people would die. Better her than one of his folk. Or one of his kin.

Garr came riding towards them from where he had been scouting the land ahead.

"What news?" asked Beobrand, his voice clipped, anxiety rasping in his throat. They had ridden so far, and now, so close to his hall, he was suddenly overcome with the fear that something terrible had happened. He half-expected Garr to speak of burnt ruins where the buildings of Ubbanford should stand. But he held his face still, showing no sign of the dark worries that flapped inside his mind like a trapped murder of crows.

"All looks well, lord," replied Garr. "No sign of Picts here. They must all be further north."

Beobrand let out his breath and nodded.

"It is good. Let us ride on then. To Ubbanford. To home."

They spurred their mounts forward into the cold breeze that came from the north. The day was dry, but dark clouds hung ominous and brooding low overhead.

Acennan and Garr cantered away, but Eowa matched pace with Beobrand. He had been a pleasant travelling companion these last days. Since that first conversation by the campfire, they had spent more time conversing; during the days of riding and at night beside crackling fires in sheltered forest glades or beside the roaring hearth fires of lords who provided them with hospitality.

Beobrand had grown to enjoy the atheling's company. He was thoughtful; a man of conviction. Not once had he attempted to flee, instead being driven by the weight of his own words. Beobrand understood that sense of duty. Understood and admired it. And yet, being bound to one's oath seemed a fickle thing as they rode ever closer to Oswald, and what would almost certainly prove the death of Eowa. Beobrand wished he could see a way to avoid the outcome he saw looming. But how could he not bring the man to justice before his king?

"These are good tidings," said Eowa, "I know you have been anxious. All the tales I hear of these Picts portray them as a savage and dangerous tribe indeed. Living on the frontier of their land must be hard."

"They are not one tribe," answered Beobrand. "There are

many folk in the north – men of Dál Riata, Ystrad Clud, Gododdin, Picts. But 'Picts' is what they call them here, in Bernicia."

"Well, it seems fitting," Eowa said. "The Waelisc call us all 'Seaxons', even though we are many tribes and folk in the different kingdoms of Albion."

"True," said Beobrand with a grin. His fear fell from him like snow from a steep roof and he was suddenly filled with the joy of homecoming. He had not known how much he had longed to return to Ubbanford until this moment. "Come, we are near my hall. Tonight we will rest in comfort and safety. We can worry of Picts and what is in store for us tomorrow."

He dug his heels into the mare's flanks and the beast, picking up on her rider's mood, reared up and then flung herself forward into a gallop. Beobrand laughed as the wind ruffled his long hair, pulling it from his face.

Home.

He missed the people. Bassus and the rest of his gesithas.

Reaghan.

With a jolt he thought of Octa, his son. He missed them all. But mostly, he was glad to be home.

Behind him he heard Eowa whoop and holler as he urged his own mount into a run. Beobrand was not a great rider and the mare was not fast. If Eowa wished for a race, Beobrand did not think he could beat the atheling. He shot a glance over his shoulder and saw Eowa closing on him. Kicking the mare's sides once more, Beobrand slapped her rump and shouted.

"Come on, girl. We can beat them! We are almost home."

He was full of the excitement of the chase. His cheeks were flushed and his eyes sparkled as they sped down the last hill towards Ubbanford. Eowa was close behind, laughing with the thrill of riding with abandon. Ubbanford was as Beobrand remembered it. Nothing had changed in the weeks they had been away. Smoke drifted from the scattered buildings, hazing over the settlement. Beyond the houses and the old hall in the valley, the broad river Tuidi flowed, deep and strong.

On the hill to his right, standing proud and imposing, was his new hall. The hall he had built with Sunniva. For a moment, he considered turning to ride up to his hall, but then he noticed Garr and Acennan had ridden down to Ubba's hall. They had dismounted before the old hall that nestled amongst the smaller huts and houses. Who was that there with them?

Beobrand leaned forward, peering.

Eowa, with a surge of speed from his horse, rode close to Beobrand. The mare was tiring. But Beobrand cared nothing now for the race. There was something wrong. Ice fingers of fear scraped down his back. Figures in dark robes milled before the hall. Who was that there?

Unthinking, he pulled gently on the reins and the mare slowed to a canter. Eowa sped past, cheering loudly. Beobrand ignored him.

And then, he recognised the foremost robe-clad figure. His forehead was shaved back to the crown of his head, leaving his long brown locks to fall behind his ears. The face was young. It was a soft face, that he knew was prone to smiling. But now it was pinched and pale. The skin below the eyes was dark and drawn.

Beobrand hauled the mare to a halt before the figure. Eowa had already leapt from his horse, joining Acennan and Garr who were surrounded by the people who had spilt out of the hall.

Sliding from the small horse's back, Beobrand grunted at

the jab of pain in his leg. It was almost healed, but just when he had all but forgotten about it, the wound reminded him of its presence.

"Coenred," said Beobrand to the young monk, who stood wide-eyed and pallid before the open doors of Ubba's hall, "what brings you to Ubbanford?" Coenred did not respond immediately. Beobrand noted other monks behind him. He recognised the new bishop of Lindisfarena, Aidan. He too had the look of a man exhausted by endless toil. Or stricken with grief.

Others crowded around them. He saw Elmer. Aethelwulf standing close to Ceawlin. Attor, whole and well, seemingly fully recovered from his wounds. Beobrand was glad to see them all, and yet he was unable to focus. Something had drawn his gaze and now he could not tear his attention away from it.

There was a dark smudge on Aidan's cheek. As the holy man walked slowly towards him, eyes deep and sorrowful, Beobrand saw that it was blood. Looking down he saw the man's hands were covered in gore.

Something awful had occurred here. Dragging in a shuddering breath, Beobrand spoke again.

"What has happened?" his voice cracked. He swallowed and blurted out: "Is it my son?" Terror lent force to the question, surprising him, but as he spoke the words he knew that was his worst fear. Something must have happened to tiny Octa and he had not been there to protect him.

Aidan stepped close and placed a bloody hand on his arm.

"Tell me, priest," Beobrand shouted. "Is my son dead? Speak, man."

All around them, the people of Ubbanford and the newly arrived warriors were silent. Coenred said some words in the tongue of the Christ priests. Aidan nodded and spoke in a calm voice, as one would to a frightened animal.

"Octa is well, Beobrand," he said, his accent strong, his words slow. "Your son is well."

Relief flooded through Beobrand and he almost fell. Aidan gripped his arm, held him upright. Beobrand's eyes returned to the blood on the bishop's face and hands.

"Then who... whose blood?" Beobrand managed at last.

"It is Bassus," Coenred said, stepping forward. "He was gravely wounded and they sent for us. We prayed and prayed. The abbot tried everything he knew. But it was no good. I am sorry, Beobrand. We were too late."

PART THREE
SIEGE OF SOULS

Chapter 27

Reaghan poured more of the good mead into Eowa's drinking horn. The lady Rowena had ordered that the best food and drink be prepared for the return of their lord. Their lord. Her lord. She blushed at the stupid thought, but she could not hide the pleasure at seeing Beobrand again. Would that the circumstances had been better. What had happened to his friend, Bassus, was terrible, but her concerns lay only with Beobrand. She flicked a glance again at the partition to the rear of the hall. Bassus lay there, away from the feasting, in a darkened room. Alone, apart from his friend Beobrand.

"Reaghan! Foolish girl. Look what you are about," snapped Rowena.

With a shock Reaghan saw that she had spilt the mead. It trickled over the board of the high table and onto Eowa's thigh.

Flushing a deeper shade of red, Reaghan used her apron to mop up the worst of the spill from the table.

"I am sorry, lord," she said, her voice quivering.

Eowa reached up and placed a calming hand on hers.

"There is no harm done here." He offered her a smile. He was handsome. She had heard them say he was the brother of Penda, an atheling of Mercia. Though why he was here in Ubbanford, she had no idea.

She pulled her hand free from his soft grasp and retreated to fetch more drink.

"Stupid girl," Rowena said.

Reaghan hurried away. These days she did all she could to keep her distance from Rowena and her daughter, Edlyn. Maida and Odelyna helped by finding her chores to do, but she could not avoid the high-born women all the time. Whenever their paths crossed she seemed to anger them. She had felt the lash of a hazel switch many times this summer. The punishments hurt her, leaving welts that Odelyna treated with leechcraft, but the pain was nothing when compared to the loneliness she felt. She was hollow. The tiny babe that had been growing inside her had been expelled by her body leaving her weak and empty. She hated thinking of that day, but it seemed to be lurking in her memories, like a wolf in a dark forest, ready to pounce whenever she lowered her guard. The cramps had been terrible, her body racked with pain. In the end, she had voided everything from her womb, leaving her with nothing. She was a thrall. Nothing was all she could ever have, and yet, when she could have had one thing, a perfect thing, she had chosen to destroy it. To kill it.

Tears welled in her eyes and she struggled to refill her jug from the barrel.

Odelyna and Maida told her she had done what was best. But they had no inkling of the devastation she felt inside.

The best days were when Maida asked her to watch the children. This kept her far from Edlyn and her mother, and she found the company of the little ones soothing. The children liked her. She had a soft way about her that they took to easily. They did what she asked of them, and in return, she would devise games to keep them amused. Octa, the baby, was her favourite. She relished the moments when he grew sleepy after suckling from Maida. Reaghan would take him with pleasure, clean him and then nestle the babe close to her body. She would close her eyes and breathe in the scent of his baby head, stroke the gossamer softness of his blond hair. Hair that would be the colour of his father's when he grew. Those moments of closeness with Beobrand's son were the times she cherished most.

Once, when she had opened her eyes after snoozing for some time with the boy snuggled on her lap, she had found Maida watching her, with a knowing expression. Reaghan had known what the goodwife had been thinking. "The child is not yours."

She had stood, placing Octa into his crib and made to leave the hut. Maida put her hand on Reaghan's arm, stopping her.

"Never speak to him about what happened this summer, Reaghan. You did what needed to be done, but he would not understand."

Reaghan had stared at the woman for a long time. Maida had been as kind to her as anyone, but she did not comprehend the guilt she felt whenever she held Octa. The guilt and the jealousy.

She nodded.

"I know," Reaghan had said.

Sunniva had given Beobrand a son. Reaghan had killed one.

She carried the jug of mead back to the benches, filling

cups and horns. Letting the noise of chatter wash over her unheeded.

Maida was right. She could not tell Beobrand of what she had done. But she needed this emptiness inside to be filled. Movement from the partition drew her gaze. Beobrand stepped from the doorway, his face drawn and haggard. The events of the past year had aged him in ways that could not easily be seen. His eyes were pinched and dark-ringed; his step heavy and full of sorrow. And yet his body was still that of a young warrior, tall and strong. A lord in his prime.

Their gazes met across the fuggy haze of the hall and, as if he could hear her thoughts, he pulled himself upright, squared his shoulders. With an imperceptible nod in her direction, he strode towards his gesithas.

"Have you spared enough of my mead for me?" he said. She watched as Acennan stood, offering Beobrand a full drinking horn. No words were said, but she saw the silent communication between them. Beobrand took the horn and drained it.

Aethelwulf stood, raising his own cup.

"Welcome back, lord," he shouted, his voice raucous with the drink he had already consumed. He emptied his cup in one quaff.

"Be sure to leave enough for my guest and I to get drunk, Aethelwulf. We have been on the road for a long time, and travel is thirsty work. Besides, we must drink our fill tonight, for tomorrow we ride north."

The warriors must have already heard this news, or guessed it, for they seemed unsurprised. They hammered the boards and cheered their returned lord, as Beobrand made his way back to the high table.

Reaghan felt her eyes prickle. She would not cry. Tears

gave no help, did nothing. But the sudden sadness that came upon her now forced her to lower her head and wipe at her eyes. He was to leave so soon. They had not even spoken since his arrival. She looked back to where he now sat talking to Eowa.

Rowena was right. She was a foolish girl. There was nothing between them. She was a thrall. He was her lord. Looking back, she realised they had seldom spoken. To him she was a mere plaything. A body on which to expend his lust. And yet, he had come for her when she had been taken by Nathair's sons. And he had asked Maida to watch over her. Her stomach twisted. He had planted his seed inside her.

She saw that Beobrand's horn was empty and he looked towards her, raising the vessel.

She blushed and felt a rush of heat throughout her body. She went to him. Did his eyes linger on her as she walked?

As she leaned in to pour the drink, his hand brushed her arm. She almost spilt the mead once more, such was the jolt of desire that ran through her. The force of it shocked her.

He turned his head to her and whispered, "Will you come to me this night?"

Her throat was closed. She could not speak. His touch burnt her skin. The smell of him, sweat, dust, horse and mead, filled her nose.

She nodded. Whether Beobrand knew it or even cared, she understood something in that moment. He may be her lord, and she merely a thrall. But he had not commanded her to go to him. And she knew something else, he would never have to, she would go to him as willingly as a goodwife goes to her husband.

*

Beobrand lay still with his eyes shut, listening to Reaghan's steady soft breathing. Her warmth enveloped him under the furs they shared. Gently, not wishing to wake her, he stroked a hand along the curve of her back. She let out a muffled moan of pleasure at his touch. He recalled the sounds of her passion the night before. At first, he had been dull with drink, exhausted and still stunned at the news about Bassus. But Reaghan had caressed and kissed his body until he could think of nothing else but her. She seemed to have made it her duty to bed him that night. Beobrand smiled. Who was he to question her duty?

In the end, their love-making had been thunderous. He had missed the touch of a woman these past weeks and once his body was inflamed, he could not hold back. Reaghan too appeared desperate to take him inside of her. She clung to him, gasping and moaning as he thrust into her until they had both screamed out their passion and collapsed into a sated, contented sleep.

Reaghan was a mystery to him. A thrall who had ensnared him somehow. He thought of what Eowa had said about women. Who was it who really held the power?

He opened his eyes and looked at the dark hair that encircled Reaghan's slim face. Not the shining gold of Sunniva's locks. In an instant, his warm contentment was gone, as if washed away with ice-cold water from the Tuidi. He sighed and stood, lifting his breeches and kirtle from the floor and pulling them on. Would he never know true happiness again? Perhaps he did not deserve it. He yet lived, while so many others had gone to the afterlife. He knew what Bassus would say. That he should not dwell on the past and merely enjoy the moment. The giant warrior was probably right, but it was not an easy thing to do.

Was Bassus now thinking of the past; of what he had lost? No. Beobrand doubted the pain of the present would allow his friend to think of anything but his current situation. The shock of seeing the huge warrior laid low was still fresh in his mind. Bassus had seemed an invincible force. Initially, when he had galloped into Ubbanford, Beobrand had believed Bassus dead, and felt great relief when Coenred managed to get through to him that his friend yet lived. But his joy had been short-lived. He had hurried into the partitioned area at the back of Ubba's hall to be confronted with the terrifying stench of flesh-rot, blood, sweat and fear. And overlying it all, the cloying scent of burnt flesh.

Bassus lay on a cot. In the dim flicker of the rush lights his sallow face showed no sign of life. The massive warrior's skin was pallid and bejewelled with fever-sweat. Leaning in close to him, Beobrand felt the heat wash off him like a forge. Or a bone-fire. He yet lived, but Aidan and Coenred had said it was in God's hands now whether he stayed on middle earth or departed. Looking at the leaf-wrapped stump of the man's left arm, Beobrand found it hard to believe that Bassus could survive. But was it truly the great warrior's wyrd to die thus, sweating and shaking after losing his arm to a wound from a treacherous Pictish arrow?

Beobrand pulled on his leather shoes and laced them as quickly as he could, silently cursing the clumsiness of his missing fingers. He had survived losing them. If anyone could live after having their arm taken, it was Bassus. Did the gods laugh to see one so mighty brought down thus?

Beholding Bassus weak, fevered and broken, had struck Beobrand like a physical blow. He had sat by his friend for a long time. Tears had slid down his face at the thought of losing another loved one. Staring at Bassus' pain-tight features in dismay, Beobrand had heard the big man's voice in his mind, as clear as if Bassus had awoken and spoken them. "Don't sit here weeping for me, boy. I can take care of myself. You have men to lead. Get out there and show them you are their lord."

And so he had scrubbed the tears from his face with his calloused hands and returned to the hall. To the chatter, food and drinking. To the riddles and boasts of his men. Gram had asked him how Bassus did, unable to conceal the fear in his voice. He too was in shock at the great warrior's decline from the arrow wound.

"Bassus will be up and drinking us out of mead before you know it," Beobrand had replied. He hoped the anguish and uncertainty behind his words were hidden by his bluff tone.

Beobrand made his way quietly to the door of the sleeping chamber. He glanced back at the slumbering form of Reaghan. She looked so small and peaceful. Would that he could share in that peace a while longer. He drew in a deep breath, turned and left her to sleep.

Coenred's eyelids drooped. He yearned for sleep, but knew it would not be allowed now until after sunset. He sipped at the weak ale in his cup, then took a bite of bread. It was hard, so he dipped it in the ale and took another bite. The food and drink slowly seeped into his body and he began to feel more alert. He had been awake for much of the night. They had prayed over Bassus and sung the offices. He wondered if he would ever grow truly accustomed to the life of a monk. He loved the prayer and the community of the brethren, but he did feel ever weary. He longed to sleep without being woken for prayers. He marvelled at how older men managed to make the life seem easy. Fearghas had been ancient and yet had never missed an office until he was too infirm to rise from his pallet.

Bishop Aidan seemed always bright-eyed and eager to do the Lord's work, no matter how much sleep he had. It seemed to Coenred that the other monks found sustenance from God in a way he did not. Surely they were holier than he. He still fought with temptations sent by Satan to pull him from the path of righteousness he should follow. Gothfraidh said it was normal for one of his age to feel urges of the flesh. Perhaps it was. The devil must be powerful indeed, for Coenred found it difficult to think of little else than their soft curves when he was in the presence of young women. How would it feel to touch them? To lie with them? He shivered, though the morning was not cold. Beobrand had no such problem. Coenred had felt a sharp pang of jealousy as the pretty thrall girl had left the hall with Beobrand the night before. He remembered the beautiful woman Beobrand had married too.

He dunked more bread into his ale, then chewed it, deep in thought.

Beobrand may have found pleasures of the flesh, but his life was also filled with sadness. Perhaps it was better to never know the loving touch of a woman, than to suffer despair at its loss.

"Would you care for some cheese?"

Coenred looked up, disturbed from his reverie. Attor, the lithe and whip-like warrior, who had ridden to Lindisfarena to ask for Aidan's help for Bassus, stood before Coenred, his face open and eager to please.

"Thank you," said Coenred, taking the proffered slice of good, creamy cheese. He placed it on his remaining bread, took a bite and swigged ale into his mouth to soften it all. He nodded appreciatively and Attor beamed back at him.

Christ had clearly touched Attor. Since he had been delivered from seemingly certain death from his own arrow wound, he had cast aside his pagan ways. Gone was the Thunor amulet he had worn about his neck, replaced by a small wooden cross. When there was no sign of Bassus' wound healing, Attor had known the only hope for him was the Christ and His new bishop.

"How does Bassus do?" Attor asked, his usual gruff tone always softened when he addressed any of the holy men. Coenred liked him, but feared him. He was like a wild wolf that had been tamed to sleep beside the hearth in a hall. He may seem soft and biddable, and yet the same sharp teeth rested within the jaws of the beast. Coenred felt the same way about Beobrand.

"We shall see, Attor. The abbot is with him now. We have prayed all the night and his life is in the hands of the Lord now. Have you also prayed?"

Attor's face paled.

"Should I have?" There was an edge of panic in his tone. "I did not know. How should I pray?"

Coenred smiled.

"Do not fear. Prayer is simple and God will always listen to prayers from believers. And you believe, do you not?"

Attor rubbed his shoulder where Aidan's poultice had drawn out the poison from his wound.

"I do."

"Then to pray all you must do is find somewhere quiet and speak to Christ as you would speak to your earthly lord. Speak and you shall be heard."

Attor looked confused.

"I am no holy man. I do not know the rites or sacrifices to make the gods hear me."

"There is only one true God," corrected Coenred. "You need not perform any secret rite or sacrifice to speak to our Lord God. But," he said, too tired to enter into a lengthy discussion with this warrior over the ways of religion, "you should speak to Abbot Aidan later. I think he would explain these matters better than I. And, perhaps you would wish to be baptised."

"Baptised?" Attor asked, yet more confused.

"It is when you wash away your sins and become a true worshipper of Christ."

"And after that God will talk to me?" Attor's eyes were wide.

"Well, it is not so simple, but God talks to us all, if we listen."

The doors to the hall swung open, letting a stream of bright daylight into the musty gloom of Ubba's hall. From the light strode Beobrand, broad and tall.

Attor's expression changed from one of intense concentration and wonder to one of abject misery. He hurried forward and fell to the rush-strewn ground before his lord.

"I am sorry, lord. If only I had slain that Pictish bastard, Torran. I have let him slip away twice. And now Bassus..." He could not bring himself to finish.

Beobrand pulled Attor to his feet.

"Brave Attor. You cannot be blamed that the craven Pict runs like a hare in the forest. No. And I hear if it were not for you, Bassus would now be dead."

Attor's face was still twisted with anguish, but he nodded.

"I rode as fast as I could to Lindisfarena. And I made the monks ride back. Aidan wanted to walk, but I would not hear of it."

"You did well, Attor. But you are right, we should have

killed Torran when we had the chance. The next time our paths cross, I swear I will take his life."

"If I don't take it first," said Attor, a thin smile twisting his mouth. The wild beast was not far beneath the surface. Coenred had not seen Attor fight, but he had heard the tales. The man was savage in battle.

Beobrand smiled and clapped Attor on the shoulder.

"So, all healed now?" he asked.

"Yes, lord." Attor's voice was full of awe. "A miracle of the Christ."

"Let us hope he can work his magic on Bassus."

Attor's face grew serious once more. With a curt nod, he padded away.

Beobrand sat beside Coenred.

"It is good to see you. How was the journey back from the lands of Wessex?"

"Easy enough," said Coenred. "We were not stopped on the river on the return. And we missed the rains. The storms began shortly after we arrived in Bebbanburg."

Attor came back and placed bread, cheese and ale before Beobrand.

Beobrand took a bite of the bread. He winced at the texture, pausing to soak it in ale before trying a second chunk.

"How was the journey with the queen?" asked Coenred, remembering the stunning daughter of Cynegils, and feeling not a small hint of envy that Beobrand had travelled long days north in her company.

Beobrand's face clouded.

"It was not without hardship," he spoke around the bread and cheese in his mouth.

Coenred awaited something further, but Beobrand continued to eat in silence.

"How does Cyneburg fare?"

Beobrand shot him a hard glance. His blue eyes were as pale as winter skies. And as cold.

"She is safe in Eoferwic. She is Oswald's worry now."

Coenred thought that such a choice beauty would be no man's worry, rather his joy, but he could see that Beobrand was unwilling to say more on the subject of the queen.

"Tell me," Beobrand said at last, "of how Aidan treated Bassus. Can he truly survive such a terrible thing?"

"Only the Lord knows if he will survive, but he is as strong as an ox. And we have prayed for his recovery all this night."

Beobrand chewed for a time before speaking.

"I have seen the strength of your god's magic, Coenred. And Aidan has great skill with wounds. I know this, but…" he hesitated. He took a draught of his ale and continued. "Did he have to take his arm?"

Coenred understood his dismay. For one such as Bassus, a great warrior, to lose an arm was a terrible thing. Never again would he be able to heft shield and spear. Never more would he stand in a shieldwall. He would see himself as less of a man. Perhaps others would too. The loss of the arm would be bad enough, but the lack of battle-fame and respect from other warriors would be worse.

"If Aidan had not taken the arm, Bassus would already be with our Father in Heaven. The wound-rot had crept into his flesh from where the arrow pierced the skin. The arm had grown black. Even now, he may yet succumb. It is dreadful for him to have lost the limb, but if he had not, he would be dead already."

Beobrand seemed mollified by the words. He took a further mouthful of bread and cheese.

"How was it done? How did he not lose all of his life blood?"

Coenred paled to remember the awful process he had witnessed. He had vomited after all was finished, but none there had belittled him for his weakness. In fact, Aidan had praised him for holding his nerve until he was no longer needed to help.

"How was it done?" Beobrand repeated.

Coenred took a deep breath.

"Abbot Aidan cut away the dead flesh. It was black and stank of decay." Coenred felt his gorge rising at the memory of that sickly smell. He swallowed and continued. "We later burnt what was cut from him, that the evil within it would be destroyed. Fire too was used to seal the wounds as they bled." It had stunk like burning boar meat. "Once the dead flesh was removed, Elmer helped us." Coenred swallowed again. He did not wish to remember. It had been a struggle to bring himself to eat, now he feared he would bring up the food again. The cheese and bread sat heavy in his stomach.

"How did he help you?"

Coenred could still hear Bassus' screams. Mead had dulled his senses, but the pain had still been terrible.

"With his axe. The arm bled a lot then. I had to stop the blood with the hot metal we had prepared. Aidan said I did well." Coenred looked to Beobrand and saw that his Cantware friend's jaw was set. His skin pale.

"After that, Bassus slept. We wrapped the stump in tender leek leaves and pounded salt, that the heat of the fire would be the sooner drawn away."

The partition at the rear of the hall opened and Aidan stepped into the room. Attor rushed to him with a cup of ale as the priest made his way to where Beobrand and Coenred sat.

Beobrand stood.

"It seems you have again aided one of my trusted gesithas. I thank you."

Coenred translated the words into Latin.

Aidan smiled but shook his head. His face was drawn and tired, but his eyes bright.

"Do not thank me," he said in the tongue of the Angelfolc. "Thank Christ, son."

"The Christ is not my god, but I will thank Him if Bassus lives. Perhaps I will build a shrine here in Christ's honour." Coenred could scarcely believe Beobrand's words. He knew that Beobrand cared little for what he thought of as a weak god.

Aidan sipped at his ale and listened to Coenred's translation. He replied, speaking fast words to the young monk.

"He says that you should build a place of worship for Christ followers. If you do this, you will be blessed."

Beobrand frowned, apparently unsure how to respond. After a time he said, "How is Bassus?"

At this, Aidan showed his teeth in a broad grin. He spoke animatedly.

Coenred explained his words, unable to keep a wide smile from his own face.

"It would seem the Lord has heard our prayers for Bassus. His recovery from last night is nothing short of a miracle. The fever has broken and Aidan bids you go in to Bassus. To see you would lift his spirits."

Bassus shivered as if he was lying naked under a drift of snow, and not covered in thick furs. And he felt hot. The dreadful pain of burning radiated from his left arm. He ground his teeth against the agony. He had never known such pain. He felt tears prick at his eyes. He had not cried since he was a child. He had suffered. Wounds, loss, death of friends and family, but he never wept. This throbbing, searing agony might change that.

He made to wipe his hand over his face and for an instant was confused. He did not feel his rough palm against his coarse beard. The pain was making him foolish. Of course he felt nothing from his hand. He no longer had a left hand. Despite the waves of shuddering nausea Bassus smiled grimly. This would be no easy thing to grow used to. He quickly rubbed his right hand over his features, removing the tears that had squeezed past his eyelids. He would not weep, by all the gods. That Pictish whoreson would not make a child of him.

Another heart-clenching throb of excruciating agony made him close his eyes. A small groan came through his gritted teeth. Gods, he had no arm now, so how did it still hurt? If he did not look, he would have sworn an oath that he was still whole. Still a warrior to be feared. And yet he knew the truth of it. He would never hold a shield again. The priest, Aidan, seemed to think he would survive. Looking down at the seeping bandage and empty space where his arm had been, Bassus was not sure he wished that.

He should never have come north again.

The door to the chamber opened with a rasp of wood against wood. Beobrand stood there. The pity on the young man's face stung almost worse than the burnt stump. Is that what he was now? What he would be? Just an object of pity. An old man with one arm.

"You look better," said Beobrand, coming to sit by his side. "Last night I feared the worst."

"What could be worse than this?" said Bassus, his voice a croak of despair.

"Do not speak so. You will heal and mend. You still have one good arm. You are not dead yet, old friend."

Bassus let out a harsh bark of laughter and looked away.

"No, I am not. But perhaps it would have been better if that Pict's arrow had found its mark."

"Better? How would that be better, Bassus?"

Something in Beobrand's voice drew Bassus' gaze back. Tears ran down the warrior's cheeks. Bassus was struck by how young he looked. Not much more than a boy. Pain again made him close his eyes and hold his breath.

"I have lost too many, Bassus," Beobrand said. Bassus opened his eyes. Beobrand cuffed the tears from his face. "I will not lose you too. You will get well and live many more years." His voice had taken on the tone of one who should be obeyed. A lord. His lord. He knew then that Beobrand would cry no more. And that he would live.

"Very well, Beobrand. If you command it, I will live." He forced a weak smile. "But there are some who need to do some dying."

"Aye," said Beobrand, gripping Bassus' remaining hand. "I swear to you I will seek out Torran, son of Nathair, and I will slay him."

"You do that," said Bassus. "That son of a Pictish pig needs killing more than most men from what I have heard."

"He will not live," said Beobrand, and Bassus heard the truth of his lord's words.

"But there is another who you must kill, Beobrand," Bassus

said, squeezing Beobrand's hand tightly at another surge of pain.

Beobrand leaned in close to Bassus to hear tell of this other walking corpse.

The day was fine. A few clouds drifted in the deep-blue sky. Beobrand walked between the houses of Ubbanford. Fragments of frost lingered in the shadows of the buildings, but in the sunlight the air was pleasant. His thoughts were like a reflection of this interplay between warm light and cool shade. One moment he was overjoyed that Bassus lived, that Reaghan was well and Octa was flourishing, the next, darkness smothered him. Torran must die. And Nelda, that whore-witch mother of Hengist could not be allowed to live after what she had done.

How he would find them he did not know. But once his duty to the king was done, he would search for them, and he would see them both dead. How many more would he add to those he had vowed to kill before the winter snows came? If it were true that Wybert had travelled to Frankia, his vengeance might take him to lands he had never seen before. Part of him wished he could be free of the killing. But no, that was not his wyrd. Perhaps one day he would be able to rest in his hall, but would he ever know peace until his sworn enemies were dead? The thought of Wybert yet living, when he had caused such misery, filled Beobrand with rage. He knew he would not be able to face his wife's defiler soon, but the fire of his anger burnt hot and slow, like a banked forge. It would never be extinguished.

His hatred of Torran and Nelda was more charcoal added to the flames.

The sound of children laughing reached him. Beobrand slowed and cautiously peered around the barn, hoping to see his son for a moment before being spotted. Octa would not even recognise him, he was sure. He was yet a babe, and Beobrand had not been with him for more than a few moments since his birth. He vowed that he would spend time with his son when he returned from fighting the Picts in the north. He did not wish Octa to grow up thinking of Beobrand as a stranger. He would be a better father than Grimgundi had been to him. He would teach the boy how to be a good man.

The grass before the house was bathed in the morning sunlight. Elmer and Maida's children frolicked and laughed, chasing one another in a circle. In the doorway, stood Reaghan. She held Octa on her hip and watched the children play contentedly.

Beobrand's stomach twisted. He knew in that instant, seeing her there, his son in her arms, that she could be a thrall no longer. He did not understand what he felt for her. It was different to how he had felt for Sunniva, but it was powerful in its own way. This fragile-looking Waelisc girl had somehow enthralled him. It was true. Women held more power than could be seen or measured.

Reaghan looked in his direction and, seeing him, smiled broadly.

Beobrand returned the grin, his memories of the previous night's passion bringing colour to his cheeks. As if she knew what he was thinking, Reaghan lowered her gaze coyly.

"My son is well?" Beobrand asked, striding forward, choosing to ignore the awkwardness between them. What did he expect? She was a thrall and he a lord. They would never be able to be at their ease before onlookers while the situation remained unchanged.

"He is, my lord. Octa is a strong, healthy boy, just like his father." A flutter of a smile played about her lips. Those rose-petal lips that had kissed his body with such intensity the night before. Beobrand felt himself stirring. The power of the girl was intoxicating. But that was not what he had come here for. Taking a deep breath, he held out his hands.

"May I hold him?"

"Of course, my lord," she replied and offered the blond babe to him. Reaghan's hands touched his as he lifted Octa. Their eyes met and spoke a truth neither would dare put into words.

Around them, the children had ceased their play and were staring up at the giant warrior who was now holding Octa. The baby seemed curious. Beobrand was unsure how to hold him, but the boy did not squirm. Instead, he looked into Beobrand's eyes with a questioning expression. Beobrand could see himself in those eyes. And the hair. He thought he could make out Sunniva's chin and cheeks too, but with a sharp pang of sorrow, he realised he was not sure. Could he have forgotten her face so soon?

Cradling Octa in his right arm, Beobrand stroked the boy's cheek with his left half-hand. Octa reached up and grasped his father's forefinger with surprising strength. Beobrand laughed.

"He is fine," Beobrand said. "You will grow up strong and proud, Octa, son of Beobrand."

Maida came out of the house, blinking in the bright sunlight.

"Maida, I thank you for caring for Octa so well."

Wiping her hands on a cloth, she blushed.

"It is my honour, lord," she said. "And Reaghan has helped a lot."

"Well, you have my thanks. Both of you." He looked pointedly at Maida. "Thank you again for caring for my own. It means much to know that when I return to Ubbanford, I will find my loved ones safe and well. This winter we shall have a feast. A symbol. And I will hand out gifts to my most trusted folk. I will forget no one."

Maida smoothed her dress and looked flustered.

"Would you care to come inside, lord? Perhaps something to eat, or drink?"

"I thank you, but no. I have broken my fast and must ride north soon. Before I go, I would talk with Reaghan."

"Of course."

He handed his son to Maida, prising his finger from the boy's tight grip.

"This fine boy can sit at my side at the feast when I return. Will he walk by then?"

"Perhaps, lord," Maida replied, but her face showed how unlikely that was. Of course, Octa was barely a half-year old. When did children learn to walk? He had no idea. He'd never really thought of it before.

"No matter," he said. "He will sit with his father at the high table and see the folk of Ubbanford in the hall."

Not knowing what to say next, Beobrand placed his hand on Reaghan's shoulder and drew her away from the house.

One of the children made to follow, but Maida shrieked at him, and he stopped in his tracks and returned to his mother's side, crying loudly.

They walked some distance from the hut in the direction of the river. To their right, on the high hill, the imposing structure of the new hall, Sunniva's hall, towered over the valley.

"I bid you safe journey, lord," Reaghan said, when they were far enough away to avoid being overheard.

"I give you thanks," Beobrand said, his tone stiff. He looked down at where the glint of the sun rippled on the waters of the Tuidi. He would be crossing the river soon. Once more riding into the unknown. Into battle perhaps. Leading men into danger. Taking Eowa to almost certain death.

"Bassus told me of the witch," Beobrand said after some time.

Reaghan became very still beside him. Gone was the shy playfulness of moments before.

"What did he say?"

"He said she met with you and tried to poison you."

"Nothing else?"

"What else is to be said? The cunning whore tried to kill you. And that Pictish whoreson, Torran, tried to slay Bassus. He believes perhaps they are together, plotting against me. Seeking to harm those I love."

With a start, he felt Reaghan's hand on his arm.

He looked down at her. Neither spoke for a long time, each drinking in the features of the other.

At last, Beobrand broke the silence.

"Do not stray from the village alone. Watch out for Octa and stay safe for my return."

She squeezed his hand and gave a small nod.

"And what of the cunning woman, and the Pict?"

Beobrand set his jaw. Somewhere, over the river, a crow cawed.

"They will die."

Chapter 28

The sun was past its zenith when they were finally ready to leave. Beobrand sat, straight-backed and sombre, on Sceadugenga. From his vantage point atop the tall stallion he watched as his small band of gesithas rode out of Ubbanford. Close to him, Acennan sat astride his smaller chestnut mare.

Beobrand surveyed the men leaving the settlement. The first of them splashed into the ford, sending up great glittering arcs of spray from his horse's hooves. The warband he took to Oswald numbered seven, counting Acennan. Eowa and Beobrand took the band to nine. Nine men heading north. All strong warriors. All killers. And all mounted. The horses they had ridden from Eoferwic were not fresh, but they were good steeds that would see his men northward.

Behind his dour, scarred face, Beobrand felt like a child playing at being a warlord. That these men would follow him filled him with shock and yet it was not without pride that he looked on them. He could scarcely believe that his retinue had grown by three just that morning. He was still reeling at the suddenness of their addition to his gesithas.

Beobrand had just bid farewell to Coenred and Bishop

Aidan. Coenred has smiled broadly at Beobrand's offer of thanks for aiding Bassus. Aidan had merely nodded and said, "Thank God, Beobrand. Not His servants." Around the settlement the warriors had been completing their preparations for leaving when three horsemen had cantered into Ubbanford, causing men to rush to their weapons.

The new-arrivals were led by Dreogan, the tattoo-faced warrior of Athelstan's. They had ridden from Eoferwic to Athelstan's hall to give the tidings of Athelstan's death to his widow. When they had left on their woeful errand, Beobrand had felt a terrible guilt that he had known nothing of Athelstan's wife. He had considered the man a friend, and yet only knew him as a shield-brother and drinking companion. They had needed no more. Beobrand had never thought to ask him of who awaited him back at his hall. The old warrior was always pawing at pretty girls; Beobrand and he had first clashed over Athelstan's treatment of Sunniva. He'd not imagined the man had a wife. It felt wrong now that his life beyond the mead hall and the shieldwall had been unknown to Beobrand.

Beobrand had been surprised to see Dreogan's dark-striped face beneath the helm of the lead rider. The grim-faced warrior and his two companions had dismounted and approached Beobrand. For a moment, he had thought they meant to attack him and Acennan and Attor had rushed forward, blocking their path. Then, to the shock of all, Dreogan and the other two men had knelt, offering their swords, hilt-first, to Beobrand.

"We would join you, Beobrand, Lord of Ubbanford," Dreogan had said. "You were friend to our lord, and we would now be your men. And swear our oath to you."

Beobrand had been shocked. He had believed that Dreogan

had despised him for a youthful upstart. He knew not what to say to them. To refuse would be a great insult, but to accept... Did they truly wish to be his men? His gesithas? Would they fight for him? Die for him?

"Mighty Dreogan," Beobrand had said, and, recognising the other men, "brave Beircheart and Renweard, you do me much honour in your offer of service. Of course I would be glad to hear your oaths." What else could he say? "But know this: I mean to deliver Eowa atheling to our lord king, Oswald. No ill may befall him. I give you my word that he will face our king's justice, but not ours. If this does not sit well with you, I understand, but you would not belong amongst my warband. Once I have heard your oaths, you will be my men, and my word is final. What say you?"

For a long while, Ubbanford had been silent. Dreogan raised his gaze and sought out Eowa. The atheling of Mercia stood beside his steed. Beobrand watched as Dreogan sized up the slayer of his erstwhile lord. Eowa was clean, and dressed in his fine warrior coat. His good sword hung scabbarded from his belt. They stared at one another and Dreogan's hatred was plain for all to see. Eowa did not lower his eyes.

At last, Dreogan looked back to Beobrand.

"If you give your word that he is to be brought before the king for what he has done, then we will plight our oath to you."

"I am the winner in this bargain. You have my word."

They had spoken their oaths clearly and he had raised them up. And so it was that Beobrand had found himself with three new warriors. Each with his own heregeat; horse, armour and weapons. He had seen them fight in Mercia and knew they had stood in the shieldwall at Hefenfelth. They were hale warriors. Shield-bearers and strong spear-men.

Now, as they splashed through the Tuidi, Beobrand could not help but feel uneasy at the haste with which they had come to him.

"We must keep a close watch on them," Acennan said, as if he could hear Beobrand's thoughts. "If we are not careful, Eowa will meet with an accident before we reach Oswald. Oaths or no oaths."

Beobrand grunted, but said nothing. It was as Acennan said. He had seen the lust for vengeance in Dreogan's eyes. He knew that fire well, for he carried a bellyful within himself. And he knew how difficult it was to keep those flames at bay, whatever promise had been made.

"And I fear Elmer may be less than pleased at being left with the women, children and old folk once more," said Acennan.

Beobrand turned towards his friend.

"Truly? I need men I can trust to stay here. To protect Ubbanford and its folk."

"Can you not trust all of your gesithas?"

"You know that is not what I meant." Beobrand sighed, though in truth he would not trust Dreogan, Beircheart or Renweard to be left at Ubbanford. Not yet. They would have to prove themselves to him first. "I would have thought Elmer would be glad to stay close to Maida. And his children. Where he can watch over them."

"I am not so sure he sees it as a gift from you. He has not ridden out with us for many months. The men have begun to jest about it."

Beobrand frowned. Why was it so hard to lead men? He would rather be staying at Ubbanford than riding north. If his duty allowed him to, he would gladly have remained in his hall, warm under blankets and furs next to Reaghan.

But was that true? Or did he lie to himself? Did he not feel his blood quickening at the thought of facing the Picts? At the chance of finding Torran amongst them?

"I will see to it that he is well-rewarded," he said, scowling. "And next time we head for battle, I will ensure Elmer is amongst my warband. Though I am not so sure Maida will thank me for it. Do the others feel the same?"

Acennan shrugged.

"Gram seemed happy enough to stay close to Bassus. I believe Garr welcomed the chance of a rest."

Beobrand nodded. He hoped he had left enough men to keep Ubbanford safe.

Attor, fully restored now, and keen to spill Pictish blood once more, was the last to ride through the ford. The others were already lost in the darkness of the trees of the northern bank.

With a final look up to the hall on the hill, and the scattering of buildings in the valley, Beobrand touched his heels to Sceadugenga's flanks. A cloud scudded before the sun, plunging the valley into shade. Beobrand shivered. Wind blew cold through the trees, dry autumn leaves rattled and flurried. The season was changing early this year. Snow would not be far off.

"Come, my friend," he said to Acennan. "Let us hope that Oswald and Oswiu have those Picts ready to be slaughtered. With any luck we can be home to the warmth of the hearth before the first snows fall."

"The warmth of the fire in your hall sounds appealing, Beobrand," said Acennan, spurring his mare forward, so that both riders hit the chill waters of the Tuidi at the same moment, drenching them in a shower of icy droplets, "but I have another warmth I crave, and I hope to find it within the walls of Eoferwic."

"There," said Attor, pointing ahead. His eyes were keen; nobody else had seen anything of note.

Beobrand reined in Sceadugenga close to the wiry warrior and peered into the distance. Was there perhaps a smudge of smoke on the horizon? It was possible, but he could not be certain.

"It could be just another farmstead," said Beobrand. They had passed several small settlements since leaving Ubbanford two days before. Each had been put to the torch. At one, they had found the charred, crow-pecked remains of four men hanging from the blackened beams of the husk of the hall. In each case, the remnants of the buildings had long since ceased to smoke.

"No, it is Din Eidyn. I am sure of it. By my reckoning it is yet a half day's ride, but we should make it by sundown. By the look of the campfire smoke, there must be a host of warriors there."

Beobrand knew not how Attor could be so sure that what he strained to see above the horizon was the smoke from Oswald's host, but he did not question him. Instead, he waved on the others.

"We shall be at Din Eidyn by nightfall."

"Let us hope they have not drunk all the mead," said Aethelwulf, spurring his steed down the slope. Attor followed him.

Beobrand cursed silently. He should have brought mead or provisions from Ubbanford. Oswiu and Oswald had long been in the field facing the Picts. Surely they would be in need of supplies. Well, there was nothing for it now.

Eowa rode past, his face set, expressionless.

Perhaps the gift Beobrand brought to his king would be enough. Though whether he would be cursed or praised for bringing bad news and trouble to his lord, he did not know.

"Don't look so glum, Beobrand," Acennan said, as his sturdy mare brought him level with Beobrand's position on the crest of the hill. Here a chill wind buffeted them as it had ever since they left Ubbanford. On the journey, they had been glad of the shelter of valleys and forests where they were afforded some protection from the wind. Beobrand recalled the biting cold the last time he had ridden this way the previous winter in search of a priest for Lindisfarena. The clouds above them flew southward, driven by the strength of the winds. It had been dry these last days, but the smell of snow was in the air.

Beobrand looked at his friend's round, smiling face. He could not return the grin.

"I wish to be at the journey's end," he said, scratching his scrubby beard with his half-hand, "but I dread bringing the tidings I carry."

Acennan reined in next to his lord.

"Aye. Giving Eowa to Oswald will be hard." They watched in silence for a moment as the Mercian rode his horse down the hill. He sat straight and prideful, in control and exuding confidence. "He's not a bad one. Stupid, maybe, but a good man, as far as I can tell. And who hasn't done stupid things for the chance at getting some warm cunny?"

Beobrand snorted.

"I don't think our lord king will be so understanding."

"I think you may be right. If Eowa was ploughing my wife's furrow I doubt I'd be too happy either."

"There is nothing for it, I know," Beobrand sighed. "And Eowa goes willingly to his doom."

"Aye," said Acennan, serious all of a sudden, "but that makes it all the harder, does it not?"

An air of despondency hung over the Northumbrian host, intermingling with the fug of dozens of campfires. The sun was touching the horizon as Beobrand rode into the settlement at the head of his small warband of mounted gesithas. They were stopped briefly by a group of desultory sentries, but once Beobrand spoke his name, they were quickly allowed passage into the camp.

The low sun bathed the men who huddled around the fires in a golden glow that belied their sombre aspect. These were men who had been too long far from their homes and fields. Beobrand knew the look.

Some recognised him and raised a hand or called a greeting. Most looked up sullenly as the warband trotted past. The ground was churned by the constant passage of feet and hooves over days and weeks. All around them were shelters. Some had been put together from the timbers of houses destroyed in the fighting. Others were well-made tents of leather pulled over wooden frames, such as he had seen in Dor earlier in the year. The luckiest, or more likely the richest and most powerful, of Oswald's host had taken up residence in the houses or barns that remained intact.

Dominating all was a huge rocky crag. Mightier than the rock of Bebbanburg, it stood thrust up from the earth rising high over the men who camped at its feet. Atop the rock the setting sun picked out walls and buildings. A stout gate. The place was imposing. It looked impregnable.

The fortress of Din Eidyn, Beobrand surmised.

He remembered riding close to the area in the winter, but

they had not ventured to this point. Instead, Oswiu and his small band had been turned away by a Pictish lord, a gruff man named Donel, whose hall was close to the vast water to the north of here. Donel had insulted Oswiu and they'd spent a miserable night in the freezing cold of the wind and rain. The atheling had been furious, promising to return. Scanning the host of grim-faced warriors camped around the jutting rock of Din Eidyn, Beobrand thought that the Pictish lord probably regretted his rudeness now. If he yet lived.

Some distance to the east another great rocky outcrop rose out of the land. Larger, with one side dropping off in sheer cliffs, there were also buildings there. Beobrand was unsure where to go. He could see no clear sign of where Oswald and his hearth-thegns would have settled in this squalid, mud-soaked encampment.

As he scanned the area, movement caught his eye. A group of horsemen approached from the direction of the cliff-edged hill to the east. Beobrand turned Sceadugenga towards the riders.

"Let us see who comes to greet us."

They spurred forward, their horses throwing up clods and splashes of muck in their wake. Someone cursed, evidently splattered by their passing.

Quickly they were free of the encampment and the air was noticeably clearer. Beobrand raised a hand and pulled Sceadugenga to a halt, allowing the other riders to close the remaining gap between them.

They numbered ten men, all armoured in iron-knit shirts and bearing shields painted red with the Christ-symbol, the rood, upon them in white. As they drew close, the leader removed his great helm. It caught the dying rays of the sun and flashed bright, like a spark in a newly kindled fire. He was not a young man, but his shoulders were broad and his hands and arms strong. His teeth showed from his full grey-streaked black beard.

"Well met, Beobrand, son of Grimgundi," he said. "I thought it might be you, but was unsure you had such a retinue of warriors. You are doing well for yourself, it seems."

Beobrand chose not to comment.

"Well met, Derian, son of Isen," he said. "It has been too long. How do you fare?"

"As well as could be expected for one who has been stuck here in this gods'-forsaken place for weeks."

"What news of the Picts?"

"There is not much to tell. Things started well here. We killed many and took the hill yonder." He indicated the cliffs behind him. "But, Donel fled with many of his hearth-warriors and they retreated to that accursed rock. Try what we might, we are unable to unseat the bastard. We have wasted too many men on trying and soon," he glanced at the darkening sky and the clouds rolling in from the north, "I fear, soon winter will be upon us. Still," he said, smiling once more, "it is good to see you, and you bring more men. Perhaps you can help us break this siege."

"I doubt we will be able to make much difference where you, Oswald and Oswiu have failed."

"Failed, is it?" Derian said, his smile twisting. "Well, I suppose we have at that." He rubbed his beard. "Well, have you come here to pass judgement on how we fight the Picts, or for some other reason?"

Beobrand could not tell whether the older man was jesting or serious, so he changed the subject.

"We bring tidings of King Oswald's queen. We have ridden

all the way from Wessex with scarcely a rest. I would speak with our king, if you would lead me to him."

Derian's smirk vanished. This was no matter for jest.

"I will take you to him. He is anxious to hear of his bride's health. Follow me." And with that, he placed his helm once more upon his head and expertly wheeled his horse around to face the cliffs. The other riders followed him. When they were moving towards the hill, their shadows streaking out before them as the sun finally fell below the earth, Derian turned in his saddle and shouted to Beobrand.

"Perhaps when you are done talking to the king, we can share a cup of mead and you can tell me how you would defeat these damned Picts." His face was hidden by his helm, but Beobrand was sure he could hear Derian's laughter over the thrum of the horses' hooves.

"Well, if it isn't the great warrior, Beobrand, returned from the south."

Oswiu, atheling of Bernicia, smirked as Beobrand trudged into the hall. Beobrand bristled with instant anger. He hated the way the king's brother addressed him. There was insult hidden close behind the joviality. Without thinking, Beobrand reached for the hilt of Hrunting and was suddenly glad that they had been made to leave their weapons at the door to the hall. None could approach the king armed. Not even his thegns. Beobrand was glad of it. Drawing a blade on the atheling would not have ended well for him. He swallowed his ire and stepped forward.

"I thank the gods that you are well, Oswiu, son of Æthelfrith," Beobrand said, his words somehow sounding like taunts.

The large round building was situated atop the bluff that overlooked the rock of Din Eidyn. Derian had told them that after the Picts fled to the fortress, Oswald, his brother and their retinues had taken up residence here. It was certainly better than the make-shift shelters of the fyrd-warriors camping around the besieged crag. It was a fine hall, not lofty or extravagant in design, but solid and warm. But it was overcrowded. The stench of many men, sweat, stale ale, spilt mead, food and smoke, hit the back of Beobrand's throat after the clear air outside on the hill.

Despite his tone, Oswiu seemed friendly enough. He ushered Beobrand forward to where Oswald sat on an elaborately carved, high-backed chair, surrounded by ealdormen and his most trusted thegns. Beobrand approached the king. Derian came with him. The rest of the men stayed back with the throng of warriors already at the boards. Thralls bustled about the hall, fetching drink and meat for the hungry men. Beobrand's mouth filled with saliva. He too was hungry. To feed so many would take prodigious amounts of provender. Once again, he cursed himself that he had not thought to bring provisions from Ubbanford.

"I had expected to see you before now, Beobrand," Oswald said. "What detained you? I trust the beautiful Cyneburg is safely in my kingdom."

Beobrand stood uncomfortably before the high-board, all eyes upon him.

"I left the queen safe within the walls of Eoferwic. She will be well-treated there and awaits your return, my lord."

The king nodded. Beobrand noted the lines around Oswald's eyes, the lankness of his usually shining hair. The king looked aged, exhausted.

"I do not see Athelstan here. Did he choose to linger at

his hall rather than come to fight the Picts with his king?" Oswald smiled, but to Beobrand it seemed forced.

Beobrand swallowed the lump that formed in his throat.

"Alas, Oswald King, I bring sad tidings." He took a deep breath, willing his voice to remain calm. "Athelstan fell."

"He is dead?" Oswald sounded incredulous. Beobrand could understand why. The old thegn had seemed invincible. But of course, such a thought was madness. No man could defeat death. This was something Beobrand had learnt all too well. Beobrand's face clearly gave all the answer Oswald needed, for the king continued: "How did he die?"

Beobrand opened his mouth to speak, then closed it again. He was painfully aware of all the watching eyes, all the listening ears. To speak of the things that had transpired could have far-reaching effects. If he told now the tale of his journey, the king would be shamed before all of his men. Such a thing would be a calamity. The fewer who knew of the events of the past weeks, the better.

"How did he die?" the king repeated.

"I will tell you, my lord, but I would speak with you alone."

For a long moment, Oswald stared at the young thegn before him. Beobrand felt as though he were being judged for his part in some terrible crime. Eventually, Oswald stood.

"Very well," he said. "Come with me. I would hear all the tidings you bring."

It was full dark as they walked from the hall to a small out-building. In the gloom Beobrand could not ascertain the usual function of the hut; a storeroom perhaps. Strong wind buffeted them. They were exposed out here on the cliff-edge. Below them, the flickering glow of dozens of campfires showed the extent of Oswald's host. Again Beobrand wondered how long so many men could be kept away from their homes. How long until the food ran out? Men would get sick. The snows would come. Then Din Eidyn would be left for another season.

Derian entered the small building, raising the guttering torch in his left hand high. After a moment, content that it was empty of eavesdroppers or would-be assailants, the bearded thegn bade them enter. Oswald's fine cloak flapped in a strong gust of wind. Oswiu and Beobrand followed him inside. Derian addressed the two men who guarded the door outside.

"None is to enter," he said, before slamming the rough wooden door against the night and the wind.

Inside it was all dancing shadows and looming shapes. Bales, sacks and barrels were stacked against the walls. Meat and smoked fish hung from the rafters. Derian silently produced a couple of tallow candles and lit them from the brand he carried. Warm light caressed the stocks of provisions, but did not reach into the shadowy crevices. The wind outside caused the walls of the hut to creak and groan. Under the wind-creak of the timber, Beobrand could make out scratching. Rats.

Beobrand shivered.

After the chill of the windy bluff the storeroom seemed warm, but it was no great hall. Nowhere fit for a king. And there were no seats.

Oswald turned to him, his face veiled in shadows, but eyes glinting.

"What news do you bring, Beobrand? I could see from your face, there is much I need to hear."

How to proceed? He did not wish to speak of these things with his king. He thought on Cyneburg, the tears streaming down her smooth skin as she imagined what would happen when her husband found out about her lover. And Beobrand liked Eowa. The Mercian seemed to be a good man. Would he not have done the same if he were in Eowa's position, blinded by love?

But he would not lie to his lord. He had given his oath, and he would stay true to his word, or he had nothing.

And yet, must he tell Oswald all of the truth?

"Speak, man," Oswiu spat, impatient to hear the tidings Beobrand brought.

Beobrand drew in a deep breath.

"Athelstan fell in the borderlands of Mercia."

"How so?" asked Oswald.

Beobrand swallowed. He would not lie, but perhaps he could skirt around some of the events, the way a traveller chooses his footing carefully around puddles and bogs.

"We were attacked." He did not mention they had been in Anwealda's hall. In Wessex.

"Who attacked you?"

"A band of Mercians."

"Mercians? But why? So quickly they break the truce? To what end?"

Beobrand chose his words with care. "I am unsure what they really believed would happen. I could only see one outcome to their actions."

"Did you slay them all?"

Beobrand hesitated, realising he had stepped from the precarious path he trod into a dangerous quagmire dotted with meres of deceit and lies.

"Well?" prompted Oswiu. "Did you slay them all?"

"We fought and several were slain."

"But not all?" asked Oswald.

"No, not all."

"Come now, man," Oswiu said, his tone sharp. "You are speaking in riddles and half-truths. What is it you hide?"

Had it been so clear then?

Oswald stepped into the candlelight. His eyes were dark, bottomless.

In a softer tone to his younger brother's, he said, "Tell me, Beobrand. Who led these Mercians?"

Beobrand could not deny his king, and he would not lie.

"Eowa, son of Pybba," he said. It was done. Eowa's fate now lay in the hands of Oswald, as he had known it would. Would the king choose to snap the threads of Eowa's wyrd this very night? Beobrand sighed.

"Brother of Penda?" Oswald seemed intrigued. He rubbed his face pensively. "And what happened to him?"

There was nothing for it now but to answer his king's questions. But perhaps he had succeeded in avoiding the matter of Cyneburg's infidelity.

"I captured him. He is now seated at the board in the hall yonder."

To his surprise, Oswald let out a laugh.

"Well, you are always a surprise, Beobrand. Who would have thought you would have brought me the atheling of Mercia here, to Din Eidyn?" He slapped Beobrand on the shoulder. "You have done well. Derian, fetch the Mercian here."

Derian nodded and made to leave.

"But Derian," the king said and the bearded thegn turned back to face his lord, "do it quietly. I would not have all of my comitatus speaking of this. If God smiles on us this night, perhaps none save Beobrand's gesithas will have discovered his name."

The candle flames flickered as Derian opened the door and then it slammed shut behind him and he was gone into the night.

"You see, Oswiu?" Oswald said, his tone still unnervingly cheery. "This is what makes the likes of Beobrand a warrior to reckon with. It is not just his sword-arm strength, his bravery and his loyalty. Many men possess such traits. It is his unpredictability and luck."

"He does not seem so lucky to me, brother," said Oswiu.

Beobrand said nothing. He agreed with Oswiu. He was not a lucky man. For a short spell the year before perhaps, he had felt differently, when Oswald had raised him up after Hefenfelth. For a few short weeks he had had everything a man could dream of – land, wealth, battle-fame and a beautiful wife. Acennan told him to be thankful for what he still had, but it was not easy to look beyond the death and torment that seemed to follow him the way gulls flock behind a plough.

"Nonsense," said Oswald, "he is as blessed as any warrior I know. But tell me, Beobrand, why did Eowa lead an attack against a band of Wessexmen, Northumbrians and my queen?"

Beobrand's throat went dry. What to say? Oh gods, he did not wish to speak.

And then, perhaps proving the king's point that he was indeed lucky, the door to the shack swung open. Eowa entered, followed by the grave-faced Derian.

"I have been told your name," Oswald said, his voice now as harsh as the wind that rattled the frame of the building, "but I would hear it from you. Who are you, stranger to my lands?"

Eowa stepped into the pool of candlelight. Derian quickly leapt forward and gripped his arm hard.

"Not too close," he growled.

Beobrand suddenly wondered if this whole series of events could have been a trick to get close to the King of Northumbria. As quickly as he thought it, he dismissed the notion. It would have been impossible to predict everything. Eowa could easily have been killed. And Beobrand believed that the Mercian and Cyneburg were truly in love. But was it possible that Eowa could seek to harm Oswald in order to save Cyneburg? Beobrand tensed and moved close to Eowa, ready to spring at the slightest suggestion of an attack on his lord.

Oswald raised his hands for calm.

"Your name?" he urged.

"I am Eowa, son of Pybba, son of Creoda, atheling of Mercia and lord of the northern marches." His voice was strong and clear, with no sign of the nervousness he must surely feel.

"Does Penda know that you are here?"

"I have no way of knowing whether my brother knows where I am, lord king" answered Eowa, the sound of a smile in his tone.

"I have had enough of games of words for this night," Oswald snapped. "Did Penda send you to attack my men?"

Eowa flashed a glance at Beobrand. Eowa's eyes were wide.

"I am sorry for my impertinence, Oswald King," said Eowa. "I thought that Beobrand would have told you of my plans. Why I did what I did."

"He has not told us. I do not know why he was reticent to do so, but as you are before me now, the tale is yours to tell, not his." Eowa nodded his thanks to Beobrand. He must have understood how hard it had been for Beobrand not to tell of his indiscretion. "So speak," continued Oswald. "Why did you attack my men, taking the life of my old friend, Athelstan? Why did you break the truce that I agreed with your brother so very recently?"

"I am truly sorry for the death of your friend. And the other brave men who fell when we fought, Northumbrian, West Seaxon and Mercian alike. None should have died for my cause. It was a fool's errand…"

"Tell me all of it. What brought you to throw away the lives of good men?"

Eowa flinched as if he had been slapped.

"Love." His voice was small now, a child standing before his elders.

"Love? Speak no more in riddles. My patience is all but vanished."

Eowa squared his shoulders.

"I love your queen," Eowa said, as if that were explanation enough.

Beobrand held his breath, unsure of his king's reaction to Eowa's words.

Oswald stood still for a long while, glowering at the Mercian. Outside the wind had picked up. As it blew through the eaves of the building it made a low moaning sound.

"And does she love you?"

"I believe so."

"And this is why you attacked my men? To rescue her from me?"

"It was madness. But I could not bear the thought of losing her."

Oswald's eyes glimmered in the flame-flicker of the greasy tallow candles.

"Is my bride... sullied?" he asked, his voice now as cold as ice-drenched steel.

Eowa hesitated.

"No, lord. Cyneburg is pure."

Oswald bent and lifted one of the candles. He raised it up close to Eowa's face and peered into his eyes. Eowa met Oswald's gaze.

For a long while they stood thus.

"Your wife is pure," Eowa repeated at last, his voice firm.

Oswald did not reply. Instead, he lowered the candle back to its place on the ground.

"My life is forfeit—" began Eowa.

As swiftly as a striking serpent, Oswald lashed out and struck a blow with the back of his hand across Eowa's face. The atheling's head snapped to the side. He staggered, then pulled himself up straight once more.

"You are right," spat Oswald, a strange calm in his voice, "your life is mine to take. But I will not kill you, Eowa, son of Pybba."

Beobrand thought he saw a glimmer of hope in Eowa's eyes.

"I have my spies amongst the Gewisse and the Mercians," continued Oswald. "I am King of Bernicia and Deira. I will soon rule the land as far north as this rock of Din Eidyn. The Gewisse of Wessex pay tribute to me. As do the East Angelfolc of Sigeberht. I am Bretwalda, lord of all Albion. Do you believe me to be blind?"

Nobody answered. A rivulet of blood trickled from Eowa's nose. Beobrand recalled the sudden beheading of Cadwallon. For all his praying to the Christ, the god of forgiveness, Oswald's calm exterior hid a ruthless killer.

"No," Oswald said, "I knew of your meetings with Cyneburg. I thought it the stuff of childish folly. I did not foresee this. I thought you would forget each other once she was safely in my kingdom. Many would take your life for what you have done. But I will let you live. But you are no longer a free man of Mercia. From this day forth, you are my man, though none shall know it save for those in this hut."

"But, my lord Oswald—" Eowa was again stopped by a savage slap from the king. He reeled backwards. Beobrand and Derian reached out and prevented him falling.

Oswald pushed his long hair back from his face.

"Yes, I will be your lord. And you will give me your oath now, Eowa." The wind outside hummed and groaned. "And know this. Should you betray me, or fail to answer when I call upon you, remember who holds the life of your beloved Cyneburg in his hands. If you forsake me, she will pay dearly for it before you do. Now speak your oath."

Eowa's eyes flicked from one man to another, seeking for some way to be free of this punishment. But of course, there was no way out. His life was no longer his. It had been Oswald's from the moment he had entered Anwealda's hall. Beobrand's mind was in turmoil. Oswald had known of Cyneburg and Eowa's love? He was amazed at how quickly the king had turned this situation to his advantage.

Seeing there was nothing for it, Eowa shrugged off the hands that held him. He knelt on the packed earth. The candle flame guttered, its light illuminating his features clearly. His eyes were full of sorrow and anguish, but he held himself still, as he gave his oath to the King of Northumbria.

When Eowa had finished speaking the words, pledging his allegiance, Oswald nodded.

"Now you are bound to me. Remember what I have said. I

hold the life of Cyneburg in my hands and if you cross me, I will destroy you both."

Beobrand shivered again. This time, he was sure it was not from the cold of the night.

"You must escape this night and hurry homeward, Eowa. To Mercia. I will send word when I need your assistance."

"Escape?"

"Yes. You will take a horse and ride off into the night. Derian, see that he has a horse and provisions."

Eowa stood, his face displaying an unhappy mix of hope and despair. Oswald strode to the door, turning his back on them. At the door he paused.

"Of course, your men must believe you escaped. You will need to show signs of a struggle. Derian, Beobrand, make sure he carries enough injuries to last him until he reaches Mercia. And," his eyes glittered in the darkness, "see that his face is marked. I would not wish for any other young, foolish princess to have her head turned by the dashing features of this atheling of Mercia."

Chapter 29

"I can see no weakness in the fortress," said Acennan. "It will not fall easily."

They had ridden around the great rock of Din Eidyn, hoping in vain that they would see some way to breach the defences. Beobrand had known it was a futile errand. Oswald and Oswiu had been camped here with a host of thegns, ealdormen and fyrd-warriors for many days. If they had not spotted a weakness, it was certain there was none.

But Beobrand was eager to mount Sceadugenga once more and to ride free of the hall where the king and his comitatus sheltered from the cutting northerly wind. Acennan would not hear of him riding alone, despite Beobrand's protestations that no harm would come to him.

"Our enemies are besieged behind the wooden walls of Din Eidyn," he'd said.

"One can never tell where enemies will strike from," Acennan had replied. Beobrand thought of the night before in the storeroom and nodded. Acennan was right. Eowa had known he was riding to his doom, but had he not thought Beobrand his friend? Or at least no longer his enemy?

Beobrand had not wished to get involved in the punishment of the atheling, but it was his king's order. How could he refuse? He gripped his reins tightly, the leather creaking within his grasp. His knuckles ached from where he had punched Eowa. Looking down, Beobrand saw a cut on one finger. He was reminded of Eowa spitting a tooth and blood onto the packed earth of the storeroom floor. Beobrand's hand was bruised and angry-looking. His memories sickened him.

When he had returned to the hall, Acennan had taken one glance at his lord's face and enquired what was wrong. Beobrand had refused to answer. He could not speak of it. His king had ordered them to remain silent, never to tell of the night's events. Beobrand had called for mead and when Dreogan had peered over the board and asked where the Mercian had gone, Beobrand had snapped.

"Eowa's whereabouts is no concern of yours, Dreogan. Drink and fill your belly and be glad of the warm hearth this night as the wind rages outside of these walls."

Dreogan had glowered and half-stood before Renweard pulled him back to the bench with a whispered word.

Acennan had stared for a long while at Beobrand, but had said no more.

Now, looking at the southern face of the crag, the bitter wind brought tears to Beobrand's eyes. He brushed them away with the back of his hand. Truth be told, he felt like weeping. He had no qualms with beating, or even slaying a man, in defence of his loved ones, but the savage attack on Eowa was something different. But was it? If he had Wybert within his power would he not wish to do the same, or worse, to him? He knew that given the chance, he would kill Wybert without any feeling of guilt. So what made this so terrible?

He clenched his jaw until his teeth ached. His stomach grumbled sourly. He had eaten sparingly in the night and had no appetite this morning.

By the end, Eowa had scarcely been able to stand. Oswiu, teeth flashing in the dim light of the candles, had grinned as he had kicked the Mercian where he lay. Beobrand had stepped forward and placed a hand on Oswiu's shoulder.

Oswiu had spun around, fists raised.

"You dare to touch me, Cantware hound?" he'd said, his eyes aflame with a savage glee. Beobrand had thought Oswald's brother would strike him. Had he done so, he knew he would not have been able to control his anger. It was all he could do to stop from shoving Oswiu away from him. But if he landed a blow on the atheling of Bernicia, his life would be worthless.

Derian had spoken into the tense silence.

"Eowa needs to be able to ride, my lord Oswiu."

Oswiu had scowled for a long while at Beobrand, perhaps willing the young thegn to swing a punch at him. It was clear that his blood was up and he was relishing inflicting pain on Eowa, who had done nothing to defend himself. It seemed to Beobrand that all the weeks of being unable to fight the Picts in open battle had changed both the sons of Æthelfrith. There was a darker, easy violence close to the surface where usually it lurked deeper, held in check.

"He needs to be able to ride," Derian had said again.

Turning away with a shake of his head, Oswiu had pulled a knife from his belt. The blade caught the candlelight, gleaming.

"Indeed, that was my brother's wish." He had knelt beside the quivering form on the ground. During all of the beating, the punches and kicks, Eowa had made hardly a sound, but as

Oswiu went to work with his knife, he had let out the feeblest of whimpering screams; a proud man unable to remain silent any longer.

"You look like one who is close to death," said Acennan, breaking into Beobrand's thoughts. "Are you ailing?"

"No," he said. But his stomach twisted as he recalled Eowa's face when finally they had lifted him from the ground and helped him mount a horse.

"Let's ride a little closer." Beobrand said, nudging Sceadugenga towards the rock. A twinge of pain throbbed in Beobrand's right leg. "But let us not get so close as to allow the Picts to test their archery skills."

The wind ushered dark clouds from the north. They were heavy with the threat of snow. Sceadugenga's hooves slipped on a patch of frost that lay in a shadowed dip in the ground. Winter was coming. Staring up at the fortress, Beobrand could not avoid thinking that the siege would fail.

"There is nowhere to attack this rock," he said. "It is like Bebbanburg; as strong as an iron-clad fist."

Acennan frowned, but nodded.

"Aye, I doubt they are just going to open the gates for us," he said. "And as many warriors as there are here, they are too few to storm all the walls at once."

Beobrand focused on the broken grey rock of the cliff and the wooden palisade atop it, searching in vain for any sign of weakness that had hitherto gone unnoticed. He tried to forget the images from the night, but his mind returned over and again, like a dog that will not cease to lick a wound, even though doing so will open it further.

Oswiu had made deep cuts to both of Eowa's cheeks. He had also sliced into the man's nostrils, splitting them. Blood sheeted down Eowa's face, soaking into his fine beard, making it black in the dim light. Beobrand had hardly been able to look upon him, such was the guilt he'd felt.

Derian had sent the door wards away, so that no one should witness Eowa's leaving and, for a moment, they'd stood alone on the hillside, buffeted by the wind. Beobrand had removed his cloak and placed it upon Eowa's shoulders. Without it, he would surely perish in the night. Oswiu had frowned, but Beobrand had ignored him.

The night air had brought some sense back to Eowa. He'd reached out and gripped Beobrand's hand. The same hand that moments before had dislodged a tooth from the Mercian's mouth.

"We will meet again, Beobrand," Eowa had said, his voice clogged with blood. He'd spat and the wind had snatched his spittle away. "And we will not be enemies, you and I. This is not your doing, I know that."

His forgiveness was more powerful than any weapon. Beobrand had staggered under the force of the wind and Eowa's words. And with that, the Mercian had kicked his heels into the horse's flanks and cantered into the wind-whipped darkness.

Acennan and Beobrand pulled their steeds to a halt and once more set about looking at the fortress of Din Eidyn. Beobrand wondered if Acennan truly believed they might find something, or was he just humouring his friend and his lord?

"So, the tale is that Eowa escaped last night," Acennan said, not looking at Beobrand, instead glaring with intensity at Din Eidyn. "They say he stole a horse and overpowered the door wardens."

Beobrand said nothing.

"I know you do not wish to speak of it, Beobrand, but

know that I am your friend. And I can keep a secret should you wish to talk."

"There is nothing to talk about," said Beobrand. He was warmed by Acennan's offer, but knew he would never speak of what had occurred in the darkened storehouse on the hill.

Acennan said something else, but Beobrand did not hear the words. The wind howled, rending leaves from bushes and trees in a flurry around them. But Beobrand hardly noticed. In an instant his attention had been pulled from the events of the night before to the present.

He nudged Sceadugenga a couple of paces closer to the fortress. Could it be true?

Acennan moved alongside him and followed his gaze.

"By the gods," he said, his voice full of amazement, "is that who I think it is?"

A great gust of wind ripped leaves from the branches of the rowan trees that huddled at the base of Din Eidyn's great rock. The tents and shelters surrounding the crag cracked and creaked in the wind. As if summoned by some arcane command, a great flock of rooks wheeled in the sky above the fortress. Beobrand's cloak – borrowed from Derian that morning – streamed out behind him. Sceadugenga, not normally nervous, whinnied and took a jostling step to the side.

Beobrand tugged on the reins harder than was necessary and the black stallion once again tossed its head and whinnied. Without thinking, Beobrand reached up with his left hand and grasped the hammer amulet that hung at his neck.

He had wondered if he would ever see her again; had expected to travel for long weeks in search of the witch, and yet here she was.

Nelda, Hengist's mother, was unmistakable even at this distance. He could never forget her lithe body, her flowing jackdaw grey-black hair. The tantalising woman scent of her.

He shuddered as the great mass of black birds circled above her head and then flew towards him. Their raucous chatter was like the clatter of dry bones. The wind was the rush of a funeral pyre.

The wind blew Nelda's hair back from her face and Beobrand saw that he had destroyed her beauty. Just as he had rendered her son ugly, so his blow had changed her face into a twisted mask. It was as if when struck, both mother and son displayed their true nature in their wounded faces.

Acennan's mount stepped close to Sceadugenga, as if seeking protection from the larger horse.

"The witch is here," Acennan whispered, his words barely loud enough to hear. The stocky warrior seldom showed fear, but Beobrand heard the tremor in his voice now. He too had been into Nelda's lair, listened to her words, as soft as gossamer and then, sudden as lightning, shrieked like a night-walker, spitting out her hatred and spite.

Beobrand finally found his own voice.

"So it would seem." His mouth was dry.

Nelda had seen them. Her stare bore into them and she raised her arms to the sky, as if invoking the heavens themselves. All around them, groups of men turned their faces towards the woman on the fortress palisade.

As if in answer to her command, the wind eased and Nelda's voice carried to them.

"Beobrand Half-hand! Foul murderer of Hengist! My

curse follows you yet. All those you love will die and leave you. You will be alone at your end." Her words struck him like poisoned barbed arrows. Had this cunning woman, this witch, taken Sunniva from him? He knew she had tried to kill Reaghan. Had she also somehow sought to slay Bassus?

Above them, the night-black rooks spun as one and winged their way southward.

Without turning his eyes from Nelda, Beobrand could sense the gaze of the fyrd on him, awaiting his response. He could not remain silent. He was a thegn of Bernicia. A leader of men. A hlaford. He must live up to the name. He swallowed the dryness from his throat.

"It is not I who is trapped within a doomed fortress," Beobrand shouted back. "Din Eidyn will fall, and I will rip your accursed heart from your chest, viper. I will see you dead long before my own end."

"Well-said," murmured Acennan, "we know she bleeds. And what bleeds can be killed. You should have let me do for her when I had the chance."

Beobrand said nothing. Acennan was right. He had held her life in his hands and yet he had not been able to bring himself to allow his friend to kill a defenceless woman. How he regretted that moment of weakness.

Unnervingly, Nelda let out a cackling laugh that carried over the gathered host like the cawing of the rooks moments before. All around them, men reached for amulets. Many made the sign of the Christ's rood over themselves. Many more spat. There was magic and power here.

Fear rippled through the despondent men of the camp. Fear was a strong weapon when wielded with cunning. Hengist had been as much a master of fear as of the blade. Beobrand saw the pale faces of the fyrd-men, wide-eyed and trembling, gazing on this witch who cursed one of their own. He did not need to ask what they were thinking. She controlled the wind and the birds of the sky, her curses would be listened to by the old gods. And she laughed at thegns of Bernicia, even from the fortress that their king said was doomed to fall.

Beobrand spurred Sceadugenga forward. Fear was the enemy. He must face it head on.

"By Tiw's cock, Beobrand," Acennan said, "you know they have archers?" Beobrand ignored his friend. Now was not the time for caution. A moment later, Acennan followed him towards the fortress. "Of course, you know there are archers," he grumbled. "But why ride close enough for them to test their aim."

"Stop your moaning, Acennan," Beobrand forced a smile, "you sound like an old woman."

With that, he kicked Sceadugenga into a gallop and rushed towards the crag of Din Eidyn. Derian's dark cloak streamed behind him, and his long fair hair blew back from his face. Beobrand knew that all eyes were on him now. The huge thegn astride the massive black steed. He tugged the reins hard, bringing the stallion to a skidding halt. Sceadugenga, angry at the treatment, reared, showering earth and leaves from his hooves into the chill air. Beobrand clutched the reins and gripped the saddle with his thighs. His right calf throbbed, but he ignored it. Sceadugenga calmed and Beobrand let out a breath at not having lost his seat.

Sceadugenga wanted to be allowed to continue galloping, but Beobrand held him in check. The stallion turned a quick circle while Beobrand clung on. He jerked the reins hard to show the beast who was in command. Sceadugenga halted his prancing and rolled his eyes balefully.

Acennan galloped up close on his smaller steed, his round

face upturned as he scanned the fortress wall for signs of danger.

Beobrand offered up a silent prayer to whichever gods might listen that it was not his wyrd to die here today, punctured by arrows from the Pictish defenders. He dragged Hrunting from its fur-lined scabbard, noticing the slight catch as a notch in the blade snagged. The blade had been nicked on the tough bones of Aengus mac Nathair. Beobrand grinned savagely. The Picts may have strong bones, but they die easily enough. He held the great sword high in the air for all to witness. The day was dull, but what light there was glimmered on the serpent-skin patterned blade.

"This is Hrunting," Beobrand bellowed. "It is the slayer of Hengist. With this blade I defeated Cadwallon, King of Gwynedd. It has drunk of the blood of many brave warriors and supped on the life of the sons of Nathair. I, Beobrand of Ubbanford, Thegn of Bernicia, servant of King Oswald of Northumbria, swear upon the mighty Hrunting that Din Eidyn will fall and my blade will taste of your blood, witch."

For an instant he thought that Nelda would respond, but there was movement on the palisade beside her. He tensed. Was this an archer, come to put an end to his show of bravery? He squinted into the wind. And in that instant he knew he had been right in his suspicions that Nelda had joined forces with another of his enemies. For the new arrival on the palisade was indeed an archer. One he recognised.

The narrow face of Torran mac Nathair peered over the rampart. His skin was pallid, as if he was sick. But his voice was powerful enough for all those gathered to hear.

"Your blade did not slay all of the sons of Nathair, you whoreson Seaxon," he screamed. Spittle flew from his lips. He was not pale from illness, he was furious almost beyond control. "You have taken my brothers, Beobrand Half-hand, but I will kill you and all you hold dear. Just as I killed your friend, Bassus."

Beobrand struggled to control his own ire. He swallowed down the acid taste of bitter fury. There was nothing for him to do here while Torran hid behind stout walls.

And the fyrd was watching.

"Bassus yet lives, Torran, as do I." A look of surprise twisted Torran's features. "It seems your arrows are not as deadly as my blade. And I swear here before all the gods and these warriors of Northumbria, that I will take your life for all you have done."

"You can do nothing," spat Torran. "Din Eidyn is too strong. We are too strong! Finola and Talorcan are safe where I brought them. Away from you Seaxon scum. Winter is coming and Din Eidyn will not fall. And then I will come for you, Beobrand. I will come for you and I will slay you."

"You bleat like a sheep, Torran oath-breaker. Torran deceiver. Torran the craven. You are a nithing. Your word has no value. You say you would slay me, but how? With an arrow from afar, like the coward that you are? This is not a man who speaks. These are the words of a worm. I speak not to worms."

Beobrand sheathed Hrunting with a flourish and turned Sceadugenga.

"Come, Acennan," he said quietly. "Time to leave."

He did not wait for a response, but trotted away. Torran's screams and insults bombarded his back as he rode beyond arrow-range. Beobrand sat tall and rigid in the saddle, expecting to feel the agony of an arrow-head ripping into the flesh between his shoulder blades at any moment. But no arrow came.

Acennan caught up with him and matched his pace.

"Well, that was fun," he said, grinning. But Beobrand could hear the strain in Acennan's voice. "What now?"

"Now we fulfil my oath."

"What do you mean?"

"We take Din Eidyn and I kill that goat-swiving son of a whore, Torran. And that whore-witch, Nelda."

"Nothing too hard then?" Acennan smiled, the tension was dissipating as they rode further from the fortress. All around them, the upturned faces of dirt-smeared warriors watched their passing with awe.

"I did not say it would not be hard," said Beobrand, spurring Sceadugenga into a canter. He laughed suddenly, the horror of the night before forgotten for the moment.

"Come on," he shouted over the rush of the wind, "I have a plan."

Chapter 30

Beobrand could not sleep. The hall was cold, the embers of the hearth fire nothing more now than a twinkling red glow surrounded by the shadow-shapes of slumbering men. He lay some way from the hearth and doubted it gave much warmth now anyway. The night was full of snow and a howling wind that sounded like the screams of the dying. The snow had begun to fall heavily as the sun went down and soon the world was engulfed in a swirling blizzard. The gods alone knew how the men in their tents and shelters around Din Eidyn would survive the night. The hall atop the cliff was chill, but he knew he was much warmer than he would have been without the walls, roof and flickering embers.

The gale raged outside and from time to time a gust of wind would shake the whole building, making it groan and creak, like an old man being asked to lift a great weight. Draughts found their way under the doors and through cracks and knotholes in the walls. They made the embers crackle and shine. The cold air caressed the back of his neck. Beobrand shivered.

And yet it was not the cold or the noise of the storm that

kept him awake. His mind was full of thoughts, as if he had somehow swallowed the great flock of rooks they had seen and now those birds were beating and scratching inside his thought-cage.

Would his plan work? Now, with the snow falling deep outside, would it be possible?

When he had taken his idea to Oswald, the king had listened patiently. He had asked a few questions, but had nodded all the while.

"It is a good plan, Beobrand."

Oswiu had scoffed.

"It will never work. It is too simple, too easily will something go amiss."

"You forget something, brother," said Oswald, his voice calm and soft, a small smile playing on his lips. "Beobrand is lucky. And more importantly, he has brought me the blessings of God with his plans in the past. I believe that God speaks through him, even if Beobrand does not know it."

Beobrand indeed knew nothing of the sort. The idea of being a mouthpiece for a god was terrifying. But he said nothing. He did not wish to offend his lord, but as soon as he had laid out his idea, he had regretted it. So much could go wrong and then who would Oswald blame? Not his precious Christ god, of that he was certain.

"Besides," Oswald had continued, seeing the scepticism in his brother's face, "we have no better plan. Once the snows begin, all will be lost until after the winter. And I would bring our brother's wife and son back to Bebbanburg, where they belong."

"Very well," Oswiu had said reluctantly, "let us see if your luck holds, Beobrand. If you can get us into Din Eidyn and I can finally confront Donel, I will reward you handsomely. You can have Finola and the boy, brother. Donel is mine. And he will regret the night he turned us away from his hall."

"And when he stood against the sons of Æthelfrith," said Oswald, his voice as cold as the wind from the north. "I have offered the cup of welcome and the embrace of peace, but no. The Picts have chosen to reject Christ and to defy me. With Beobrand's help, we will make them see the mistake they have made." Again, Beobrand had been reminded of the steel-hard edge to Oswald that seemed to have been brought out over recent months. It was as if Oswald had been a blunt blade, but the events of the last year had honed and sharpened him, making him more deadly.

For an instant, Beobrand had remembered Eowa's blood-slick face. Yes, the Picts would be sorry for not swearing allegiance to the heir of Æthelfrith.

A huge gust of wind rattled under the eaves of the Pictish hall, making the whole building shake and moan. Somewhere off to the other side of the hall someone coughed and rolled over. Beobrand hoped his men were able to sleep. They would need all their strength on the morrow. Though if this snowstorm continued, the plan would have failed before it began.

"Do not fret so," said a hushed voice from close by. Acennan. So he could not sleep either.

"How can I not worry?" answered Beobrand in a whisper that no one else would hear above the wind. "Brave men will surely die tomorrow. At my behest." His stomach churned with the weight of the risks they would face.

"Brave men die all the time. It is the manner of their deaths that is important. If they follow a good lord, and fight with all their might, then they can die content."

Beobrand said nothing. The burden of leading men was terrible.

"And you are a good lord, Beobrand," said Acennan. "We will follow you tomorrow. We know your life too will be in the balance. Our wyrds are all entwined. The men trust you to bring them a great victory. I trust you. Even the king trusts you. You should trust in yourself. As Scand would have said, you have cast the dice now, tomorrow we will see how they land. Until then, rest."

Beobrand swallowed the lump in his throat. He could not bring himself to answer for fear his voice would crack. He rolled himself in his borrowed cloak and closed his eyes. Moments later, Acennan's snoring added another sound to the noise-filled night.

Beobrand lay there listening to the sounds of the sleeping men and the maelstrom of the storm outside. He knew that Acennan was right; there was nothing to be gained from worry. All the pieces were in place and the day would come soon enough. And yet it was a long time until his own breathing slowed and sleep took him.

His dreams were filled with clouds of squawking black ravens and deadly showers of white-fletched arrows that seared through flesh and bone.

Chapter 31

Beobrand squinted up at the fortress of Din Eidyn. The glare from the snow made his head ache. The storm had blown itself out while he had slept. On awakening, he had stepped out of the hall into a world of brilliant white. Drifts of snow rose against walls, rocks and shelters. The bright sun in the pale, cloud-free sky shone down with a chill, biting light. Everything had changed in the blizzard. The world was now a softer, cleaner place. But Din Eidyn was still home to Torran and Nelda.

If the gods smiled on him, Beobrand would see them both dead before nightfall.

"Is everything in place?" he asked, his voice as clipped and sharp as the icy puddles that lay hidden beneath the snow. Plumes of breath-smoke blew from his mouth and drifted away on the light breeze. His words and the crunch of his boots in the freshly fallen snow were loud, jarring in this muffled, soft, white land.

"Aye," answered Acennan. "Everyone is ready. Do what you must, and they will do their part, lord." He only ever called Beobrand "lord" when he was angry or nervous.

Beobrand nodded. He too was uneasy. His stomach growled and gurgled. He had been unable to swallow anything that morning, anxiously donning his battle-harness while other men ate. Now he wished he'd heeded the calls from his gesithas to sit with them. He could have settled his stomach with some bread and ale. And he might never have another chance to a share a moment with them. Too late now. He had paced impatiently by the doors waiting for the others to prepare.

Beobrand glanced over his shoulder to where Oswald and Oswiu stood. They were flanked by their hearth-warriors, all bedecked in their finest war gear. To one side he marked where most of his gesithas were gathered. Further away, other warriors stood around small fires. They stamped their feet and coughed into the still morning. They had survived the torment of the night and now looked around them with dark-rimmed eyes.

"Do you think it possible? With this thick coat of snow?" he asked, absently rubbing his half-hand against his left side. His ribs hurt. His byrnie was cold and heavy under his calloused hand.

"Too late to worry about that now, lord."

Too late. So many things were too late.

Beobrand stood silently for a moment, contemplating the fortress. There was a sloping path that made its way up to the gate. The path was smooth and perfect in the stark sunlight. As untouched and pale as a virgin's thigh.

"If I fall, swear to me you will kill him. The witch too, if you can."

"You will not fall," answered Acennan.

"Promise me this thing."

Acennan sighed, his breath steaming.

"Very well, I give you my oath. If you fall, I will finish the deed." He laughed then, suddenly. "I plan on killing the witch anyway. I should never have listened to you back on Muile."

Beobrand nodded his thanks and held out his left arm. Acennan lifted his shield and helped his lord fit his arm through the leather straps. The stocky warrior then handed Beobrand his polished battle-helm. He took it in his right hand and strode forward. His boots made deep prints in the snow. His leg bindings were already soaked through. The throbbing ache in his right leg reminded him of Torran's skill with a bow.

He stopped at the point where the path began to slope upwards to the entrance of Din Eidyn fortress. Here, his men had cleared the snow from a patch of flat ground. It was the size of a stretched-out cloak. To one side was a brown-streaked pile of slushy snow. He was alone and exposed on the dark, flattened-grass and earth, surrounded by white. The world seemed not to draw breath. All was still and silent. Beobrand took in a deep lungful of frigid air.

"Torran mac Nathair!" he bellowed in a voice that would carry over the tumult and death of a shieldwall. "Torran mac Nathair, show yourself."

Faces lined the fortress palisade, but there was no reply. He could not see Torran amongst the besieged watchers.

"Torran mac Nathair! Are you so craven? Do you not dare to confront your enemies as men do, face to face, with blade and board? I have felt the bite of your arrows, shot from afar, but I would face you now. Before all these men of Bernicia, Deira and Dál Riata." He waved his hand in the direction of the gathered host and the warriors let out a cheer. "Before all these men and your own Pictish Gododdin, I challenge you. Face me now or all shall know that you are the most cowardly of the sons of Nathair. I took the life of your brothers. I give you the chance to take mine. Fight me here, or let all men know, you are a nithing."

There was no movement from Din Eidyn. Would this be enough to goad Torran out? To be marked as a nithing and a craven before all was a terrible thing. But walking out to face a thegn of Bernicia, clad in battle-byrnie and polished helm, would call for a bravery Beobrand was unsure Torran possessed.

Beobrand stood there, all eyes on him, for a long while. His breath tattered in the breeze. The damp and cold seeped into his boots and leggings. The big toe on his right foot pained him.

This was not working. Torran would not put himself at such risk. He preferred the shot in the dark, the arrow from the shade of trees across a river, not the clash of blades in sunlight.

"I see it is as I had supposed," Beobrand shouted. "You are too scared to face me."

"How do I know there is not some deceit here?" a voice called from the battlements. Torran. At last. Perhaps he would prove Beobrand wrong.

"There is no deceit, Torran. It is not I who lies in wait in the shadows. Not I who shoots silent barbs from the forest like an elf. I am Beobrand of Ubbanford, and I look into the eyes of my enemies."

A pause.

"And if I do this thing? If I face you in a duel and vanquish you?"

"Then you can return to Din Eidyn with your head held high, knowing you are the only son of Nathair to fight me and live."

Again silence. Beobrand stamped his feet against the cold. The sun was softening the earth. It would turn to mud soon enough if Torran decided to fight.

Beobrand turned and sought out Acennan. His friend raised his eyebrows and shrugged, but gestured with his hands palm down for Beobrand to wait a while longer.

Beobrand looked up at the rock once more and with a jolt of surprise, realised that Acennan was right. The still air carried to him the sound of a bar being removed from the heavy, oaken doors of the palisade. Then, with barely a sound as they pushed against the drifts of snow, they were opened just enough to allow a figure to emerge. The doors closed, leaving Torran standing alone at the top of the slope.

Oswald's host cheered once more. They would see a duel this day.

The Pict stood for a moment, perhaps surveying the host from this new vantage point outside the palisade, or maybe he merely savoured not being within the overcrowded fortress. Beobrand knew how such cramped living conditions could prey on one's mind.

Or mayhap he was wondering if this bright day might be his last on middle earth.

After a moment, Torran threw his cloak over his shoulder and began the slow trudge down the slope towards Beobrand.

Beobrand watched him keenly. He was sure-footed, lithe and fast. Smaller than Beobrand, and full of cunning and guile. Beobrand hefted his shield, feeling the ache as his muscles bulged against the wound Torran's brother, Broden, had given him. Broden had been huge and savage. Torran was much slighter of build, but Beobrand wondered whether he was not the more dangerous of the brothers.

As Torran reached the half-way point towards Beobrand,

the Picts could see him clearly from the walls. They let out a cheer. Beobrand noticed there were more faces there than before, the Picts must have been desperate to see one of their own defeat an accursed Seaxon.

Torran was close now. He wore a small helm of polished iron. His eyes glowered from the helm's shadow, piercing and hate-filled. His shield was small, the leather covering daubed a deep blue, with yellow swirls painted around the sharp central boss. On his body he wore a tight-fitting metal-knit shirt. At his side hung a sword. Its hilt was plain, its scabbard unadorned. The sword blade was shorter that Hrunting's. Torran would have less reach than Beobrand, but he would be fast. He was slimmer, his blade lighter, his shield more manoeuvrable.

Torran stopped before Beobrand, on the edge of the cleared snow.

"So, Beobrand Half-hand, you mean to slay me, as you did my brothers?" He spoke quietly. The onlookers would not hear. He seemed calm. His confidence was unnerving.

"You have sought my death. You have hurt those I love. There is only one end to this, Torran. This feud can only be settled with blood." Beobrand dragged Hrunting from its scabbard and held it aloft. The sunlight glinted on its patterned blade.

"Yes, with blood," said Torran, smiling. He stepped into the cleared area; the cloak-sized parcel of land that would be their killing ground. "One way or another, this will be settled with blood." Torran drew his sword from its sheath and raised it high. It was not as polished as Hrunting's fine blade. It did not glow and glisten with the light from sun and snow. Torran slashed with the blade in an intricate pattern that reminded Beobrand of Broden, and how the Pict had wielded his great axe. Torran appeared relaxed, sure of himself and his weapon-skill. His speeding sword blade whispered as it cut through the chill air.

A sliver of doubt needled Beobrand. Could he defeat this confident Pict, who seemed to know no fear?

Like so much, it was too late to be concerned with that now.

Too late.

Beobrand placed his war-helm upon his head.

As if he'd awaited that moment, Torran sprang forward, scything down with his sword.

The speed of the Pict was astonishing. Beobrand flung Hrunting into the path of Torran's sword, uncaring for the damage to the fine blade's edge. He staggered back, but quickly regained his balance. The blades crashed together with an anvil-clang.

The sword-song had begun and there could only be one end to this.

There would be blood.

Beobrand brought his shield round quickly to take the brunt of another savage attack from Torran's blade. His feet slipped in the wet earth as he was pushed back. The jarring strike on his shield sent stabs of pain along his left forearm. Gritting his teeth, he hoped for a pause; a chance to take stock. But Torran came on, attempting to press home his advantage with a flurry of quick, chopping cuts of his sword. Beobrand's shield soaked up the power from Torran's assault. Splinters flew, and the leather covering began to tear. He took another sliding step backward, until his heel touched the bank of snow at the edge of the duelling-square. Torran's eyes glinted with cold delight, perhaps believing Beobrand's retreating steps were a sign that he was weak.

Beobrand bared his teeth. The caged animal that lived within him was tearing at its leash. It would be so easy to release it; to launch himself upon Torran with all his strength and battle-skill. But he must hold the beast back. It would not do to slay the Pict so soon.

Torran screamed his anger and threw himself at Beobrand again.

Beobrand could not give in to the battle lust, but he dared not allow Torran to get the upper-hand. Lowering himself into a crouch, Beobrand pushed himself forward to meet Torran. He held his shoulder behind his shield and shoved. His timing was perfect. Shield smashed into shield, iron bosses ringing. Beobrand grunted at the jabbing pain in his left arm, but he did not slow. Using his bulk, he pushed Torran backwards. Torran leaned his own body weight behind his shield and pushed with all his strength. Beobrand dug the toes of his shoes into the softening earth and heaved. One step. Two. Beobrand was heavier. This was a battle he would not lose. Then, before Torran could reach that same conclusion, Beobrand jump back and to the right. For an instant, Torran was off balance. His sword arm was exposed, but Beobrand chose not to sever the limb; not to deliver the killing blow. He swung Hrunting into Torran's back. He hit hard, but did not use the sharp edge of the noble sword. Torran must die, but he must live awhile yet.

A cheer rose from the watching host.

The Pict staggered a step, groaning at the bruising blow he had received. Once again Beobrand was surprised at his adversary's speed. As fast as a cat, Torran spun round to face Beobrand once more, shield raised, sword held firm and ready.

"You believed me easy prey, Beobrand?" Torran spat. His breath steamed. He was scarcely breathing heavily. "It is not just with the bow that I am skilled."

"Indeed, it is good to see Broden was not the only son of Nathair who was brave. I had thought you to be more like Aengus. A snivelling wretch who would weep and shit himself before standing toe to toe in a fight."

"He was just a boy," said Torran, his voice taking on an edge of sorrow. His sword point dipped. All the strength seemed to sap from him. "Just a boy," he repeated quietly, as if to himself. "Just a boy!" he screamed the words a third time and leapt forward, sword flicking up at Beobrand's armoured midriff. Beobrand had expected the attack, but still Torran's agility almost caught him by surprise. He stepped back and pushed the sword blade away with the edge of his shield.

The Picts watching from the walls of Din Eidyn cheered to see their champion attacking once more.

Beobrand sprang towards Torran, who raised his shield to catch Hrunting. Beobrand took another step forward, again swinging his blade into Torran's board. A third time he swung at the Pict's left side, but as Torran raised his shield, Beobrand twisted his body and punched forward with his left arm. He could not have performed the move without the straps that helped him hold the board fast, but with them, the shield became an extension of his arm and hand. The toughened rim of the shield connected hard with Torran's face. The Pict staggered back, falling to one knee.

Rather than finishing him, chopping down into his exposed neck, Beobrand took three steps back quickly, giving Torran a moment to recover.

Torran spat blood and shards of teeth into the mud.

Again Oswald's host cheered. From Din Eidyn, men shouted

their support of Torran, or their hatred for Beobrand. They spoke in their own tongue, so he could not tell which.

Slowly, Torran pushed himself upright and stood. He spat again, then wiped his mouth with the back of his sword hand. He looked down at the red smear on his hand before turning his gaze upon Beobrand. To Beobrand's surprise, Torran's mouth opened in a wide grin. His broken teeth were hidden by blood. He began to chuckle.

A shiver of unease ran up Beobrand's spine. What madness was this? He must have known that he was outmatched. And yet he was laughing.

"I will kill you," said Beobrand, taking a pace forward.

Torran was pale beneath the blood-splatter on his face. But still he laughed.

"Aye, you probably will, but I will take you with me to the afterlife, Half-hand."

"It is not my wyrd to die here today," Beobrand said. A moment before he had believed it, but there was something in Torran's face. Why was he still smiling?

"Do you not feel it yet?" Torran asked. "Can you not feel it burning? She said it would burn."

Beobrand looked down, following Torran's gaze. He saw a small stain of crimson on his breeches, just about his left knee. Torran must have nicked him when he had lunged under his shield. He had not felt a cut. It must be small, judging from the tiny amount of blood. But all of a sudden Beobrand noticed a stinging sensation emanating from the wound. His thigh burnt, but the rest of him felt as if he had been plunged into a snow drift. He shuddered, turning his attention to Torran's blade. It did not shine in the sun the way that Hrunting did. It was dull and dim. And with a sickening feeling, he understood why.

"What have you done?" he asked, cursing the tremble he heard in his voice.

Torran spat another gobbet of bloody spittle into the earth.

"She gave me something. Told me to dip my arrows in it. Said the wounds would burn, and you would die."

The stinging burn was getting worse. His thigh was throbbing with each heartbeat, pain radiating from the cut.

"When you called me a coward before all those warriors," Torran continued, "I knew I could not refuse your challenge. But I could put to use Nelda's deadly dew. My blade is soaked in the stuff."

Poison. Like a serpent's bite.

Beobrand recalled a summer years before in Cantware when his friend, Scrydan, was bitten by a viper. Uncle Selwyn had been close to where they had been playing in the bracken. He had cut and bled the wound, sucking out the poison and spitting it upon the earth. He said by doing so he had saved Scrydan's life. The boy had moaned and his leg had become swollen and bruised. But he had lived.

Beobrand's leg was hot now, the pain becoming worse by the moment. It was only a small cut. Perhaps all was not lost. If he could put an end to Torran quickly, maybe he could bleed the wound. But the wound, small as it was, already sent pangs of pain shooting up his leg.

There was no time to be wasted. He could hold himself in check no longer. With every heartbeat, death drew closer.

Beobrand sprang forward, swinging Hrunting in a savage arc, hoping to take Torran's head from his shoulders. The pain in his leg was searing agony now, slowing him. Torran skipped back from the swing easily. Ignoring the pain, he rushed Torran, hacking with Hrunting again and again. At last Beobrand gave in to the creature that dwelt within him. He welcomed the lust for battle with a snarl.

As Torran deflected Beobrand's blows with his shield, Beobrand prayed he had not left it too late.

Chapter 32

"The mighty Beobrand," scoffed Torran, grinning. Blood trickled down his chin. Easily, the Pict once again parried Beobrand's attack. "It seems you will not slay the last of the sons of Nathair. I can see you are weakening. Slowing."

Beobrand did not reply. He needed all of his strength for the fight. He hefted the shield that now seemed to weigh down his arm and rushed at Torran. Ignoring the pain in his leg, he sought out Torran's throat with the tip of Hrunting's patterned blade. Torran skipped back, avoiding the sword, and then launched a counter-attack. Horrified by his own sluggishness, Beobrand watched as the poison-slick blade flickered towards his face. At the last possible moment, Beobrand summoned enough strength to throw himself backwards and raise his linden board. Torran's death-bearing sword scraped across the shield, clattering off the iron boss. Beobrand's boots slipped on the treacherous ground, yet somehow he kept his footing.

Torran was right. He would not win this fight. The animal battle-speed that had won him so many confrontations before had left him now. The beast had been tamed by Nelda's poison.

Or the beast was dying.

Torran came on, battering his sword into Beobrand's shield. Splintered cracks began to show. If the blade passed through the wood, it could easily cut his bare arm, just as Broden's axe had done. It was possible that the gods would allow him to live with one small envenomed cut. Perhaps his wyrd would see him survive against the odds. But he was certain that a second wound would spell his death, as sure as a snowflake melts when it lands on a fire.

The Picts jeered and screamed from the rock of Din Eidyn. The men of Oswald's host seemed to hold their breath. Their appetite for this duel had fled. He was not surprised. They could see that their huge thegn, Beobrand of Ubbanford, was struggling for his very life. He had been a fool to tempt wyrd thus. His pride would be his undoing. Oswald praised him for his luck. Where was that luck now? His leg smarted and his vision blurred.

They were both breathing heavily now. Beobrand's whole body felt as though it belonged to another. Plumes of steaming breath drifted around them like morning mist. Torran, all terrifying bloody smile, confidence and slashing sword, smashed another blow at Beobrand's head. Beobrand's feet crunched into the snowy edge of the killing square. Without thought, he lifted his tattered shield. He was slow. Much slower than he should be. Too slow. But still fast enough to halt this blow. Torran's blade cracked into the linden and split the board. It moved into the wood and Torran's grin widened.

"Now you die!" he screamed. The Picts above them were in an ecstasy of rage and pride as their man hacked into the Seaxon warrior's shield. They could sense the end was close.

But the poisoned blade did not reach Beobrand's unprotected flesh. It slid into the grain of the wood and then held firm, wedged hard between the two sides of shield board.

Torran's grin faded. Desperately he tried to free his sword. He yanked savagely, pulling the blade left and right, up and down. But Beobrand, even in his weakened state, was still the stronger of the two. He pulled the shield hard to the left, dragging the sword with it. Torran clung to the weapon, but he could not prevent Beobrand from pulling him with the blade. In that instant he understood his mistake, while focusing on reclaiming his sword, he had left himself open to attack.

Beobrand did not hesitate, he swung with all his might at Torran's exposed stomach. He was not as fast as a striking snake. Gone was his uncanny speed, but he did not miss. Hrunting's blade connected with a jarring force. Rings from Torran's byrnie burst asunder, but the Pict's battle-harness was good; the blade did not cut deeply.

Torran staggered back several paces and fell. His hand had been wrapped tightly around the grip of his sword and his weight tugged it free of its wooden shield-prison.

"Kill him! Kill him!" Dimly Beobrand made out the cries of Acennan over the clamour of hundreds of voices.

And yet he did not move. He panted, the chill air burning his throat. He watched as Torran pulled himself up with an effort and rose to his feet. Beobrand blinked and shook his head. The world was dimming. He had failed. He would not get another chance to slay Torran.

His luck had left him as had all his loved ones. Death would not be so terrible. Perhaps he would see Sunniva again. Octa. Their sisters and mother. No, it would not be so bad to enter death's embrace.

Torran bent over and drew in a shuddering breath. He reached down to his side and gingerly felt for blood. His hand came up clean. Torran smiled again.

"That hurt," he said, "but it did not pierce my flesh. I will live. And you will die."

Torran raised his sword and shield. Warily, but with determination, he paced towards Beobrand. Death was coming and Beobrand knew he could not prevent it.

But if he were to face death, he would die fighting as best he could. His arms were as heavy and dull as rocks. He lifted them slowly. Agonising waves of pain washed up his leg. Wavering where he stood, he willed himself to remain upright.

Torran stepped closer. Beobrand could not take his gaze from the poison-soaked blade as it swished back and forth through the bright morning air. And then the sword seemed to hesitate. Torran had stopped walking. Beobrand looked up. Torran was looking behind Beobrand. His grin had gone, replaced by slack-jawed disbelief.

Beobrand shook his head to clear it. Could it be? Was it possible that his plan had worked?

He looked beyond Torran, up towards the fortress of Din Eidyn and what he saw there brought a smirk to his lips.

He may well die, but if the gods smiled upon Oswald and the host, Din Eidyn would fall.

Beobrand could hear them approaching. The sound of hundreds of men running, the jangle of harness, the crunch and stamp of boots through deep snow, the roar of unbridled battle-rage of a host of warriors that had been waiting for weeks to unleash their fury. It was the sound of battle. The sound of the shieldwall. The sound of death.

He did not turn to see them; he knew their destination. He did not dare take his gaze from Torran and his deadly blade. In moments the host of Angelfolc and Dál Riatans would be upon them. Torran's eyes were wide. He turned quickly to look up at the castle. Sure that for that moment the Pict would not attack, Beobrand followed Torran's disbelieving stare. The gates were open and there were men fighting there. As they watched a Pictish warrior was thrown from the palisade beside the gates. A heartbeat later the piercing sound of his scream reached them over the din of the charging host. The falling man smashed into the snow-covered rocks below Din Eidyn, trailing a splash of red as he slipped down the crag-face.

The besieging host ran past Beobrand and Torran. None interfered with them. The two men the gathered host had watched battling for their lives moments before had been forgotten like nightmares after a trouble sleep. Oswald and Oswiu led the charge, surrounded by their comitatus. Their great helms glinted in the sun as they surged up the sloping path towards the opened gates of Din Eidyn. The fighting at the gates grew more savage. Blood sprayed in the air and painted the snow. The gates swung wide. It was clear now that the roaring tide of men would reach the open gates. And then all would be lost for the Picts.

Torran slowly turned back to face Beobrand.

"You lied," he said, his voice aghast. "You said there was no deceit."

"And you poisoned your blade, like the craven I knew you to be." Beobrand raised his voice to be heard over the clamour of battle and the tumult of the warriors who yet streamed past the small plot of snow-cleared mud where Torran and he stood.

Torran shook his head, as if trying to free it of cobwebs. "No," he said. "No."

He looked into Beobrand's face. His eyes were dark, haunted.

Beobrand knew that look. It was the look of one who had seen everything taken from him and believed his life was already lost. He recognised the look for he had worn it on his own features two years earlier. Then he had stood before Hengist in the shadow of Bebbanburg. Hengist had murdered his brother and taken so much more from him. Unbidden, Beobrand clenched his left hand more tightly around the boss-handle of his shield.

Torran and he fought in the shadow of a different crag and this time it was Beobrand who was the kin slayer. But the scene was familiar to him. The gods must be laughing as they watched. The gods loved their mischief.

Torran's eyes narrowed. In that instant, Beobrand knew what the Pict would do. A calmness descended upon him. The pain in his leg yet burnt and throbbed, but it seemed more distant, less sharp. They each would play their role here. But Beobrand had lived this scene before. In another time. Before a different fortress. With a different foe.

Despite the slowness of his limbs, Beobrand was not surprised when Torran flew at him, sword-arm outstretched, poisoned blade thrusting towards his throat. He had expected the attack and knew what he should do. Summoning all of his remaining strength, he dropped to his knee and punched Hrunting forward. Torran came on, unable to halt his rushing attack. His poison-slick blade scraped harmlessly across Beobrand's helm. Hrunting did not miss its mark. It found the patch of broken rings in Torran's battle-shirt and pierced his flesh as easily as if it were water. Torran groaned and sagged against Beobrand. Blood bubbled around Hrunting's blade. Beobrand grunted and pushed Torran away from him. The Pict gasped and fell onto his back on the dark, churned mud. He looked small and bewildered now. All the confidence fled as the cold hand of death gripped him.

Beobrand stood, his leg shrieking with agony.

The sounds of the distant fighting at the fortress echoed in his head. For a moment, he looked towards Din Eidyn, but he didn't seem able to focus on what was happening there.

Swaying slightly, Beobrand gazed down at Torran. Blood gushed from the wound, black and thick. The gaping sword-thrust oozed and steamed.

"How?" whispered Torran. His face was white as the snow that covered the land. Soon it would be as cold. "How could you…? You should be dead."

"Perhaps," answered Beobrand with difficulty, his tongue was too big, his lips slack and difficult to control. "Perhaps," he slurred again, trying to smile, as he recalled Oswald's words, "but I am lucky."

He gazed up once more at the fortress, but his eyes refused to work.

"I am lucky," he repeated.

And collapsed onto the soft earth beside Torran's corpse.

Chapter 33

Beobrand's dreams had been filled with burning brands and howling screams of pain. Perhaps it was his own voice he heard, but it sounded to his fevered mind that a multitude of men were being slain in horrific ways. And all the while his leg was buried under the crackling embers of a hearth fire. He thought he must surely die, such was the pain. Perhaps he was already dead and was even now in the Hell that Coenred and the Christ followers spoke of. A place of endless burning torment for those who had not lived a life of virtue.

When he finally awoke, it was slowly. He dragged himself up from the bog of nightmares in which he had become enmired. He was yet on middle earth, surrounded by living men. The screams of horrific torture were replaced by the hubbub of feasting and laughter. His left leg still felt as though it were smothered in smouldering coals.

He opened his eyes. A great fire raged on a central hearth, sparks flew upwards towards the roof of the hall. The beams above his head were bare apart from tendrils of soot that wafted gently in the smoky air.

With difficulty, Beobrand raised himself on an elbow. He

lay on a pallet, off to one side of a long hall. All around were benches and boards. Men ate and drank. Laughed and talked. Beobrand lifted the blanket that covered his legs. For an instant he was convinced that his leg would have been removed. He was to be a cripple. He would not be fit for the shieldwall. He would not be fit for anything. Terror gripped him. Death would surely have been better than this. Then a shuddering relief washed through him like soothing rain after a summer drought. He was whole. Both his legs were intact. The left leg was bandaged, and the cloth was surrounded by mottled bruises. But he would walk again.

"Ah, Beobrand awakens at long last," said a voice he knew well. Oswald. The room grew still.

Beobrand shifted his position to see his king. A stabbing pain jolted down his leg. Oswald, Oswiu, Derian and a few others sat at the high table. Beobrand realised with a start that the pallet in which he lay was set next to the king's board. A position of honour. He looked around the hall. All eyes were on him. His guts churned. He could barely support his weight, propped up as he was. Rarely had he felt so weak. He prayed that he would not disgrace himself before all these hardened warriors, these noble-blooded thegns, and the king.

"We have prayed for you this day, Beobrand," Oswald said. "It is as I foresaw. You are God's instrument."

"The plan worked?" Beobrand croaked.

Oswald laughed.

"Yes, it worked, did it not, my thegns?" The hall erupted in a cacophony of approbation. The men cheered, hammered knives and fists into the boards.

"I am glad, my king," said Beobrand, his voice fading as he struggled to maintain himself in a sitting position. He was so tired. His eyelids drooped.

"Rest now, Beobrand. That Pictish poison yet weakens you. Rest and we will talk when you are recovered. You have earned your rest, and other rewards of which we can speak on the morrow."

Beside the king, Oswiu scowled and sipped from a metal-tipped drinking horn.

Beobrand allowed himself to fall back onto the thin, straw-filled mattress. His eyes were heavy. He would sleep some more. He hoped he would not dream of Hell again. A shadow fell over him, pulling him back from the brink of slumber. Acennan, his face pale and drawn.

"You should eat and drink," his friend said. "You must regain your strength."

All Beobrand wanted was to sleep, but he could see from the set of his jaw that Acennan would not allow that without him taking some nourishment first. Beobrand sighed.

"Very well, then. Fetch me a few morsels and you can recount the day to me while I eat." Beobrand's voice cracked. "And bring me some ale. My throat feels as though I have swallowed sand."

Acennan brought provender and pulled up a stool beside Beobrand. Around them the hall was awash with sound and movement. Beobrand turned his attention to the small cuts of bread, cheese and meat that Acennan had provided. His mouth filled with liquid. Acennan was right, he must eat, he was famished. He drank a deep draught of cool ale that tasted softly of heather and asked, "So, Acennan, tell me how I ended this day here." He glanced at the high table. Behind it a great shaggy bearskin hung from the wall beside a horse's skull. He shuddered. "And where is here?"

"This is the fortress hall of Din Eidyn. Your plan worked. When you fought Torran before the gates, all of the Picts came to witness the duel. When we gave the signal of the second cheer Attor and his band began to scale the cliffs at the far side of the rock."

"Thank the gods Attor was able to climb, despite the snow. I had feared the snow would make the ascent impossible."

"By all accounts it was not easy. Aethelwulf fell."

Beobrand ceased chewing, the food was ash in his mouth. He swallowed with difficulty.

"Was he the only of my gesithas to be slain?" Please let there be no others.

To his surprise, Acennan laughed.

"No, Aethelwulf is not dead. He fell from the rock. Slipped on the ice. He twisted his ankle and banged his knee, but he is as alive as ever. See, he is there, doing his best to drink whatever mead has been found for this feast. He was furious at missing the fight at the gates."

Beobrand saw that at one of the benches sat Aethelwulf and the rest of his gesithas. They had clearly been waiting for him to notice them, for they raised their cups and horns and cheered. His heart swelled. Grinning, he lifted his own drinking horn in toast to them.

"My brave gesithas!" he called, his voice hoarse, but loud enough to carry over the din. "I am the luckiest of lords!"

Again they cheered.

"You are truly lucky, Beo," Acennan said. He reached over and took one of the chunks of cheese from Beobrand's trencher. "I know you well, and I know your thoughts. You are thinking of all the things you have lost, counting the ways in which you are not lucky."

Beobrand said nothing. Acennan truly knew him well.

"But know this," Acennan continued. "Your gesithas scaled that rock and then fought like giants to open the gates. They did that for battle-fame and glory and for their king, but mostly, they did it for you. And they all yet live. You believed in them and that gave them strength and the luck to conquer all before them."

"What of Dreogan and Athelstan's men? How did they fare?"

"They are Athelstan's men no longer. They battled as hard as any. Dreogan saved Attor's life at the gates. See how they drink together now?"

Beobrand looked to see Dreogan, teeth flashing starkly against his soot-darkened cheeks, pouring ale from a pitcher into Attor's cup. Attor's head was bandaged, but he seemed hale enough beneath the stained rag. The fire of battle had forged the men into a single force. Beobrand nodded.

"It is good to see them. You speak true – my wyrd is woven with a strong thread of luck." He just wished it was not so tangled with strands of sorrow and loss.

"And I know at times you wonder whether death would be a welcome escape. But one who cared not about dying would not fight so hard to live. I thought we had lost you. The poison was working deep into your leg by the time I reached you. I cut your skin and let as much of the foulness out as I could. It tasted like pig shit."

Beobrand spat his ale onto the rushes of the floor. "You... sucked... me?"

"Your leg, Beobrand!" Acennan chortled. "Likely you would have died had I not done so," Acennan laughed. "But I am not lying when I say it tasted like shit."

"How do you know what shit tastes like?"

"Have you not tried Maida's pottage?"

They both laughed. It felt good.

"Well, I thank you," Beobrand said, wiping the tears from

his eyes. "You are right. I have thought of death these past months, but I do not wish to die now. I have much to live for." He thought of Ubbanford. Of Octa. Reaghan.

A thought came to him suddenly, like an icy blast from an opened door during a blizzard.

"What of Nelda?"

Acennan shook his head.

"She was not in the fortress. Neither was Finola, or the boy, Talorcan."

"How could that be? The rock has been surrounded all the while."

"Aye, but they escaped. That witch is cunning beyond measure. When we did not find them, Oswald was furious. Lord Donel told him how they had done it. They had wrapped themselves in white cloaks and left during the blizzard. In the night and the snow, none saw them pass. Whether merely cunning or witchcraft, they are gone. Donel laughed at having thwarted Oswald. But he did not laugh for long. Oswald took his head from his shoulders right there in the yard before the hall. Oswiu was furious. Said Donel had been his. For a moment I thought the sons of Æthelfrith would come to blows. In the end, Oswald gave his brother the fortress and Donel's hearth-warriors, those that remained alive."

Acennan hesitated. His gaze grew distant.

"What did he do, Acennan?"

Acennan rubbed a hand over his bearded face. He let out a sigh.

"He slew them all. Like cattle. Stripped them and had them hacked down. It was like Blotmonath in the yard." Acennan leaned in close and lowered his voice so none save Beobrand would hear. "Oswiu has a wild streak in him. Like a crazed dog. Oswald is a great warrior and king, and I would never wish to have him as my enemy. But his brother? The rage within him grows. He frightens me."

Beobrand looked at the high table. Oswiu was watching him through the haze. The atheling raised his ornate drinking horn in toast, a smile playing on his lips. His eyes were hard as flint.

Chill fingers scraped down Beobrand's back.

Ignoring the pain in his leg, he swung his feet to the ground. "Help me walk."

"Of course," Acennan said, reaching out to help Beobrand stand, "but where? You need to rest."

All thoughts of sleep had fled. He could not stomach lying here under the gaze of Oswiu. He wished to be surrounded by men he loved and trusted.

"Take me to my gesithas. I would drink with them this night. We must celebrate our victory. That we yet live. And our luck."

In the end, Beobrand had not managed to stay awake for long. His body needed rest and after a couple of horns of mead his head had nodded while the men around him told tales of the battle at the gates of Din Eidyn. He vaguely recalled Acennan and Dreogan half-lifting him and laying him tenderly on the cot that they had brought from the end of the hall to rest by their benches. The message was clear to all. They were Beobrand's men. And he was their lord.

He awoke in the morning feeling surprisingly refreshed. Around him men yet snored. A Pictish slave stirred the embers on the hearth, rekindling the fire. Beobrand sat on the cot and placed his bare feet on the rush-strewn ground. His left leg still ached, but the pain was much decreased. Placing a hand on a bench, he pulled himself upright. The leg throbbed, but it obeyed his commands and held his weight.

"Where are you going?" whispered Acennan, rousing himself from where he had lain, wrapped in his cloak.

"I would breathe fresh air," answered Beobrand in a hushed tone. "But where are my shoes?"

"Sit still for a moment. I will bring your clothes."

Beobrand sat and allowed Acennan to fuss over him. The stocky warrior helped him on with his shoes. He laced them and wrapped Beobrand's leg bindings tightly. For a moment Beobrand was far away, in Hithe, as his older brother, Octa, had helped him tie his shoes before they went out to help plough the top field. He closed his eyes and could almost hear his brother's laughter.

"Come on then," said Acennan, "you've woken me up, so you cannot go back to sleep. Lean on me and we can walk together."

Beobrand smiled and pulled himself up again. He placed a hand on Acennan's shoulder, but found he could walk quite well.

"Your leg seems much healed," said Acennan.

"Thanks to you sucking it," Beobrand replied, laughter creeping into his voice.

"If the winter is ever bad enough that we have no food, I would rather starve than eat you. Tasted like shit, I tell you."

"That was the poison." Beobrand grinned. "I am sure I would taste good enough. With plenty of mead to wash me down."

They stepped over the detritus of the feast and swung the hall doors open enough to allow them to walk into the cool morning. The door wards, grim-faced and silent, nodded to them as they passed. The sight that greeted them dispelled the mood of good cheer.

The thick snow that had cloaked the land, giving it a clean and soft aspect, had begun to melt. The brilliant white of the day before was replaced by brown, mud-churned slush. The sun was low in the sky. The yard, surrounded by the high palisade, was in shadow. To one side of the courtyard lay the grisly reminder of Oswiu's rage. A dozen corpses piled in a heap of butchery. Limbs entwined like obscene, grey-skinned lovers. Gaping wounds parted like lips of horrific mouths. Blood, shit and piss had congealed and pooled around the charnel heap, making a swamp of death. Atop this ghastly mound sat several ravens. They feasted on the flesh, pecking at eyes and dipping beaks into the softs maws of the sword-strokes that had killed these men.

Beobrand turned from the scene. His stomach clenched.

On the other side of the walled enclosure a severed head had been placed on the point of a spear. The spear haft had been dug into the ground so that the head could gaze upon the massacred hearth-warriors with unseeing eyes.

"Donel had little time to regret laughing at Oswald," Acennan said. He picked up a pebble and threw it at the pile of corpses. The ravens flapped lazily up from their feast, cawing angrily. Beobrand spat.

"There is no fresh air here," he said, walking towards the huge oaken gates where the fighting had been fierce. There was a ladder up to the palisade. He remembered the Pict falling, splashing red on the rocks beneath the walls. He tested his leg on the first rung and pulled himself up the creaking ladder, one step at a time. Acennan followed him.

Beobrand's leg was stiff, and ached, but it was a dull pain now. Gone was the savage burning of the day before.

From the palisade, he could see far. The day would be fine. There was no more chill wind from the north. No snow-laden clouds.

"It's as if winter lasted but one day," he said, breathing deeply of the cool air. The sun warmed his face.

"Perhaps we will have good weather for our journey southward."

All around the rock were scattered the shelters of the fyrd. Wisps of smoke drifted from dozens of campfires. The scent of woodsmoke reached them on the soft breeze. Those men would be wishing to return to their families. To their farms.

Their homes.

Back in the courtyard, the ravens had returned, their croaking cries harsh reminders of the end that awaits all warriors. Something in the birds' voices recalled to him Eowa's pitiful moans. Beobrand sighed. He closed his eyes and leaned forward, resting his head against the rough-hewn wood of the wall.

"What is it?" Acennan asked, reaching out a steadying hand to Beobrand. "You should not have climbed up here with that leg."

"My leg is fine," Beobrand lied. "But I am tired of all this." He waved his hand, indicating everything and nothing. "I do not wish to spend another moment here, surrounded by all this death. Rouse the men and send for the horses. By midday I would be gone from this accursed rock."

"Oswald wishes to bestow treasure on you. You have earned the battle-fame and you should claim your reward."

Beobrand straightened and faced his friend. Forcing a smile, he said, "I did not say I would forgo treasure or riches. Let Oswald King and his brother bedeck me in jewels and gold before we depart. But depart we will. And soon."

He looked down at the black-feathered birds that hopped, squawked and fluttered in the yard. He frowned, a sliver of fear pricking the back of his neck.

"I would return to Ubbanford. Too long have I been away. Too long has death surrounded us. I miss peace." He thought of Sunniva, her fair hair glowing in the warm sun of the meadow above Gefrin.

Acennan descended the ladder.

Cyneburg's hair was the same hue of gold. He recalled how she had cried for the loss of Eowa. They had been mad. It could never have worked between them. And yet Beobrand understood their madness. He understood it and yearned to know it again.

"I miss love," he whispered to himself, and began climbing slowly down to the death-strewn yard.

Chapter 34

"Ride ahead, Attor," said Beobrand. "Inform the lady Rowena of our return. We shall be home before nightfall."

Attor nodded. The bandage on his head had been changed by one of Oswald's priests before they left. After three days of travel it was stained, but his wound had ceased bleeding. He did not complain of any pain.

"I will see that the women prepare food and drink, lord."

Grinning, Attor dug his heels into his mount's flanks. The beast's hooves threw up clods of earth as it carried him out of the sunshine and into the gloom of the forest.

The day was pleasantly warm. There was no trace of the snow that had fallen so suddenly only days before. Perhaps it had not snowed this far south. Not for the first time, Beobrand wondered at the sudden storm and Nelda's escape. Had she called on the gods to send the blizzard? Was her power so great?

He shrugged. It would do no good to wonder. He just hoped she had headed north with her precious companions; to King Gartnait. When Beobrand next saw her, he vowed he would take her life, but there was no urgency. For now he would be content that one more enemy was dead. He looked around the ruins of the settlement where they had paused before entering the final forest that would take them to the Tuidi and to Ubbanford.

The charred bones of Nathair's great hall jutted from the ground. Some of the other houses had also burnt. A few huts yet stood, and the smoke drifting from one spoke of some of Nathair's people still residing here. But they had seen nobody and Beobrand did not care to look. They were welcome to scrape together a living from the land here, as long as they did not cause mischief. He would return in time and find them; let them know who their new lord was.

Nathair and all his sons were no more. Perhaps they had uncles and cousins; men who would continue the bloodfeud. But Beobrand hoped he was done with the kin of Nathair.

"Come, if we wish to beat the setting of the sun, we must ride," Beobrand said. The return journey from Din Eidyn had taken longer, despite the warmer weather. Yet, Beobrand could not begrudge the slow pace. Renweard and Beircheart led a heavily-laden donkey apiece. The stubborn creatures had been gifts from the king, as had their baggage. Oswald had lavished riches on Beobrand.

"Din Eidyn would yet be held against me if not for you, Beobrand, son of Grimgundi," the king had said with a warm smile. "I give you my thanks, and these tokens of my favour." Fine weapons, byrnies, helms and even a pot of golden coins from a faraway land were loaded onto a donkey.

Beobrand, feeling a mixture of embarrassment and pride at being singled out for praise in this way, had mumbled his thanks.

"I have given you wealth, as your ring-giving lord and

king," Oswald had continued, "and yet there is another who promised you riches and also owes you much. My brother Oswiu, now lord of Din Eidyn, will match my gifts to you."

Oswiu had offered something close to a grimace. He had not addressed Beobrand, instead he had clicked his fingers and another donkey was brought into the yard where Beobrand and his gesithas were preparing to leave. The second beast was similarly laden with all manner of items of value.

Oswiu had glared at Beobrand, who had wished that the king had not chosen to force his younger brother to do this thing. Oswiu had no love for Beobrand, but this gesture had merely served to push his feelings towards Beobrand closer to loathing.

"I thank you both for these generous gifts," Beobrand had said. "My sword and my life are yours."

"We value both," Oswald had replied, "but we hope we have no need of either for some time. The lands of Nathair are forfeit and I declare that they are now yours. Return to your lands and rest."

"I thank you again, my lord and king."

More land. More riches. He should have been overjoyed. This was the stuff of dreams. And yet, he could not bring himself to even smile.

Grim-faced he'd made to mount Sceadugenga, but his leg still pained him too much. Quickly, Acennan had come to his aid, heaving him up into the saddle.

His leg was now much improved and that morning he had been able to pull himself into the saddle unaided.

With a last look at the ruins of the settlement, Beobrand turned Sceadugenga's head to the forest path.

"It seems like an age ago when we fought the sons of

Nathair here," he said. The night of fire, screams and death was like a distant nightmare.

"Aye, much has happened since," said Acennan, nudging his steed closer to Beobrand so that they could talk without having to raise their voices. "And life is never boring around you, my friend." Acennan grinned, clearly happy to be riding south again.

"You think it possible there will be peace now? When I came to Bernicia I dreamt of becoming a warrior. Of battle-glory and fame. I knew nothing then."

Acennan sniffed and spat.

"I hope there is peace, for a while at least," he said. "But I do not believe this island of Albion will be tamed in our lifetime. We must rest and feast while we can, for war is never far away."

"I would enjoy some days of quiet in Ubbanford. I have seen too little of my son."

"Or of a certain slave girl." Acennan chortled.

Beobrand had been thinking much of Reaghan these past days. He did miss her. Her warm, comforting touch. Her passion. An image of glowing golden hair flitted in his mind, whether Sunniva's or Cyneburg's he could not be sure. But did he love Reaghan?

"Yes," he smiled, "I will need to do something about Reaghan."

"Something about her? Or with her?" Acennan's eyes twinkled in the dappled sunlight that filtered through the trees.

"Probably both!"

"Well, enjoy her while you can," Acennan said, "I think by next Eostremonath we will be called once more to stand with Oswald in battle."

"I fear you speak true," said Beobrand, frowning. "Penda will not be content with Mercia. We will fight him again, I would wager."

"It is for the best, Beobrand."

"Why? I am sick of the killing."

"You think that now, while your wounds still smart, but mark my words. You are not a man to sit happily on your gift-stool, passing judgement on the boundaries of neighbours' turnip patches."

Beobrand snorted.

"My wyrd's threads do seem to be woven into war and blood. Perhaps that is all I will ever know." His face took on a dark aspect. "Whether war comes in the spring, there are still those I must seek out. I will never forget Wybert's wrong to me. I have sworn the bloodfeud and his life is mine."

Acennan, serious now, turned his face to his lord.

"And I will travel with you to find the wretch, Beobrand. Together we shall run him to ground and he will pay in blood for what he did." He reached over and clapped Beobrand on the shoulder. "But that will be after the turning of the year. Till then, you must regain your strength. And practise your sword-skill. I watched you as you fought Torran. You have rusted like an unused seax. You must rebuild your sinews and that speed that makes you the deadliest of foes. Luck will take you only so far."

"I was poisoned, you know?"

"Yes, and now you must rest, but do not neglect to take the whetstone to that rusty seax. You will need its edge come the spring."

Ahead of them, a deer trotted out of the trees and ambled along the path, its white tail bobbing in the forest gloom. Dreogan and Aethelwulf touched their spurs to their mounts and galloped after the creature. The deer, as quick as thought, bounded away and sprang into the cover of the trees. The two warriors whooped and gave chase.

His gesithas too were pleased to be returning to the hall. And a rest from battle.

"Scand would be proud of you," said Beobrand, pulling Sceadugenga back. The stallion, always keen to run, wished to speed off after the others. "Remember how he made us train? We will all rest and build our strength over the winter."

"You can all rest," Acennan replied. "But first, I have something I must do."

"Indeed?" Beobrand watched as Dreogan and Aethelwulf returned, laughing but empty-handed from the forest.

"With your leave, I will be heading south. To Eoferwic. There is someone I must see there."

Beobrand laughed, reminded of Eadgyth's dark-haired beauty. He hoped his friend would find happiness with her.

"Of course. Perhaps Wulfgar will have returned. But do not tarry too long there."

"I will return soon, Beobrand. The gods alone know what trouble you will fall into without me to look out for you!"

"Would you like me to fetch you another cloak?" Reaghan asked. Despite the bright afternoon sun, it was cool here on the porch of the new hall. Sunniva's hall, the people of Ubbanford called it. Beobrand's lady. The mother of his son. Reaghan looked down to where the babe slept in a wooden crib. He had bellowed for an age before he succumbed to sleep. He was a stubborn one and strong. Just like his father.

"I am no gum-sucking greybeard that needs to be wrapped

in blankets and furs," growled Bassus. She knew he would say something of the sort, but she could see that he was uncomfortable. Next time she would not ask. So stubborn, all these warriors. Even the old ones who would never fight again.

"The Christ priests said that you should keep warm and rest," she said, her tone soothing. "God will heal you now. But to catch a cold would do no good. I will bring a cloak."

Bassus grunted, but did not reply further.

Reaghan went into the hall in search of a cloak. There was one with wolf-fur trim that would be perfect. She hurried to where it hung from a peg. Taking the heavy garment down, she ran her fingers through the thick pelt. She wondered how Beobrand fared in the north. She missed him. She could not speak of her longings or desires, but Maida and Odelyna knew. They smiled to her secretly and ever since that dark summer day, they had been kind to her.

These last days had been calm. She had taken to caring for Bassus, seeing that he was fed and the poultice on his stump was changed regularly. Rowena and Edlyn had seemed content to remain in the old hall in the valley and thus, Reaghan's days had been quite pleasant. Bassus was gruff, but he was not mean. He did not talk a lot, but when he spoke he treated her with respect. Each day, Maida brought Octa to Reaghan. She would walk with her gaggle of children up the hill and hand her Beobrand's son. Maida said it was so that she could have a rest from the babe, but Reaghan saw the smile in her eyes and knew Maida did this thing for her.

She carried the warm cloak outside and draped it around Bassus' shoulders. He reached up with his right hand and pulled the fur-trimmed wool clumsily into place. He winced.

He still tried to move the arm that was no longer attached. She said nothing. If she tried to help him, she knew he would only get angry. He was a proud man. She looked at him sidelong. Bassus had aged in this last week. More grey frosted the hair at his temples and his skin was sallow. He had lost weight too. For a time, she had feared he would not recover, that the wound-rot had not been removed in time and he would slip away. She did not know how to pray to the new Christ god, but she had left an offering of food and meat for the old gods in the forest.

And Bassus had started to get better.

She liked Bassus and she had witnessed how much Beobrand loved him. She was glad he would live, though she saw the sorrow in the huge warrior's eyes every day when he remembered that he was no longer whole.

Without warning, Bassus leapt to his feet, dropping the fur-lined cloak to the earth. Reaghan cursed. The ground was wet and to brush mud out of the fur would be a tiresome task.

"See there?" Bassus shouted in a huge voice. "I told you I saw Attor before. He must have stayed down at Ubba's hall."

Octa awoke at the sound of Bassus' booming voice. Reaghan flashed Bassus a sharp look and scooped up the baby.

"There, there," she cooed, rocking Octa on her hip.

"What did I tell you?" Bassus continued, more excitement in his voice than she had heard since he had been wounded. "They are returned."

Reaghan followed Bassus' gaze and all worries about the sullied cloak and Octa's crying vanished like mist under a hot sun.

Splashing through the ford, sending up a great spray, came a fair-haired warrior astride a massive black steed. Unbidden,

Reaghan felt her face stretch into a broad grin. She stroked Octa's pink cheek and the babe ceased bawling.

"That's right, Octa," she said, joy shining in her voice, "your father is home."

Historical Note

As usual in my stories about Beobrand's adventures in seventh-century Britain, despite being fiction, there is much that is true in this book. King Oswald did marry the daughter of Cynegils, King of Wessex. She may have been called Cyneburg, but she is not mentioned by name until later chroniclers write of her. Oswald also became Cynegils' Godfather, thus cementing an important relationship with an ally through both marriage and religion. Oswald grew up surrounded by the monks of Iona and was renowned for his piety by the likes of Bede, but I am sure that he must also have been an astute statesman who used the newly resurgent religion to further his own ends. The fact that the Christian monks and priests could read and write may well have provided an added benefit, as Oswald could use the network of scribes to carry messages that were guaranteed to be accurate and that very few possible interceptors could decipher.

On their journey south, Beobrand and Oswald meet King Sigeberht (later Saint Sigeberht) of East Anglia at a place called Dommoc. I don't believe there is any evidence for this meeting, but the pious East Anglian was too interesting not to mention. His story is complex and, as with many kings of the time, ends in violence. He may well be the subject of a future tale, so I will not give away all the details here. The location of Dommoc is debated by historians, with rival claims being staked by different groups of monks much later in the Middle Ages. I have plumped for Dunwich, in Suffolk.

The appearance of a second King Sigeberht, this time of Essex, is also factual. The spelling of names is very fluid at this time, and it would have been possible to have each of these kings with clearly different spellings to their names, thus avoiding confusion. But I liked the idea of the mistake being made, and this is a small nod to all the times that students of the Anglo-Saxon period (or writers of historical fiction!) bemoan the fact that all the characters have very similar names. Funnily enough, the Sigeberht of Essex mentioned here (known as Sigeberht the Little), was succeeded by yet another Sigeberht – Sigeberht the Good.

Bishop Birinus was one of a number of European missionaries who came to the British Isles and is recognised as being responsible for the conversion of the West Saxons, or Gewisse, as the tribe was known. However, despite being called Wessex, the kingdom at this time did not match that occupied by later generations and that most famous of Wessex kings – Alfred. The Wessex of the early seventh century is a smaller expanse of land, nestled between Mercia and what would become the later larger kingdom of Wessex. Its capital was Dorchester-on-Thames (Dorcic), not to be confused with Dorchester in modern-day Dorset.

Eowa, brother of Penda, existed. His story will reappear in

Oswald's tale, though his connection with Cynegils and his unfortunate meeting with the King of Northumbria is pure fiction on my part.

Abbot Aidan (later Saint Aidan) is one of the most famous Christian figures in the north-east of Britain, perhaps only second to Cuthbert. It is recorded that he liked to walk everywhere and it is a matter of folklore that he crossed the Tweed (Tuidi) at Norham (Ubbanford) on his way to Lindisfarne. When I read this, how could I resist having him appear at just the right time to save the day? More than once I show the practical worth of the educated Christian clergy in terms of their knowledge of healing. I am sure there are many reasons for Christianity taking sway over the populace, but I think that the assistance offered to communities would certainly have helped the cause. The description of the amputation of Bassus' arm and the subsequent treatment of the affected area comes from *Bald's Leechbook*, a medical text probably compiled sometime in the ninth century. It is the source of many strange and wonderful cures and treatments. The *Leechbook* has recently been the focus of renewed study as, in March 2015, one of its recipes, which included garlic and the bile from a cow's stomach, was found to kill the hospital "superbug", Methicillin-resistant Staphylococcus aureus (MRSA). It seems the Anglo-Saxons knew a thing or two about medicine!

Details of the siege of Din Eidyn (Edinburgh) are sketchy, and I have employed some artistic licence. The siege probably occurred a little later (around 638), but I have chosen to compress the events to make the story more compelling. Little is known of what led up to the siege or even its outcome, although it is known that Oswald became the over-king of Northumbria and Gododdin (the kingdom in which Din

Eidyn lay), making it most likely that the siege did not end well for the defenders.

I've chosen to have the Angelfolc (the people of Oswald and Beobrand) refer to all of the people north of the Tweed as Picts. This is of course a gross simplification of the situation, as is having all of the Anglo-Saxons referred to as either Angelfolc or Seaxons. However, I think it is important to be able to tell a gripping tale without getting bogged down in all the specifics of the different tribes and peoples interacting at the time. In the same way, Beobrand and the other "Anglo-Saxons" refer to all those who are foreign to them (i.e. native Britons) as Waelisc.

The term Wealh (with the same derivation as Waelisc and the connotation of foreigner) was a common term for thrall, or slave. Slavery was accepted and commonplace, and a way of generating wealth from victory over one's enemies. Reaghan is such a foreign slave, captured in a raid. It was possible to give slaves their freedom, something that perhaps Beobrand is considering towards the end of this tale.

Poisons play an important part in the story. Many deadly poisons were known, such as aconite, belladonna, hemlock and mandrake. Cunning women, or witches, would have had a wide-ranging knowledge of how herbs could be used for both good and nefarious ends. Poison on the blade of a weapon is judged by most experts to be a dubious method of delivery and unlikely to be very effective. However, I used the story of the attack on King Edwin's life in 626 by a West Saxon assassin wielding a dagger dipped in poison as inspiration for Torran's envenomed sword blade.

Another moment in the story that is inspired by a real historical event, but from a different time and place, is that of Nelda's escape from the fortress of Din Eidyn. In 1142, Queen

Matilda escaped the siege of Oxford Castle during a blizzard. It is said she was wrapped in a white cloak to avoid detection. This just seemed too good a story not to use for Nelda, Finola and Talorcan to elude Oswald and the Northumbrian host.

Beobrand's story is far from over. King Oswald's ambitions will not allow there to be peace for long, and where there are battles, you can be sure that Beobrand will be there standing shoulder-to-shoulder with his gesithas in the shieldwall. And of course, there is the matter of vengeance and bloodfeud. Beobrand will not rest until he sees Wybert and Nelda providing carrion for the crows.

But that is for another tale, and another book.

Acknowledgements

First of all, I must thank you, dear reader, for buying this book and reading it. I sincerely hope you have been entertained and enjoyed this chapter in Beobrand's ongoing saga. If you have, please tell your friends and family and help to spread the word. The best ways of doing this are to leave a review online or to give the book a mention on social media. Of course, the old-fashioned word of mouth is good too!

No novel is written in complete isolation, and I would like to thank those who have helped with the creation of this book.

Special thanks to my daughter, Iona Harffy, who gave me some great ideas for the siege of Din Eidyn and Beobrand's distraction of the besieged Picts.

Thanks to my trusty test readers, Gareth Jones, Simon Blunsdon, Rich Ward, Shane Smart, Alex Forbes, Clive Harffy and Angela Harffy. I must not forget to mention Graham Glendinning, who provided me with feedback on my first two books and whom I missed out of both acknowledgements! Sorry, Graham!

A big thanks goes to the team at Aria and Head of Zeus.

Thank you to Caroline Ridding, Nia Beynon, Geo Willis, Yasemin Turan, Blake Brooks, Sarah Ritherdon, Paul King and everyone else on the team that has worked on getting the book ready for publication and also for the hard work of marketing and publicising the books once released. It's great to be part of such a wonderful team.

As always, thanks go to my agent, Robin Wade, for his steadfast support and belief in my writing and for his tireless search for a publisher.

Over the last few years I have become part of a lively online community of historical fiction authors, readers and reviewers. There are too many people to mention them all here, but I am indebted to everyone who has shared my posts and tweets, offered support, written reviews and generally provided a network of like-minded people with whom to talk about history and writing.

And lastly, as always my thanks go to my ever-loving family. I am never sure how much impact my writing has on my daughters, Elora and Iona, but I know that I am not always the most patient of people when I am trying to pin down the muse and get the words written, so thank you for putting up with me, not that you have much of a choice! And of course, to my wonderfully patient and supportive wife, Maite. You not only put up with me, but encourage me and champion me every day. For that I love you even more than I already did, if that's possible.

KILLER of KINGS

THE BERNICIA CHRONICLES: IV

MATTHEW HARFFY

Frankia AD 635

"Be careful there, you two!"

The cry came from old Halig. He worried like a maid.

Wuscfrea ignored him, leaping up to the next branch of the gnarled oak. The bark was damp and cold, but the sun was warm on his face as he looked for the next handhold. They had been enclosed in the hall for endless days of storms. Great gusts of wind had made the hall creak and moan as if it would collapse and when they had peered through the windows, the world had been hidden beneath the sheeting rain.

After so long inside it felt wonderful to be able to run free in the open air.

A crow cawed angrily at Wuscfrea from a perch high in the canopy of the trees. The boy laughed, echoing the bird's call.

"Away with you," Wuscfrea shouted at the creature. "You have wings, so use them. The sun is shining and the world is warm." The crow gazed at him with its beady eyes, but did not leave its branch. Wuscfrea looked down. Fair-haired Yffi was some way below, but was grinning up at him.

"Wait for me," Yffi shouted, his voice high and excited.

"Wait for me, *uncle*," Wuscfrea corrected him, smiling. He

knew how it angered Yffi to be reminded that Wuscfrea was the son of Edwin, the king, while he was only the son of the atheling, Osfrid. The son of the king's son.

"I'll get you," yelled Yffi and renewed his exertions, reaching for a thick branch and pulling himself up.

Wuscfrea saw a perfect path between the next few branches that would take him to the uppermost limbs of the oak. Beyond that he was not sure the branches would hold his weight. He scrambled up, his seven-year-old muscles strong and his body lithe.

The crow croaked again and lazily flapped into the sky. It seemed to observe him with a cold fury at being disturbed, but Wuscfrea merely spat at the bird. Today was a day to enjoy the fresh air and the warmth of the sun, not to worry about silly birds. For a moment, he frowned. He hoped Yffi had not seen the crow. Crows were the birds of war. Whenever he saw them Yffi recalled the tales of the battle of Elmet, and how the corpse-strewn bog had been covered by great clouds of the birds. The boys had frightened themselves by imagining how the birds had eaten so much man-flesh that they could barely fly. It was a black thought. As black as the wings of the crows. To think of the death of their fathers brought them nothing but grief. Wuscfrea shook the thoughts away. He would not allow himself to be made sad on such a bright day.

Glancing down, he saw that Yffi was struggling to reach a branch. He was a year younger than Wuscfrea, and shorter.

"Come on, nephew," Wuscfrea goaded him. "Are you too small to join me up here? The views are fit for a king." Wuscfrea laughed at the frustrated roar that came from Yffi. Yet there was no malice in his words. Despite being uncle and nephew, the two boys were more like brothers, and the best of friends. Still, it was good to be the superior climber. Yffi, even though younger, was better at most things. The long storm-riven days had seen the younger boy beat Wuscfrea ceaselessly at tafl and Yffi had joked that someone with turnips for brains would only be good to rule over pigs. The words had stung and Wuscfrea had sulked for a while until Yffi had brought him some of Berit's cheese as an offering of truce. Wuscfrea loved the salty tang of the cheese and the insult was quickly put aside.

Now, as he pulled his head and shoulders above the thick leaves of the oak, Wuscfrea wondered whether he would ever be king of anything. Certainly not of this land, rich and lush as it was. This was Uncle Dagobert's kingdom. Far to the south of Bernicia and Deira, the kingdoms his father had forged into the single realm of Northumbria. Far away and over the sea. A safe distance from the new king.

Wuscfrea breathed in deeply of the cool, crisp air. The treetops on the rolling hills all around swayed in the gentle breeze. The leaves sparkled and glistened in the sunlight. High in the sky to the north, wisps of white clouds floated like half-remembered dreams.

One day, he would travel north with a great warband, with Yffi at his side. They would have ships built from the wood of this great forest and they would ride the Whale Road to Northumbria. They would avenge their fathers' slaying and take back the kingdom that should have been theirs. Wuscfrea's chest swelled at the thought.

"Vengeance is a potent brew," Halig had said to him when they had spoken of the battle of Elmet one night over a year before. "Drink of it and let it ferment in your belly. And one day you will wreak your revenge on the usurper, Oswald," the old warrior had touched the iron cross at his neck. Wuscfrea had thought of how Jesu told his followers to turn the other cheek when struck and wondered what the Christ would think of the lust for revenge that burnt and bubbled inside him. But then Wuscfrea was the son of a great king, descended from the old gods themselves so they said, so why should he care what one god thought?

Glancing to the south, a smear of smoke told of the cooking fires of the great hall. They had walked far and would need to return soon. Suddenly hungry, Wuscfrea's stomach grumbled. Several woodpigeons flew into the bright sunshine. Where was Yffi?

Wuscfrea peered down into the dappled darkness beneath him, but there was no sign of his younger nephew now. Had he gone too far with the jibes? He sighed. He would ask for Yffi's pardon and let him beat him at a running race. He did not want the day spoilt by Yffi's pouting.

"Yffi!" he called. "Come on. I'll help you up so that you too can see the kingly view." He couldn't help himself from continuing the jest. "Yffi!"

No answer came. The crow flew close and cawed. The pigeons circled in the air above the wood, but did not settle.

"Yffi!" he shouted again. Silence.

Letting out a long sigh, Wuscfrea began to climb down. It seemed Yffi was not in a forgiving mood. Perhaps they should return to the hall and find something to eat. When hungry, Yffi was impossible.

Carefully picking his way back down from branch to branch, Wuscfrea shivered at the shift in temperature. It was much cooler in the shade of the trees and he would have liked to have spent a while longer basking in the warm sun-glow.

Dropping down to the leaf mould of the forest floor, Wuscfrea scanned around for signs of Yffi. Surely he had not run back to the hall without him. Halig would not have allowed him even if he had wanted to. The grizzled warrior was as protective of them as a she-wolf of her cubs. But where was Halig? All Wuscfrea could see were the boles of oak and elm.

"Come on, Yffi," he said in a loud voice that he hoped veiled the beginning whispers of unease he felt. "I'm sorry. Let's go back and get some of Berit's honey-cakes."

No answer came and Wuscfrea strained to hear any indication of movement. But there was no sound save for the wind-rustle of the trees.

Cold fingers of dread clawed at his back.

"Yffi! Halig!" He didn't care now if they heard the fear in his voice.

What was that noise? Relief rushed through him. He had heard a stifled sound, choked off as one of them tried to remain silent. Perhaps Yffi suppressed his giggles from where he hid with Halig to teach Wuscfrea a lesson in humility.

He had them now.

Wuscfrea ran in the direction of the sound. Did they seek to make a fool of him? He would show them. His soft leather shoes slipped in the loamy soil as he skidded around the gnarly oak trunk. His face was flushed with excitement.

He passed the massive tree, laughter ready to burst forth from his lips. But the laughter never came. Instead, a whimpering moan issued from him. He skidded to a halt, his feet throwing up leaves and twigs. He lost his footing and landed on his behind. Hard.

Yffi and Halig were both there, but there were others behind the tree too. Strangers. Wuscfrea's gaze first fell on a giant of a man, with a great, flame-red beard and hard eyes. In the man's meaty grip was a huge axe, the head dripping with fresh blood. The corpse of old Halig lay propped against the tree, sword un-blooded in his hand, a great gash in his chest.

The old warrior's lifeless eyes stared up at the light shining down from the warm sun above the trees.

Some movement pulled his attention to another man. He was broad-shouldered, dark and scowling, his black hair in stark contrast to his fine blue warrior-jacket with its rich woven hem of yellow and red. In his left hand, this second stranger held the small figure of Yffi by the hair. Wuscfrea's eyes met those of his nephew. He saw his own terror reflected there a hundredfold. The stranger's right hand was moving. There was a knife in his hand. With a hideous sucking sound the knife sawed across Yffi's throat and bit deeply. Yffi's eyes widened and a gurgled scream keened from him. Hot blood spouted in the forest gloom. The knife cut through flesh and arteries and with each beat of the boy's heart, his lifeblood gushed out and over Wuscfrea in a crimson arc.

Wuscfrea felt the hot wetness of the slaughter-dew soak him. His nephew's blood covered his face, his chest, his outstretched legs. Wuscfrea could not move. He wanted to scream. He knew he should bellow his defiance of this dark-haired warrior and the red-bearded giant who had given him more deaths to avenge. A king would leap up from the cold leaf-strewn ground and launch himself at these strangers. He would scoop up the sword from his fallen gesith and slay the man's murderers.

But Wuscfrea just stared. His breath came in short panting gasps as he watched the dark-haired man casually throw Yffi's twitching body onto Halig's corpse. Halig slid to one side, his dead hand finally losing its grip on the sword.

Wuscfrea knew he should do something. Anything. To die lying here was not the death of a great man. Not the death of a king for scops to sing of in mead halls.

Hot tears streamed down his face, smearing and mingling

with Yffi's blood. But he was yet a boy. He was no man. No king.

And, as the death-bringing stranger stepped towards him, an almost apologetic smile on his face and the gore-slick knife held tight in his grip, Wuscfrea knew he would never rule Northumbria.

From the fungus-encrusted trunk of a fallen elm the crow looked on with its cold black eyes as the bloody knife blade fell again and again.